PHANTOM WHEEL

PHANTOM WHEEL

A HACKERS NOVEL

TRACY DEEBS

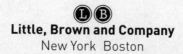

Little, Brown and Company

New York Boston

Copyright © 2018 by Hachette Book Group, Inc.

Front cover: Face 1: © BonNontawat/Shutterstock.com; face 2: © Kaylas_33/Shutterstock .com; face 3: © kostudio/Shutterstock.com; face 4: © Armin Staudt/Shutterstock.com; face 5: © Vladimir Arndt/Shutterstock.com; face 6: © Ilike/Shutterstock.com; turned girl: © Svetlana Bekyarova/Trevillion Images; running boy: © Stephen Carroll/Trevillion Images

Cover design by Tom Sanderson
Cover copyright © 2018 by Hachette Book Group, Inc.

Little, Brown and Company
Hachette Book Group
1290 Avenue of the Americas, New York, NY 10104
Visit us at LBYR.com

First Edition: October 2018

Little, Brown and Company is a division of Hachette Book Group, Inc. The Little, Brown name and logo are trademarks of Hachette Book Group, Inc.

The publisher is not responsible for websites (or their content) that are not owned by the publisher.

Library of Congress Cataloging-in-Publication Data
Names: Deebs, Tracy, author.
Title: Phantom Wheel : a Hackers novel / Tracy Deebs.
Description: First edition. | New York ; Boston : Little, Brown and Company, 2018. | Summary: "A group of teenage hackers has been conned into creating the most devastating virus the world has ever seen, and now it's up to them to take down the shadowy corporation behind it before it's too late." —Provided by publisher.
Identifiers: LCCN 2017051342| ISBN 9780316474412 (hardcover) | ISBN 9780316474436 (ebook) | ISBN 9780316474405 (library edition ebook)
Subjects: | CYAC: Hackers—Fiction. | Computer viruses—Fiction. | Friendship—Fiction. | Adventure and adventurers—Fiction. | Science fiction.
Classification: LCC PZ7.D358695 Ph 2018 | DDC [Fic]—dc23
LC record available at https://lccn.loc.gov/2017051342

ISBNs: 978-0-316-47441-2 (hardcover), 978-0-316-47444-3 (pbk.),
978-0-316-47443-6 (ebook)

Printed in the United States of America

LSC-C

Hardcover: 10 9 8 7 6 5 4 3 2 1
Paperback: 10 9 8 7 6 5 4 3 2 1

For Martin Torres,
the best man I know

• • • • •

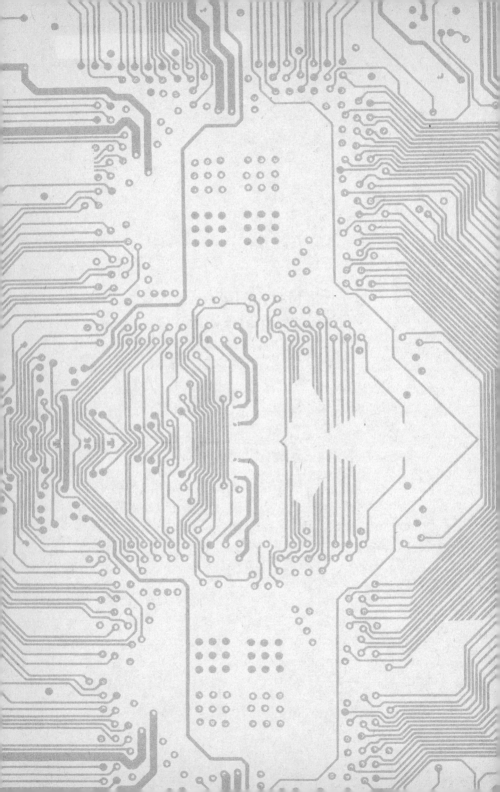

1

Issa
(Pr1m4 D0nn4)

I can't believe I'm here.

Seriously. I. Can't. Believe. I'm. HERE!!!!!!!!!!!!!!!!!

Three days ago I was changing my little sister's dirty diapers in between calculus problems in our crappy apartment in San Antonio, and now I'm climbing out of the back seat of a limo in L.A. It doesn't seem real.

But it is real, I tell myself as I thank the driver before making my way up the sidewalk to the security guard who waits for me at the open door. Discreetly, I reach down and pinch myself.

The pinch hurts, but not enough, so I do it again. Just to be sure that this is real. Just to be sure that I really have a shot at making my dreams come true—if I don't screw up.

Not that screwing up is an option, because it isn't.

With that thought in mind, I plaster a smile onto my face as I approach the security guard, who watches me make my way into the building with narrowed eyes.

"I'm here for the college program," I tell him, forcing a steadiness into my voice that I'm far from feeling. "My name is—"

"I know who you are, Ms. Torres." If possible, his eyes narrow even further as he looks me over from head to toe like I'm some kind of criminal.

Which I am, I suppose. One more reason why it's so unnerving to be waltzing through the front door of the CIA's Los Angeles headquarters.

"You can check in with the receptionist at the desk. She'll get you a name tag, and then an agent will escort you up to the conference room."

Escort, of course. Because letting a bunch of hackers run around on their own in a major CIA office isn't the smartest move. Even if you are auditioning those hackers for some top-secret intelligence program...

"Thanks," I tell him with a nod before doing as he says. I kind of expected there to be a line, a bunch of kids like me waiting for their big chance to impress the CIA in return for a full ride to college and a guaranteed job upon graduation.

But there's no one in the lobby who doesn't appear to work here. Two security guards, the receptionist, and a janitor cleaning the big picture windows at the front. I hope it means I'm early and not late....

"ID, please?" the receptionist says as soon as I approach the long wraparound counter where she's sitting.

I fumble in my bag for my wallet. As I pull out my license, I notice the receptionist—who is dressed in the most boring gray suit ever—glaring at the colorful sugar skulls and safety-pin chains on the front of my purse.

Note to self: The CIA really isn't into creative expression.

I prop my purse up on the counter so she can get a better look at what she so clearly disapproves of. Then wait semi-patiently for her to run my license through a thousand-dollar ID scanner. Seconds later, a badge pops out. I nearly freak when I realize it has not only my name on it, but also my handle: Pr1m4 D0nn4.

Seeing it out there like that makes me sweat a little. I mean, obviously they know who I am or I wouldn't be here, but still. I've never claimed my handle publicly before, and I'm not crazy about doing it now. In a government building.

Then again, that could be the point, right? This is the CIA, and maybe they want to see how I react to having a curveball like this thrown at me.

The receptionist watches, eagle-eyed, as I peel the backing off the label and start to press the tag onto my hip. No need to advertise any more than necessary, after all.

But she stops me with a shake of her head and a sharp, "No! It needs to go on your chest." She pats her own gray tweed lapel to ensure that I understand. I do.

After my name tag is in its CIA-approved place, she gestures toward the elevators to our right. "Agent Carstairs will escort you upstairs."

Before she's even done speaking, the elevator doors glide open, and a tall, dark-skinned man in a navy suit is standing there, face carefully blank, eyes alert.

I try to introduce myself, but I don't get any further than "Hi, I'm Issa—" before he cuts me off.

"I know who you are, Ms. Torres. Please come with me."

Ooooooookay. So everyone here is in we-know-more-than-you-do mode. Which is true—I'm not denying that. But it still makes me want to pull out my gear and take them down a few pegs. They aren't the only ones who know things, like how to access information that others can't.

I step onto the elevator instead. This is an audition, after all. I'll get to show them exactly what I know—and what I can do—soon enough.

Agent Carstairs doesn't speak as the elevator swishes us up to the fourth floor. Nor does he speak as he leads me down a long hallway lined with official-looking pictures of official-looking people—former CIA directors, according to the plaques beneath the frames.

The enormity of where I am sinks in a little more with each step I take, with each picture we pass, and my stomach starts to flip-flop. Normally I've got mad confidence in my skills, but I want this too much. Suddenly I'm terrified that I'm going to make a mistake and end up back in San Antonio, hacking test sites to help my dad make ends meet.

Don't screw this up.

Don't. Screw. This. Up.

Don'tscrewthisup.

The words are a mantra in my head, a beat in my blood, and they're ramping me up a little higher with each step we take. Thank God we get to the end of the hall before I go into total and complete freak-out mode. It's close, though, and I concentrate on taking deep breaths as we pause outside a door labeled CONFERENCE ROOM 1A.

Agent Carstairs glances at me before he pushes the door open. I expect him to lead the way, but he gestures for me to cross the threshold, so I do, trying my hardest to look like I belong here.

Seconds later the door closes firmly behind me.

I am on my own.

• ● • ● • ●

A man in a brown suit at the front of the conference room turns to look at me, as do the five people sitting around a long table. My stomach sinks a little as I look back and forth among them, but I don't let it show. Instead, I square my shoulders and paint a badass look on my face, trying not to notice that there's only one seat left—which means I'm the last to arrive. Late, not early. Fantastic.

"Issa, glad you're here," the man at the front of the room says as he gestures me closer. "We've been waiting for you. Please take a seat so we can get started."

"Sorry I'm late," I say. "My flight was a little delayed." I couldn't control that, so I don't know why I'm apologizing, but I feel like I'm at a disadvantage walking in last.

"You're not late," he assures me with what I think is supposed to be a smile but most definitely is not. "But please do take a seat so we can begin."

"Wouldn't want to get a minute off schedule," one of the guys mutters as I pass. He's big, with mocha-colored skin and killer dreads. He also looks like he's about to get a root canal instead of audition for an all-expenses-paid trip to college with a job waiting for him after graduation.

5

He's hot, I'll give him that, but he's wearing his bad attitude like a shield, and I *so* can't afford to be associated with that right now. Which is why, when I take the empty seat next to him, I try to subtly scoot my chair as far away from him as I can. The smirk on his face tells me that he notices. I subtly try to scope out his name tag, but I can't read it without being really obvious.

"All right, then. Let's get started," the agent at the front of the room says. "For those of you who just got here"—he glances at me—"I'm Agent Shane Donovan, and I'll be guiding you through the activities today. First of all, I'd like to say how pleased we are that you accepted our invitation to join us. Because we need people like you to help us find our way through the difficult years ahead."

His voice is booming now, bouncing off the oatmeal-colored walls, and I try to block out everything else and listen carefully.

"We're at war, ladies and gentlemen, right now, this very minute. Not just in Afghanistan. Not just against ISIS. But against cyber terrorists who want to bring down the United States of America for political, economic, and social reasons. And have no doubt—they *are* everywhere, and they *are* gunning for us. We are in jeopardy. Our way of life and our place in the world are in very real danger, and we're looking to you, and others like you, to help save us."

He pauses and takes a sip of coffee from a plain white mug. He remains silent as we wait for him to continue, then drains his coffee before very deliberately setting the cup on the table.

"We're only looking for the best for this program," he tells us, turning his head so that he can take turns looking each one of us in the eye. "And according to our research, you six are the very best in your age group at what you do. Which—if you pass our tests—is why we want the chance to train you over the next several years and eventually give you a place at Langley, *if* you're good enough."

A guy at the front of the room—who looks more slick than any hacker I've ever seen—shifts at that, like he wants to say of course he's good enough. He doesn't, though, and Agent Donovan continues.

"These are dark and dangerous days," he tells us, voice grave and body ramrod straight. "Your country needs people like you to act as our last line of defense against those who want to bring it down."

All of this sets my teeth on edge a little, if I'm being honest. I don't like the CIA—no hacker does—but I dislike being poor even more. And since we're talking about access to the best equipment in the world here, I can overlook the rest. Especially since all our activities will actually be government sanctioned.

No more looking over my shoulder.

No more waiting to be arrested for hacking my way into some classified database to make a few bucks to help put food on the table at home.

No more worrying about what will happen to my family if I'm not there to watch out for them.

Add a college scholarship to the mix and a job after graduation, and it's like I've won the lottery. If listening to a bunch of pro-government propaganda is the price of the ticket, I will gladly pay it.

Still, he's droning on and on about stuff that doesn't seem to have anything to do with the actual test we're here to take, so I let my mind wander just a bit, making sure to keep one ear open for when he actually starts to give us instructions.

I glance around the room. Photos of the president, the CIA director, *and* the deputy director hang at perfectly spaced intervals on the walls, along with all five (former and present) directors of national intelligence. At the front of the room is the official seal of the president of the United States, and underneath is the official motto of the CIA: "The work of a Nation. The Center of Intelligence." Meanwhile, the back wall is covered with what my research on the CIA has taught me is the agency's unofficial motto, written in huge black letters that stand out against the light-colored walls: AND YOU SHALL KNOW THE TRUTH AND THE TRUTH SHALL MAKE YOU FREE. (JOHN 8:32)

Seeing those words puts me a little at ease, since hacking is all about truth. Most people think hackers are bad, and some definitely are. But most of us are in it because we don't like secrets. We want to know everything, want to see everything. Curiosity might have killed the cat, but it's fueled just about every hacker who ever lived.

A quick glance at the others as they perch on the edges of their red leather rolling chairs tells me they look as excited to be here as I am. Well, except for the guy with dreads, who looks more and more like he swallowed a lemon with each word that comes out of Agent Donovan's mouth.

He even goes so far as to pull out his phone and scroll through it. I watch him surreptitiously, a little amazed that he's got the guts to be screwing around in front of Agent Donovan. Then again, I don't know anything about him, nor do I care. I'm here for me.

Agent Donovan pulls out some black folders and begins handing them out.

"What are these?" the guy with dreads asks as he shoves his phone back in his pocket.

"Your assignment," Agent Donovan answers, handing me the last folder.

I take it with trembling hands. This is it. This is my big chance, right here. Right now.

I flip open the folder and start to read, but before I can do much more than glance at what's inside, the guy beside me tosses his folder on the table and grabs his bag.

"What are you doing?" Agent Donovan demands.

"Not wasting my day doing this BS, that's for sure." He stands up and rips off his name tag and shoves it into his pocket before I can even see what it says. Then he heads for the door.

I'm staring at him in shock—as are the rest of the people in the room—when suddenly Agent Donovan moves to block his way. The fact that the guy is four inches taller than the agent makes their whole nose-to-nose showdown kind of comical— or it would if I could stop trying to figure out what's happening and just enjoy the show.

"You need to sit down," Agent Donovan orders.

"Like I'm going to listen to you," the guy responds.

"You're here for an audition."

"Yeah, well, I just got stage fright. Sue me." He shrugs like he doesn't have a care in the world.

"You need to do what I say." Agent Donovan sounds as angry as he looks.

"No, I don't. But you *do* need to move before I move you." He doesn't even flinch as he waits to see what the CIA agent is going to do.

The rest of us wait too, breath held and shoulders tense.

A stare-down ensues, and I swear you could hear a pin drop in the room as we all wait for the explosion. Agent Donovan doesn't look like the kind of guy who's used to people giving him attitude. Plus, the CIA paid for us to come all this way for an audition. The least this guy can do is hold up his end of the bargain.

In the end, though, Agent Donovan just steps aside and lets him leave. "Don't count on us to give you a ride back to the airport."

The guy just laughs. "Dude, I wouldn't count on you to know what a command prompt is, let alone how to access it, and neither should anyone else in this room."

He turns and looks straight at me. For a second it seems like he wants to lay into me—into all of us—but he just shakes his head and says, "When something seems too good to be true, it probably is."

And then he's gone, closing the door behind him with a firm *thud* and leaving the rest of us to stare anywhere but at Agent Donovan as we try to figure out what just happened.

As I wait for Agent Donovan to say something, anything, the guy's words replay over and over again in my head.

When something seems too good to be true, it probably is. When something seems too good to be true, it probably is. When something…

I try to block them out—try to block *him* out. Because he can't be right. He just can't be. I need this to be true too much.

"All right, now that we've gotten rid of the deadweight," Agent Donovan finally says, "grab some snacks off the table in the back, and I'll show each of you to the rooms where you'll be working." He walks to the door and opens it, steps into the hall, and waits for us to pick up drinks or candy bars and follow him like good little soldiers.

Which we do. All five of us.

Just the thought grates a little—I'm not big on making waves for no reason, but I don't like not knowing what's going on either. Especially after what just happened. But what else are we supposed to do but follow Agent Donovan wherever he wants to take us?

I need this program and the scholarship it provides way too badly to mess it up just to make a point. Better to keep my head down and my mouth shut, at least until I've done what they brought me here to do.

I'm so busy concentrating on the floor and trying to avoid my own thoughts that I bump into one of the other good little soldiers.

The guy jumps a little, then apologizes to me—even though I very clearly bumped into him—with a smile on his face. I smile back. I like him, and the well-trimmed red Mohawk he's sporting. His badge says his name is Seth Prentiss.

I think about introducing myself, but Agent Donovan is walking fast, his polished mahogany wingtips eating up the hallway one decisive click at a time. He stops suddenly and gestures to a room on his right. "Issa, this is your room. Everything you need to accomplish your task should be in there. If you're missing anything, you can call me on the number provided inside your folder, or you can improvise." His tone tells me which of those I should do.

"Thanks," I answer, opening the door and stepping inside. I turn, start to ask about a password on the computer, but Agent Donovan is already making his way down the hall with the others.

Okay, so no questions and no lifeline. No problem. I've been making my own lifelines for a while now. Why should today be any different?

As I move to close the door, another man walks down the hallway. He's tall and old looking—silver hair, wrinkly face—and if I were somewhere else, I probably wouldn't even notice him. But considering his suit looks like it cost more than a year of college tuition, I can't help being interested. I thought government employees didn't get paid enough to afford clothes like that.

He nods when he notices me staring, but doesn't say anything. Neither do I. I just watch as he walks by like he owns the place—head up, shoulders back, face totally impassive.

I close the door, then take a moment to stretch out my neck and fingers and look around the room. Everything in it is government-issue gray—the desk, the chair, the carpet, the state-of-the-art Jacento computer, even the walls.

Who paints walls gray, anyway? I wonder as I slowly make my way to the desk. And yes, I'm well aware that I'm stalling. Now that it's all spread out before me, I'm nervous. Really, really nervous.

Not because of my task—I glanced through the folder when Agent Donovan handed it to me, and I'm pretty sure it's not going to be a problem—but because so much is riding on this. This offer dropped out of the sky when I needed it most, and if I blow it, then I've got nothing.

I'm not going to let that happen, not going to spend the rest of my life like my father, pining for a future that slipped through my fingers. This is my golden ticket, and I'm holding on to it with everything I've got.

This thought is the reminder I need, and it steadies me. It also gives me the courage to sit down in the ergonomically correct gray chair.

I flip open the folder, take a few deep breaths, and study the instructions more closely. My nerves settle. Because while there are a lot of big words that make the hack sound super complicated, the truth is, it's really not. I've run this kind of game hundreds of times in hundreds of different systems. It's all about the code, and I have a bunch of pretty, pretty codes up my sleeves.

Usually I'm all about finesse—I like my hacks to be as stylish as they are effective. But even though it says on the first page in the folder to take our time, that doing it right is more important than doing it fast, I can't help feeling like this is a race. Four other people are out there, all of whom are probably doing this exact same thing. I don't want to be the last one in the door—especially when I don't know how many open spots they have in the program.

With that thought in mind, I turn on the computer. I'll do whatever it takes to get my shot, even if it means brute-forcing my way into this thing.

The second the screen comes up, I bite back a groan. Seriously? They seriously gave me a computer that runs *Windows* to do this stuff? It's bad enough that they don't have Wi-Fi, that they keep us tethered to Ethernet like a bunch of lamers. But Windows? It's like they're some small-town sheriff's office instead of the freaking CIA.

For a moment I wonder about the practicality of wiping the computer—installing Linux in place of Windows so I can actually do what I need to do with about a million times less hassle. But the clock keeps ticking in the back of my head, and doing that will take waaaaaaay too long, no matter how state of the art the system is.

Maybe that's part of the test. Windows takes triple the time Linux does because of the way I have to format commands—but maybe that's what they want. To measure how we do when we're not in our comfort zone, using equipment that isn't our own and an operating system that sucks.

The computer is password protected, just as I thought. A quick look through the desk shows that there's nothing in it at all—they either emptied it out for us or this office is dedicated to auditions and interviews.

The thought makes me even more nervous, and I give up on finding the password and turn my focus instead to breaking in. It's not the easiest thing to do, but it's not impossible either—if you know what you're doing.

I've spent years making sure I know exactly what I'm doing.

I strike a few keys, get to the command prompt behind Windows. Then I enter a few lines of code that let me establish a back door into the system. A few more lines of code help the OS recognize the back door, and from there it's a simple matter to circumvent the password.

"Automagic, baby," I crow before it registers that they might be recording me. Once it does, I keep my fist pump to myself, but it's hard. I glance at the clock on the wall—less than five minutes and I'm in.

Once I've got control of the system, I write a few lines of code in Python just to test things out. I can program in the C languages and Java, but I much prefer Python since it cuts repetition down to bare bones—and the time saved is totally worth the installation time.

As soon as I'm up and running, I search the network's IP addresses with my favorite mapping tool, looking for any open ports. Every single server they gave me has at least one open port, and though I have no idea where the servers lead (they're just blind addresses to me), I spend a minute ranking how easy they are to access based on my own strengths and weaknesses. It's not foolproof considering I'm not in any of their systems yet, but I'm betting when all is said and done, I'll only be off by one or two, at most.

I've been doing this long enough to know what I'm talking about.

Grabbing a clip from my bag, I push my hair up and out of my eyes. And then I get to work.

I've always been a girl who likes a challenge, so I tackle the hardest first.

I start by Burp Suiteing it. I prefer Aircrack-ng, but Windows. Ugh. I bite back a groan and start searching for a point to exploit.

Time begins to fly by, as it always does when I do my thing. The hack is a lot of munching. I didn't expect to have to do so much exploration when I first saw the gig, but I roll with it, IRPing where I can and patching where I can't. I eventually hit my groove, and three and a half hours later, I'm Netcatting the last server.

I don't want to make any mistakes, so I'm taking my time. But it's hard once I start hearing doors open in the hall. The others are finishing, and I'm still in here, working on this last stupid exploit.

And the exploit is harder than I expect. Still, I stick with it, using my standard Python code to strong-arm a path to where I want to go. But the vulnerability I originally found isn't nearly as wide open as I thought, and I'm starting to worry I'm going to have to find a zero day—which will take way more time than I've got. Hours, or even days.

I'm trying a bunch of different things—codes I've written through the years to get me through almost anything—when my phone pings. I want to ignore it, stay buried in what I'm doing, but I can't.

I swipe it open, and my stomach falls through the floor when I see the text from my sister.

C has fever of 102

Not now, not now. Please not now.

Where's Dad?

But even as I wait for an answer, I know what she's going to type. Sure enough:

Dad's sleeping

Is she drinking water or formula?

No

She's really hot

God, God, God. Think, Issa, think.

OK. Give her baby Tylenol, from the bathroom cabinet. READ THE DIRECTIONS. I can't remember how much to give her

Then rub her all over with a cool washcloth and let her stay in her diaper

Try to get three ounces of Pedialyte into her

Text me in forty minutes if she's not better

Ok

I wait for her to text more, but she doesn't, and I have a minor freak-out. Since my mom died, my dad's been kind of out of it…okay, a lot out of it. Which is understandable. I mean, I get it. He takes his wife to the hospital, thinking he's going to be bringing her and a baby home. Instead, he gets the baby and loses the wife to some freak complication during childbirth.

Within a few months of my mom's death, my dad stopped working—I'm still not sure if he quit or was fired or is, I hope, on some sort of leave until he snaps out of this depression. All he does most days is sleep. I've begged him to see a doctor, to get help for his very obvious depression, but he keeps telling me he just needs time.

I'm not okay with any of this—I wasn't a few months ago, and I'm not now—but it's not like I get a choice. There's a baby to take care of, plus the other kids. And since my dad can't do the job right now, I do it. Most of the time, anyway.

Today is…an anomaly. Leaving Lettie in charge for the day shouldn't be a big deal—she's fifteen and has helped me out a bunch of times. But now Chloe's sick, and Lettie shouldn't have to deal with that alone. God. I need to finish this code so I can get out of here and back home.

Forty minutes later, I finally make it through the firewall. From there it only takes a couple of minutes to cover my tracks, blowing up my point of entry and erasing any trace that I was even here. I'm about to shut down when my phone goes off again.

I grab it so fast that I nearly drop it, then shudder in relief when I read what Lettie wrote.

Fever's down

She just drank some pedialyte

Great! Keep me posted

Make sure you give her next dose of Tylenol on time

Ok

How's it going

Good

Yay!

How's everyone else?

Twins are good and so is Ricky

Good. I'll be home really late tonight but text me if you need anything.

I give myself a second or two to relax after all the drama. Then I shove my phone in my bag before shutting down the computer.

I've got this, I tell myself as I make my way down the hall. *I've got this.*

2

Harper
[5p3ct3r]

A little thrill of excitement shoots through me as I realize the conference room is empty. I'm the first one done.

That has to count for something, right?

I mean, this *is* a competition. And the prize is a full ride to the university of my choice, courtesy of the American intelligence community, with a job doing what I love waiting for me when I get out.

Thank you very much, CIA.

Just thinking it feels like a betrayal, considering how difficult the agency usually makes things for people like me. If someone had told me a month ago that I'd be here, tucked up tight in the belly of the beast, I would have called them a liar. And then hacked into their personal stuff just to make a point. Just because I could.

But here I am, soda in one hand and Skittles in the other, all courtesy of the United States government. It feels like a really bad trip . . . or a really good one. If I make it.

I really, really want to make it.

Being chosen for the program means no more pretending. No more hiding. No more worrying that someone, somewhere, is going to see through my hacks and drag me—kicking and screaming—back into the system.

I'd rather die than be sent to another foster home. Or worse, to one of those group homes where survival of the fittest is more than just a lesson in a biology book.

Keenly aware of the cameras in the corners of the room, I pick my seat carefully. All the way at the far end, back against the wall, with a perfect view of the door. Sure, it puts me right in the middle of both cameras' range, but that's the point.

The best place to hide is almost always in plain sight.

I drop my backpack at my feet, rest my soda on the table in front of me, and take out my phone. I pull up a random app, angle the device so the cameras can pick up what I'm doing, then let my thumbs fly as I pretend to be totally absorbed in—I glance at the screen for the first time—a rousing game of Candy Crush.

I lean forward a little, looking to all the world like I'm totally into the game, and let my hair fall into my face just enough to obscure my eyes from view. And then I watch.

There's a large window opposite me, with a long hallway just beyond it. It's the hallway I walked down to get here, and it's the hallway everyone else will have to walk down too. So far it's empty, but it won't stay that way for long.

As I wait, eyes trained on that window, I pull my phone in close to shield the screen, all the while keeping up the Candy Crush pretense. Then I key in a second password, one that gets

21

me into a highly encrypted area of my phone that is invisible to anyone who doesn't know it's there.

I swipe across another app—one I designed, this time—and let it do its job. Within seconds, it's identified three bugs strategically placed in the room. I could fry them in a second, but I don't. No use tipping my hand. Besides, it's not exactly a surprise that they're listening to us. It's what the CIA does.

I'm just closing out of the program when Silver Spoon steps into the hallway. According to his name tag, his name is Ezra Hernandez, but with his designer clothes and state-of-the-art everything, my nickname fits him better.

Everything about him is arrogant as hell—his walk, his eyes, even the way he talks. He's got life by the balls, and he knows it. Everyone else knows it too.

He opens the door with a triumphant flourish, eyes sweeping the room. He pauses when his gaze lands on me, an indecipherable look crossing his face before the conquering-hero smile is fixed firmly in place.

"You're fast," he says, sauntering across the room toward me.

I've got a million answers to that on the tip of my tongue, but thinking them and saying them are two very different things. So I just nod.

"The equipment was stellar, though, right?" he continues. "My setup at home is pretty sweet, but this next-gen Jacento stuff is a whole different level."

"I didn't use it."

One of his brows goes up in that way you only read about in books. It's sexy, I suppose, but it only makes me distrust him more. Never trust a guy who's that good-looking. Best advice I ever got—even if I gave it to myself.

"You didn't use it? Why not?"

"I've got my own kit." I nod to the backpack at my feet. "I like it."

Which is true, but it's also true that I don't trust anyone else's system. Ever. Call me paranoid, but paranoia is better than prison. Second-best advice I ever gave myself.

"Yeah, but..."

His eyes light up as Snow White walks in. Of course they do. These two speak the same language, and I don't mean C++.

"Hey, Alika." Silver Spoon waves casually. If Silver Spoon can't be trusted because of his looks, the same goes for Snow White and then some. She's hands down the most perfect-looking girl I've ever seen in real life.

"Hey." She too does a quick sweep of the room, then smiles at us. That it's a genuine smile doesn't surprise me. That it's meant for both of us does. Then again, Snow White has no reason to fear the competition. Her designer clothes make it obvious she doesn't need this job the way I do.

"Three down, two to go, huh?" She plops into the chair across from mine.

"Four down." I nod toward the door just as Issa walks in. I don't have a nickname for her yet, but I'm thinking of going with Buffy. With her affinity for nineties fashion, she's certainly got the look of the vampire slayer from the old TV show. And the attitude.

She doesn't bother to check out the room, just heads straight for us. She takes the seat one over from me, flannel-clad arms folded over her chest and legs stretched out in front of her. She's got a pretty impressive resting bitch face and more holes in her jeans than I have encryptions on my phone. I like her more than I should.

The same can't be said for Silver Spoon.

"Don't feel bad about coming in fourth, Issa," he tells her in a tone that says pretty much the opposite. "At least you aren't last."

"Nothing to feel bad about. After all, genius takes time." She shoots him a look that would have made a less arrogant guy crumble on the spot. "Then again, so do a lot of things. You sure you want to keep bragging about how fast you are?"

"Hey, I've got no shame about coming in second out of five." But his cheeks flush just a little.

"Haven't you heard?" she shoots back. And yep, I'm definitely going with Buffy. At the moment she looks like she would love nothing more than to drive a stake straight through Silver Spoon's Armani-loving heart. "There are no points for second place."

He just laughs, though. "That's the worst *Top Gun* impression I've ever heard."

She looks at him, baffled, and I'm about to explain the scene—Silver Spoon isn't the only one here who loves old movies—when the door crashes open.

It's the first time I've been caught unawares since we got here, and the fact that Mad Max—who looks like a character from the movie, with his flaming red Mohawk and bright green skinny jeans—is the one to do it blows me away. I can't help but watch in astonishment as he skitters across the room, all nervous energy and abundant enthusiasm.

"You're last, Seth." Silver Spoon's look is pure superiority.

But Mad Max isn't biting. "Nothing wrong with saving the best for last, baby." Buffy reaches over and fist-bumps him. I'm definitely not the only one Silver Spoon irritates.

"What's with you and the superiority complex?" she asks. "You came in second. That means Harper or Alika beat *you*."

I suck in a breath so fast that I nearly choke. And when Buffy holds up a fist for me to bump, I freeze. I'm not used to people knowing my name, let alone talking about me. It's how I like it— easier to fly under the radar if no one knows you exist. But I can't just leave her hanging either. Not when she's standing up to Silver Spoon, something I've been wanting to do since I got here.

Long seconds pass before I drop my phone into my lap and awkwardly press my knuckles against hers.

"How do we even know it was a race?" Mad Max asks, eyes trying to conceal either laughter or indignation. Or both. It's hard to tell because, for all his easygoing attitude, his eyes are as shuttered as mine. "Maybe I just got the hardest task."

"Yeah, right," Silver Spoon replies with an eye roll. "Because the CIA is going to give the hardest job to a guy who looks like a matchstick."

"You never know. I had to crack through triple encryption and design a kick-ass sniffer to hit the payload. Not to mention duplicate a double hash—that's one hundred and twenty-eight characters, for those of you used to playing in the kiddie pool."

Buffy fakes a yawn. "Is that all? I had to brute-force my way into—"

"Maybe we shouldn't be talking about this." Snow White speaks up for the first time.

"What do you mean?" Mad Max's brows hit his hairline.

I get his incredulity. I mean, this is what hackers *do* when we get together. We brag about what we cracked and how we cracked it. We can't tell anyone else—at least not if we don't want to end up in prison—so the whole tale-swapping thing is a time-honored tradition.

But at the same time, I'm totally aware of the three bugs in the room and what they mean. I'm trying to think of a way to tell the rest of them without giving anything away to the CIA when I catch sight of Agent Donovan through the window. He's practically sprinting down the hallway toward us, and I can't help wondering if his sudden appearance is because he doesn't like that we're showing *and* telling.

"I just think the CIA probably expects discretion from us," Snow White continues. "Maybe the next step is—"

Agent Donovan pushes open the door. "Hey, hey, the gang's all here," he jokes as he heads our way.

Silver Spoon fakes a little laugh—of course he does—but the rest of us just kind of stare at Agent Donovan, waiting to see what he'll say. He's got our futures in his hands, and suddenly the butterflies in my stomach feel an awful lot like pterodactyls.

"First of all, I'd like to thank all of you for coming today. We're just getting started going over your work, but I can tell you we like what we see so far. Do any of you guys have questions for me?"

I wait for the others to speak up, but no one does. Which means—no matter how much I hate it—I'm going to have to. Because I really, really want to know. "How long before we'll know if we're accepted into the program?"

"Three or four weeks, probably."

Four weeks feels like forever when my whole future hangs in the balance. I'm trying not to show my disappointment, but I must not be doing a very good job because Mad Max bumps his knee against mine in an unmistakable gesture of comfort. It doesn't lessen my disappointment, but it does comfort me more than I expect. He may look like a human matchstick, but he seems like a really good guy.

"Any other questions?" Agent Donovan asks. When no one else says anything, he continues, "Okay, then. You've all got your plane tickets. There's a car downstairs that will take you back to the airport. Feel free to help yourselves to the food we've stocked in the back for you." He starts ushering us toward the door.

"That's it?" Buffy asks, a little incredulously.

"That's it," he answers crisply. "Except, of course, I'm sure you all understand that we expect you to keep what you did here today completely confidential. Even from each other. You may have only been running simulations, but the work we do here is serious. We need to keep it under wraps. Understand?"

We all nod like good little girls and boys, but I can't help glancing at Snow White. And I realize the others are looking at her too. Does she know about the bugs too? Is she just better at this than the rest of us? Or is she just a really good guesser?

I'm still pondering the answers to my questions when we climb into the back of the limo. Seems like a huge waste of taxpayer dollars, shuttling us back and forth from the airport in a limo, but then, they did pay to fly us all here. Renting a limo for a day is probably nothing.

For a second, just a second, I think of the guy who walked out—Owen, I think his name tag said. He warned us about things being too good to be true, and as I settle into the luxurious interior of the limo, I can't help wondering if he was right. Is this all just a little too much?

I don't want him to be right, though, so I shove the thought out of my mind and concentrate on what's going on around me instead.

There's a stack of boxed lunches—or dinners, considering the time—next to the mini bar and Mad Max whoops when he sees them. He passes one to everybody, then digs in to his before the limo is even moving. Silver Spoon and Buffy do the same.

Snow White and I exchange a look, and though we both open our boxes, neither of us makes a move to eat anything. I'm too nervous about the three to four weeks we've got to wait to even attempt eating, and I wonder if that's her problem too. She may not *need* to make this program the way I do, but she obviously wants it.

Suddenly, Silver Spoon asks, "Anybody else think it strange that Agent Donovan warned us not to talk about anything, then put us all in the back of a limo together? I mean, it's the CIA. They could have arranged for us all to go separately."

"Maybe this is still part of the test," Mad Max tells him. "Maybe the limo's bugged, and they're waiting to see what we do."

"Maybe. Or maybe it's…" He looks like he's trying to find the right words.

"*The Usual Suspects*," I contribute, figuring that since he likes old movies, he'll get it even if no one else does.

I'm right. "You think?" he says, his eyes suddenly locked on mine.

"What's that?" Buffy asks, her fingers already flying over her screen. "A 1995 movie—seriously, you two need to update your viewing choices—where a group of criminals are all left together in one jail cell in the hope that they'll take the bait and bond together to carry out a crime." She looks up, incredulous. "You really think that's what this is about? They want us to talk about what we did?"

"I don't know what I think," Silver Spoon answers. "I'm just throwing ideas out there."

"Well, stop." Snow White closes her box and drops it on the floor.

"Stop?" He looks at her like he can't believe she just said that.

"Yes, stop. Agent Donovan told us not to talk about anything we did, and I'm going to take him at his word. I want to get into this program, and I'm not going to blow it just because the rest of you can't follow directions."

"Hey! What did I do?" Mad Max squawks. "I'm just sitting

here eating my sandwich. It's those three that are going all conspiracy theory over there."

"Way to sell us out, matchstick boy," Buffy tells him with a roll of her eyes.

"I just call 'em like I see 'em."

"Yeah, well, so do I. And—as much as it pains me—I agree with Ezra on this. Why put us together if they don't want us to talk?" Buffy asks.

"But what's there to talk about?" Snow White suddenly looks agitated as she runs her hands through her long dark hair. "We ran a bunch of simulations for them. So what?"

"That's what I'm trying to figure out," Silver Spoon replies.

"Yeah, well, do us all a favor, Ezra, and figure it out yourself." She opens her purse and pulls out a pair of pristine white earbuds. "I've got better things to do."

After putting in the earbuds and swiping her fingers across her phone a few times, she leans her head back against the seat. Closes her eyes.

And leaves the rest of us staring uneasily at one another as we try to figure out just what—if anything—we've suddenly become a part of.

3

Issa
[Pr1m4 D0nn4]

"It's kind of weird that we're on the same flight home, isn't it?" Seth asks as he shoves half a Snickers bar down his throat. "I mean, we couldn't have been on the same flight in, because you said your flight was late and mine was definitely on time. Weird we'd end up on the same flight home after being on different flights here...."

I swear, there hasn't been more than ten minutes all day when he wasn't eating something. I'm pretty sure Freud would have a field day with his oral fixation.

"I don't see what's so weird about it," I tell him as I step into an empty row and prepare to take the window seat. This morning was the first time I'd ever been on an airplane, and I was too scared to take the window then. Now, I can't wait to watch as we barrel down the runway before gradually pulling up through the clouds. If this flight goes as smoothly as my first, I'm pretty sure flying might unseat hacking as my second favorite activity in the world. Cuddling Chloe is still first, but then, she's pretty much the cutest baby on the planet.

As I shove my backpack under the seat, I realize Seth is still talking, babbling on about fate versus coincidence. I want to tell him it's neither—that we're on the same plane bound for Southwest's Houston hub because he lives in Austin and I live in San Antonio—but lashing out at him would feel an awful lot like kicking a puppy, so I just nod along and pray he decides to keep moving.

I know it's a pipe dream even as the thought crosses my mind, and sure enough, Seth joins me in the row before I can so much as fumble my seat belt on. He even goes so far as to plant himself in the middle seat, in an obvious commitment to our newfound friendship.

Lucky, lucky me.

Something tells me Seth isn't the type to let three hours pass in silence. I barely resist the urge to snicker. Who am I kidding? He's not the type to let three *minutes* pass in silence. I can feel my plans to sleep once the plane is in the air slipping away.

Sure enough, once he's settled, he pulls out a pack of M&M's and offers me some—seriously, it's like he's got Willy Wonka's entire factory in his ridiculous backpack.

I just shake my head, bemused, but he grins. "Oh, come on. I saw you earlier—I know you're a blue M&M girl. I won't even say anything if you want to dig through and pick out only the blue ones."

"Wow, you're observant," I answer, taking the pack because it feels like I'd be rejecting him if I didn't. And while normally I'm okay with that, he's trying so hard that I just can't. Instead, I comb through the pack until I pick out seven blues.

So sue me; I have siblings who take their M&M's very seriously. I'm usually lucky if I get the last one in the pack—and it's almost never blue.

I hold up my palm, which is full of the small chocolate candies. "This is some serious friendship right here."

"No doubt," he agrees, and damn if there isn't something completely endearing in the look he gives me. I find myself responding despite my best intentions. I mean, I don't have a lot of time for friends—what with school and hacking and taking care of four kids under the age of ten, plus Lettie—but if I did, I think I'd like to have Seth as a friend. He's sweet and good, and I'm pretty sure that with him what you see is what you get. He's not boyfriend material, but that's a good thing considering I swore off boys eleven months ago.

"So, what do you think of this whole CIA program thing?" he stage-whispers after ingesting two handfuls of candy.

I kind of want to ask if he's planning on telling the entire plane what we spent the day doing—his whispers are like normal people's shouts—but he's holding out three more blue M&M's, and I just don't have it in me.

We talk for a few more minutes as the rest of the plane gets settled—mostly about the many, many ways that Austin is cooler than San Antonio—and then we're barreling down the runway before I can even prepare for it.

Within seconds we're airborne, and less than a minute after that we're pulling through the lower levels of clouds. I watch, fascinated, wishing Chloe was here—she's got a fluffy white cat Lettie and I bought her right after she was born, and she loves the thing so much. She'd squeal the second she saw the clouds, then try to pat them the way she does her cat. It would be so adorable.

But we've barely made it through the clouds—Seth babbling on about some music festival he went to a few weeks ago in Austin—when the plane drops several feet.

A few gasps echo through the cabin, mine included, as we start bumping up and down. I remind myself that air travel is completely safe, that the plane we're in is an Airbus, which means they're probably running an Integrity OS on the in-flight comps. And since Integrity is one of the best and most secure systems, running an encryption system so good it's pretty much unhackable—I should know, I tried before I ever agreed to get on a plane to L.A.—we're good to go. Especially since the military runs it in a lot of their planes because it more than meets the standards set forth in the DO-178B.

The plane drops again—even a sweet OS like Integrity can't control turbulence, I guess—and seconds later, the captain's voice comes over the loudspeaker. "Ladies and gentlemen, it looks like we're going to be in for some turbulence for the next several minutes. Please make sure your seat belts are fastened and that you remain in your seats. Sorry for the inconvenience, and I'll do what I can to steer us out of it as soon as possible."

The plane drops one more time, and suddenly the second flight of my life doesn't seem like such fun. State-of-the-art in-flight computers or not, I'm in what amounts to a tin can in the sky. The precariousness of our position hits home as the plane starts to buck and rock.

My hands grab on to the armrests of their own volition, my fingernails digging in as I try to keep the plane in the air through sheer will alone.

"You know, the chance of turbulence bringing down an airplane is really slim," Seth says, and this time when he speaks, his voice is low and soothing.

"I know," I answer him. But that knowledge doesn't have me relaxing my grip on our shared armrest one little bit.

Slowly, he pries my fingers away. "You're going to hurt yourself," he says, and I realize I've actually broken a nail on the stupid thing. Not that I have long nails—because hacker, please—but still... my hands actually hurt from how tight I was squeezing.

Seth pats my hand. "It's going to be okay," he tells me, and he sounds confident even though the plane's bouncing around like a basketball at the NBA championship.

I'm too busy trying not to freak out to answer him.

The turbulence continues, and we sit like that for a couple of minutes, with him patting my hand and me pretending I'm anywhere but in a really big tin can that could crash at any second.

"So," he finally asks, "have you heard the Harry Styles album?"

"Excuse me?" Not even fear of imminent death can keep the horror out of my voice.

"Harry Styles? 'Sign of the Times'? 'Two Ghosts'?"

"Do I look like a One Direction fan to you?" I demand, a little breathless and even more outraged.

Seth shrugs. "I'm a One Direction fan. But Harry Styles's solo stuff is more glam anyway—like David Bowie meets Lana Del Rey. It's one of my favorite albums of the past couple of years."

I just stare at him. "I can't believe we're actually having this conversation."

"Oh, don't tell me you're a music snob!" He genuinely looks like I've just admitted to sacrificing kittens under a full moon.

"Good music is good music," I answer. "Nothing snobbish about that."

"Exactly!"

Because I still have a death grip on his hand, Seth rests his phone on his knee and starts scrolling through it. Seconds later, he's holding out his earbuds for me.

I shake my head and try not to roll my eyes. "I'm good, thanks."

"What? Afraid you'll be proven wrong?"

"More like afraid I'll go into a sugar coma from all the sweetness."

"Hey, now, don't be music-ist!" he scolds me.

"Music-ist?"

"Yeah, you know. Prejudiced against music."

Now I'm just appalled. "Seriously, Harry Styles? Aren't you afraid they'll revoke your man card?"

"I'm secure enough in my masculinity that I think I can handle it." He holds out the earbud again. "Now come on. Try it."

It's pretty obvious he isn't going to give up on this, so I sigh and make a big deal of taking one of the stupid earbuds and putting it in my right ear. He grins at me, face close, and puts the second one in his left ear. He hits Play, and I brace myself for bubblegum pop.

What comes on instead is a slow, soulful ballad. I turn to look at Seth, eyes wide, and he just grins at me, mouthing *Told ya.*

We listen to the whole thing through, twice, and when it's done, I can't help saying, "Okay, you win."

"I always do," he answers.

"Now who's being jerk-ist?" I joke.

"Jerk-ist means I'm prejudiced against jerks. I'm actually totally okay with that."

I roll my eyes. "You really don't quit, do you?"

"Never." He grins. "It's part of my charm."

"Just keep telling yourself that."

"I plan on it."

Suddenly, the captain comes on and says, "Okay, folks, we've been out of the turbulence for a couple of minutes, so I'm going to turn off the fasten seat belts sign so you can move about the cabin. Please remember to keep your seat belts fastened when you're seated."

Seth slowly releases my hand, and that's when it finally hits me that he's been distracting me all along. "Thanks," I tell him softly.

He just smiles that ridiculous grin of his. "Anytime." Then he pulls out a pack of Twix and offers me one.

I take it without comment. And can't help thinking that maybe being friends with this guy isn't the worst move in the world.

Case Study:
Owen Heath aka 1nf1n173 5h4d3

DOB: 3/21/00

Sex: Male

Height: 6'3"

Weight: 230 lbs.

Eye Color: Green

Hair Color: Black (wears in dreads)

Race: Mixed (African American and white)

School: Francis J. Worth Academy (private), Boston

Parents: Caleb and Althea Heath

Personal Net Worth: $1 mil (trust fund)

Family Net Worth: $25 mil

Most Notorious Hack: Seizing control of livestream during playoff game and running fake (and hilarious) stats for players.

OBSERVATIONS:

Owen Heath is, as Winston Churchill once said, "a riddle, wrapped in a mystery, inside an enigma." Except I'd add that he's all that underneath a paradox too. Which is probably why I've spent so much time thinking about him. From the minute he walked out of that room in L.A., I've been trying to figure him out. Trying to get inside his head and see who he is— and what he saw that made him leave when the rest of us didn't even think about it. Trying to see what I'm missing as I wait for an acceptance letter he seemed so sure wouldn't come.

I've hacked into as much of his life as I could get into: checked out his grades on his expensive prep school server, creeped his classmates' social media, even hacked his coach's emails. And all I've done is confuse myself even more. The kid makes absolutely no sense.

Honor student and star quarterback.

Black hat hacker and member of the school honor guard.

Philanthropist and total misanthrope all rolled into one.

So who *is* the real Owen Heath? A bad boy with a heart of gold or a good boy with a **really** bad attitude?

Most people are easy—even the ones who like to play it close to the vest have tells. Little phrases, actions, attitudes that give them away. A double blink here, a finger tap there. Little signs that fill you in on who they are, what they're thinking, and—most important—what they want.

Heath has tells. He has lots of tells. The only problem is they're so contradictory that it's impossible to figure out which ones are real and which ones are deliberate, just to throw you off the scent.

In a business where everything depends on figuring out what your mark wants, and tricking them into thinking you're the only one who can provide it, ambiguity is a superpower. The only question is, is Owen Heath a sociopath or a prophet?

SURVEILLANCE FOOTAGE:
11/24/18
09:37
BOSTON, MASSACHUSETTS

Footage begins, courtesy of security camera F12, in the lobby of the main headquarters for the Boston Stars football team. The lobby is empty, save for two very large security guards, Roger Browning and David Shilling, and a receptionist, Beth Gracen.

Thirty male students from Francis J. Worth's varsity football team enter the building at 09:42, accompanied by school coaches Charlie O'Connell and Mick Adams. Owen Heath is one of these students.

The group encounters Browning at 09:44, who greets Heath like an old friend. The two talk for three minutes and twenty-three seconds as Shilling begins checking in the rest of the team. Browning and Heath are sideways to the camera, but the way Browning gestures repeatedly to one of the jerseys hung under glass on the wall (HEATH 23) suggests they are talking about Heath's father for much of the conversation.

At 09:50, Chuck Monahan, Boston Stars offensive line coach, enters the lobby and greets the high school team. He talks for two minutes and twenty seconds, giving what looks like a rousing introductory speech, then takes a minute to speak to Heath, who looks unhappy with the conversation.

The tour of the facilities begins at 09:55. Security camera F16 picks up the group on the practice field seven minutes and twelve seconds later, where numerous Stars players are running drills. Students are allowed on the field to run a few drills (tackling dummies, sprints) with the professional athletes. Selfies and autographs commence.

At 10:41, the tour continues, hitting the offices and the locker room over the course of the next thirty-six minutes (footage provided via cameras F2, F2, F4, and 09).

Monahan and the boys enter the training center at 11:17 (camera F7), where he introduces the boys to therapists Vik Adobe and Marcella White. They greet Heath warmly, but Heath's body language is *very* hostile toward both.

Camera F18 picks the group up entering the weight room at 11:32. Monahan allows the boys to try out the equipment, and as they divide up, Heath—who has been noticeably subdued through the tour—takes the opportunity to approach Monahan. Monahan and he talk animatedly for a few minutes. (This is considerably different from Heath's interaction with him in the lobby.) Eventually, Monahan pulls Heath in for a one-armed hug. Heath allows it, using the moment to lift Monahan's access badge. (He does it so smoothly that I had to watch the footage several times to catch it.) Heath then excuses himself to use the bathroom in the corner of the room.

Surveillance ceases as he enters the bathroom.

At 11:56, security camera F1 picks up Heath outside the building as he uses Monahan's pass to reenter via one of the player-access doors. Review of public-record blueprints suggests that he climbed out the second-story window in the bathroom and dropped to the practice field.

It takes Heath one minute and thirty-one seconds to climb three flights of stairs and swipe his way into the fourth-floor offices. He keeps a low profile as he winds through cubicles and open space—head down, shoulders hunched. For a guy as large and good looking as he is, he does an admirable job of blending in and not getting noticed.

At 12:02, he scans his way into Steve Blayback's office (general manager of the Stars). Once in the office (camera C7), he heads straight for Blayback's computer. A quick check of the drawers yields what I assume is a password list because seconds later, Heath is logging into the computer. As soon as he's in, he pulls an R2-D2 thumb drive from his pocket (once a geek, always a geek) and inserts it into the computer. My guess is that he took all the files on the computer, seeing how long they took to download and how he didn't look through them, just immediately started downloading.

Seven minutes and fourteen seconds later, Heath ejects the drive and leaves the office, just as Blayback enters the fourth floor from the elevator (camera C3). At 12:10, Heath heads back down two flights of stairs, and at 12:12, he slips (completely unnoticed) back into the weight room via the main door, just as his teammates finish their impromptu workout. The kid is definitely a chameleon—his ability to blend in is incredible.

The tour continues with no further incidences, and at 13:01, the boys exit the main lobby.

◆ ◆ ◆

UPDATE: 11/25/2018

The *Boston Globe*'s online site is hacked by 1nf1n173 5h4d3 at 02:47, and numerous Boston Stars case files are posted under its breaking news section, providing reports of suspected CTE among several retired Stars players—as well as documentation of the team's efforts to keep said reports from public (and current player) consumption.

UPDATE: 11/26/2018

Owen Heath quits the Worth football team and walks away from dozens of college scholarship offers. Lots of people want answers; he gives none.

UPDATE: 11/26/2018

Neighbors call police regarding a domestic disturbance at 287 Seaport Lane in the Beacon Hill neighborhood of Boston, home of Caleb and Althea Heath. No arrests are made.

4

Owen
(1nf1n173 5h4d3)

"Yo, dude, we sure could have used you tonight," Jerome tells me as he offers up a fist bump. I meet him halfway—of course I do—but I can feel the accusation in his words even as our fists bounce off each other.

Murmurs of agreement go up from the group as we make our way to the parking lot, and I think about defending myself, think about telling them just how screwed up things have gotten and how football doesn't mean jack to me anymore.

But they won't get it. They've been in the locker room with me for years, have seen how bad the bruises have gotten in recent months, and still they won't get it. How can they, when most of them get freaking stars in their eyes every time my dad's name comes up? Stars that are even more blinding since he arranged that visit to his old headquarters two weeks ago.

"Sorry, man," I tell Jerome as I click open the locks on the top-of-the-line truck my dad got me for my birthday last year. "Couldn't do it anymore."

No one asks exactly what it is I couldn't do, and I don't

volunteer anything else. There's a fine line between sharing and being a total loser, and I feel like lately I've been coasting precariously close to the latter.

But what else was I supposed to do? Keep playing that stupid game even though just the sight of it makes me sick? Keep staying out of the house for all hours at brutal varsity practices, leaving my mom alone and vulnerable with my dad?

Options are not something I have in abundance right now.

Maybe that'll change when Northwestern's winter break starts next week and Damon comes home. But until then, I'm toeing the line. Doing whatever I need to do to keep things calm.

"Hey, you know what we should do?" Scooter says as he climbs into the back seat. "We should head over to the water, mourn our playoff defeat in style. It's been months since we've been up there."

He's right, it has been. We used to hang at my family's waterfront house, thirty miles north of Boston, all the time after games. Used to hole up partying and then spend the night passed out on whatever surface happened to be available.

But that was last year, when things were relatively normal. Now just the idea of being gone overnight freaks me out. The only way I even got to go to L.A. a few weeks ago was because my aunt came to stay for the weekend and Dad's always pretty chill when his baby sister's around.

"Come on, Owen—that's a great idea!" Jerome says. "Matt and Justin already have supplies in the trunks of their cars. We can head up there right now."

Their excitement fills the cab, and I can feel it crushing

me—just like the rest of my life. A party's the last thing I feel like right now, but I've disappointed them enough this year. The idea of doing it again makes me feel like ass.

Pulling out my phone, I fire off a text to my mom before starting the engine.

U good?

If she's not, there's no way I'll even think about going anywhere but home.

She answers a few seconds later.

Yeah ☺

How was the game?

We lost

Where's Dad?

He fell asleep half an hour ago

Everything's fine, Owen. He's in a good mood tonight

U sure?

YES

We had a nice dinner out, saw a movie

He's good

OK

Can we use the beach house for the night?

Absolutely, but you know the rules

Yeah, I know

I'll be home tomorrow morning

Have fun!

xoxoxox

"Text the others," I tell Jerome as I drop my phone onto the console beneath the dash. "Tell them to meet us at the beach."

Jerome whoops and hollers and talks freaking nonstop the whole way. Even stopping for snacks at the local market doesn't shut him up. By the time we get to the beach house, I'm not sure who wants to smother him more—Scooter or me.

Moments later, I'm turning off the alarm and giving the all clear to the others. They pile in, loaded down with enough supplies to last out the apocalypse.

According to Austin, the girls should be here soon, so Justin gets the music cranking while Scooter and Blake set up everything else. I walk around facilitating everything, helping Justin hook into my dad's monster stereo and grabbing bowls so Tyler can set out the snacks. "Girls like it when you're a little classy," he tells me over the *thump thump thump* of Justin's bass.

Sure enough, the girls show up a few minutes later, and Ashley makes a beeline for me. I think about taking her up on her very blatant offer, but the truth is, I'm just not into it. Not into her, not into any of this same old BS right now. Not with everything else that's going on.

I dodge her two or three times—claiming the whole gotta-be-a-good-host thing—but as the night wears on, I start running out of excuses. *Screw it.* There's only one thing I really want to be doing right now anyway—and it's not messing around with a girl I don't even like when the lights are on.

After going out to the car and grabbing my backpack, I sneak up the back stairs to my parents' room. All the guys know it's off-limits, so I should be safe there, but I lock the door anyway—just in case Ashley comes looking.

Pulling out the laptop that goes absolutely everywhere with me, I settle in the middle of the bed. And pull up the file folder I've been working on for a while.

The first thing I do is connect to my computer at home and check the facial recognition program I've got running twenty-four seven. I created it a while ago for fun, but now that I have an actual purpose for it, I've been working out the last of the bugs.

My program's nowhere near as fancy as the FBI's—theirs tends to focus on criminal databases, DMV photos, things like that—but mine still gets the job done. Besides, the chances of getting caught go up exponentially (as does the amount of time required to even attempt it) when you have to break into that many high-security databases.

Which is why I went a totally different route, one that hits sites with security so ridiculously easy to bypass that it's a little embarrassing to admit I'm even bothering with it. But the honeypot's so good that I couldn't resist hacking into every high school yearbook in the country.

Sure, the hack has its flaws—it's limited to the last twenty years or so, because this stuff wasn't online before that. But right now that little flaw doesn't matter, since the person I'm looking for isn't any older than early to mid-thirties.

My program hasn't hit on anything yet, so I keep it grinding away while I pull up another folder—one that contains the ownership and financial details of the building I visited in L.A., 2367 Sepulveda. I've been digging around in between school and family crap, and I really don't like what I've found so far: mainly that the building is owned by a mom-and-pop property management company that does short-term leases on properties all over Southern California. It tends to lease the Sepulveda building out to film companies that need an office location to shoot in.

I've managed to uncover the name of the company that leased the building during the week in November we were there, but when I dig on the company, all I get is a bunch of nothing. It's definitely a shell corporation—and a good one at that. I've dug down three layers so far, and I'm still no closer to finding out who actually rented the building than I was a month ago.

I start digging again now, following the money trail between the latest corporate iteration I've managed to find and the parent company that's trying so hard to stay hidden. The difficulty in itself tells me something. Nobody tries this hard to hide unless they've got a reason for it. Looks like I made the right decision walking out of that room.

Downstairs, someone turns the music up so high that I swear I can feel the walls shaking. I consider going down and telling people to chill a little bit, but I'm not that kind of guy.

Besides, they deserve to blow off some steam with everything they've been through the last few weeks.

So instead of complaining, I pull out my earbuds and plug them in.

An hour and a half later, my computer dings, and I'm so deep down my latest rabbit hole on this bogus corporation that I almost miss that my facial recognition program just went off. When my brain registers what's happening, I click over and nearly lose it, because Agent Shane Donovan is staring at me from my computer screen.

Only his name isn't Shane Donovan. According to the 2001 yearbook from Salvation High—in Salvation, North Dakota—Shane is actually Daniel Davies.

Armed with this new information, I dig a little more—and that's when I hit the jackpot. Because Salvation, North Dakota, is the hometown of Franklin Enterprises, where Daniel Davies got his first job in 2006—and where he is still employed to this day. Franklin Enterprises, it turns out, is a little-known subsidiary of global communications conglomerate Jacento.

I think back on the code they wanted me to write when I showed up at 2367 Sepulveda, code that sent me running out the door because I didn't want any part in creating code like that for the CIA—even if they already employ half a dozen people who could do it.

But the CIA seems like child's play now, because why the hell would a communications company want code like that? A communications company that has access to tens of millions of cell phones and tablets all over the world. Just the thought is enough to make my blood run cold.

Especially considering the way Jacento pretended to be the freaking CIA . . . which I'm pretty sure is a crime all on its own. Besides, if what they were doing was on the up and up, why'd they have to lie about it?

Suddenly I'm very, very interested in what skills the other five people in that room had—and what tasks they were asked to complete.

The bad feeling intensifies, and now it's so overwhelming that my hands shake a little as I pull up another file, one I've labeled SELLOUTS.

I'd been pissed as hell at the crap they pulled with those ID stickers—names and handles—but when we were mixing and mingling before Issa showed up, I made sure to memorize everyone's. Not that it was hard. There was a ton of talent in that room—everyone Jacento picked for that little "audition" already has a rep in the hacker world.

I pull up the profiles I've started building on Ezra/EazyH, Seth/5c0ut60, Alika/W4rrl0r W0m4n, Harper/5p3ct3r, and Issa/Pr1m4 D0nn4. I start looking at some of their old hacks that I've compiled, trying to figure out what each might have done during the "audition." But it's not like the hacks are a tell-all—like me, what they've claimed credit for is probably only a tenth of what they're capable of.

Which means I am completely screwed.

Sure, given enough time, I could probably hack their personal accounts—no matter how good their defenses are. But common sense, and the sinking sensation in my stomach, tell me there is no time. Not now, when I've already wasted a month gathering intel.

I study the profiles again, looking for anything I might have missed. But there's nothing. Which means I've got no other option. I need to know exactly what these guys did.

But which one of them do I trust? And who can I get to trust me? It's not like I made a great impression when I stormed out before the "testing" even began.

In the end, I go with my gut. A quick Google search turns up a school email address in her city of residence, so I fire off a quick email that I hope doesn't make me sound like an idiot. And then I wait, hoping like hell that she'll decide to answer....

$$\bullet \ \bullet \ \cdot \ \bullet \ \cdot \ \bullet \ \cdot$$

Five excruciating hours later, Alika emails me back. It's seven in the morning, and I haven't slept all night, too afraid I'd miss a response from her. And too determined to dig up as much as I can on Jacento and any shadowy connections it might have.

Turns out there's a lot of them, if you know where to look. But that's another part of the story—right now I just need to know what Alika knows and how her part of the audition fits with mine. I swipe on the email, wait impatiently for it to load. But when it finally comes up on the screen, my stomach sinks.

> Why is it any of your business what I did for my
> audition? You didn't even stick around for yours.
> Please don't contact me again.

Damn. Just damn. It's exactly the answer I was afraid of—and exactly the answer I deserve. This girl doesn't know me at all—not that I know her either, but at least I've learned something about her over the last few weeks as I was digging into who she and the others are and what the CIA/Jacento might be using them for.

But that's exactly why I'm not ready to let this go yet. Not ready to move on to Seth, who's the next one on my list. Because I *have* researched this girl and I've figured out enough about her to know that I want her on my side during this. And not just because her daddy is secretary of state.

Without giving myself time to think, I hit Reply. And then I just type.

> Please, Alika, hear me out. Something's really wrong with this whole situation, and I need help to piece it together. It's why I left to begin with— because something didn't feel right. I just found out the place they took us to didn't belong to the CIA at all. It belongs to a real estate company that rents it out to movies when they need an office building. Basically, it's a soundstage—the whole thing is fake. And the week we were there, it wasn't rented by the CIA or anything affiliated with them.
>
> Please. Here's my number. Call me and I'll explain more.
>
> 617-555-0166
>
> Owen

I hit Send and I wait. And wait. And wait.

After about fifteen minutes, I hear the first stirrings of life in the house. I head downstairs, where the noise is coming from, and hear Jerome in the shower, singing at the top of his lungs. Awesome.

A quick tour tells me everyone else is still sleeping—in the living room, the family room, on the enclosed patio. Back inside I find Scooter passed out in the middle of my dad's pool table, and for a second I think about waking him for no other reason than his face is planted on the ball rack and I'm pretty damn sure that can't be comfortable. I'm also sure it's going to leave a hell of a bruise.

But I just leave him—if I wake him up, I've got to deal with him, and right now I've got enough going on without having to entertain a bunch of starving football players. They're my friends, sure, but they're still assholes at least half the time.

I screw around for a few minutes, make myself a cup of coffee and a couple of Pop-Tarts. But by the time I scarf one down I'm pretty damn close to jumping out of my skin, so I pull out my phone and head back up to my parents' room. A quick stop by my own room reveals Blake lying on my bed, with a girl on either side of him. I'm not even surprised.

It's no use checking my email—I'd know if Alika replied— so I pull up my messages instead. And fire off a quick one to my mother, just checking in.

She answers within seconds.

Everything's good

I feel my shoulders sag a little in relief. Usually—not always, but usually—it's apparent pretty early on how the day's going to go. The fact that it's about eight now and things are calm, even though my dad never sleeps past five anymore, is a good sign. Not absolute or anything—because that's way too much to hope for—but good.

Which means I can give everyone a couple more hours to sleep before waking them up and herding them out.

Then again, time's ticking by so slowly at this point that I might lose my mind before those hours are up.

Screw it. I pull up the files I've been keeping on this audition thing and start digging again—I want to tie Jacento directly into that whole debacle in L.A., and I want to do it with more than just fake Agent Shane Donovan.

I'm deep down another rabbit hole, working my way through layers of code so crunch I think my head might explode, when my phone rings, completely splitting the silence. I nearly jump out of my skin and fumble for it with hands that are suddenly clumsy as hell. My friends are pretty much all in the house right now, so it's either my mom calling to tell me something's gone really, really wrong at home, or...

A quick look at the screen shows it's an unknown number. I swipe to accept the call, with my heart pounding a little faster as I do.

"Hello?"

"Owen?" The voice on the other end of the line is huskier than I expect it to be. Alika looks so prim and proper, but she sounds anything but.

"Alika?"

"Yes." She pauses. "I'm not even sure why I'm calling you."

"I'm glad you are. Have you heard from the CIA yet, about your audition?"

"No, not yet." She sounds hesitant. "But they said three or four weeks. . . ."

"You won't hear from them. The CIA had nothing to do with that trip to L.A."

There's a long silence, then, "What are you even talking about? We were all there—"

"Yeah, but it was just a front." I grab my laptop, start attaching some of the research I've uncovered. "I'm about to send you some information. Look it over and you'll see what I'm talking about."

I hit Send before I even finish the sentence.

"Why should I trust you?"

"Why should you trust *them*? The whole reason I walked out is because I didn't like what they wanted me to hack. It didn't seem like a test. It seemed like a real hack, and I didn't trust them."

"What did they want you to do?"

My brain is screaming caution—I don't really know if I can trust this girl. But I know I can't trust Jacento, just like I know I'm not going to get anywhere if I don't trust *someone*, so after a few seconds, I say, "They wanted me to write the code that would help a worm spread as quickly as possible in anything that runs macOS."

"I don't believe you." There's no hesitation in her voice.

I shove down my annoyance at the matter-of-fact statement, concentrate instead on getting her to listen to me. "Why would I lie? There's no point."

"There's no way you could write code like that in a day. Or a month. The whole idea is absurd, no matter how good you are."

"I actually have a lot of the code written already, so it wouldn't be nearly as hard as you're implying."

"You've already got the code?" Now she sounds more than skeptical. She sounds worried.

"I hacked iTunes a while ago, after the big Sony hack, just to see if I could. I wasn't looking to steal info, though—just wanted a good look at their encryption and what they were running."

"Which wasn't enough, obviously."

"Obviously."

"I've got the info you sent," she says, and there's a long silence as she opens the docs, looks through them.

I force myself to give her time.

Finally Alika starts talking again, and this time she sounds way more concerned. "I don't understand. What does Jacento want with us?"

"The bigger question is, what does Jacento want that they're willing to hack iTunes and who knows what else to get?"

Another long silence. Alika's definitely a look-before-she-leaps kind of girl—it's why I picked her—but it's frustrating as hell when I'm sitting on the other end of the line trying to figure out what she's thinking.

"They wanted a new blended threat, one that piggybacked off Stuxnet and could infect iOS," she finally says.

"And you could do that? Just pull Stuxnet code out of your ass and create a worm for a whole different operating system based on it?"

"I did a major research paper on Stuxnet at the end of my junior year—I know the code inside and out. A lot of it doesn't work in this situation because the zero-day exploits were designed for Siemens control systems, but the theory behind the code is solid, obviously. It was just a matter of adapting it to a different OS, especially since I didn't have to find the back door in—"

"Because that was somebody else's job." I can't help thinking about the skill sets of the other four people in the room with us. Any one of them could have found that back door without breaking a sweat.

Another few moments of silence and then, "Yes. Probably."

"How detailed was this research project of yours? And how could Jacento have known about it?"

"Very detailed," Alika says with a sigh. "It was actually a discussion of how the principal properties of Stuxnet could be adapted to other operating systems—I spent a considerable amount of time working up code to prove it, though that was part of the project and not included in the actual paper."

"Which is how you could do something like this in a day. Because you'd already done it, basically."

"Basically, yeah."

"And your paper is published? I mean, how did Jacento figure out you'd done this?"

"It's not published, but it was my big junior year IB project, so it was sent out to be judged by a committee. Plus I used it in all my college applications, so..."

"So it's not exactly a secret."

"Nowhere near a secret," she agrees.

"They must have known what I did with iTunes too. Otherwise, why would they come to me for it? I mean, they didn't say, 'We want you to hack iTunes,' but I recognized the system right away from what they were asking—it's pretty unique."

"I bet. So, Owen, what does this..." Her voice trails off, like she can't even figure out what to ask.

"What does this mean? I'm not sure, but it's not good, right? I mean, what does Jacento need with this kind of access? And if they had us on Apple, does that mean the others were working on exploiting Android?"

She swallows audibly. "I don't know."

"Yeah, well, we should probably figure it out, don't you think?"

"I guess...."

"You guess? These assholes used us to do God only knows. How do you think that's going to work out for us once everything's in place and they get what they want? I've seen *Live Free or Die Hard*. Trust me, in cases like this, it does *not* go well for the hackers."

"What is it with you guys and old movies?"

"What do you mean?"

"Never mind." She pauses. "So, you think we should contact them?"

"I think we have to contact them, yeah."

"Okay. How? I don't even know their last names—"

"I do. I memorized their name tags. I'll dig for their numbers, set us up in a group chat."

"You think that's smart? Won't the CIA—"

"You mean Jacento?"

"Yeah, right. Jacento." She sighs. "Won't Jacento be watching for that?"

"I'm on a Jacento phone right now," I tell her even as unease crawls through me at the thought.

"Yeah, me too. I'm betting all of us have Jacento phones."

"You want me to set up a ghost chat instead?"

"Actually, yeah. That's probably the best idea. Can you get their IPs?"

"Are you deliberately trying to insult me?" I demand, and I'm only half-teasing.

"Umm, no?"

"Is that a question, or a statement?"

"At this point, I don't know what it is. I feel like my brain's about to blow up."

"Yeah, well, I've felt that way for the last month, so—" A crash from downstairs has me springing to my feet. "Look, I've got to go. But I'll put something together in the next couple of hours. Keep an eye out."

"Yeah, okay."

There's another long silence, and I start to hang up, but then Alika surprises me. She says, "Thank you."

"For what?" I can hear footsteps thundering up the stairs.

"For being suspicious while the rest of us were blinded by what we wanted the truth to be. So thanks for digging. And for reaching out to me."

"Yeah, umm, you're welcome." There's another crash. "Okay, I really, really have to go."

I hang up and rush downstairs, just in time to see Blake race through the living room and out to the backyard, clutching a throw pillow under his arm like a football.

"Seriously?" I look at the table he knocked over during the impromptu game of football. "Aren't you all still tired from your big night of partying?"

"Never too tired to play football," Scooter tells me as he jumps up and catches the pillow that Blake just sent soaring.

"Yeah, well, try to wrap it up in ten minutes, will you?" I roll my eyes as I head back upstairs for my gear. "I need to get home."

"Hey, where you going?" Jerome calls from his spot near the door. "Aren't you going to play?"

"What's more important than football?" Scooter calls after me.

I think about my dad, about hacking, about the mess I'm currently caught up in. "A lot of things."

It takes some wrangling, but I manage to get the guys up and out of the house pretty quickly after that. As soon as I get home and check on my mom, I head up to my room. Once I'm back at my laptop, it takes me about twenty minutes to get the info I need to set up the ghost chat. The only problem is, what do I say to get their attention? And to get them to respond?

I think about it for a while, but I don't want to overexplain right away, so in the end, I just type one sentence. Then I hit Send before I can change my mind.

5

Harper
[5p3ct3r]

YOU'VE BEEN PLAYED

The words show up in a box at the bottom of my screen on an otherwise ordinary Sunday, sent from a phantom chat account that identifies only as OH. I stare at them for long seconds, trying to figure out who sent them—and what they're in reference to.

Not to mention how someone managed to pull me into a ghost chat without my permission. *And* how they know who I am.

It's the last thing that has me freaking out a little. I guard my identity *very* closely, and I really don't like somebody finding a way around my security and dragging me into who knows what. I stare at the message box, blank now since the words disappeared seconds after showing up, and try to decide if I want to log out or click on the box—and let whoever sent this know that I've seen the message and am watching—when someone else chimes in.

AI: Listen to him. Please.

OH and AI…meaning what? Original Hacker? Artificial Intelligence? Origami Hamster? My finger hovers over the trackball as I try to decide. Stay or leave? Keep watching or close out the chat?

Suddenly, a third person joins.

EH: Dude, I never get played

Then a fourth.

IT: Who is this? What do you want?

AI: It's Alika. And Owen. From the audition a few weeks ago

Okay, now things are starting to make more sense. Owen Heath, the kid who walked out early, not Origami Hamster. More's the pity—hamsters don't have nearly the attitude this guy does.

But how did he go from being the Lone Ranger with attitude to teaming up with Snow White, of all people? She's the original good girl and team player while he…he, very definitely, is not.

I must not be the only one who's surprised, because the chat comes to a stop for a good minute or so, as the others are probably trying to work out the same stuff I am. The others being EH, i.e., Silver Spoon/Ezra Hernandez, and IT, who is Buffy/Issa Torres. The only one missing is Mad Max/Seth Prentiss. And, of course, me.

I still don't know if I want to join, even though reading the conversation in single lines at the bottom of my screen is getting annoying. But until I actually click into the chat, that one disappearing line is all I'm going to see.

> EH: Hey, Alika, aren't you the one who said we shouldn't be talking?
> EH: I'm pretty sure this little chat breaks ALL of Agent Donovan's rules
> OH: Lay off her, man
> EH: It doesn't look like I'm the one who's on her

Ugh. I roll my eyes, very nearly stop reading. If there's one thing I hate, it's chest-beating testosterone jockeys. Especially when one only cares about himself, and the other...I still don't have a clue what the other one cares about. And I sure as hell don't know why he's bothering to contact us now, when he didn't stick around for much more than introductions at the audition. If I was part of the chat, I'd be tempted to ask, but since I'm lurking, I just sigh and wait for it to be over.

I guess I'm not the only one who's annoyed by the testosterone overdose, because Snow White ignores all the posturing and takes the conversation back to its main point.

> AI: The rules don't matter if everything's fake
> AI: There is no CIA program and there are no college scholarships

The words disappear as soon as she types them, but they hang in the air around me, so huge that I can almost see them. So monumental that I can feel them lighting up a caution sign inside my brain.

> IT: **What are you talking about?**
>
> IT: **Of course there's a scholarship. They said**
>
> OH: **They lied**
>
> IT: **Why would they do that?**
>
> EH: **Because we got played**

That's a big admission coming from Silver Spoon. It gets my radar up, has me wondering just what he did for the "audition" that has him caving so easily from his "I never get played" stance. Then again, he's obviously a smart guy—one who's smart enough to recognize the truth when he sees it and honest enough not to try to hide it.

A begrudging kind of respect kindles deep inside me. I ignore it, at least for now. One moment of self-awareness does not a decent person make. Besides, I still don't know if the Lone Ranger and Snow White are lying to us.

My gut says no, but I never believe my gut. At least not without a lot of research to back it up.

> EH: **So, what'd they want with this little charade?**
>
> SP: **Hey! Who is this?**
>
> SP: **What'd I miss?**
>
> SP: **Whoa, catching up now**
>
> SP: **You can't be serious**

So Mad Max is in now too. I'm the only holdout. Again, my fingers hover over the trackball. In or out? In or out?

OH: If we wanna know what their goal is, we need to figure out what we did for them

IT: Don't you mean, what WE did? You ran away

OH: Seriously? You're going to blame me for that when you're the ones who let yourselves get used by Jacento????

SP: Jacento? What do they have to do with this?

IT: Jacento? Are you SERIOUS?

The name Jacento rings a bell for me—well, rings a bell for everyone, I'm pretty sure, as they're one of the largest telecommunications and computer equipment manufacturers in the world. Half the country has a Jacento phone or tablet or laptop, as does most of Europe and Africa. They're just breaking into the markets in Asia and South America, but it won't be long before they're huge there too.

Global domination is pretty much their mission statement, after all.

The thought rings another bell for me, as I stare at my own laptop and phone, both of which are from Jacento. Sure, we're in a ghost chat, which should be invisible to Android or any other OS, but *should be* are famous last words for a reason.

The thought has me googling something I remember reading a couple of weeks ago, even as I wonder what to do to make sure my Jacento equipment is safe. Call me paranoid, but paranoid is better than screwed. And definitely better than caught.

I keep an eye on the text box now, as I skim through the results of my search, looking for the article.

OH: Serious as a Trojan horse in your inbox

OH: We need to know what you did for them

IT: How do we even know you're who you say you are?

IT: How do we know this isn't just another test?

OH: Are you freaking kidding me, Issa?

OH: Are you really that brainwashed?

Not that *brainwashed*, I think, as I wait for Buffy to answer. That *desperate*. I know because I'm just as desperate. I can make enough with my hacking to support myself, but support myself *and* pay for Harvard? Tuition alone is over forty-three thousand dollars a year, and applying for financial aid is out, since it would raise all kinds of questions.

But there's no way I can do that without help. Or without some major black hat hack, which...no. I've already done enough covering up of records, moving stuff around in the system, getting paid by my classmates to hack their school tablets for food and rent money. I'm not ready to move from that to stealing from people.

But, unlike Buffy, I'm not into self-delusion. Like Silver Spoon, once I know the truth, I don't have the time or interest to hide from it. I'm too busy trying to find out *why* something happened to spend time or energy denying that it did....

OH: Check this out

He posts a file for download, and I grab it before it disappears. As always, I use my VPN to download it so that it won't be recorded in my history. But as the data streams onto my screen, I can feel my stomach start to sink.

The building we were in last month is nothing but a soundstage rented by some shell corporation the Lone Ranger managed to trace back to Jacento. Which is bad news for SO. MANY. REASONS.

A million questions zip through my brain, the most important one being, why did Jacento lie? Why did they feel the need to pretend to be the CIA? If they wanted work done, why didn't they just hire us—or other, more experienced hackers—to do it instead of going through the trouble of the whole CIA ruse?

The only way it makes sense is if they're planning something illegal. And not just a little illegal, but totally, completely, can't-be-defended-in-a-court-of-law illegal.

And if that's the case, then sure, I can totally see what they were thinking. Pick some stupid (but very skilled) teen hackers, let us do whatever they need done, and then tell us, "Thanks, but you haven't been selected for the program, blah blah blah." They figured it'd be like any other job or college application—we'd cry into our keyboards a little bit and then move on, no harm done.

Except they made one miscalculation. One huge miscalculation. They forgot that hackers aren't like normal people. We don't just move on from something that interests us, and we rarely forget anything—especially if it matters to us.

Most important, we're curious. Really, really, *really* curious. And in a world where technology is God, we've got the skills to indulge our curiosity in a way that few others do.

Which means that, unlike other kids our age, when crazy stuff happens, we tend to want to know why. And we dig until we do.

Hence the Lone Ranger finding all this out even though he didn't even stick around for the audition. Something obviously felt off to him that day, and this mess of information is the result.

The others seem to be reading, and absorbing, what he sent too, because the chat is quiet for a couple more minutes—which gives me enough time to finally find the article I was looking for.

I pull it up on a split screen, start to skim it to make sure I'm remembering correctly. As I do, I keep an eye on the bottom right corner of my screen, waiting for the others to catch up as I try to piece together what I know with what the Lone Ranger just showed us.

Freaking out's not really my thing—I prefer the calm and cool approach—but I've got to say that what I'm thinking is making me nervous. Really, really nervous.

So nervous, in fact, that I jump into the chat without thinking any more about it.

> **HB: I created an infection propagator that works on Red Hat Enterprise Linux**
>
> **EH: There she is**
>
> **EH: I always figured you for a lurker**

EH: Also, Houston, we have a problem

EH: Because I created the same thing for Ubuntu

OH: They wanted me to create one for macOS

OH: It's why I walked

IT: I created back doors into several large servers running Windows

SP: Uh-oh

SP: Houston, we have a BIG problem

SP: Because I created target locators and a tracking system for a polymorphic worm

SP: Also a suicide switch

AI: And I created a polymorphic payload

Her words go off like a bomb. Utter screen silence for several long seconds. Then:

EH: I repeat

EH: Houston, we have a BIG FREAKING PROBLEM

IT: Oh God

IT: What did we do?

EH: You want to know what we did?

EH: We created the apocalypse

EH: That's what we did

6

Owen
(1nf1n173 5h4d3)

Ezra's right.

I go over the list of what everyone did for the tenth time, trying not to tear my damn dreads out. Because come on. Just COME ON.

OH: What the hell were you guys thinking?

I type the words before I can think better of it, but once they're out there, I don't regret them. Because who does this crap? I took one look at what they wanted me to do and walked out. Why the hell didn't the rest of them?

AI: Okay, let's everybody calm down here

AI: We're a far cry from a digital apocalypse

EH: Yeah, right

EH: Tell yourself that often enough and you might actually believe it

EH: Isn't that how the government always gets

into trouble, State Department Girl? By deciding
something isn't a problem and ignoring it until
it's a disaster?

AI: Don't call me that! I'm not some government
stooge, no matter who my dad is

EH: Then don't act like one

EH: Do you even know who runs on Red Hat and
Ubuntu?

AI: What am I, stupid?

EH: I don't know, are you?

OH: From where I'm sitting, you're all morons

SP: Okay, enough with the name calling

SP: We get it, we screwed up

SP: And the answer is everybody

SP: Everybody runs on Red Hat and Ubuntu

IT: Obviously not, or my part wouldn't have been
necessary

HB: Almost everybody important does

OH: Google runs on Ubuntu

SP: Technically it's Goobuntu

OH: Really? Are you just screwing with me now?

SP: I was only trying to be accurate, jeez

IT: Amazon runs Red Hat

OH: Half the world runs Red Hat, including Social
Security and the Department of Defense

SP: The DoD runs SELinux, actually, using their own
code that's totally classified

OH: Yeah, you just go on believing that, dude

IT: You hacked the DoD?

OH: Like I'm going to answer that

AI: And Apple runs macOS. Obviously

EH: Like I said

EH: The apocalypse

IT: That depends on the payload

Issa's right, but she's also wrong. The actual apocalypse might depend on what the payload is, but even the least malicious worm in the world will wreak total and complete havoc if it's uploaded into even one of those systems. Loaded into all of them…it would take months, maybe even years, to sort out.

And that's before common sense kicks in and says we're not dealing with a bunch of gray hats here. We're dealing with a major corporation who went through the trouble of creating a blind scenario to pull off their dirty work. There's no way this code isn't bad freaking news.

Because this is what I need right now, on top of everything else. Jesus. I just wish I knew how all five of them could have been so damn blind.

I split the screen so I can keep an eye on where this is going, then pull up a code I worked on months ago. I have a feeling we're all going to need it before today is through.

EH: What's the payload do, Alika?

She doesn't answer right away. I'm not sure if it's because she's scared or if she's just trying to wrap her head around the ramifications of what she did. Either way, I can feel the impatience—and the fear—emanating from the others. Maybe it's my imagination. Maybe it's just me magnifying my own feelings.

But I don't think so. Not when it feels like the whole group of us is holding our collective breath.

SP: What's the payload do?

IT: What's the payload do?

Even Harper gets in on the act, all three questions going up at pretty much the same damn second.

HB: What's the payload do?

AI: Information gathering, mostly

AI: It's really not that complicated

EH: A simple smash and grab?

EH: You want us to believe that a major corp like Jacento went through all this trouble just to get people's credit card info?

EH: No freaking way

AI: It's not credit card info they're after

SP: What, purchase histories then?

SP: That's ridiculous. Companies share that stuff all the time

SP: Plus with Congress making it legal to sell browser history, what's the point of all this cloak-and-dagger stuff?

IT: None of this makes sense

IT: I mean, we've got infection propagators, but how are they going to deliver the payload? How are they going to get in?

IT: None of us actually hacked these companies' security, did we?

EH: No, but there's no guarantee we were the only group they put together to do this

AI: Maybe not, but why get more people involved than absolutely necessary?

AI: The more people who know, the bigger the chance for a leak

SP: So what are they planning?

SP: To get in the back doors Issa put in the smaller servers?

IT: That's risky

EH: Right?

EH: The places we're talking about have way too much security for that to work

HB: They're not going in through the servers

HB: Check this out

HB: FILE UPLOAD

I click the button to download the file with a really bad feeling in my gut. It's a feeling that only gets worse as the headline is revealed.

No Charger?
No Problem

Jacento to roll out charging kiosks throughout North America & Europe on New Year's Day

I start to skim the article quickly, looking for the highlights. But by the third paragraph the bad feeling is no longer contained to my stomach. It's crawling on my skin like lice, wriggling around all over me and making me twitchy as hell.

So I start back at the beginning, and this time I read every word. Carefully.

When I'm done, I go back and read it again. Because if Harper is implying what I think she is, then this is worse than I ever imagined. Depending on what Jacento is going for, digital apocalypse might be too mild a term for what can happen.

IT: **Oh my God**

EH: **They're going to upload it through the phones?**

SP: **That's impossible**

AI: **No, it's brilliant**

OH: **Yeah, it is**

OH: **Think of how many people in America use Amazon, iTunes, Google Play, on a daily basis**

OH: **Now think of all those people's phones hooked up to chargers at the same time**

IT: But it won't be at the same time

IT: I mean, how many people are actually going to need to charge their phones at any given moment?

SP: In big cities around the globe? It's practically infinite

SP: I mean, not really. But a lot

HB: Think about events

HB: Music festivals, antigovernment marches, conferences

OH: Professional sporting events, hot spots, airports, and train stations

OH: The list is endless

OH: People will use the kiosks in droves for their phones, tablets, laptops

They won't even think twice about it. Except to be grateful a charger is there, within easy reach so that their phone doesn't die before they can check their email or pull up their movie tickets or check in for their flight. Seth is right. The number of people who will use these things is a lot closer to infinite than it is to zero.

I look at my own phone with disgust—and some horror. What's to say they aren't in there already? What's to say they didn't crack all our phones when we were in that crappy fake office building in L.A.? Sure, I left early, but the others didn't. What if they used their own equipment in conjunction with the stuff Jacento had there? It's not a stretch to wonder if Jacento's already in their phones or laptops.

The thought gives me the creeps—and has me redoubling my efforts on my old code.

IT: And then what? You can't deliver a worm this sophisticated via a charging cable

EH: Who says it's sophisticated?

AI: I do

SP: It's polymorphic, right? What construct did you use, Alika?

AI: I used my own

AI: I developed it last year. Basically it's Russian roulette, if every chamber had a bullet

IT: Umm, I'm pretty sure they call that a loaded gun

AI: More like a Gatling gun. It keeps rapid-fire pinging the system over and over again until it wears it down and the server decides it recognizes it

OH: Like a wheel. It just keeps spinning until it gets where it wants to go

AI: Exactly

EH: That's pretty dope

HB: It's brilliant, just like she said

HB: Terrifying, but brilliant

IT: The charging cables can activate the worm, get it so that every phone attached to them whose user has an account at any of the big sites is pinging those sites at the same time

EH: Wearing them down, like she said, until the site starts to recognize the worm as normal

IT: Yeah, but that still doesn't explain how the worm gets *on* the phone to begin with

OH: Are you kidding me? It's Jacento

OH: All you need is one update

OH: And you won't even have to hack to do it

OH: The phone—and its user—will invite you right on in

SP: At that point the worm's just a phantom

SP: I designed a complicated target-specific set of locators that lets the worm ghost certain apps, then hides inside until the app is activated, and then uses it to target and infect other app users

IT: So that even those who don't use the charging stations can eventually be targeted by other apps, once someone who *is* infected opens the app?

AI: Like I said

AI: Brilliant

HB: Terrifying

EH: But freaking brilliant

IT: So then what? This phantom wheel just runs amok until every system in the world is infected?

IT: For what purpose?

That's about the time everyone gets quiet. Because, yeah. That's the part I haven't been able to figure out—and from the lack of messaging going on, I'm pretty sure they haven't either. But you can be damn sure I'm going to.

I put the finishing touches on my code and then shoot it out to the others over the chat.

AI: What's that?

OH: Something I've had worked up for a while

OH: I just modified it to protect all Jacento products from intrusion. At least for now

OH: Thought you guys might be interested, considering what we're talking about

EH: I'm interested

HB: Me too

SP: Whoa, didn't realize we were at the point where we trust each other enough to just run some random code

OH: Run it, don't run it

OH: I don't care

SP: Yeah, but that's what anyone who wants us to run their code would say

SP: How do we know it's legit?

AI: It's legit

SP: How do you know?

AI: Because he's been the one warning us all along

AI: And because I just uploaded it and it's really sweet

AI: Pretty sure it turned my whole phone ghost

OH: It did

IT: You just uploaded it without checking it out first?

AI: I trust Owen. Plus, my phone's running the
heaviest protection out there

AI: Can't risk the secretary of state getting
his secure phone infected by his daughter's
phone....

In the grand scheme of things, it's not much trust. But she's
a hacker and any trust at all is above the norm, so I'll take it. The
fact that it's the very hot Alika who went out on a limb for me...
yeah, not going to let that matter.

At least not right now, when there's too much to do.

I split the screen again, start to pull up info on Jacento.
Financial data, shareholder reports, stuff like that. If hacking's
taught me nothing else, it's to follow the money. In the end, it'll
show us everything we need to know.

EH: We need to figure out what they're doing with
this worm

HB: And then what?

EH: And then we stop it

EH: I'm no white hat, but come on. We can't just let
this go

IT: Right? There's a difference between hacking
something to poke around, maybe get some
useful info

SP: But giving Jacento the right to get inside
every single one of their customers' phones?

SP: And then using those phones to get inside
three of the largest corporations in the
world?

SP: With the most users?

AI: That's not okay. That's...

OH: Infinite power

OH: In a world where information makes you a king, it's infinite, *unchecked* power

IT: But for what?

Her frustration comes across loud and clear, but I don't know what to tell her. I don't know what to tell any of them. When I first started digging, I wasn't sure I'd even get to this point, let alone a place where we're actually trying to stop the destruction we wrought.

Well, the destruction *they* wrought. I'm the only one who was smart enough to walk away.

I think about doing that now, about washing my hands of this whole thing.

I didn't do anything wrong, after all. This isn't my mess to clean up, and I've got a lot of other stuff going on in my life right now. Taking this on too? It's a lot.

Maybe even too much.

But the alternative? Just walking away and letting these guys bumble their way through it? How can I do that when they weren't even clued in enough to figure out what they were doing in L.A.?

Besides, I have a vested interest.

Once again, I glance down at my Jacento phone, sitting right next to my Jacento tablet. I'm protected, at least for now. But still, the idea of some freaking corporation doing whatever they want with my accounts, my data?

OH: We need to break the research up

OH: Jacento is huge, and we don't have time to duplicate—the article says they're going to roll out the kiosks on New Year's Day

SP: That's in three weeks

OH: I am aware

AI: Owen's right. We need to do this fast

AI: I'll take the kiosks, find out everything I can about them

OH: I'll take the financial data. I'm good with numbers

IT: I can help you with that

OH: I've got it

IT: Don't be like that

IT: There's a lot of subsidiaries and shell corporations. It's too much for one person to do, at least with the timetable we've got

EH: I'll start sniffing around patents and other proprietary info

EH: Check out what Jacento has coming down the pike

HB: I'll hack the officers, see what I can pick up from their emails and texts

SP: Alika, send me what you've got of the payload, and I'll take Phantom Wheel out for a spin

SP: See what it can do

SP: Metaphorically speaking, I mean

OH: Is that what we're calling this thing? Phantom Wheel?

IT: I like it

HB: It's better than Stuxnet

AI: Anything is better than Stuxnet, but yeah, I like it too

EH: It's almost as flashy as loveletter

IT: But cooler

SP: So Phantom Wheel it is

AI: How long do we have?

EH: I say a week

IT: A week?

EH: If we've only got three weeks to actually stop this thing, then yeah

EH: A week on reconnaissance is about all we can spare

AI: Especially since finals are coming up and then Christmas Eve is in two weeks

SP: How about ten days

SP: We get everything we can on Jacento between now and December 19

I'm about to jump in, try to stretch it to two weeks, when a crash sounds from downstairs. It's followed immediately by my father yelling, and then another crash. By then I'm at my door, Phantom Wheel suddenly the last thing on my mind.

"Caleb, please. Stop!" my mom screams.

Forget the stairs. I vault over the bannister when I'm halfway down, and hit the ground running. They're in the family room, and it only takes me a few seconds to realize what's happening. My mom's standing near the couch, a wineglass broken at her feet as red wine stains the rug. A wine bottle broken against the wall across the room, liquid puddling under the dark green shards.

And my father standing over her, fist raised and face livid. The scariest part, though, is the way his eyes are checked out, completely blank, like he's just not there.

Experience has taught me that's when he's at his worst, and I pretty much jump across the room in an effort to put myself between him and my mom. I make it just in time, his fist slamming into my shoulder instead of her face.

He still packs a hell of a punch, but I hold my ground since the alternative is falling onto my five-foot-three-inch mom.

"Owen, no! Don't!" she cries out, trying to put herself between us. "He's not okay right now."

"Yeah, I got that." Still, I don't move. This is one more thing I can't walk away from. One more fight I'm determined to win.

No matter what it costs.

Case Study:
Alika Izumi aka W4rr10r W0m4n

DOB: 8/1/00
Sex: Female
Height: 5'1"
Weight: 97 lbs.
Eye Color: Brown
Hair Color: Black
Race: Asian (of Japanese descent)
School: Georgetown Prep (private), Washington, DC
Parents: Ted and Maki Izumi
Personal Net Worth: $100K college fund
Family Net Worth: $5.5 mil
Interesting Fact: Her father has served behind the scenes of three presidencies and is currently secretary of state, his most high-profile job to date. But rumor has it he's got his eye on running for office in 2020.
Most Notorious Hack: Created virus that hacked congressional databases and revealed campaign donation irregularities for several members of Congress opposed to net neutrality.

OBSERVATIONS:

Never trust perfection. That's essentially the warning Owen gave us that first day, and it's one I would have heeded if I hadn't so badly wanted to believe the CIA lie. After all, perfection being a lie is a lesson I learned early in life, and one that's stood me in good stead through the years. I forgot it once, and look at the mess we're in now. No way am I going to forget it again.... Which is why I keep side-eyeing the hell out of this girl, who is as close to perfect as I've ever seen.

Here are just a few of her recent accomplishments:

- *In line to be valedictorian of her class*

- *Applications in to Harvard, Yale, Vassar, and Princeton, no applications to safety schools*

- *Captain of the debate team*

- *President of student council*

- *Editor of the school newspaper*

- *Not a piano prodigy, but pretty damn close*

- *And oh yeah, hacker extraordinaire*

Of that whole list, the thing I find most interesting is...I don't think she even likes playing the piano. And I don't mean a love-hate relationship here. I mean a hate-hate relationship. I've watched about ten hours of performance videos of her in major competitions in the US and Europe (snore), and it's really obvious that she hates everything about it. Being on stage, playing piano, competing—I'm not even sure she likes the music. And yet she takes lessons from a master teacher two evenings a week and practices at least two hours every day of her life, often in the middle of the night because that's the only time she can fit it in.

She's a dedicated, ambitious girl who gives everything she does 210 percent, as evidenced by the three AM practice sessions and the Ivy League applications. Add in exclusive private schools, a politician daddy, and perfect SAT scores (that she got the old-fashioned way), and it's obvious she's setting herself up to be a major power player down the line.

And yet… there's the hacking. She's good at it, really good, but it doesn't go with her perfect image at all. Not to mention if anyone finds out, her daddy's career won't look too good— and neither will her future. So why risk it? Why jeopardize everything she's worked so hard for?

SURVEILLANCE FOOTAGE:
12/19/18
19:32
WASHINGTON, DC

Footage begins at 17743 Cherry Tree Lane, in the prestigious Georgetown neighborhood of DC, at 19:32, when the front-door security camera picks up Alika Izumi and her parents arriving at the home of Brady Masters, secretary of the Treasury in the current administration. Masters and his wife, Sandra, are throwing a Christmas party for Washington's movers and shakers, and Ted Izumi is definitely on that list. It should be noted that several members of the US Secret Service are present. Also to be noted is that the Izumis will be referred to by their first names in this report to avoid confusion.

Before dinner, there's a cocktail hour in the main salon, brought to us—with audio—courtesy of nanny cam 1 (hidden in a plant near the baby grand piano that dominates a corner of the room). Alika is definitely the youngest person at the party, but she holds her own.

At 20:04, Alika excuses herself to go to the restroom. She is followed by Brady Masters. The nanny cam loses sight of them at 20:05.

At 20:15, nanny cam 2 picks up Alika and Brady Masters strolling into the library. He is telling her a funny story about his long-ago Princeton interview, urging her to relax over the one she has scheduled at the beginning of January.

She thanks him for the alumni recommendation he gave her, but he shrugs it off as not a big deal. Then he walks to one of the bookshelves and pulls out a very old-looking book. The title is obscured, but later comments by Alika and Masters reveal that it is a 1687 edition of Cervantes's *Don Quixote*. It is obvious from her enthusiasm that this is what Alika came into the library to see.

She opens the book and starts poring over it. Two minutes and fourteen seconds later, Masters crosses to the bar in the corner and pours two drinks, which appear to be whiskey. He carries them back to where Alika is still absorbed in the book, and tries to hand her one. She refuses with a smile, then points to something in the book and reads, "Finally, from so little sleeping and so much reading, his brain dried up and he went completely out of his mind." She laughs, then comments that Cervantes obviously knew what it was like to be a high school senior trying to get into an Ivy League school.

Masters tells her not to worry about her acceptance, that it's in the bag. Then he pulls the book out of her hands and lets it fall to the table in front of her.

Alika stiffens, starts to move away. But he wraps his hands around her waist and holds her in place as he leans down so his mouth is pressed against her neck.

The following conversation occurs:

Alika: What are you doing? Stop! (*She pulls away from him, looking appalled.*)

Masters: Do you know how beautiful you are? (*He reaches for her again.*)

Alika: Are you serious right now? (*She knocks his hand away.*) I'm going back to the party.

Masters: What's your hurry? (*He grabs her arm as she starts toward the door, and then he pulls her against him.*) I thought you wanted to talk about the Princeton interview?

Alika: Let go of me.

Masters: Don't get so worked up, baby.

Alika: Don't call me baby. (*She struggles against him in earnest now.*)

Masters: Come on, now. You've got to know this is how the world works. You do something for me, and I'll do something for you. No one needs to know— Hey! What did you do that for? (*A closer look at nanny cam 2 reveals that Alika gave him a hard kick in the shin.*)

Alika: Don't ever touch me again.

Masters: You really don't get it, do you? (*Masters is glaring at her as he bends down and rubs at his shin.*)

Alika: You're the one who doesn't get it. I'm valedictorian of my class, editor of the school

paper, student council president, and captain of
the debate team. I'll get myself into Princeton,
thank you very much. And the next time you try
to grab me? I won't aim for your shin.

She heads for the door; Masters—who is visibly fuming—
calls after her.

Masters: You just made a big mistake. You know who
was more appreciative of my help? Your sister.

Alika (*turning back to him*): What did you say?

Masters crosses his arms and smirks, looking very
pleased with himself. Alika seems so shaken by the mention of her sister that she visibly trembles for a moment
before quickly steeling herself.

Alika: You don't talk about my sister. You don't *think*
about my sister. Do you understand me?

Masters's posture and body language change so that
he once again becomes the arrogant, confident man who
entered the room with Alika a few minutes ago. He believes
he has the upper hand.

Masters: Get out of my library, little girl. I've grown
bored of you.

Alika stands stock-still for a moment, and when she
speaks next, her voice is steady and low.

Alika: There's going to be a day, in the not very
distant future, when you look back at this
moment and realize what a big mistake *you* just
made.

She walks out of the room, and at 20:25 is picked back up by nanny cam 1.

The rest of the party is uneventful, until 21:48, when Alika excuses herself from the dining table and makes her way to Masters's office. Security camera 3A shows that it takes her seventeen seconds to pick the lock. Surveillance picks up—audio and video—as she walks into the office and heads straight to Masters's laptop.

At 21:54, she picks the lock on Masters's desk drawer and riffles through the papers until she finds a small index card taped on the outside bottom of the drawer. Seconds later she logs into the computer.

For the next twelve minutes and twenty-three seconds, Alika alternates between typing and reading whatever comes across the screen. At 22:07, she logs off and rejoins the party.

◆ ◆ ◆

UPDATE: 12/22/18

The *Washington Post* breaks a story about massive corruption in the Treasury Department.

UPDATE: 12/23/18

News breaks that three congresspeople are calling for Secretary Masters to face hearings on Capitol Hill when Congress is back from the holiday break.

IT: Are you there?

OH: I'm here

OH: Have you been working all night?

IT: Haven't you?

OH: No. I've been doing other stuff

IT: What other stuff?

OH: Seriously?

IT: Sorry. It's just, this is important

OH: You're telling me that?

IT: Sorry

IT: I found something that doesn't make much sense. I wanted to shoot it over for you to look at

OH: What is it?

IT: Some weird numbers I found on the comp for the CFO of Franklin

IT: They look like payouts, but I can't tell to whom

OH: Shoot it over. I'll follow the trail

IT: Thanks. I'm going to keep digging here, see what else turns up

EH: Got a minute?

AI: Yeah. What's wrong?

EH: They're really putting all their eggs in this charging kiosk basket

AI: Yeah, I'm getting that too

EH: Have you found the rollout schedule yet?

EH: It looks like they're starting in their headquarter cities. New York, San Francisco, and Helsinki

EH: But I want to know what cities come next

AI: Why?

EH: Just a hunch I'm following up on

AI: I don't know. I'll find the schedule and shoot it to you in a little

EH: Cool. Thanks

9:14 AM, CST

SP: This is some kind of worm you built

AI: Do you need help with it?

SP: Nah. I'm just impressed

SP: And a little scared of you

AI: Oh

AI: Thanks, I guess

SP: Definitely a compliment

10:41 AM, CST

SP: Any idea who specifically we can blame for this yet?

HB: You mean besides us?

SP: Yes, besides us. Obviously

HB: Just made it through the firewall at Franklin

SP: I thought you were concentrating on Jacento?

HB: I am

SP: Ooooooooooookay

1:30 PM, EST

AI: Sending the rollout schedule now

AI: They're hitting every major city in Europe and America within fifteen days of the first kiosk going live

EH: Who's next?

EH: Barcelona?

AI: How did you know?

EH: Cuz I'm that good, baby

AI: Don't call me baby

EH: Whatever you say

EH: Baby

AI: DON'T

AI: Seriously, how did you know?

EH: I only share that info with people who let me call them baby....

10:38 AM, PST

EH: Hello?

EH: Hello?

EH: Okay, okay. Sorry I insulted you.

EH: Baby

OH: You might want to start by checking out Daniel
Davies

OH: He works for Franklin

OH: Hello???

OH: In the middle of this, you have something more
important to do? Really?

OH: Must be nice

HB: Don't get your panties all twisted up, I'm here

HB: Who is Daniel Davies?

OH: Agent Shane Donovan, from the audition

OH: You didn't even check him out?

OH: You give hackers everywhere a bad name

HB: Bite me

HB: Shane's not even his real first name? Why
would he pick Shane for a fake first name?

OH: Seriously? In the middle of all this, that's what
surprises you?

HB: Bite me again

EH: Tell me you've got something

SP: You mean besides the fact that Alika is a
freaking genius?

EH: Let me clarify

EH: Tell me you've got something I don't already know

SP: No really. Phantom Wheel is freaking art

EH: Is it art we can kill?

SP: That's the problem

SP: She programmed in a kill switch, but it's not that hard to find

SP: If they've even got someone decent looking at the thing

EH: They'll change it up and we'll be screwed

SP: I'm pretty sure we're already screwed

EH: Now where's that positive spirit we admire so much?

SP: Okay, I'm positive we're screwed!!!!

SP: Better?

EH: Dude...

7:10 PM, PST

EH: Jacento has planned a whole new product line aimed at old people

EH: Do you know about it?

SP: Dude, I'm out of orange soda

EH: And that matters because...

SP: I don't hack without orange soda

EH: Well, can you read without it?

SP: Not while I'm driving

EH: Jesus. Amateur

SP: Forgive me for wanting to live

EH: So not forgiven

SP: Okay, I'm back

SP: Hello?

SP: HELLOOOOOOOOOOOOO

EH: And obviously properly hydrated

SP: You know it, baby

EH: See! It's totally an expression!

SP: What's an expression?

EH: Never mind

EH: Now that you're hyped on orange soda and no longer incoherent, did you know about the new product line?

SP: Why would I know about it?

EH: Because your dad's company is partnering with Jacento on it

SP: No way. Really?

SP: Hey, how do you know what company my dad works for?

EH: The same way you know what company my family owns

SP: Touché

EH: So, what do you know about it?

SP: Nothing

SP: Yet

HB: These guys are gross

IT: Did you really expect anything else?

HB: No. I mean criminally gross

HB: This one guy, Koskinen, in San Fran, is into some really creepy stuff

IT: You got in?

HB: To a few accounts

HB: The passwords are crap

HB: Most of them are total jerks, but Koskinen is sick

IT: What are you going to do about it?

HB: What can I do about it right now?

HB: We don't want to tip them off

IT: Screw tipping them off

IT: Sometimes you've got to step up

IT: What's this K guy doing?

HB: I have stepped up

HB: I'm here, aren't I?

IT: Looks like you are

HB: What does that mean?

IT: It means these jerks get away with enough. They don't need us letting them slide too

IT: WHAT. DID. YOU. FIND?

HB: His pics. There's no way all the girls are eighteen.

IT: Ugh. Gross

HB: Told you

IT: You need to turn him in

HB: How?

IT: What do you mean how? Just do it!

HB: He'll know someone was in his stuff

IT: I guarantee you, that won't occur to him for a while

IT: He'll be too busy lying to his wife and his lawyer

IT: San Fran PD must have an anonymous tipline. Use that. He won't know what happened until it's too late for him and all his little friends

HB: You hope

IT: I know. Do it

4:21 am, EST

AI: You there?

AI: Hello?

AI: Ping me back when you wake up

4:34 am, EST

OH: Don't you ever sleep?

AI: Not when I might be partially responsible for the apocalypse

OH: It won't get that far

AI: So you say

AI: Where's the money lead?

OH: Everywhere

AI: That's not exactly helpful

OH: Was I supposed to be helpful?

OH: Sorry, baby, I'm still asleep

AI: Don't call me baby

OH: Don't call me baby

AI: You're mimicking me now?

OH: Typing at the same time isn't mimicking. It's logic—or precognition

AI: Where's the money going?

OH: Where it always goes

OH: To big houses and crooked politicians

AI: So, what are we going to do?

OH: Get it back. Obviously.

AI: How?

OH: I'm still working on that part

6:37 ᴀᴍ, CST

IT: I've been thinking

OH: Spit it out. I've got to get to school

IT: You're going to school?

OH: I don't have a choice. It's the last day before winter break. I've got finals

IT: Where's the money?

OH: Alika and I just did this

IT: Well, since you haven't solved the problem, do it again

OH: Ooooh, I like being bossed around

IT: And I like a guy who listens, so . . .

IT: Where's the real money?

IT: I don't mean what's being funneled around for this whole thing

IT: I mean, in the end, who benefits

OH: That's what I've been saying!!

OH: Maybe you're the one who needs to listen

IT: Can we forget your ego for a minute and just follow this through?

OH: Yes, Mom

IT: Seriously?

OH: Sorry. I'm a little loopy from lack of sleep

IT: It's about business and politics

OH: It's always about business and politics

IT: Just give me a minute

IT: The real money is in swaying governments to do what you want, right? To pass legislation that will somehow benefit your company

IT: I looked it up. Jacento has at least a dozen lobbyists working in the US alone, plus Europe, Africa, Asia

OH: Alika and I kind of batted this around earlier, but we were talking about the money going to the politicians

IT: But the money only goes to the politicians so that in the end the laws benefit big business

OH: I'm not sure I'm following you

IT: What if this is just a smash and grab?

OH: Of course it's a smash and grab!

OH: Jacento wouldn't be doing it if it didn't benefit them. The question is how???

IT: What if they're paying the government in info instead of in dollars?

OH: WTF?

IT: I don't know yet. I'm just thinking...

10:55 AM, CST

SP: Hey, have any of you guys heard of Oxford Analytics?????

OH: No. What is it?

SP: Took me a while to get to the bottom of it, believe it or not, but it's actually... big data

IT: Oh no

OH: Oh no is right

HB: What'd I miss?

AI: Is that what we've been missing?

OH: I think so

IT: Definitely

EH: Anyone want to let the rest of us in on what's going on here?

SP: Oxford Analytics is this big data firm out of London

HB: They're an advertising firm? Isn't that what big data is used for?

OH: Big data's used for EVERYTHING

EH: It's why likes on social media are private now

AI: What is it? Ten FB likes and they know you better than your best friend?

IT: Something like that

SP: So, what if Jacento's going beyond social media?

SP: What if the reason they want into everything is because they want the information those companies can give them on us

HP: But for what purpose?

HP: You really think they're going to traffic in information with the US government?

SP: I think it's a possibility

IT: A really big, really scary possibility

AI: That's not just scary. It's downright terrifying

OH: Right?

IT: I don't want those people running around in my business

EH: It's not about them running around in your business. It's about them running around in your HEAD

EH: They get access to all this, they get access to you

AI: We don't know for sure that's what they're going to do with this info

OH: We don't know for sure that it's not

OH: You got a better idea of what's happening here?

AI: No, but I don't think we should decide that Jacento plans on using info as currency until we know for sure

HB: We can't know for sure, not unless we get inside

EH: I thought you were hacking the officers

HB: I am. But it's not so easy. Their CEO may be a visionary, but he's also paranoid. There's only so much info I can gather outside of Jacento's actual headquarters. They've got a lot of stuff that stays in-house, that never leaves the building, even through cyberspace

OH: So what's that mean? We've got to go there?

IT: We can't just go there. I'm in San Antonio!

SP: Not to mention, it's Christmas in four days

SP: We can't just take off for San Francisco

OH: Okay, but we've got to do something

OH: I've got to go. I have another test

EH: You're still in school right now?!?!?!

OH: Dude, it's New England

EH: I have no idea what that means

AI: It means they invented the whole walk uphill, in the snow, barefoot, for two miles to get to school thing

OH: Exactly

AI: I've got to go too

AI: Same reason

SP: Wait! Have we settled this?

IT: There's nothing to settle!

IT: No way can I just take off for San Francisco!!!!

OH: Yeah, well, I don't think we're going to be able to figure out what's going on if we don't

OH: I'm out, but I'm down for San Fran

AI: Me too

EH: Let me see what I can work out

IT: What does that even mean?

IT: Ezra? Hello?

SP: My parents are going to freak

HB: Tell them you're saving the world

HB: Aren't your parents all about that?

SP: Yeah, the other 364 days of the year

SP: My mom takes Christmas really seriously

IT: Why are we even still talking about this?

IT: I CAN'T GO TO SAN FRANCISCO

IT: Hello?

IT: Hello?

IT: SERIOUSLY? YOU GUYS?

Case Study:
Ezra Hernandez aka EazyH

DOB: 7/2/00	
Sex: Male	
Height: 6'1"	
Weight: 175 lbs.	
Eye Color: Brown	
Hair Color: Black	
Race: Hispanic (Colombian descent)	
School: The Bishop's School (private), San Diego	
Parents: Victor and Hilda Hernandez	
Personal Net Worth: $20 mil (trust fund)	
Family Net Worth: $975 mil	
Interesting Fact: His parents own hotels. Lots and lots of hotels, in more than fifty countries around the world. There's rich and then there's Ezra. He's on another level.	
Most Notorious Hack: Honestly? This one.	

OBSERVATIONS:
The kid moves like he thinks he's a badass.

*I take that back. He moves like he **knows** he's a badass.*

It's in the way he holds himself, in the way he speaks, in the way he looks at everyone around him—not like they're inferior, but like he knows he's just a little bit better. Better looking, better at talking his way into and out of things. Just better, all the way around. And after watching him in these surveillance videos, it's hard to disagree.

No doubt, he's hit the genetic lottery. Not just with his looks, although those are good too. The shaggy hair is an absolute "screw you" to the social conventions for which he's otherwise a walking, talking poster boy. That it's obviously courtesy of a two-hundred-dollar haircut doesn't really go with his rebel-without-a-cause vibe. Then again, maybe I've got the vibe wrong—Ezra doesn't seem the type to make such a blatant mistake.

But no, when I say he's won the genetic lottery, I'm talking about what's behind those dark brown eyes of his. Because the boy is SMART. Anyone who looks can see the intelligence in his eyes. And anyone who looks closely can see how he uses that intelligence—by figuring out how to best everyone else in the room, whenever and however he wants to.

This kid's a grifter, pure and simple. He may call himself a social engineer. A facilitator. Sometimes even a hustler. But deep down, if you ask me, he's just an old-fashioned con man, looking for the next sucker—and the next big score. It's not my game, but I'd be lying if I said I didn't admire him for it. Just like I'd be lying if I tried to pretend there wasn't a part of me that wanted to be him, just for a little while. Just for a day . . . or two.

SURVEILLANCE FOOTAGE:
12/24/18
23:42
CORONADO, CALIFORNIA

Footage begins in parking lot A of Coronado Country Club and Marina. Security is lax-a guard is sleeping in a golf cart-and traffic is nonexistent (foot, automobile, and boat).

A 2017 Cadillac Escalade (California license plate 622E991) pulls into the parking lot via the Silver Strand entrance and parks in the first row of the empty lot, facing the Starfish Isle exit. Three people in hoodies and jeans exit the vehicle, including Ezra Hernandez from the driver's door.

The three make their way through the empty parking lot under the full moon. When they come to the first security gate, Incidental 1 (identified as Maxwell Singley) takes out his cell phone and hacks their way in. They continue on their way, making a left at the path that takes them to what employees call Money Row, so named because it has the deepest and the biggest slips and is home to the most expensive yachts in San Diego. Including *La Vida Aqua*, the largest yacht in the marina and the pride and joy of current US vice president Richard Harris.

Camera 27, parking lot A, loses sight of them at 23:48 as they turn toward Money Row. Camera 13 picks them up at 23:49 as they approach the second security booth. This one is manned by Marcus Briggs, who stops them in their tracks.

Hernandez talks to Briggs in a jovial, easygoing manner that transforms the security guard from belligerent to amused.

Two minutes and twenty-seven seconds after the conversation starts, Hernandez and his two accomplices walk right through the manned security gate.

At 23:57, they board *La Vida Aqua*.

At 00:02, the bridge security camera and recorder picks them up (transcription follows).

Singley: Dude, this is epic! I still can't believe you got us on board!

Robert Carrera: Right? When that guy demanded ID, I figured we were toast!

Singley: Yes! I nearly pissed my pants.

Hernandez is at the yacht's instrumentation panel, flipping switches.

Carrera: So what are we going to steal, man? So we can prove we actually made it on board?

Singley: I think we should steal a bottle of our vice president's finest liquor.

Carrera: No way, man. Liquor can come from anywhere.

Singley: Yeah, but a picture can't.

Hernandez: No photos.

Hernandez moves between his phone and the instrument panel as he flips switches and checks gauges.

Singley: I'm going to take a pic of me sprawled in the captain's chair with a bottle of the ship's best tequila.

Hernandez doesn't answer, but he does spin the chair Singley is going to sit on so that Singley ends up sprawled on the floor.

Singley: So what are we stealing, then?

Hernandez: You mean you haven't figured it out?

Carrera: Figured what out?

Hernandez: We're stealing the boat.

A string of expletives spans the next thirty-one straight seconds.

Hernandez: We're ready to go. Go untie the yacht.

Carrera and Singley leave the bridge, as instructed, at 00:19.

Hernandez gets a text at 00:23, at which point he climbs behind the wheel and starts guiding *La Vida Aqua* from the slip.

Voice recording ceases until 00:36, though video recording shows Hernandez navigating the boat through the bay.

At 00:48, Hernandez slows the yacht down. Audio recording picks back up.

Hernandez: Get out on deck and look for two boats
           off the starboard bow.

Carrera: Which one's the starboard bow?

Singley: Boats? What boats?

Hernandez: The right side, dipshit.

Carrera: What boats, Ezra?

Hernandez: The two that should show up near our
    starboard bow sometime in the next two minutes.

Carrera: I see them! What's going on, Ezra?

Hernandez: You didn't think this was just a joyride, did
    you? Here, take the wheel.

Singley: Me?

Hernandez: Don't worry, I'm dropping anchor.

Hernandez drops anchor at 00:56, then leaves the bridge. At 00:58, security camera 1 picks him up on the lowest starboard deck, lowering a ladder toward the water. Security footage doesn't show what is happening in the water, but at 01:02, a teenage girl appears at the top of the ladder.

Twenty-five people (unidentified at this time but with approximate ages between sixteen and twenty) climb onto the yacht with several coolers filled with beverages and snack foods.

From 01:02 until 04:27, a Christmas party ensues, complete with mistletoe and spiked eggnog.

At 04:30, Hernandez ends the party. There is no audio recording, but it's very obvious that he's closing the party down, despite the complaints of many on board. I think it's important to note that no one refuses to leave when ordered.

The yacht is cleared of all but Hernandez, Singley, and Carrera at 04:41.

Hernandez returns to the bridge at 04:43, where he turns the yacht back toward shore while security camera 1 shows Singley and Carrera cleaning up stray trash. And at 05:17, Hernandez pulls *La Vida Aqua* back into slip 27 at CCCM.

Hernandez, Singley, and Carrera disembark at 05:21. Before he leaves, Hernandez looks straight into the camera and blows it a kiss.

Security camera 13 reveals Hernandez, Singley, and Carrera after securing the yacht from 05:21 until 05:26. Security camera 27 picks them up as they leave the marina at 05:28. They reach the Cadillac Escalade at 05:33.

Hernandez climbs into the driver's seat at 05:34. He starts the SUV, then pulls out of the parking lot and onto Starfish Isle Road.

Surveillance ceases.

7

Issa
[Pr1m4 D0nn4]

I can't believe I'm doing this.

I can't believe I'm freaking doing this.

"Make sure you watch your new Legos," I tell Ricky as I roll my suitcase down the hallway of our apartment. "You can't leave them on the floor, or Chloe might eat one and choke."

Just the thought has me panicking—not to mention rethinking this terrible, horrible, absolute mistake of a trip.

"Her bottles for the next two days are in the fridge," I tell my sister, who is dozing on the couch. Not that I blame her—it's pretty much the crack of dawn right now. Still. "Lettie! Are you listening to me?"

"Bottles. Fridge. Got it."

"I bought a couple of the liquid cans of formula so you don't have to worry about messing with the powdered stuff. Just make sure you don't leave the formula in the cans after you open them. Pour it all into bottles and make sure you—"

"Use them within forty-eight hours. I got it." Her eyes open for the first time. "How long are you going to be gone, anyway?"

"I don't know. I told you it depends on how far I get."

"I can't believe the CIA is making you compete for this scholarship like you're in some kind of reality TV show. It's ridiculous."

"Maybe it is," I tell her, the lie twisting sourly in my stomach. "But I need the scholarship, so they get to call the shots."

I lean down and kiss the top of Lettie's head. The fact that she lets me tells me exactly how discombobulated she is about me leaving. Then Ricky's there, wrapping his arms around my waist and holding on tight.

"I love you, Issa."

I kiss his forehead next. "I love you too, guys."

"Don't go. Pleeeeeease. It's still Christmas!!!"

I glance at the old clock on the wall. "Christmas ended five hours ago, bud. And I'll be back before you miss me."

"I already miss you! Plus Chloe's going to freak when you don't come home tonight."

"Chloe will be fine as long as you guys remember to feed her on time," I say loudly, so Lettie can hear. And so I can maybe even convince myself. *She'll be fine*, I tell myself as I roll my suitcase toward the door. They all will. It's just for a few days. Lettie can handle it—and maybe, with me gone, Dad will actually step up and take some responsibility for Chloe. "And don't let the twins sleep past nine or they won't sleep tonight."

Everything's going to be fine. It is.

"When Dad gets up, tell him I left money for groceries in his top drawer. There's also money for pizza for dinner tomorrow night, once the leftovers run out. Make sure you buy extra so you'll have some for lunch a couple of days this week."

"I know, I know." Lettie finally deigns to sit up. "You told me this three times already. Just like the bottle stuff."

"And text me if you have any questions. Except for the three and a half hours I'm on the plane, I'll answer you right away."

"We're fiiiiiiiiine," Lettie says as she climbs off the sofa and follows me to the door. "Now go kick some serious hacker butt."

It's not the hackers I'm worried about, but I don't tell her that. The only way I got my dad to agree to this whole trip is because he thinks I've still got a chance at the CIA scholarship. When this is all over, I don't know how I'm going to tell him I didn't get it.

I push that thought out of my brain. There will be enough time to think about it later, just like there will be enough time to think about how guilty I feel for lying to my family. But right now I have to get on that plane and get to San Francisco so I can stop this whole disaster I helped set in motion. And while it would be nice to leave this to the others, the truth is I don't trust them not to screw it up.

Besides, this is as much my fault as it is theirs. More, if you count Owen, who didn't have anything to do with Phantom Wheel but is still doing his best to fix it.

It still bugs me that he somehow knew and I didn't. That he took one look in that folder and saw how this was going to go down, while I just let Jacento and "Shane" play me.

Then again, he must not need the scholarship the way I do. If he did, he probably wouldn't have seen so clearly either....

"Make sure you lock up after me," I tell Lettie. "And don't open the door for anyone unless Dad is here. And check on Chloe in an hour, make sure she's doing okay. And—"

"I'm fifteen, Issa! I've got this!" She practically shoves me out the door. "Go get that scholarship!"

The door slams in my face, and I'm left standing in the hallway, light bulb flickering above my head as I try to convince myself that everything is going to be okay. I'm halfway to accepting it when Chloe starts to cry.

Damn.

I start to go back in, just to calm her down a little, but my phone beeps. My ride is here.

I hear Lettie murmuring to Chloe through the thin walls, and the crying stops as soon as it started. *Lettie can do this*, I tell myself as I head for the four flights of stairs between me and the street. *Everything's going to be okay.*

I say those five words over and over again as I get in the car, as we drive through the nearly deserted San Antonio streets, as I climb out of the car at the airport. I'm still saying it twenty minutes later as I make my way through security to my gate and forty minutes later when I line up to get on the plane.

It's my mantra of sorts, my promise to myself and to the world as I gingerly settle into my window seat and pray for no turbulence.

Everything's going to be okay.

8

Harper
[5p3ct3r]

What exactly have I gotten myself into? I wonder as I stop outside the address Silver Spoon gave us in downtown San Francisco. I look up at the two luxurious buildings shooting into the sky like the sleekest silver bullets and can't believe I'm in the right place.

We can stay at my family's apartment in the city, he said.

No big deal, he said.

It's smaller than the house my parents keep in Woodside, so my parents rarely stay there even when they're in town—which they aren't right now, as they're spending Christmas in Hawaii, he said.

The apartment will be PERFECT for us, he said.

These luxury towers are about the opposite of perfect, in my opinion. They demand attention from anyone who sees them. And since I've spent the last few years of my life doing anything but that, just the idea of going inside makes me tremble.

The idea of actually staying here... well, let's just say it'll be a miracle if I don't break out in hives.

I glance down at my phone again, just to make sure I've got the address right. Maybe I got off at the wrong BART station, or maybe...nope. This is it: 201 Folsom Street.

Okay, then.

Hefting my backpack a little more solidly over my shoulder, I start into the bigger tower, as Silver Spoon instructed. As I do, a man dressed in the most ridiculous suit I've ever seen—all orange lines and navy checks, with flowers inside each square—strolls out in front of me. At his feet is a tiny white poodle, dancing on a sparkly purple leash.

The dog starts yapping as soon as it sees me, running around in circles like it's trying to tangle me up in its leash.

"It's okay, girl," I say, squatting to pet the mop-headed thing. Dogs are so much easier than people. "I won't hurt you."

"I'm so sorry! Muffy is a little high-strung," her owner tells me.

"She's great," I answer, keeping my head down so that my hair falls in my face. Old habits and all that. "Full of energy."

"You have no idea. She just ate my partner's Gucci loafers, and he is not impressed. This walk is kind of a mission of mercy, you know what I mean?"

"Was this a first offense, or is she a repeat—"

The dog barks, interrupting me. Her bright eyes make it obvious that she's done with me and ready to explore her little bit of the city. "I should let you get on with your mission."

"And I, you." He gives me a cheery wave, and the two head up the street. I watch them for a few seconds before turning back to the building. He doesn't know how true his words are.

I shove my hands in my pockets and hunch my shoulders a little as I head inside.

But I barely make it two steps before I hear, "Hey, Harper, right?"

I freeze for one second, two, wondering who could possibly know me here. But as the panic recedes, I realize it's a tall guy with mocha-colored skin and a few neatly kept dreads poking out of his hoodie who's talking to me. The sunglasses he's wearing throw me for a moment, and then it hits me.

The Lone Ranger. Of course.

"Hey, L— Owen. How are you?"

"Glad as hell you're here. So far, it's just Ezra and me, and let me tell you, that's been . . . interesting."

I can't help laughing. It feels strange, considering how my normal life goes. And considering what we're here for. "I can only imagine."

"Come on, I'll take you up." He waves at the man behind the counter who's checking people in, before pointing my way and mouthing, *She's with me.*

I'm a little surprised at how chummy he is with the doorman already, since he only got here this morning. I don't say anything— I rarely do—but my curiosity must show on my face because he shrugs as we step onto the elevator. "He's a fan of my dad's."

Oh. Right. The star football player. No wonder the Lone Ranger looks so comfortable in this place.

"So, did you find the place okay?" he asks as he pushes the button for the forty-second floor. It's the top button on the panel. Of course it is.

Of course Silver Spoon would have a penthouse as one of his secondary homes.

When we take off, we shoot up fast—so fast that I stumble a little, fall against the Lone Ranger. He steadies me with an arm around my shoulders, and I stiffen. I don't love being touched by people I barely know. And I'm so not interested.

He removes his arm a moment later, thank God, and says, "That got me the first time too. You good?"

I nod. "Thanks."

"No problem." He grins. "San Francisco's a brand-new world, huh?"

"At least the Lumina towers are."

That draws a startled laugh out of him. "Right? This place is something else. It's got all the comforts of home—if your home is a five-star hotel."

The elevator picks that moment to stop, and when it opens, we step out into an opulent lobby, all gleaming white and silver.

Directly in front of us is a set of double doors, and I watch as the Lone Ranger punches in a code. Seconds later we're standing in the middle of a huge living room, with sleek white furniture and seemingly endless glass windows lining the walls in all directions. Beyond the windows in front of us is a terrace, and beyond that is the big, beautiful Pacific.

I glance around, expecting to see Silver Spoon, but the room—which basically extends from one end of the building to the other in one wide-open space—is empty.

"Ezra's probably upstairs," the Lone Ranger says, nodding at the ornate circular staircase to the right of where we're standing. "Want to go see him, find your room?"

"I, um—"

"Yeah. I know what you mean." He puts a light hand on my shoulder, propels me forward. "Come on. I'll protect you."

I try not to stiffen, reminding myself it's just a hand on my shoulder, no big deal. "I *don't* need protection."

"Okay. Then you can protect me. Ezra is . . . a lot."

Yeah, he is. But then, so is the Lone Ranger. So are all of them, in their own ways.

Buffy with her confidence and don't-mess-with-me attitude.

Snow White with the oh-so-perfect vibe and underlying core of steel.

Mad Max with his over-the-top heart and the overt goodness that comes across even in his messages.

They're all going to take some getting used to. Especially the Lone Ranger, with his killer smile and the harmless flirting that he's probably not even aware of. I'm immune, but I can't help wondering what it's going to do to the other girls.

I nod a little, remember to smile because it's the right social response. Then nearly jump out of my skin when a door slams open somewhere upstairs.

Seconds later, Silver Spoon and Snow White come strolling onto the landing at the top of the stairs. "Harper!" she exclaims, waving when she sees me. "Come on up and pick your room!"

"I didn't know you were here," the Lone Ranger says from

next to me, and suddenly he's a lot less easygoing and a lot more wary. I can feel it in the way he stiffens beside me, see it in the smile that goes from wide open to politely inquiring.

I don't know what's brought on the change, can't help wondering if the two of them have had words privately or something, since they are the ones who approached us together with the whole Phantom Wheel information.

Body language only gets me so far, though, especially since we just met. Until he takes those stupid glasses off, I don't have a chance of figuring out what he's really thinking.

Then again, maybe that's the point.

Intrigued, I step back a little and just kind of watch, waiting to see how Snow White's going to react.

But she seems cool, and just as happy to see him as she is me. "Owen! It's nice to actually meet you!" she calls. "Even if you did take the room with the best view."

"It's where Ezra put me," he answers, and at least he sounds normal as we head up the stairs. Or at least as normal as he can sound with that deep bass voice of his.

"It's the one that's farthest from mine." Silver Spoon lifts a brow at me, as if to say, *Can you blame me?* "But Harper can have her pick of the three remaining rooms."

So we each get our own room, then. *Wow.* Silver Spoon wasn't kidding when he said this place would be perfect for us— if you don't count the intimidation factor, of course. Which, he wouldn't.

Neither of the other two looks intimidated, though, and I'm reminded again of just how wide the gulf between us is. Of how these three people don't need a CIA scholarship—or the hacking—to survive. They do it for fun, or just because they can.

If someone had told me a few months ago that I'd be standing in one of the most expensive penthouses in San Francisco with the son of a hotel magnate, the daughter of the secretary of state, and the son of a famous football player, I would have told them they were delirious. Not to mention a lot of other things. And yet here I am.

Here *we* are.

"Pick a room for me," I say as I get to the top of the stairs. "I'm sure they're all great."

Silver Spoon studies me for a second, those dark eyes of his surprisingly shrewd. "You can have my sister's room. It's next to Alika's." He heads to the left, and for the first time I realize that the upstairs is divided into two wings. Big surprise.

"Thanks," I answer with a nod as I follow him into the east wing. I'm picturing some powder-pink monstrosity, complete with crystal chandeliers and zebra print, but the room is surprisingly understated. Done in light shades of aqua and gray, there's a huge bed in the middle—covered by about two dozen pillows—and a crazy comfortable-looking chair in the corner. The strongest colors in the room are the black frames on the grayscale artwork hanging on the walls.

"This is really nice," I tell him after a second.

"It seemed like it would suit you."

I shoot him a quick look at that—I don't like the idea of anybody being close enough to form an opinion about me, let alone one that is actually right—and find him watching me again. As our eyes meet, I wonder for the first time if there's more to Ezra Miguel Hernandez than meets the eye.

I've barely put my backpack down on the chair when the elevator dings down below. I hear Silver Spoon's footsteps as he heads downstairs to answer the door. A few moments later I tromp down to see who it is now—Mad Max or Buffy—and find both of them standing in the middle of the living room looking a little lost.

Mad Max looks impressed but not intimidated, and I'm reminded again of who his parents are—it's a little crazy how much money is represented by the people in this penthouse—but Buffy looks completely shell-shocked. I can relate.

Silver Spoon heads back to the landing—I think it's his favorite greeting spot, probably because he gets to play lord of the manor and ruler of all he surveys—and beckons them up the stairs.

Mad Max is carrying a backpack, but Buffy is toting a suitcase of considerable heft. She looks at the stairs a little defiantly, then moves to pick it up. Mad Max cuts off the movement and lifts the suitcase himself before heading up the spiral staircase.

To his credit, he might look like a stiff wind will knock him over, but he's actually surprisingly strong. He doesn't hesitate once on his way up the stairs.

"There's two rooms left," Silver Spoon says, pointing to the first door on either side of the stairs. "Claim one and then meet us downstairs to talk strategy."

Mad Max looks at Buffy, brows raised, but when she doesn't say anything he heads to the left. Seconds later, I hear him drop her suitcase on the floor. "You take this room," he suggests, "and I'll take the other one."

She nods but still doesn't say anything, even after she gets to the door of her room and pauses, like she's in shock.

"I'm ordering Indian for lunch. If anyone's vegan or doesn't like curry, let me know now." Silver Spoon waits, eyebrows raised, waiting for objections. When none come, he grins and heads back downstairs—but not before winking at me. Or maybe it was at Snow White. Or Buffy. Or, hell, it could have been one of the guys. Or it could have been all of us. With him, you never know.

Once he moves, it seems to give the rest of us permission to do the same. Even Buffy seems released from whatever spell she was under, shooting me a quick grin before heading into her room.

I do the same, moving straight to the en suite bathroom and splashing cold water on my face. The trip from Vegas was short, but I still feel grimy. I think it has more to do with being in this fancy apartment, though, than it does with traveling.

Now that everyone's gone, I take a moment to really look around the room, at the plush bedding and the expensive art and the other exclusive touches—like real crystal perfume atomizers and hundred-dollar candles—that only the uber rich can afford to have lying around one of their "spare places."

I sink down on the bed, bury my head in my hands. Wonder what I've gotten myself into here—and how the hell I'm going to get myself out of it.

9

Issa
(Pr1m4 D0nn4)

It's too much.

He's too much.

They all are. I've never felt so overwhelmed, so out of place, in my life.

I mean, seriously. This is the kind of apartment you see on TV, homes of the rich and freaking famous.

My whole apartment would probably fit in the bedroom I'm currently standing in, and yet I've never felt more trapped. It makes no sense, but then, none of this does. All I know is that this apartment, these people, the job we have in front of us—it all scares the hell out of me.

Because it does, I open my suitcase and pull out my makeup bag. I rummage through it until I find my favorite lipstick—so purple it's almost black—and paint it across my lips.

As far as armor goes, it's not the best, but it makes me feel better.

So does shrugging into my "I'm no damsel in distress, I'm a dragon in a dress" hoodie. It's the first thing I bought with my hacking money, and it never fails to make me feel legit.

A quick fluff of my hair and a wash of my hands, and I'm as ready as I'm ever going to get. I may not feel like a badass right now, but I look like one, and that's at least half the battle.

Or so I tell myself.

A quick check of my phone shows that Lettie's answered my texts from the train.

Chloe's fine and so are the twins and Ricky.

Dad got up an hour ago and is watching TV before he goes grocery shopping.

They're having leftover spaghetti for lunch.

Chloe had a really messy diaper, and Lettie does not appreciate it.

The little bit of normalcy in the middle of this whole screwed-up mess grounds me, reminds me what's important—and it's not this place. It's not the fact that Ezra paid for Harper's and my plane tickets and is now paying for lunch. It's not even that I'm back to square one when it comes to paying for college.

No, what's important is that my family is safe and what I'm doing here—what we're all doing here—is going to help keep that a reality. For all of us.

It's that thought that finally settles me—and gets me moving, out of my fancy room and down the circular staircase that takes me to the main level. I'd be lying if I said I didn't feel a little like J.Lo walking down it, all diva sleek and chic, but that just helps me dig deep for the badass inside me. As does the Pixies' "I Bleed," which is playing on the sound system. I'm pleasantly surprised by Ezra's taste in music.

I'm the last one down, and they all turn to look at me as I

hit the bottom step. I look at them right back, eyebrows raised. Seth immediately glances down at his hands when our eyes meet, and I feel a little like I kicked a puppy. Owen grins, Alika raises her brows, Harper's face doesn't change—it rarely does, I'm coming to realize—and Ezra, Ezra looks me over from head to toe just slowly enough to make sure I know he's doing it.

The leisurely once-over leaves a little trail of heat in its wake, a little ball of…something…in my stomach, and that just pisses me off. *God.* Why does he have to be such a jerk? And so freaking good-looking at the same time?

I ignore him, which isn't hard to do considering he's on the phone, and walk over to the main sitting area, where they've all congregated. They've left an open chair for me—some strange, modern-art thing that looks both terrifying and oddly comfortable—but I keep walking, over to the huge expanse of windows instead.

It's the first time I've ever seen the ocean.

It's beautiful. And big. Really, really big. I stand there for a little while, watching the waves endlessly roll in. Not thinking, really, just watching.

I'm so absorbed in the view—and the emotions it's bringing out in me—that I don't notice Owen is standing next to me until he says, "I'm always surprised at how different it is from the Atlantic."

I nod, because what am I going to say? That despite living in Texas I've never even seen the Gulf, let alone the Atlantic? Admitting the truth means making myself deliberately vulnerable, and that's not how this is going to go down.

"I'm Owen." He holds a hand out like he expects me to shake it. In his own way he's as overwhelming, and gorgeous, as Ezra—even with his very painful-looking black eye. I can't help wondering who was brave enough to punch him. The dude is huge.

I don't ask, and I don't shake his hand. Instead, I eye him, glancing from his hand to his face. "I know who you are."

I expect the attitude to put him off, but he just grins wider. "I know who you are too."

"Good." I stretch a little. "Now that that's settled, can we get to work?"

"By all means," Ezra says, flowing to his feet in a move so smooth that it's kind of hard not to stare. "We were waiting for you."

"Sorry." I toss my hair, deliberately insolent. "It's not easy being beautiful."

"Oh, I think you manage all right," Ezra murmurs.

I turn to look at him, startled, but he's already walking toward another part of the room, the only area in the whole downstairs that's completely walled off.

He pauses when he gets to the big beveled glass doors at the end. He types a code into the small keypad to the left, then waits for the door to swing open.

"Step into my parlor," he says with a wave of his hand and a cheesy accent.

And still I can't help thinking, *Said the spider to the fly....*

It's another ridiculously luxurious room, and I'm not sure why we needed to move in here until I see the small conference table at one end of the curved room—and the Promethean board that takes up the wall closest to it.

"The Wi-Fi password is strawberryLemonade27 star, exclam, all lowercase except the *L*," Ezra says as we all grab a seat at the table. "You don't have to use our Wi-Fi if you don't want, but my dad had a secure server installed as soon as we moved in."

"Dude. You've got your own server?" Owen sounds impressed.

Ezra shrugs. "My dad's a little paranoid."

"More like smart. When you own three thousand luxury hotels around the world, you never know who's out to get you." Seth's fingers fly over his keyboard. "Speaking of, I made a few minor adjustments to Owen's code. Just to make sure we can keep Jacento out of our equipment—without setting off any alarms. The last thing we want them to know is that we're coming for them."

"We're not actually coming for them," I answer. "I mean, we don't know that all of Jacento is behind this mess."

"And we don't know that they aren't either," Seth counters. "I vote for not taking any chances."

"I'm with Seth," Owen says. "Send that code out so we can update, will you?"

"I already have," he answers smugly.

"Since we're going after Jacento," Ezra says after we've all installed Seth's update on every device we have, "I've taken the liberty of doing some reconnaissance. I've got a map of Jacento's headquarters, blueprints of all the main buildings, shift changes and guard schedules—"

"You already did all this?" Alika asks. She doesn't sound impressed so much as surprised. "When?"

Ezra's eyes narrow as if she's deliberately insulted him. Maybe she has—I'm learning that rich people have their own language. But all he says is, "You guys had to rearrange your lives to get here. I just had to hop on my dad's jet for a forty-five minute flight. I took advantage of the time."

"You did all this in a few hours?" Seth asks as the first blueprints flash across the smartboard. He whistles, impressed, before pulling a pack of M&M's out of his pocket. "That's a lot of security to get through."

"Turns out I'm not just a pretty face," Ezra deadpans. "Who knew?"

"Well, let's not get ahead of ourselves," I tell him, equally straight-faced.

It breaks the ice, as does the food delivery a few minutes later. It's not long before we're all hunched over plates loaded with samosas, paneer masala, veg curry, and naan, tossing ideas—and insults—at one another with every other bite.

"How many buildings are there in this place, anyway?" Owen asks in between mouthfuls. And, damn, the boy can eat.

"Seven," Seth answers before Ezra can. It looks like crazy rich boy isn't the only one who did his homework.

But when I look at Seth, eyebrows raised, he just shrugs. "Planes are boring. I needed something to do."

"And hacking into one of the world's largest and most secure corporations kept you from getting bored?" Alika teases.

"For at least half the flight, anyway," Seth tells her, tongue in cheek.

"Wow!" Owen cackles. "Look at the balls on this one."

"Want to put your money where your mouth is, dude?" Ezra asks.

"I don't know," Harper interjects in her quiet way. "I kind of love the smell of arrogance in the afternoon."

"'The horror,'" Ezra answers her with a roll of his eyes.

"Hey, it's better than napalm, anyway." Seth grins like an idiot, not fazed by the teasing at all.

I'm lost, but then I remember the old-movie thing they did in the car on the way to the airport. Sure enough, a quick Google search turns up the references to *Apocalypse Now.*

I bookmark it as a reminder to check it out more fully later, then say, "I really hope your choice of movie isn't a bad omen."

"Right?" Owen agrees, softly elbowing Harper, who, I've noticed, squirms a little when he does that. "Next time pick some Disney crap or something."

Her poker face is flawless when she answers, "You mean like, 'Memo to me: Maim you after my meeting'?"

"Actually, yes, that's exactly what I meant. Obviously." He grabs another samosa from the center of the table. "Jeez, tough room."

"Right?" Seth echoes. "We've been here an hour, and she's already invoking Hades."

"You know your old movies," Harper tells him with obvious approval.

"I know my Disney. I've been to every Disney park in the world."

Ezra's laughing so hard now that he almost chokes on his samosa. "Jesus, dude, does admitting that get you laid a lot?"

"Sadly, no," Seth says. "But there's always a first time."

"No," Owen tells him with a shake of his head. "Sometimes,

there really isn't. This is definitely one of those times when there isn't."

"I disagree," Alika says, batting her eyes at Seth playfully. "I love Disneyland. So many things for a girl to ride." And that shuts both Ezra and Owen right up, so fast that I kind of wish I'd thought of it.

"Anyway…" Ezra says in the tone of someone determined to change the subject. "What we're looking for is in this building right here."

He punches a few keys on his laptop so that the tallest building lights up. It's also the one that sits deepest inside the compound—and borders the ocean, just to make it extra challenging. Big surprise. "It's where they keep the backup servers. Any information that flows through headquarters—emails, financial data, classified product info, nefarious plots, etc., etc.—will all be stored here."

"Do we really have to get *in* there?" Alika asks. "Why can't we just hack it from the outside, like we've done everything else?"

"Because it's unhackable," he tells her.

"Maybe for you," I say. "Maybe not for the rest of us."

"By all means," he answers, kicking back in his chair, "have at it, oh great hacking guru. The fact that it's not connected to the outside in any way would be a problem in the hands of a lesser woman, but it shouldn't impede your genius at all."

"Great hacking guru. I like it. I think you should call me that from now on."

"Whatever you say." Ezra lifts his brows at me. "I do like to give a lady what she wants."

"As long as it doesn't involve any fast rides," Alika cracks, and for the second time in as many minutes, I'm kind of shocked by the dirty mind on Little Miss Perfect.

"How about giving me what *I* want?" Harper asks as she reaches for the veg curry. "Pull up the blueprints to that building. I want to find the best way in."

"The best way in is going to depend on how we get there," Owen says.

"We've got two days to figure it out," Ezra says as he hits a few more keys and lights up all available ways into the building.

"Two days?" I exclaim, dismayed. I was hoping to be on my way home by then.

"Disappointed you won't have more time with me?" Ezra asks with a grin.

"Obviously. Who wouldn't want that?" I roll my eyes. Still, I study the plans, trying to see what's so complicated.

It only takes a minute.

"Are you telling me we're going up against a Vector?" I ask, referring to one of the best security systems in the world. It's considered practically unhackable, partly because it runs an eight-digit encryption code that takes way too long to even try to crack and partly because it employs a rudimentary type of AI. "That's impossible."

"Not impossible," Ezra answers.

"No, it's impossible," I argue. "I mean, unless it's a bagbiter, which it won't be. The system's a dragon, like five times over." I do a quick backdoor search on my laptop and skim the results.

It only takes a few seconds to find what I'm looking for.

"See?" I continue, turning my laptop around so that everyone can see the screen. "The Vector forms a complex neural net that adjusts to what we're doing."

"I know that," Ezra tells me.

"Do you? Do you really? Because from where I'm sitting, it seems like this whole trip out here has been a total waste of my time. Time I couldn't afford to waste."

"There's a way around it," Owen assures me. "There always is."

"Is there?" I answer sarcastically. "Because I'm in the middle of doing my senior project on Vector's new systems, and there's a reason they call them unhackable. It's because the AI they utilize is some of the top in the world. It learns from every attempt we make to circumvent the security. Which means—"

"We make it stronger every time we try to get past it," Seth adds quietly.

"Exactly!" I nod. "Which is why I say it's unhackable."

"You don't need to sound quite so triumphant," Owen tells me drily. "The goal is to beat the thing, after all."

At the same time, Alika assures me, "Nothing's unhackable. Some things just take longer than others."

I don't agree, but at this point I'm willing to back off and give them all their say. After all, I've never been in a room with five other hackers as good as I am before. Maybe Alika's right. Maybe nothing is impossible.

"This is the other problem," Ezra says, lighting up a perimeter around the entire compound for the first time. "You've got two or three armed guards at each of these guardhouses, as well as a minimum of five patrolling the grounds at any given time.

I mean, just in case an eight-digit encryption code isn't enough to back you off."

Owen whistles. "Overkill much?"

"I'm pretty sure two days is optimistic," Seth agrees as he starts gathering up the empty food containers. "Hey, Ezra, where's your recycle?"

"Downstairs, but I don't know what the cleaning people did with our bin. Just dump it in the trash."

Seth looks horrified. "Umm, no. The planet is dying, dude. You really want to kill it faster?"

Ezra rolls his eyes. "Fine. I think there's some green bags under the sink in the kitchen. Put it in there and I'll run it down later." Then, problem solved, he turns back to the rest of us. "We haven't even gotten to the security unique to each of the buildings, particularly the one that houses the servers."

"Are we sure Jacento *isn't* some cover for the CIA?" Alika asks incredulously. "Even Langley doesn't have security this tight."

"Kind of makes you wonder what they're hiding, doesn't it?" Harper crosses to the minifridge built into the cabinets along the back wall and pulls out a LaCroix. She lifts her brow in silent inquiry as the rest of us nod, and I hold my hand out for the cold blue can.

"If it's as complicated as it looks, what are we realistically going to be able to do in two days?" I demand, getting more freaked out with every second. School doesn't start for two weeks, but I can't be away that long. There's no way Lettie and my dad can handle things for more than a few days without me. "Eight-digit encryption and AI—"

"Won't be a problem," Ezra interrupts. "Because in two days, they're closing the whole compound down for a party—half holiday bash for employees, half celebration of the soft open for the kiosks on New Year's Eve. Tons of people are invited—including the press and caterers and influential members of the tech community. It's our best chance to get in."

"Wait a minute. You're telling me they have this kind of security, and in two days they're just going to open the whole compound to half of San Francisco?" Owen asks.

"It's a little more selective than that, but yeah. Basically. We'll still have to get through the building security, which is pretty freaking intense, but we'll be able to concentrate on that if we don't have to also figure out how to get through the outer ring of security."

"Two days it is, then," Harper says.

"Yeah," Seth agrees. "Besides, who doesn't like a party?"

Alika and Owen nod, and even I have to admit it's the best chance we've got. That doesn't mean I'm happy about it.

"How are we going to get in, though?" I ask. "They're not just going to open the place up for whoever wants to come."

"Leave that part to me," Ezra tells me. "I'll get us in."

"How?"

"Don't worry about it."

"Don't tell me not to worry about it!" I push to my feet. "I don't know you, and therefore I don't trust you, so if you expect us to have your back—and to believe you'll have ours—you need to be a little more forthcoming than 'Don't worry about it.' "

Silence reigns after my little outburst, but I don't apologize, and I don't take it back. If we get caught breaking into this place—let alone hacking its unhackable system—we'll be in the kind of trouble that isn't easily fixed.

A quick glance at the others tells me most of them feel the same way, even if they haven't said it yet.

Ezra looks pissed, all locked jaw and simmering dark eyes as our gazes meet. I think he expects me to back down, but that's not going to happen. Especially when we're talking about doing something so illegal that it could land us in jail for decades— even if it is for a good cause.

"Fine," he finally says, after the silence stretches past awkward into downright uncomfortable. "You'd be surprised what being Victor Hernandez's son will get me. Getting an invite to the Jacento party is no problem. The PR people will love the photo op, if nothing else. It sounds douchey to say it, though, so I wasn't going to." The sarcastic *Thanks for making me do it anyway* is totally implied.

I can tell he's waiting for an apology, but he's not getting it. He might be embarrassed of his pedigree, but it is what it is. And right now, I'll take any advantage we can get. "You're right. It does, but I'll take douchey and honest over sketchy and polite anytime."

"Me too," Seth contributes, and it breaks the tension. "And I don't know about anyone else, but I feel better knowing you've got an in."

"I don't have one yet, but I will." The look he shoots me is half-amused and half-exasperated. "Good enough?"

"For now," I answer with a nod.

"Then let's get back to work."

"So, do we have the party schematics?" Alika asks. "Where they're going to set up, what kind of stuff they're going to have?"

"We do, courtesy of the party planner's ridiculously easy password." He pops up the graphic.

"It's a circus theme?" Owen says incredulously.

"How do you know that?" Seth leans closer, as if proximity to the screen will make everything clear.

"It says 'Big Top' over the huge striped-tent schematic. I'd say that was self-explanatory."

"So who gets to be the clown?" Harper wonders.

"Dude." Seth almost topples out of his chair in his vehemence. "I don't do clowns."

"No one's asking you to do one," Ezra deadpans.

"You know what I mean." Seth looks seriously spooked. "I'll do anything else, but I am not dressing up like a clown. Those things are evil!"

"Because Stephen King says so?" Alika teases.

"Umm, yeah. The man knows some really freaky stuff, and if he says clowns are evil possessed beings, I'm totally okay with believing him."

"You know, Seth, just because you put on a clown costume doesn't mean you suddenly become evil. It's still you, in the costume," I tell him.

"Yeah, well, I'm not taking any chances: I say let Ezra be the clown."

"But then how would we ever know if Stephen King was right?" Harper is all wide-eyed innocence as she scrolls through her phone.

Alika bursts out laughing.

"Wow." Ezra leans back in his chair and folds his arms over his chest. "This is not how I thought this afternoon would go."

"Don't pout. It's so unbecoming," I tell him and have to stop myself from smiling at his wounded expression. "But seriously, Ezra, you'd make a great clown."

He looks like he's about to say something back and then seems to change his mind and starts scrolling through the info he hacked from the party planner.

"Can you split the screen, keep the party schematic on one side and the map of the headquarters on the other?" Owen asks.

"Call me an evil clown all you want, but I'm going to start getting really insulted if you people keep doubting my skills," Ezra complains as he does what Owen asks with a couple of keystrokes.

"Rich, good-looking, *and* useful," I mock, even as I study the maps, looking for weaknesses. "I'm sooooooo impressed."

"No doubt." He tears off a small piece of his naan, tosses it at me. "I can tell."

I dodge the bread, and Seth picks it out of the air before popping it into his mouth with a grin. "Yum."

I laugh despite myself—we all do—and then we roll up our metaphorical sleeves and get to work.

Case Study:
Seth Prentiss aka 5c0ut60

DOB: 2/2/01

Sex: Male

Height: 6'

Weight: 150 lbs.

Eye Color: Blue

Hair Color: Red (dyed)

Race: White

School: Westlake High School (public), Austin

Parents: Michael and Sarah Prentiss

Personal Net Worth: $10K + large college fund

Family Net Worth: Varies depending on company stock prices, but A LOT

Interesting Fact: His parents are part of the new tech revolution, nerds from Stanford and Berkeley who pretty much helped invent social media more than a decade ago.

Most Notorious Hack: Freaking Metrobank, where he took one dollar from each account and donated it to Doctors Without Borders. Seriously. That's who this guy is.

OBSERVATIONS:

Nobody, I repeat nobody, is this nice—not even the son of techie do-gooders determined to make the world a better place. Seriously. Nobody. Except, it seems, Seth Prentiss. I've been digging for weeks on the kid, and everything I turn up points to him actually being the "nicest person ever."

He volunteers at his local Austin food pantry, has been on two trips with Habitat for Humanity this year alone, teaches about composting and water reclamation at various community centers in Austin, and is a mentor at the local middle school. Even his hacking has a whole Robin Hood vibe going on—steal from the rich, give to the poor—a redistribution of wealth that has nothing to do with lining his own pockets.

I mean, seriously, his CV is enough to send a person like me into sugar shock . . . or it would be if I believed it. Which I don't.

I don't care what the research says or how his college rec letters gush about how amazing he is. There's got to be more here than meets the eye. Some people might be okay with the amount of sweetness and light Prentiss gives off, but mark my words. This kid has a giant skeleton in his closet somewhere. I guarantee it.

I just hope I figure out what it is before it brings the rest of us down.

SURVEILLANCE FOOTAGE:
12/27/18
07:06
FISHERMAN'S WHARF
SAN FRANCISCO, CALIFORNIA

Footage begins at 07:06 in the Starbucks on the outskirts of Fisherman's Wharf (security camera 52). Seth Prentiss waits in a very long line.

At 07:14, an altercation breaks out at the front of said line—started by a customer, Robert Macentire, and directed at Rosa Menendez, employee. Macentire is not facing the surveillance camera, so it's not possible to lip-read, but he is visibly upset. At one point, he opens the top of what is later revealed to be an iced latte and spills the cup across the counter. Menendez is splashed with coffee.

At 07:18, Prentiss makes it to the counter, where he orders a Venti black coffee and two blueberry scones. He pays with a twenty-dollar bill and leaves the change in the tip jar.

At 07:23, he heads out of the Starbucks, order in hand, and turns left (security camera GS1). He walks quickly toward Hyde and turns right, scanning the crowd, obviously looking for something. He finds it at 07:29 at Hyde Street Pier (security camera FW15), where Macentire is sitting on a park bench drinking a new iced latte, this one made with whatever specifications he apparently felt were missing from his first drink.

Prentiss sits next to Macentire on the bench and strikes up a conversation. At one point he must ask to borrow his phone because Macentire hands it over. Prentiss dials a number. (A check of Macentire's phone records shows that the call was actually to Prentiss's own phone.) As he calls, he swipes the phone past his own device, in a way that suggests cloning. He then deletes the call from Macentire's log and hands the phone back to Macentire with a shrug that implies "No answer."

Prentiss guzzles his coffee and eats his scones, then—after making sure to put his trash in the appropriate recycling containers—heads back down Hyde in the direction he came from (security camera G3), turns left on Beach, and reenters the still-busy Starbucks at 07:46 (security camera S2). A search of phone activity shows that at 07:49, while he waits in line, he cracks Macentire's Starbucks account. At 08:02, he orders two more blueberry scones and pays with Macentire's account. He then uses said account to leave employee Menendez a five-hundred-dollar tip.

At 08:05, he eats his scones in two bites each and walks out onto Beach Street, turning right this time. He interacts with no one else until he enters 201 Folsom Street at 08:35.

10

Harper
[5p3ct3r]

"I'm hungry," Mad Max says, breaking the silence in the room—and my concentration.

"How is that possible?" I ask him. "Weren't you just at Starbucks?"

"Umm, everyone knows Starbucks isn't real food. They're a warm-up, like an amuse-bouche for breakfast."

"Pretty sure there's no such thing," Snow White tells him drily.

"Sure there is," he answers. "Besides, I've eaten every Snickers bar in the place *and* my emergency stash of M&M's. Which means it's time to take a break before I waste away."

"We don't have time for a break." Buffy doesn't even bother to look up from her keyboard. "In less than twenty-four hours we'll be breaking into Jacento, and we still haven't come up with a plan that won't get us caught."

"A fifteen-minute break isn't going to stop us from fixing that," Mad Max tells her as he stretches his long, lean frame so thoroughly that I swear I hear his spine pop.

"You don't know that." She still doesn't glance his way.

"You're right. I don't. But I do know if I have to go any longer without snacks, I'm going to gnaw off my own hand. And then I'll be no use to you at all. Must have sustenance."

He heads to the kitchen, pausing only long enough to turn on the very large TV mounted on one of the few interior walls on the first floor of Silver Spoon's family's penthouse.

The TV's tuned to MSNBC, and as Mad Max walks away, I look up just in time to see Roderick Olsen, global CEO of none other than Jacento, take over the screen.

"Hey!" I call out as I make a grab for the remote to turn up the volume. "Look."

Even Buffy stops what she's doing as we gather around the TV to watch Olsen talk about Jacento's numerous holiday donations and the new series of internships they're making available to American college students. It's a puff piece, pure and simple, one meant to make everyone feel good about using and gifting Jacento products this holiday. After all, it's hard to feel like a capitalistic pig if just the act of buying or receiving a smartphone helps combat hunger and disease in developing nations. And if that message comes from a notoriously reclusive CEO known for being an eccentric genius? It just makes the message that much stronger.

Even as I think it, I can imagine Mad Max saying, *Wow, cynical much?*

At the same time, Buffy asks, "Do you think he knows?"

Snow White laughs. "Of course he knows. That's how these things work."

So I'm definitely not the only cynical one in the room. Good to know. Except...

"Not necessarily," Mad Max tells her, right on schedule. "He's actually a really good person. I have trouble believing he'd be a part of something like this."

"Just because a guy gives money to charity doesn't make him a decent person," the Lone Ranger says. "Look at Ezra."

"Exactly," Silver Spoon agrees from the kitchen, where he's working on a plan to get us into Jacento's server room. "Rich people are always scum."

The sarcasm is so thick I can cut it with a knife.

"Maybe," Mad Max agrees earnestly, because of course he does. "But my dad knows Olsen and—"

"Wait. Your dad knows him?" I demand. "How?"

"They went to grad school together, and they used to hang out a lot when I was a kid. It's been years since I've seen him, but I remember him being a cool guy."

"They're friends?" Silver Spoon asks, incredulous. "And you didn't see fit to tell us about this sooner?"

"Why would I tell you?" Mad Max asks as he grabs a bag of chips from the pantry and starts chowing down. "I don't see what the big deal is. He's the global CEO, not the American one. He's not even in the country right now."

"Your dad and he are close enough friends that you know where he's spending the holidays?" It takes a lot to get me worked up, but right now it feels like the top of my head is going to blow off.

"Uh, no." He points at the TV as the show comes back on.

"It says right there that the interview was done this morning at his home in Helsinki."

"Oh." The blood pounding in my head starts to go down a little. "Right. Sorry."

"Don't be sorry," Snow White says. "He still should have told us."

"Why?" Mad Max asks. "He's not involved."

"Of course he's involved!" Silver Spoon slams a hand down on the kitchen counter. "That's how these things work. And if you think otherwise, you've either got a blind spot a mile wide or you're stupid. And I know you're not stupid."

"You don't know—"

"I *do* know. My dad's CEO of Majestic, and I guarantee you, nothing major happens in that company without him knowing about it. Nothing."

"That's different. It's a family business. He hasn't even mentioned the kiosks—" Mad Max breaks off as Olsen does just that.

We stand in silence for the next two minutes as Olsen sells the kiosk superchargers like they're the greatest thing since the invention of democracy and the personal computer all rolled into one, ending with the admonishment that "everyone, and I mean *everyone*, should try one at least once."

"That guy!" Buffy suddenly yells, diving for the remote so she can freeze the screen seconds after it cuts to a shot of Olsen at one of the company's shareholder meetings. "He was in L.A.!"

"Who, Shane?" I ask, searching the screen for the fake Agent Donovan.

"No. That one." She walks up to the TV and points at an older man with silver hair and a rugged face. "I saw him in the hallway when I was doing my hack."

"That guy?" Silver Spoon points to the same guy Buffy just picked out. "Are you sure?"

"I'm positive. I wouldn't forget a face like that. Who is he?"

"I don't know," the Lone Ranger says as he gets close enough to snap a pic of the guy's face with his phone. "But I'm going to find out."

"Still think Olsen's not involved?" Snow White asks.

"The CEO is always involved," Silver Spoon repeats his earlier point before Mad Max has a chance to respond. "There might be two or three people between him and taking the fall, but he's always involved. Take it from someone who knows all about how corporations like this function behind the scenes."

Mad Max looks like he wants to argue, but in the end, he just shrugs with a sad frown. "I don't want you to be right."

"None of us want to be right on this," the Lone Ranger says as he claps him on the back. "But you know we are."

Buffy unfreezes the TV, and as Olsen goes on about the safety features built in to every new Mirage 8—features that will sweep through the 6 and 7 models in a series of rolling updates—my chest gets tight.

I know we're protected, know that the Lone Ranger's fix, and Mad Max's update to it, will keep our devices hidden from

Jacento, but I still feel the need to reach for my phone. To run a scan on it and then manually check the dozens of hiding places a sneaky virus like Phantom Wheel might try to take root. I don't find anything. Still, I do it again.

This is too important, and I've got too much to lose if I get caught. Just the idea of someone hacking us and finding out what I've done to keep myself out of the system makes me sick. I can't go back to some foster home, can't deal with the spin of the wheel that comes with wondering what kind of family I'll end up with.

I'm doing fine on my own—better than fine—and there's no way I'm going back. I'd rather die first.

I've put some things in motion, have some checks and balances to keep that from happening. But if this thing with Jacento blows wide open, if they come after us, there's no guaranteeing my safeguards will hold up in the light of day. And then I'll be completely screwed.

I put down my phone and reach for my laptop. I run the same check on my computer and my tablet while the others continue to debate the best way to get out of the Jacento compound if things go wrong.

Their voices ebb and flow around me, making a kind of nice background noise, at least until Silver Spoon drops a hand on my shoulder. I jump even as he asks, "Hey, Harper, you zoned out or something?"

"No, I'm just checking some stuff. What's up?"

He gives me a look that says he doesn't believe me, but all he says is, "We're ordering in Mexican. What do you want?"

I give him my order, then make a concerted effort to join the conversation as we wait for the food to arrive.

"We need costumes," Mad Max says as he twists off the top of yet another bottle of orange soda. "They can help to disguise us."

"Costumes will look totally out of place," Snow White argues. "It's not that kind of party."

"It's a circus," he shoots back. "That's pretty much the definition of a costume party."

"For the entertainers," she counters. "Not for the guests. We'll look ridiculous and draw way too much attention to ourselves."

"Wait until you see how much attention we draw once they've got our real faces," Mad Max says, flopping down on the sofa and kicking his feet up on the very expensive-looking coffee table. "We're going into the building, and while we're going to try not to get caught—"

"I vote for doing more than trying," Buffy interjects.

"Obviously." He rolls his eyes. "But if things go bad and they figure out something is up, the last thing we can afford is for our real faces to be caught on camera. I mean, look at me. I'm man enough to admit I wouldn't last two minutes in juvie."

"Plus a couple of you are eighteen," I say, adding weight to his argument. "You won't go to juvie. Not to mention some of you will pop instantly," I say, nodding to Silver Spoon and Snow White. "Your faces may not be instantly recognizable, but come on. How many pictures are out there of Victor Hernandez's jet-setting son living it up? Or the secretary of state's daughter doing charity work?"

I turn to the Lone Ranger. "Or you at your father's games? Facial recognition software will hit on the three of you the second they enter your picture, and you know it."

"Which means disguises," Mad Max crows triumphantly.

"Sunglasses," Silver Spoon offers. "I can totally do sunglasses."

"And a hoodie," the Lone Ranger says.

"I'm not sure that's enough," Buffy says, chiming in for the first time.

"It's going to have to be," Snow White tells her firmly. "Because dressing us up as circus freaks will only make things worse."

I'm trying to think of another argument to sway them when the doorbell rings with dinner (Silver Spoon called down and cleared the delivery person as soon as he ordered). Snow White answers the door, and I scramble to get silverware and drinks. And as we settle around the table, I decide to let the subject of more sophisticated disguises go.

After all, better to spend my time making sure we don't get seen than worrying about what we look like if we do....

11

Owen
(1nf1n173 5h4d3)

"Here goes nothing." I rest my head against my seat and pray we're not making a huge mistake. If we get caught, not only am I screwed, but my whole family is.

"Owen! Don't say that!" Seth hisses. "I mean, at least say, 'Here goes something.' Or, 'Here goes a lot.'"

"'Here goes a lot'?" Harper whispers. "That's not even a thing!"

"Who cares if it's a thing? We're trying to break into a party with more security than the Pentagon. Negative vibes are the last thing we need right now."

"God forbid we mess with the freaking vibes," I tell him. "Who knows what will happen then?"

"I'm just saying. You get back what you put out into the universe," Seth replies. "So if you put out bad vibes, what do you think is going to come back to you?"

I stare at him for several long seconds, trying to decide if he's serious with this or not. The problem is, I've come to learn that with Seth, he's almost always serious—no matter how absurd what he says is.

And this whole sending-good-vibes-into-the-universe thing will save us all? It's pretty absurd. God knows, my mom puts the best vibes out there of anyone I know, and look at what her life has become.

We're about to trust Ezra "Pretty Boy" Hernandez with what could be our safety, our liberty, and what might just be our asses, and Seth is worried about good vibes? In my opinion, he should be more worried about whether or not he's got a good lawyer on speed dial.

A quick glance at Harper tells me she feels the way I do, but somehow she manages to bite back whatever she's thinking. Which gives me the strength to do the same. The last thing we need is to get Seth in a tizzy before anything goes down.

Our headsets aren't on yet, and we're keeping our voices low, but Ezra must sense our unease because he turns around from the driver's seat of his giant SUV and says, "Don't worry. I've got this."

"Not worried," Issa tells him, but I can see the way her hands are clenched in her lap. Can feel the tension rolling off her in waves.

Then again, I could just be projecting, because, well...this whole putting-my-trust-in-someone-else thing is so *not* how I like to live my life. Especially not when that person is Ezra Hernandez. I know he hasn't done anything suspicious since we got to San Francisco, but I can't help being suspicious anyway. Maybe it's his attitude, maybe it's his money and his big-name connections, but I can't help wondering if he's cut from the same cloth as Olsen and all those other CEO types who care more about money and power than they do about people. More,

I can't help wondering if he's doing all this as a joke and that maybe, just maybe, he's on big business's side instead of ours.

"Totally worried," Alika tells him from the seat next to his. "So don't screw it up."

"I won't," he says with a grin. "I mean, come on. None of you would last two minutes in jail. I mean, except for Harper. She'd last at least seven minutes."

She flips him off without ever looking up from her phone.

So many things to like about that girl.

We're in line at one of the three main guard shacks outside Jacento headquarters, waiting to get onto the property for the party. Ezra came through with the invite, just like he said he would, but it's a you-plus-one thing, not a you-plus-five.

He swears it's not a problem, and normally I'd agree with him, but the security here is wild. In a very *If you get out of line, we'll murder you and your children and your children's children* kind of way.

It's finally our turn, and I can feel everyone in the SUV take a collective deep breath. Ezra reaches over and turns up the radio really loud so that it's blasting Drake as we roll up to the guard shack. Alika leans over to turn it down, but he gives her a warning look seconds before he slides down his window.

And in those seconds, the Ezra Hernandez we've known the past couple of days disappears. And is replaced by a much douchier, much more obnoxious kid-playing-dress-up version of himself.

"Yo, man, how you doing?" he asks the guard, reaching out for a handshake. "Having a good day?"

For a second the guy just stares at him, clipboard in hand,

like he's trying to assess the threat level. He must decide it's pretty freaking high because he shifts a little, puts his free hand on the gun strapped to his waist.

Firearms three seconds in is not how this thing is supposed to go.

"Can I help you, sir?"

"We're here for the par-tay. Free booze and smartphones, am I right? What's not to love?"

Even Seth is tense beside me now.

"Do you have an invitation? Because it's a closed party—"

"Course I got an invite. Who do you think I am?" Ezra points his finger at him like it's a gun, then brings his thumb down in the universal firing gesture at the same time he makes some *I'm hot and I know it* clicking sound with his mouth. "Ezra Hernandez, Majestic Hotels. Look it up, my man."

The guard looks anything but amused, and I brace myself to be dragged out of the SUV. We all do. What the hell is wrong with Ezra?

But in the end, the guard just mad dogs him for one second, two, before glancing down at the list on his clipboard. "I see you've RSVP'd, but it says two people." He glances in the window, makes eye contact with me for one brief second. "How many people are in that SUV?"

"Two?" Ezra squawks. "I never go anywhere with just one person—surely not to a fine-ass party like this. I need my crew to back me up."

His crew? Jesus, he sounds like every bad movie representation of the rich kid trying to be gangster I've ever seen, and

I'm embarrassed for him if this is his big move. His big con. Because, frankly, this is humiliating.

"Your *crew*"—the guard says the word like it's a sexually transmitted disease—"is not on the list."

"That's impossible. We're always on the list, cuz we bring the par-tay with us." He nods at the guy, easygoing grin still in place. But there's a hint of petulance—and a hint of *Don't screw with me*—beneath the party-boy exterior when he says, "Why don't you look again."

It's obvious that the guard is holding on to his patience by a thread. "I already checked, sir. Your name is here with a plus one. Which means you and the young lady"—he nods toward Alika—"can either ditch the rest of your *crew* or you can turn around and find something else to do."

"Check again." There's real steel in the command this time.

"I already checked." He holds up the clipboard. "Now—"

"Not on that stupid piece of paper." Ezra reaches out and sends the clipboard flying. It bounces off the car, then hits the ground with a clatter. "On the computer, where the real list is."

The guard's pretty much bent on murder by this point—and I don't even blame him. I kind of want to kick Ezra's ass myself, even if we are on the same side.

Except, before the guard can say more than "All right, that's it," his supervisor inside the shack steps toward the car, all puffed-up chest and *I'm the boss here* attitude.

Which is never good.

"Excuse me. Is there a problem?"

"Yeah, there's a big freaking problem!" Ezra tells him. "I

talked to Randy myself last week, and he assured me that my friends could attend this little soiree with me. Now this guy"—he curls his lip like he just smelled something bad—"tells me we're not welcome. We drove all the way out here from the city, through brutal traffic, and we want to go to the damn party."

The supervisor's eyes go flat at his tone, but all he does is bend down and pick up the clipboard. "You're on the list?"

"Yeah, I'm on the damn list. I'm right there." He slaps at the clipboard again, but this time it's more for emphasis than to actually send the thing crashing to the ground.

"What's your name, sir?"

Ezra sighs heavily, like it's the biggest imposition in the world. "Ezra Hernandez. That's H-E-R-N-A-N-D-E-Z, from Majestic Hotels. Now, are you going to call Randy and get this all straightened out, or am I?" He yanks his phone out of his front jeans pocket and brandishes it like a weapon.

The new guard doesn't respond for several seconds, just leans in the window and looks from one of us to the next. I'm so embarrassed that I can barely meet his eyes.

But Ezra just huffs impatiently and says, "Looks like it's going to be me, then." He pulls up his address book, presses Call.

As the sound of a phone ringing replaces the obnoxiously loud music in the car, the guard steps back. "You're good to go," he says, waving so the third guard will lift the barrier. "Follow the orange-and-white signs to the parking lot. And enjoy the party."

"Yeah, I'll try," Ezra snarls. "Thank the other guy for nothing, will you?" Then he hits the gas, and we're barreling into the compound.

"What. The. Hell. Was. That?" Issa hisses when we're several hundred yards away from the guard station. "You almost blew the whole thing before it even started."

Ezra just turns his head and smirks at her. Smirks at all of us, really, and the light of triumph is definitely in his eyes. "Never underestimate the total and complete douchebaggery of a second-gen Silicon Valley rich kid," he tells us. "On the plus side, no one wants to deal with you if they think you are one, so you get everything you want in life and then some."

"Does it also give you a soul?" Alika asks as he pulls the Escalade into the parking lot earmarked for party guests. "Because that was gross."

"Haven't you heard? Souls are like privacy in the twenty-first century," Ezra tells her as he finds a parking spot near the lot's exit, just as we planned. "Highly overrated and pretty much dead anyway."

"That's a terrible way of looking at the world!" she answers as we climb out of the Escalade.

"I never said it wasn't, but terrible doesn't mean untrue. If it did, we wouldn't be here trying to stop a money-hungry, power-mad corporation from exploiting the work we did for it under false pretenses. So save the Disney-princess attitude for Seth, will you, and let's get to work."

12

Issa
(Pr1m4 D0nn4)

"Hey, how'd I get in the middle of this?" Seth squawks as he slides his laptop into his backpack. "I'm just sitting here minding my own business."

"Really?" Owen glares at Ezra as he steps out of the SUV. "We're really going to do this now?"

"I'm pretty sure I made it clear we don't have time to do anything now, except get this hack done," Ezra replies.

From anyone else it might sound like he was backing down, but the look on Ezra's face is a giant screw-you to the whole group of us. And even though he's put my teeth on edge from the first time we met, there's a part of me that doesn't blame him.

Sure, Alika looks like a puppy who just got a boot to the face, but accusing Ezra of being soulless was a pretty crappy move on her part too. Especially when he's gone out of his way to be accommodating from the moment we first got to San Francisco. The food, the place to stay, taking Harper and me shopping for the types of outfits and all the equipment we'd need to run this con.

Which only makes it stranger that he sets all of us on edge. But he does, most of the time without even trying.

It's not the money, because Harper and I are the only two here who aren't loaded. I mean, sure, no one else has the kind of money Ezra's family has, but once you break the million-dollar mark, I feel it's pretty hard to quibble.

It's not the looks—even though he's probably the hottest guy I've ever seen. But Owen's crazy hot too, and he doesn't get my back up the same way, and neither does Seth, who is also really cute in his own way.

So what exactly is it? I wonder as I double-check to make sure I've got everything I need for my portion of the plan. His smoothness? His attitude? The fact that none of us is good at following orders—except maybe Alika—yet somehow we find ourselves following Ezra's more often than not?

That doesn't seem right either, though. Sure, it bugs me sometimes, but it's not Ezra's fault that he knows San Francisco better than anyone else—and that he's so good at taking control.

Still, it bothers me that I can't figure this out. I don't like mysteries I can't solve, and I definitely don't like questions I can't answer.

How can you trust something when you don't know what makes it tick?

"It's two o'clock," Harper says, breaking into my reverie. "The big entertainment starts at three, which means we've got one hour to do what we need to do and make it to the rendezvous spot. So can we shelve the petty BS for right now and just get on with it?"

"Consider it shelved," Alika says as she shrugs out of her coat for the first time since she came down the stairs this morning. And all I can say is . . . *Wow. Just wow.*

I'm pretty sure if Ezra had seen her like this five minutes ago, he never would have made that Disney-princess crack. Because there's nothing princess about the vibe she's throwing off right now. I don't swing that way, and even I'm having a hard time looking away. I've got no clue how Alika is actually going to run in that red leather dress if we need to, but she'll definitely cause a diversion.

"You look amazing," I tell her.

Harper nods.

All three guys stare like they've never seen a hot girl before.

Alika smiles sweetly at me and says, "I chose this dress for a very specific purpose."

Before I can ask her to elaborate, Ezra takes my elbow. "You ready?" he asks me as he nods toward the party.

"As I'll ever be."

Alika makes a point of knocking into him, hard, as we start to walk away. He looks at her in a *Do we have a problem?* kind of way, but she just raises a *Do you have a problem?* brow at him in return. I'd be lying if I tried to pretend I didn't love the whole exchange.

Alika may look like Little Miss Perfect, but that doesn't mean she's a pushover. The more I get to know her, the more I realize the girl has big brass ovaries.

After leaving the others to their parts of the plan, Ezra and I make our way toward the people milling around the huge stone fountain at the center of the compound.

"Remember, we can get what we need from four people," he murmurs as he guides me through the well-dressed crowd. "So keep your eyes peeled. Whoever we spot first is the lucky winner."

"I got it," I tell him, trying to ignore the way his palm feels pressed against my lower back. My dress has a dip in the back low enough that the tips of his fingers brush against my bare skin with each step we take. I know he's just sticking close because he doesn't want to lose me in the crowd, but a little shiver goes through me every time our skin touches.

I may hate it, but I can't help it.

Any more than I can help how out of place I feel at this party. And not just because we're running a con. I've never been anywhere like this before, have never seen anything like it outside of movies and magazines. We're supposed to blend in, be invisible, but how can I do that when I have no idea how to act? And when I'm with the hottest guy here?

Maybe Ezra and Alika should have teamed up. They'd be a hell of a distraction. The rest of us could walk straight into the server room stark naked, and no one would notice.

"Let's get a drink," Ezra says, guiding me toward the mobile drink station set up a few feet away. As we make our way there, I get a glimpse of Niklas Otto. He's IT director of Jacento's North American branch, and one of the four people who can help us get past security for the internal servers.

"There's Otto," I hiss as I stop dead in my tracks.

"Where?" Ezra scans the crowd with sharp eyes.

"Near the main bar," I tell him. The tiny earbud in my ear

comes alive as Seth and Harper find their target too. I block them out so I can focus on what we're supposed to be doing. "To the left. Do you see him?"

"I do." His eyes narrow as they lock on our prey.

I fluff up my hair and smooth my dress. "Do you want me to—"

"Change of plans," he says with a grin so sharp that it's almost feral. "I've got this."

"Wait, what? I thought we agreed I'd—"

But I'm left talking to myself, as he's already making his way toward Otto like the man's got a homing device in his back pocket.

I stay where I am, not wanting to blow the con, but I shift a little to the left so I can keep both Ezra and Otto in my sights. I don't have a clue what game Ezra's got planned, but he looks so confident that I'm not worried. He might have shaken up the game plan, but if he's proven nothing else over the last few days, it's that he knows what he's doing.

After grabbing a bottle of water from a nearby display, I settle in to watch the show. Then I nearly choke on my first sip as Ezra approaches Otto and says, "Well, hello there, gorgeous."

Otto's eyes widen at the greeting. But then he's looking Ezra up and down, a slight grin on his face as he leans back against the bar. "Hello yourself, stranger."

"I'm Elliott," Ezra tells him as he crowds up close to Otto, hip to hip. "And you are?"

It takes a minute for him to get his name out, but that's because the guy's almost choking on his own tongue. I'd feel sorry for him—being the object of all that sex appeal—if he wasn't at least peripherally involved in Jacento's horrible plot.

"Niklas," he finally gets out. "I'm Niklas."

"Nice to meet you, Niklas." Ezra slips Otto's drink out of his hand and drains it in one long swallow. "And see? Now we aren't strangers anymore."

"Umm, I guess not." As Ezra crowds even closer, the guy looks like he's hit the lottery on Christmas morning. Not that I blame him. Sure, he's okay-looking, but definitely not in Ezra's league. "Can I, umm, get you another drink?"

"You can." Ezra eyes him like he wants to eat him up. Not going to lie, it's hot. Really hot, and that's just from a spectator's perspective. I can't imagine what it would be like to actually have him look at me like that. I'd probably melt on the spot.

Ezra spends the next ten minutes flirting so outrageously that I expect Otto to catch on. I mean, come on. Sure, having all that intensity focused on you addles the brain a little, but at some point you have to get used to it, right? And start wondering what the guy wants because he can't actually want you....

Obviously not everyone thinks the way I do, because Jacento's IT director is eating it up. So much so that when Ezra asks for his number, it looks like he's going to swoon right there. He doesn't, though. Instead, he holds it together long enough to rattle off his digits so Ezra can add them to his phone. And when Ezra asks to take a picture to go with the number, Otto never hesitates. He just gives the camera—and Ezra—what I'm sure he thinks is a sultry smile, though it actually looks more like indigestion.

I should know. Chloe gets that look a lot.

Ezra keeps him chatting for a couple more minutes—mostly about imaginary dates they can go on—before slipping away "to find the restroom."

I meet up with him around the corner of the nearest building.

"I've already sent the photos to your phone," he says as he blocks me from view.

"I didn't know you were gay," I comment as I pull up the text attachments with steady fingers.

"Who said I was gay?" he responds with a shrug. "People are people. Why limit yourself any more than you have to?"

I grab the best picture, then enlarge it so I can see what we've got to work with. "That's a very enlightened attitude."

"I'm a very enlightened guy." He leans closer, trying to get a look at what I'm doing. But he's so close that it freaks me out a little, even makes my fingers tremble as I isolate what we need.

"Is it good enough?" His breath is hot against my cheek.

"I think so." I pull up the scan I got when I finally managed to hack into the system yesterday morning. Once I do, I superimpose the picture Ezra took over the scan and play with it a little bit, cleaning things up the best I can. "But I've never done this before, so I won't be sure if I've chomped it until we're actually at the door."

Still, I've read every article I could get my hands on about this over the last two days, so I'm hoping for the best. Even before Ezra runs a hand down my back and says, "You'll get it. I've got total faith in you."

"We'll see." I hold the picture up to him, refusing to let myself react to all the sexy heat pouring off him. He was throwing so much of it at Niklas Otto that he probably hasn't had a chance to rein it all in yet. Or at least that's my story and I'm sticking to it.

"You were a lot closer than I was. Does this color look right?"

"It looks perfect." For the first time, he sounds excited. "You're really good at this."

As he steps back, he takes the blatant sensuality down about ten notches, and I can finally breathe again.

And that's when it hits me, what has me so on edge around him all the time. What has all of us so suspicious of him, no matter how many nice things he does.

It's that even after all the time we have spent with him, none of us has any idea who the real Ezra Hernandez is.

Maybe it's the guy whose place we've been staying at for the past two days.

Maybe it's the douchebag who got us into this party.

Maybe it's the supersmooth, supersexy operator who just had Niklas Otto—a man our research never identified as anything but straight—eating right out of his hand.

Or maybe he's all those things—and so many more that there is no "real" Ezra Hernandez. Maybe he really is just the human version of a chameleon—someone who can so easily become anything to anybody that it's impossible to know who he really is outside that. Or if he even exists outside it at all.

The realization is enough to blow my brain wide open, so

I shove the idea back into the dark corners of my mind and focus instead on finishing my task. A few more clicks, and I'm printing out the photo on my Polaroid Zip and holding it up for Ezra's approval.

"Good?"

"Beautiful," he answers, but his eyes are on me.

As we walk toward the cordoned-off area—and the building where the servers are housed—I pretend he was talking about the picture.

It's not as exciting, but it is easier. And right now it'd be really nice if just one thing in my life could be easy....

13

Harper
[5p3ct3r]

I don't have a clue how we're going to do this. I mean, the technology is there, but I've never used it before, and neither have any of others. There's a first time for everything, but still. I'm more nervous than I want to admit.

Mad Max seems optimistic, but that's kind of like saying the sun is hot. I'm not sure the boy has any other mode.

He's tamped down his style a little bit for the party—instead of his usual outrageous color combinations, he's dressed in a pair of dark jeans and a button-down, limiting the loud colors to the funky bow tie he's wearing. With his usual red Mohawk in place and the addition of a pair of designer sunglasses he borrowed from Silver Spoon, he looks every bit the cool California hipster.

What surprises me is how much I miss his typical goofy appearance. Who knew it was even possible to miss checkered pants?

We work our way through the crowd, listening through our earbuds as Silver Spoon charms some guy out of his mind, among other things.

"I can't believe they're already working their target," Mad Max says in a stage whisper so loud that it'd be a miracle if half the party didn't hear it. "We haven't even found ours."

"They had four to choose from," I remind him. "We've got one."

"Still, how hard can it be to find a six-foot-three Samoan woman in this crowd?"

"Obviously harder than we anticipated." I just hope Talia Latu didn't skip out on the party. If she did, this whole thing is going to take a lot longer than we hoped.

Maybe too long.

Thinking that way isn't going to do us any good, however, so I keep working my way through the crowd, scanning, scanning, scanning. And pretending that Mad Max's optimism hasn't already started to rub off on me.

As we pass the new product booth they've got set up on the lawn, I notice a video of Roderick Olsen running on a loop. He's talking about the kiosks and how they'll make Jacento more than a household name. How they'll make the brand—the company—as indispensable to people as their wallets. Jacento will be at the top of their minds all day, every day.

Considering what those kiosks—and Phantom Wheel—will give Jacento control of, listening to him talk about world domination freaks me out, to say the least. No way is this guy innocent.

"There she is!" Mad Max crows about ten minutes later, so excited that he nearly spills his cranberry juice down my light gray dress. I dodge, but it's a close call, and he mutters his apologies over and over again as we weave our way toward the very tall, very large woman standing with an equally tall, equally large man right outside the circus tent.

They're engaged in a pretty animated conversation. Great— just great. That's going to make this a whole lot harder than I was hoping it would be.

"Let's go." Mad Max starts all but dragging me her way.

"What are we going to say to her?" I demand, digging my heels into the grass to stop his forward momentum. "I thought she'd be by herself—we can't just break into their conversation!"

He looks at me like I'm crazy. "Of course we can. Now turn your recorder on and come on!"

Seconds later, we're standing in front of Talia, and I still have no idea how to get her attention off the man I think is her husband and on to us. Mad Max, thankfully, doesn't have the same problem.

"Excuse me, ma'am, do you know what time the entertainment is supposed to start?" he asks, all wide eyes and innocence.

"Three o'clock," her husband answers. Of course he does. So glad Mad Max thought this was going to be easy.

I'm already frustrated, but he looks completely relaxed as he continues, "Thanks so much. Do you know where we're supposed to line up or—"

"The entrance is right over there." The man answers again. Fantastic.

"But there's no line," Talia adds. "I think you just wander in and find a seat whenever you're ready."

I perk up a little—at least she's talking. Maybe this won't be a total disaster after all.

"Cool. I'm really excited to see it—I've never been to the circus before. Have you?"

Talia chuckles. "Many times. But I agree, it is exciting." She's an older woman and, for whatever reason, seems totally charmed by Mad Max's enthusiasm.

"As long as there are no clowns. Clowns completely freak me out."

"Right?" Her husband jumps back into the conversation. "I told Talia to make sure there were no clowns. They give our grandchildren nightmares."

"They give *me* nightmares!" Mad Max answers enthusiastically. "Though I did hear they were going to have zebras, which sounds totally cool."

"Zebras?" Talia's husband shakes his head. "I don't think there are going to be any zebras. Are there, hon?"

"Nope. Not a one. But there will be horses."

"Oh, that's cool." Mad Max manages to look just the right amount of disappointed. "I love horses."

"Me too," Talia agrees. "We used to have a couple."

"Wow! Me too! What were your horses' names?" He pauses, then before they can answer, says, "No, wait. Let me guess. Zephyr and…"

"Nope. Definitely not Zephyr—they weren't near fast enough for that," Talia's husband says.

By this time, my nerves are stretched to the breaking point. But Mad Max stays cool. "Really? I always thought that'd be a great name for a horse. My sister"—he nods to me—"would never go for it, though. She threw a fit until we named the horse Zinnia."

Talia's grinning now, and so is her husband. "Zinnia's a great name! Our kids went with Bert and Ernie, even though the horses were both girls. Those two loved *Sesame Street*."

My whole body sags with relief.

"Bert and Ernie were always my favorites too," Mad Max tells them. "I loved their shirts."

Then he makes a show of looking at his phone. "Oh man, my mom just texted. She's looking for us. Thanks for the help, though. It was great talking to you."

"You too, young man. I hope you enjoy the show."

"Oh, we will. Absolutely!" He gives her a spontaneous hug that she returns, even going so far as to pat him on the back a few times.

Then we walk away slowly when all I want to do is run until we make it to the only open building on the compound. It's supposed to be for restroom use only, but I scouted out a room earlier that we should be able to use for a few minutes.

"I can't believe you got it!" I tell him as we settle behind the desk in the dark, so no one can see us.

"Told you I would. But, jeez, do you know how hard it is to think up *Z* words on the fly? I was sure the zebra thing would work."

"It did—just on the wrong person." I pull out my phone and send the audio recording to my laptop. Then I open my computer and pull up the sound software that will help me isolate—and combine—different sounds from Talia's speech so that I can duplicate her verbal password: zydeco two.

"Did you get the badge?" I ask as I start pulling apart the recording. I spent most of last night practicing, but as there's nothing voice protected in Silver Spoon's whole apartment, it was impossible to test my new skills.

"I'm really beginning to get my feelings hurt," he answers, dangling the badge in front of me.

"Sorry. It's just that we've got one chance at this, and I don't want to blow it."

"I know. I feel the same way. Plus, Ezra and Issa already got their stuff. Can't let them beat us."

"There's no world where Silver Spoon beats me," I tell him, and I'm concentrating so hard on what I'm doing that I don't even realize I slipped up until he lets out a bark of laughter.

"Silver Spoon?" he repeats. "That's a brilliant nickname for Ezra."

"Yeah, well, he's definitely got one. More than one, in fact."

"He really does." He laughs a little more, repeats the name to himself three more times. Then says, "Hey! Do you have nick-names for the rest of us too?"

I pretend to be absorbed in what I'm doing so I don't have to answer. Well, half pretend. I need a long O sound and I'll be done with zydeco—and there it is. *Nope*. It takes a minute, but I manage to isolate the O. Getting the P out was easy since it's such a hard sound, but the N took some work.

I've got it, though, and since Mad Max got her to say *too*, I should be able to lift that directly and—

"You do! You do have nicknames for us! What are they?"

"Dude, I'm trying to finish this like, yesterday. Can you give me a minute here?"

"Yeah, sure, of course. Sorry." He settles back against the desk next to me, muttering softly to himself. "Luke Cage…The Rock…"

"What are you mumbling?" I ask.

"Trying to figure out Owen's nickname."

"Oh." I go back to work.

"Seriously? That's all you're going to say? Come on, just tell me. I won't tell anyone."

The *too* slides into place just like I hoped it would. I play the whole thing back a couple of times, just to make sure the sounds all blend together.

Zydeco two.

Zydeco two.

Zydeco two.

"There's too big a space between the words," he tells me. "You need to smooth it out a little more so it doesn't trip an alarm."

I shoot him a look. "You *are* paying attention."

"Of course I am! Unlike some people in this partnership, I can actually multitask."

"Multitasking is highly overrated."

It takes me about ten tries, but I finally manage to blend the sounds together perfectly. As soon as I do, the tension leeches from my shoulders.

"Owen's the Lone Ranger," I tell him as I save everything and then slide my laptop into my backpack. "Obviously."

"Obviously!" he crows. "You're really good at this. So, what's mine?"

"Like I'm going to tell you."

"Come on, I won't get mad. I promise. Unless it's like Rooster or something. Because that's not cool."

"It's not Rooster." I head for the door.

"Good." He grins. "Okay, then. Porcupine?"

I shoot him an appalled look. "Definitely not."

"See? As long as those two are off the table, there's nowhere to go but up. Right?"

"Sure."

"You're still not going to tell me, are you?"

"Nope."

"What if I guess?"

"Yeah," I say with a snort. "Because you've been so good at that so far, Porcupine."

"Hey, I didn't mean for you to start calling me that." He pushes the door open, waits for me to go through first.

"And I didn't mean for you to start bugging me about this, but we don't always get what we want, do we?"

"Maybe I should start calling *you* porcupine."

"And maybe I should start punching you in the face."

We walk out of the building, and I pause for a second to get my bearings before turning toward the meeting point.

"Is it Spinosaurus?"

"You have a real issue with that Mohawk of yours, you know that?"

"Come on, Harper, tell me."

"No."

"Pleease."

"No."

"Pleeeeeeease."

I stop and look at him. He gives me his most winning smile. "No."

"That stinks."

"Not as much as you do . . . Porcupine."

"Haaaaaaarpeeeeeeer!"

"Por-cu-piiiiiiiine."

We dodge a couple of kids more interested in their ice cream cones than looking where they're going.

"You know I'm going to keep bugging you about this."

"As long as you know I'm going to keep saying no."

"I'll wear you down eventually."

"Every boy needs a dream, I guess."

14

Owen
(1nf1n173 5h4d3)

"Are you sure that's the guy you want to go after?" Alika asks. "He's huge."

She's standing next to me, her hand holding my elbow as we weave our way through the crowd. She says it's for appearance, but I'm pretty sure it's because she can't walk over the grass in those ridiculous shoes she has on.

Not that I don't appreciate them, because they're sexy as hell. Just like that dress. And I get that appearances are important—hell, they're everything during a con like this—but still, it makes me a little uncomfortable seeing her dressed like this, because it's so different from her usual style. Guys have been practically breaking their necks checking her out. Alika seems oblivious to it, but it's seriously pissing me off, and I think maybe she's just pretending not to notice all the lewd looks she's getting.

"Of course he's huge," I say as I guide her toward Michael Jenks. "He used to play for the Raiders."

"And now he works for Jacento?" She sounds incredulous. "As a security guard?"

"Security supervisor," I correct. "And not all football players are loaded, you know. Or stupid."

The last part comes out a little harsher than I intend it to, and she must pick up on it, because her eyes go wide. "I'm sorry, I wasn't implying—"

"I know. Don't worry about it."

Jenks is speaking into a walkie-talkie, his eyes constantly scanning the crowd for some disturbance—real or imagined. He's doing his job to the best of his ability, but he has no idea what's about to hit him. Or that hyper vigilance out here in the crowd isn't going to save him—or Jacento.

Part of me feels bad for the guy, considering the havoc we're about to wreak on his perfectly planned day, but life is rough all over. Besides, when you work for a company like this, you've already sold your soul. Especially if you're a security supervisor who knows way more about how things operate than the average administrative assistant.

"Showtime," I murmur to Alika as we get close. "You ready?"

"Let's do this." Tossing her long black hair over her shoulder, she takes a few steps away from me, then spins in a couple of circles while looking up at the sky. "I love this song." She glances over her shoulder at me. "Come dance with me."

I shoot her an exasperated look. "There's no dance floor."

"Who needs a dance floor when they've got music like this?" She shimmies a little, takes a few rocking steps to the side. And plows right into Security Supervisor Jenks.

"Oh, I'm so sorry!" she says, grabbing his arms to steady herself. Most guys' natural inclination might be to help, but not

Jenks. He's too busy checking her out to actually play the gentleman.

Gritting my teeth, I make my way forward, trying to ignore the way he's looking at her—like she's a treat he can't wait to gobble up, despite the fact that she's a good twenty years younger than he is.

"You okay, babe? I told you not to wear those stupid shoes." I glance up at Jenks like it's the first time and continue, "Thanks so much for catching her. She insists on wearing crazy shoes to places like this and— Hey, wait a minute. Aren't you Michael Jenks?"

His eyebrows shoot to his hairline. "Yeah, I am. Why?"

"Oh my God! Michael Jenks from the Raiders, right? You played for them from 1999 to 2010. I'm a huge fan!"

"No offense, kid, but you don't look old enough to be a fan of mine."

"Are you kidding me? My dad loves the Raiders—he took me to my first game before I could walk. And you were definitely one of his favorites. I knew all your stats growing up." I rattle off a few just to salt the story, to prove that I'm the superfan I'm claiming to be.

Then, because I'm also playing the role of concerned boyfriend, I glance at Alika. Check her over with my eyes. And ignore the uncomfortable heat that slides through my veins as she looks up at me with that beautiful face of hers. "You all right, baby? You didn't sprain your ankle or anything?"

"I'm good," she answers, shifting her gaze to Jenks. "Oh my gosh, I just realized. This is the guy from the poster you have hanging in you room. Number seventy-two, right?"

"Right." Jenks's surprise is fading, his ego taking over. Not that it's exactly a shock. Most of these guys are the same once the limelight fades—they're always looking for something to remind them of the glory days, someone to remember who they used to be back when they were "important."

Having grown up with a very "important" dad, one who people have done all manner of crazy things to meet, I know the syndrome well. But considering what that "importance" has done to my dad over the last few years, I don't have much patience for it.

Still, it's going to get us what we want, so I keep my mouth shut and my annoyance on simmer. Buttering this guy up is totally the name of this afternoon's game.

"Man, you were such an amazing defensive end. Seriously, one of the best in the game. It's a real shame what happened to you during that Green Bay game."

His face clouds a little as he remembers the game-ending knee injury. "Yeah, well, shit happens, you know." His walkie-talkie goes off, and suddenly he remembers that he has a job to do. "I've got to get going. Hope you two have a good time today."

He takes another lingering look at Alika—one that makes me want to punch him in the face—and then moves to step around us.

We haven't gotten what we need from him yet, though, so I put myself in his path. Give him a look designed to make him feel like a god—the same look I've seen on the faces of my father's fans a million times through the years. "I know you're busy, and I'm sorry to even ask, but could you maybe sign an autograph for me? And maybe take a selfie with me? My father will freak out if I bring home a picture of the two of us. Like seriously, freak the hell out."

His walkie-talkie goes off a second time, and he looks torn. But the siren song of fame gets him in the end—just like it always gets them—and he grins. "Sure. No problem."

"That's amazing. Thanks so much." I pretend to fumble in my backpack, looking for something for him to sign, then come up with the specially treated notebook and pen.

"What's your name, kid?" he asks as he starts to sign.

"Owen."

"Cool." He signs with a flourish, and when he hands it back to me, I make a big deal of oohing and aahing over his illiterate scrawl.

"Selfie time?" he asks.

"Absolutely!"

"You want your girl in the picture?" he asks as I crowd in close.

The answer is no, I don't want Alika anywhere near this guy who keeps looking at her with his horndog thoughts written all over his face. But that's not part of the con, and two chances are better than one, so I bite my tongue as Alika smiles and allows Jenks to pull her close.

"Of course I want in the picture!" she says. "I'm going to plaster it all over social media. My friends will freak when they find out I met a real, live professional athlete!"

He doesn't remind her that he's a former pro, but then, it's not like I expect him to.

Alika cuddles into Jenks on one side while I squeeze in on the other. I press my free hand to Jenks's back as I hold up my camera, hoping he'll do the same to me. But he never does, no matter how many selfies I take, or how many times I clap him on the back.

And when his walkie-talkie goes off a third time, he disengages from both of us. "I really do have to go now," he says a little regretfully. "But it was so nice meeting you guys." He punches me lightly on the shoulder as he walks away. "Keep it real, man. Keep it real."

"Oh, I will," I promise like a total starstruck jerk, even as my mind is racing, trying to figure out what to do next.

"I didn't get it," I tell Alika as she loops an arm through mine and pulls me away.

"Maybe not," she says with a grimace. "But I did."

"You sure? I was watching pretty closely, and I didn't see him put his hand on your back either."

"Yeah, he was pretty slick about it, but then again, it wasn't my back he was touching."

It takes a minute for her words to sink in. "Your ass?" I say as she starts dragging me toward the building with the open restrooms. "That jerk touched your *ass*?"

The thought makes me see red. I turn around, scan the crowds, looking for his big head floating above the others, but the jerk is nowhere in sight. "I'm sorry—"

"Why are you apologizing, Owen? You didn't just maul me, he did."

"Yeah, but still…!"

"It's not the first time that has happened to me, and it won't be the last," Alika tells me.

"That doesn't make it okay."

"Of course it doesn't." Alika looks me straight in the eye. "I appreciate your outrage—I do. But we got what we needed, so let's just keep moving here."

I don't know what to say. Or how to understand that she can appear so calm about what just happened to her. But it's not about me. It's about Alika, so I just nod and go along with it.

She grabs her backpack off my shoulder and slips into the women's restroom to change, leaving me staring after her.

15

Harper
(5p3ct3r)

"Where have you guys been?" Snow White asks the second we make it to the rendezvous point. "We've been waiting for you forever."

Mad Max flushes a little. "We're sorr—"

"We're three minutes late, not thirty," I interrupt, making a point of looking at my phone. "And we had a situation to handle."

Silver Spoon's gaze sharpens. "What kind of situation? Everything okay?"

"Everything's fine. We just had to meet some clowns." I nod toward the twenty-story building looming several hundred feet in front of us. "You ready to do this?"

"Clowns?" the Lone Ranger asks. "You had to meet clowns?"

"It's a long story," Mad Max answers. "I'll tell you when we don't have a state-of-the-art security system to hack."

"Make sure you tell me too," Buffy says, bumping shoulders with him in that way she has. "I'm dying to hear about how you faced your fears."

"Yeah." Now he's full-on blushing. "That wasn't quite how it happened."

"Yes, it is." I don't like the way he's always so self-deprecating, especially since I've decided he's the best person here. I know for sure that he's better than me, anyway. "You were great."

"Great enough to—"

"No." I make eye contact with Silver Spoon, quirk a brow. "Shall we?"

"By all means." He waves an arm in a ladies-first gesture, and I step forward, more than ready to lead the way.

More than ready to get this over with.

It's not that I'm nervous exactly. I may not have done anything like this before, but I've got total faith in my skills. I've even got faith in *their* skills. But trusting five other people not to let me down? Putting my fate in their hands? It's hard, and I really wish that it was over with and that we were back at Silver Spoon's apartment doing the postmortem.

We keep it casual as we walk in a nothing-to-see-here kind of way. We're just a group of friends in designer sunglasses and cool clothes, taking time out from the party to walk along the ocean— it's a beautiful day, after all. The sun is shining, the weather is crisp but not cold, and the sky is a deep, unending blue. It's a wonder there aren't more people over here walking with us, really.

When we finally make it to the sidewalk that winds around to the front of the main building, Silver Spoon glances at Buffy and Snow White. "You guys ready?"

"What's there to be ready for?" Buffy rolls her eyes. "We're just the bait. The real question is are *you* ready?"

"I was born ready," he deadpans back.

"We take what we want and leave the rest," Mad Max suddenly pipes up. "Just like your salad bar."

Buffy and Snow White look at him like *WTF, dude*, but the rest of us crack up.

Mad Max grins proudly. "I've been brushing up."

Buffy shakes her head. "I don't even want to know what that means."

"*Big Trouble in Little China*. It's where the 'I was born ready' line comes from." He looks at them inquiringly, but when they stare back blankly, he sighs. "It's a great movie—you two should totally watch it sometime."

"Yeah, we'll get on that as soon as we get out of prison for hacking a major corporation," Buffy tells him.

"Don't say the *P* word," he answers, wide-eyed. "Don't even think the *P* word. It's really bad karma."

"Really?" Snow White speaks up for the first time. "Hacking the corporation isn't bad karma but saying pr—"

"Don't!" he warns.

"But saying 'the *P* word' is?"

"Well, it's not like we're doing this for no reason, right? They started it."

"Like that isn't justification for every kindergarten fight ever?" Buffy chimes in. "I'm beginning to worry about you, Seth."

"Awww, that means you like me." He beams at her.

She tries to stare him down, but ends up cracking up instead.

"So, are we ready to do this or what?" Silver Spoon asks.

"We were—" Mad Max starts.

"Born ready," the rest of us chime in. With eye rolls, but still. His level of ridiculousness is somehow really hard to resist.

Snow White and Buffy start heading up the sidewalk to the building's front doors, while the rest of us pick out a spot to lounge on the grass, overlooking the ocean. As we do, we click our earpieces back on so we can communicate during the break-in.

Mad Max pulls out his laptop and gets to work.

"You in?" Silver Spoon asks after about thirty seconds.

"Almost," he answers.

"What's taking so long? You already brute-forced the password."

"Yeah, well, it's not working." Mad Max's fingers fly over his keyboard as he stares grimly at the screen.

"What do you mean it's not working?" the Lone Ranger hisses. "We just sent Alika and Issa—"

"They must have gotten spooked with the party. Don't worry about it. I'll get it—"

"Fast enough not to leave them hanging?" Silver Spoon demands.

"Should we wait?" Snow White asks.

"Yes!" the Lone Ranger says.

"No!" Mad Max overrides him. "I'm in."

"That was fast," Buffy says.

"What can I say? I'm just that good." He mock buffs his nails against his shirt, then dives right back in.

Seconds later, the sound of knocking on glass comes clearly through our earbuds.

"Please, please, please," Snow White whimpers, and it's clear she's talking to the guards and not to us.

"Seriously?" Buffy hisses. "Why are you squirming around like that?"

"It's the universal pee-pee dance. Don't you know anything?"

"Maybe if you're three. But I'd like to think you'd have a little more self-control."

"Not if you're trying to convince guards to let you in when they're staring at you through a glass door. You should try it."

"I'd rather go to jail."

"Issa!" Mad Max starts, but she cuts him off.

"I didn't say the *P* word."

"Okay, get ready," Snow White warns. "They're coming!"

"Both of them?" I clarify.

"Yes. Looks like Owen was right, though I don't know how he knew they'd both come check on us."

"Because there are two hot girls standing in front of their doors," Silver Spoon says like it's the most obvious thing in the world.

"Meaning?" I ask.

"Bro code," all three guys say at the same time.

"So there's no one at the desk right now, watching the cameras?" I clarify.

"All clear," Buffy replies.

"Don't make any weird moves for the next two minutes," Mad Max says. "I'm recording."

"And here I planned on doing the chicken dance," Silver Spoon deadpans.

"Well, with you one never knows."

Exactly two minutes later, he says, "Okay, got it. I need one more minute and...all clear."

The Lone Ranger, Silver Spoon, and I spring into action, jumping up and running toward the side corridor we all decided would make the best access point due to its seclusion and proximity. As we do, we can hear Snow White working really hard to convince the guards to let her use the lobby restroom.

They don't sound like they're budging, but worrying isn't going to help anything, so I concentrate on what we can control.

"Make sure you keep your phone clipped to your belt," Mad Max reminds me as we race toward the door, hoods up and sunglasses on. "So I can see when to move the security cameras."

"Already done," I tell him. "You just need to connect."

We're at the bank of windows now, ducking behind the huge row of bushes that hide them from view, and the Lone Ranger drops to his knees, pulling what looks like a long silver flashlight out of his bag.

"You sure you've got this?" Silver Spoon asks.

"No, but I'm the only one who's practiced with it, so..."

The Lone Ranger bends down, fastens two suction cups on the glass, complete with a long thin wire between them, the end of which he hands to me.

Then we wait.

One of the guards finally relents. He lets Snow White go to the bathroom, but insists that Buffy stay with him. Which is what we were hoping for, actually—if I've learned anything at all in the last three days, it's that Buffy can be a hell of a distraction when she wants to be.

Two minutes later, the mini blinds go up, and Snow White's face appears inside the window next to where the Lone Ranger is waiting. She's got her purse open and is pulling out her own suction cups. She fastens them to the glass, then pulls back, applying pressure from her side.

I pull back on our side as the Lone Ranger takes a moment to adjust his sunglasses a little. Then he turns the silver flashlight thing on, aims it at the door, and slowly, slowly, slowly gets to work, cutting a hole in the bottom half of the glass door just large enough for us to crawl through.

As soon as he finishes cutting the circle and turns the laser off, Snow White slowly pulls the cut glass into the building.

"Ladies first," Silver Spoon tells me, and I climb through, careful not to touch the edges with any part of my body.

The Lone Ranger is next, with Silver Spoon bringing up the rear. But he's barely got his upper body in the hole when Buffy says, "Where's your friend going?"

"Uh-oh," Mad Max chimes in. "He's looking for Alika. He just knocked on the bathroom door."

"That's my cue!" she says, shooting up and taking off down the hall at a full-out sprint.

"Hurry up!" I tell Silver Spoon, barely resisting the urge to grab hold and pull him through the hole. He's quick when he wants to be, though, and seconds later he's standing next to me.

"Quick, put the blinds down," the Lone Ranger orders as he

looks for someplace to hide the glass in the long, empty hallway we're currently standing in.

I get the blinds back into place just as Snow White says, "Oh, thank God you found me! I think I went out the wrong bathroom door, because I got so lost!"

The guard murmurs something that I can't quite hear.

But then Snow White says loud and clear, "Do you really have to do rounds now? I was having so much fun talking to you!"

"Let's go!" the Lone Ranger exclaims, shoving the glass under the closest set of double doors.

"Already gone," Silver Spoon answers, grabbing my arm and propelling me down the hallway with him.

"Can I go with you?" Snow White asks in our ears. "I've always wanted to do rounds!"

"Which way?" Silver Spoon hisses.

I think he's talking to us at first, but then Mad Max answers, "To the left. And move! It doesn't look like Alika's going to be able to stop him."

"So not what I want to hear right now!" The Lone Ranger sprints until he's several feet ahead of us, and I can tell he's planning on taking the heat if we get caught.

Meanwhile, Mad Max is calling out directions superfast. "Left, right, left, another left, right," as he uses the cameras to keep us out of the guard's sight while also guiding us toward the staircase that will take us right next to the server room.

We're almost there, running full tilt down a hallway toward the EXIT/STAIRS sign directly in front of us, when suddenly a side door opens and a man steps out.

I'm not sure who is more shocked—him or us—as the Lone Ranger swerves to avoid slamming into him.

"Hey, what are you kids doing in here!" he demands, stepping between the Lone Ranger and Silver Spoon and me. "Russ!" he starts yelling for the security guard. "Russ…"

We all exchange panicked glances, and then I do the only thing I can think of to shut him up. I slam my fist into his face as hard as I can.

His eyes roll back in his head, and he hits the ground.

16

Owen
[1nf1n173 5h4d3]

For a long second, nobody moves as Ezra and I stare, open-mouthed, at the random guy now passed out on the floor at our feet.

We don't snap out of it until Seth starts squawking, "What happened? What happened? Are you okay?"

"Where the hell did that come from, Harper?" Ezra looks like he's about to tear his hair out.

"He was gearing up to scream the building down. I had to do something."

"What happened?" Seth repeats.

Because I'm afraid he'll forget what his job is and actually turn the cameras our way to see what's going on, I answer. "She hit him. Knocked the guy clear out."

"Oh my God!" Alika says from wherever she is. "Is he okay?"

"He's breathing," Ezra says, from where he's crouched down, checking the guy's pulse. "Which is something, I guess. Assault is better than murder."

"Nobody's murdering anyone. It was one punch." Harper crouches next to him. "Come on. We can't just leave him here for the guard to find. Help me get him back into his office."

"I've got him," I say, grabbing the guy beneath his arms and dragging him back through the open door. As I do, I try not to stare at Harper. She's the quietest, calmest one of all of us—who the hell would have guessed she had it in her to be such a badass?

"Hey, guys," Seth suddenly starts screeching at us through our earbuds. "Not to rush you or anything, but that guard is only one hallway away from you."

"Get in here!" I growl.

But Harper and Ezra must have had the same idea, because they're already in motion, diving into this guy's office and closing the door behind them as quietly as they can.

"Turn the lights off," I hiss, but again Ezra's already there.

I start to lift the guy up—I don't want to chance making any noise by dragging him—but I've barely gotten his torso off the ground when he moans.

"Shut him up!" Ezra snaps from where he's locking the door.

I don't want to hit the guy again—the last thing I want is to give anyone a concussion—but our options are limited. Harper's on the ground, rummaging through her backpack, when suddenly she comes up, triumphantly brandishing duct tape.

"Good idea!" I whisper as she tears off a piece and slaps it over the guy's mouth.

"He's in the hallway," Seth hisses through our earbuds. "Don't move."

Easier said than done, considering the guy chooses that moment to open his freaking eyes. He takes one look at me looming above him and starts to thrash around.

I really don't want to hit him, but I don't think I've got much choice at this point—

"Here!" Harper whispers urgently, and she's across the room, holding open the door to what looks like a small closet.

I glance at Ezra and he's already moving. He swoops in next to me, grabs the struggling guy's feet, and helps me carry him into the closet.

Harper crowds in after us, duct tape in hand, just as the guard knocks on the office door. "Mr. Willis, are you okay in there? I thought I heard you yell."

The guy—Mr. Willis, apparently—starts struggling in earnest now, and I've had enough. I'm about to hit him, concussion be damned, and put us all out of our misery, when Ezra reaches past me and grabs his neck. Willis's eyes go wide for one second, two, and then his whole body goes limp. Thank God.

"Mr. Willis?" The guard knocks again, rattles the door handle a couple of times.

"Don't move," Seth whispers almost silently in our ears.

Eventually the guard stops knocking and rattling, and I start to breathe a sigh of relief—at least until I hear the office door creak open. Of course he has a universal swipe card for non-classified areas of the building. Why freaking wouldn't he?

I hold my breath, and so do Ezra and Harper as we all stare, wide- and wild-eyed, at one another. *Come on, man,* I silently urge the guard. *Decide Willis has left for the day.* It's a reasonable conclusion—the office is dark and locked up, and there's a party going on on the other side of the compound.

Come on, I urge again. *Just do it.*

But this guy has some kind of work ethic, because instead of just backing out of the room, he gets on his walkie-talkie and says, "Yo, Joseph, did you see Mr. Willis head out?"

There are a few seconds of silence followed by, "No, Russ. He hasn't come this way."

"His office is dark, and it was locked up."

"Maybe he went to the bathroom. Or to raid the vending machines." Joseph's answer crackles a little at the end.

"Maybe. Hey, did that girl ever return to the lobby?"

"Yeah, she's here now. She and her friend are just hanging out, talking to me."

"Can you see Mr. Willis on the cameras anywhere?" Russ asks.

The answer comes back as nothing but static.

"Joe, you there?"

More static.

"Joe?"

Still more static.

"It's ridiculous," Russ grumbles to himself as he walks around the office. "Major telecom company, and we've got these stupid walkie-talkies that don't even work."

"Russ?" Joe's voice comes through loud and clear this time.

"Joe. Do you see Mr. Willis anywhere in the building?"

More static and then "at vending machines."

Harper, Ezra, and I all stare at one another mystified, considering Mr. Willis is currently passed out at our feet.

It seems to satisfy Russ, though, because he says, "Okay, thanks for checking." Then he finally—finally—walks toward the office door. Seconds later, the light clicks back off and the door closes behind him.

We wait for several seconds in a kind of suspended animation, just in case it's a trick—though, honestly, Russ doesn't seem smart enough for that. Then Seth says, "He just turned down the other hallway. You're in the clear."

I release a big, pent-up breath. "Damn. When he called over to Joe, I thought we were toast for sure."

"Nah, I got your back," Seth says.

"Wait, all that static was you?" Ezra asks.

"Course it was. So was the last little bit of the conversation. Had to get him moving along somehow."

"You're the best, Seth," Harper tells him. She's grinning hugely as she kneels down next to Willis.

"Yeah, well, you know how you can thank me, right?" he responds.

"The hell?" Ezra says before I can even close my mouth from the shock. "You save her ass once, and you think sexual harassment's the way to go here?"

"No!" Seth nearly trips over his tongue in his effort to get the words out. "I meant— Harper, tell them— I was just..."

Harper laughs, even as she puts him out of his misery. "That really isn't what he meant, guys." She glances at Ezra. "But, hey, thanks for sticking up for me."

"We're a team," he answers, like that says everything.

And maybe it does, for him. I'm still wary, though. My dad was part of a team for a long time, and no one had his back. At least not when it mattered most. No matter how important what we're doing is, I can't afford to let the same thing happen to me. If I do, who knows what will happen to my mom.

Harper doesn't seem to have the same worries, as she smiles up at us. "Go ahead and grab his feet, then, teammates. And hold them together while I tape him up."

"You're seriously going to leave him taped up in the closet?" Seth asks.

"You got any better ideas, Porcupine?"

Porcupine? I mouth to Ezra, but he just shakes his head and shrugs.

"You could stop calling me that, for one. I did just save your ass."

"That's so five minutes ago," she teases as she duct-tapes Willis's feet like a pro. "What have you done for me lately?"

"Remind me not to get on her bad side," Ezra murmurs to me, before moving up to grab Willis's hands.

"No kidding."

"You know what, I think I'm done surveilling," Seth says. "I think I'm going to go see if I can catch the circus. A horde of psychotic clowns *has* to be nicer than you."

"Good luck with that. Try not to get eaten or chopped into

little pieces." Harper turns to Ezra. "No, hold his hands by his sides. We want to tape his arms to his body so he can't use them at all."

"Jesus. Who are you?" he asks, even as he follows her directions.

Harper doesn't answer, just concentrates on taping Willis up so securely that it'll take three days and an army to get him undone. I can't help wondering if maybe I've misjudged the whole situation. All this time, I've been wariest of Ezra and Issa, not sure if I could trust either of them. But maybe Harper's the one I should have been watching all along.

17

Harper
(5p3ct3r)

Obviously, I'm not in as good a shape as I think I am.

Or, conversely, Silver Spoon and the Lone Ranger are in crazy incredible shape.

Either way, we've just run up seventeen flights of stairs, and they're barely winded. I, on the other hand, am so lightheaded from lack of oxygen that I'm afraid I'm going to pass out at any moment. Which is *so* not an option—partly because they need me for this next portion of the plan, and partly because I'm afraid I'll end up taped up somewhere like poor Mr. Willis.

Like Mad Max constantly reminds me, karma is a total bitch.

I stagger up the last flight of stairs like a ninety-year-old, only to find Silver Spoon and the Lone Ranger waiting for me at the top with grins on their faces. Neither of them is even sweating, the jerks.

"Remind me again, Porcupine, why I'm not the one sitting on the grass right now, moving a few security cameras around?" I gasp out between shuddering breaths.

"Because you have control issues and wanted to be the one to go in?" he answers. "And, oh yeah, you've never hacked this many security cameras at once before."

"The fact that you have disturbs me on so many levels."

"A boy's gotta get his kicks somehow."

"Playtime's over, children." Buffy's voice comes through the earbuds loud and clear. "Russ finished his rounds, and delightful as Alika and I are, he's decided he and Joe have to get back to work. So we're out, and they're heading back to the desk."

"Where they've got live video feed from every camera in the building," Snow White reminds us.

"Damn. How long have I got?" Mad Max asks. "Never mind, I see them. Okay, I'm turning the cameras in every unsecured hallway on the eighteenth floor toward the corners. Stay in the middle of the hallway and close to the opposite wall when you make turns, and they shouldn't pick you up. And, if luck is with us, Frick and Frack in the control booth won't notice until you've gotten what we came for."

"That's a lot of *should*s and *if*s," the Lone Ranger says.

"Yeah, well, you want the truth or some made-up BS? I'm not a fortune-teller, you know."

The three of us look at one another, brows raised. Despite the nickname, Mad Max has the most even temperament of all of us, and if he's frazzled . . .

"We're definitely not in Kansas anymore," Silver Spoon tells us.

"Ha! Even I know that one!" Buffy interjects. "Is this the part where I say we'll 'get you and your little dog too'?"

"Considering where we are, I really hope not," the Lone Ranger tells her.

"Right? Nobody is getting anybody at this point," Mad Max agrees.

"Fine." Buffy sounds totally disgruntled. "Can I at least say, 'Lions and tigers and bears, oh my'?"

"More like, cameras and servers and guards, oh my." Mad Max snickers.

We all groan.

"You should probably never say that again," Snow White tells him, and I can all but see her patting his arm in her good-girl way.

"You ready?" Silver Spoon asks me as everybody laughs. And it's not embarrassing *at all* that I'm the one he has to ask, especially since he looks braced to catch me if I collapse.

Definitely time to start exercising more. I take a couple of deep breaths, eventually get my head to stop swimming and the rest of me to stop shaking from oxygen deprivation.

Then I nod. "Yeah, I'm ready."

"Let's do it, then."

"No, wait," Mad Max says. "I've been working out a way to help you, if you give me a minute."

"You mean beyond stick to the middle and hope for the best?" the Lone Ranger asks.

"Or I could go check out the psychotic clowns. Which-ever you prefer…" The threat is as empty as his first one, his absent tone telling us he's already deep into his plan. "So, the station downstairs has twelve screens, which means they can only watch twelve cameras at any given second. There are two hundred and seven cameras on the system, so the thing cycles through all of them every ninety seconds."

"You want us to try to run in between the cycles?"

"No, that's too complicated. But I've been working on figuring out the pattern for the last twenty minutes, and I think I've got it. So if I can loop footage in to each of the cameras on the eighteenth floor while the system is circling through the other cameras…"

He pauses for several interminable seconds. "Well?" Silver Spoon is the one who breaks first. Of course. "Can you do it?"

"Calm down," Mad Max tells him. "I *am* doing it."

"You are?"

"Five more to go…okay, three more…and two…and done! Unless I missed one, you guys should be golden. At least until you get to the server. Those cameras are on another system, one I can't hack."

"Awesome," the Lone Ranger says as we jog down the hallway, a lot more confident than we were just two minutes ago. "So, why exactly didn't we do this with the cameras on the ground floor?"

"Because one of the weird little tics of this system is that the cameras go blind once you loop them. So if you wanted me to be able to help you out by, say, letting you know where that security guard was, I had to have a live feed going." He sounds a little insulted, like we're doubting his skills.

"Hey, we didn't mean—" I start.

"Apologize later," he interrupts. "Right now, just concentrate on getting into that server room undetected."

"We're on it," Silver Spoon assures him, even as we approach the half of the floor where security gets extra tight.

The whole area is walled off, a steel door attached to an oral recognition system the only way in. There's also a large camera pointed at the big set of double doors.

"You've got this, right?" I ask Mad Max as we stand just out of range. It's not that I don't trust him.... It's that I don't trust anybody.

"I've got you," he assures me, and though the wording is casual, the sincerity in his tone is absolute. It gets to me, as does the change in pronoun. No one has had me since my parents died, and the fact that he can say so confidently that he does...

I shove the stray thought to the back of my head. No time for that now, not when everything is on the line. I unclip my phone from my belt, shrug off my backpack. Then I open the front pocket and pull out Talia's badge. She's the administrative assistant for Jacento's American chief technology officer and, as such, has access to all of the eighteenth floor.

With my hand shaking only a little, I step forward—right into camera range—and swipe the badge. No going back now. An incorrect password try will alert the front desk and send them running, especially now that the looped cameras block them from seeing what's actually going on.

"Please say your password now."

I press Play on the recording I put together earlier, breath stuck in my throat as we wait to hear if it will pass muster. Seconds later the system says, "Welcome, Talia." The greeting is followed quickly by the sound of a deadbolt unlocking and the three short beeps that tell us it's okay to enter.

Silver Spoon grabs the door and pulls it open. This time he doesn't gesture me through ahead of him—I guess ladies first only counts when he's certain there's no danger. I'm not sure how I feel about that—endemic sexism and all—but I'm not about to stand here and argue, so I let him go ahead of me, just like I let the Lone Ranger bring up the rear. If they want to pretend like they're protecting me, who am I to tell them different? At least for now.

"Don't forget!" Mad Max says as we take our first steps into Jacento's forbidden land. "I can't control the cameras in there. You've got to be careful."

"Believe me," Silver Spoon answers, "we haven't forgotten."

"The first one is about ten steps in front of you. It's to the left, on the side hallway you have to pass to get to the inner door."

I know. We all know, because we all memorized the layout of this area from the blueprints—paying particular attention to anything that might trip us up, like unhackable security cameras. But it's nice to know that in their own way the others are right here with us, doing what they can to make sure we get through this unscathed.

"We need to get a look at that camera," I tell the guys, and they both nod as we inch forward.

The system in here is different from the rest of the building, not just because it's offline and unhackable, but because the actual cameras are different too. Instead of being focused on a fixed point, they move, sweeping back and forth across a certain area so that no part of any room or hallway is unsurveilled for more than a few seconds at a time.

Which means we have to be exact if we have any chance of moving between cameras undetected.

We crowd up close to the corner of the hallway where the first camera is, making sure to stay out of range of the second camera that's about three hundred feet in front of us. Eventually, we'll have to deal with that one too, but first we have to get past this hallway undetected.

"Okay, so we need to time the one in front of us," I tell the guys. "Then pray that the one down that side hallway has the same timing."

"I've got a better idea," the Lone Ranger says, his phone already in his hands, along with—

"Is that a selfie stick?" Silver Spoon asks incredulously.

"It is." He slides his phone into place. "And before you start, I picked it up yesterday because I thought it would come in handy here."

After the phone is secure, he crouches down and starts his video recorder. Then slowly, slowly, slowly he extends his phone into the hallway, just far enough for the lens to record.

It takes him a few seconds to get the phone angled correctly, but once he does we can see the camera doing its job from its spot halfway down the hallway.

Silver Spoon and I crowd in closer so we can get a better look.

"Let's just watch it a couple of times," I suggest. "So we know where to start timing from."

"Good idea," Silver Spoon agrees as he pulls out his own phone and prepares to time the sweeps.

The Lone Ranger doesn't say anything, just continues to watch the camera move. After about two minutes, he says, "Okay, I need you to start timing...now."

Silver Spoon starts the stopwatch on his phone's clock, and we wait, impatiently, as the camera runs through its cycle. And 19.3 seconds later, the Lone Ranger gives the signal to stop timing.

"That's better than I thought it'd be," he says. "We can do a lot in nineteen seconds."

"Depends on where the camera is, but yeah," I agree. "It's totally doable. Do you think we should time this one again, just to be sure?"

"I would," Silver Spoon agrees. "Considering the extra twenty seconds might be what keeps our asses out of pri—"

"Don't say it!" Mad Max, Snow White, and Buffy all shout at the same time.

"There you are!" Silver Spoon says. "I was beginning to think you guys had cut and run."

"We thought about it," Buffy deadpans, "but you've got the car keys."

Silver Spoon ignores her, but he's grinning as he times the camera a second time, and then a third and a fourth. Once we've verified that it's got a nineteen-second sweep, there's really nothing to do but go for it and hope for the best.

"The range of the camera in front of us stops at the red door," I tell the guys as we get ready to run. "I've been watching while you've been working on this one. And it's also on a nineteen-second loop."

"Here goes nothing, then," the Lone Ranger says.

This time none of us correct him. Instead, I push onto the balls of my feet, and the second Silver Spoon says "Go," I take off running. We slide past the camera with several seconds to spare, then grind to a halt right before the red door to avoid the other one catching us.

And that's when the flaw in our plan catches up with us. "We don't know what the camera's doing on the hall we want to turn into," Silver Spoon says. "So even if we manage to avoid this one—"

"We could very well get caught on that one," I finish up. "Crap."

"We're going to have to risk it," the Lone Ranger says. "We'll assume it's on the same program as the one on the hallway behind us."

"And if it's not?"

"If it's not, we're screwed. But we're screwed anyway, so I say let's think positive."

"That's not exactly my strong suit," I tell him.

"Yeah, well, fake it 'til you make it," he answers.

"We need to get right under that camera," Silver Spoon says, pointing to the one in front of us. "That'll give us a couple of seconds to figure out what the other one is doing...if we're lucky."

"All the luck in the world isn't going to make it possible for the three of us to hide under that camera. It's going to pick us up," I tell him.

"So what do you suggest?"

"We do it one at a time, which helps us hide and gives us the best chance of getting the timing right all the way around."

"She's right," the Lone Ranger says. "I'll go first."

"Wait—"

But it's too late, he's already gone. Seconds later he stops right under the camera, then dodges back a couple of yards while it's still pointed away from us. "The other one isn't quite where it needs to—" He takes off again without finishing the sentence. About two seconds later, so do I.

We tag team like this all the way down three hallways and around two corners, until we get to the second barrier to the server. The Lone Ranger gets there first, and he's already got what he needs in his hand. He holds it up to the palm-print scanner, and one, two, three interminable seconds later, the lock clicks open.

He makes it inside, then turns to watch the last camera. It takes thirty seconds before the coast is clear, and I run, full out, sliding through the door right before the camera catches me. Another thirty seconds and Silver Spoon races in behind me. As soon as he clears the frame, he lets the door slam behind him.

We all take a minute then to slump against the walls and just kind of grin at one another in relief. Jacento's so paranoid that there are no cameras in with the servers, no way for anyone to record anything that goes on in there that they don't want recorded. Which works out perfectly for us, no matter how suspicious the practice is.

"Hot damn! You made it!" Buffy whoops in our ears. "I'm not going to lie. I was a little worried there for a minute."

"We were all worried," Snow White says.

"Not me," Mad Max chimes in. "I never doubted you guys for a second."

"Well, that makes one of us," Silver Spoon says, even as he holds his fist up to the Lone Ranger and me for a bump.

"Hey, I have a question," I say as I pull from my backpack the photo that will get us past the third security gate. Hopefully. "What was that red thing you had the handprint on? I was trying to figure it out, but I was too far away to see."

The Lone Ranger frowns as he holds up a scrap of red leather.

"Wait a minute." Silver Spoon takes it from him. "Was this part of Alika's dress?" He looks at me. "That was part of Alika's dress!"

"Which part?" Buffy asks.

"Don't ask," Snow White replies.

There's a few seconds of silence, and then Snow White speaks again, all business. "I'm fine. We got what we needed."

I'm not sure what to say, so I scoot around row after row of the filing cabinets that make up this hard-copy storage room and walk the hundred feet or so that separate us from the last scanner. As I do, I can't help but notice the huge picture of Jacento's CEO, Roderick Olsen, hanging next to the door— the third portrait I've seen of him since we made it inside the building. *What kind of megalomaniac needs that many portraits of himself in one place?* I wonder as I stop in front of the scanner. No wonder he's so proud of the damn kiosks. Anyone with an ego that big surely thinks he deserves to rule the world.

"Everything okay?" the Lone Ranger asks when I pause.

"It's fine," I tell him as I hold the enhanced photo up to the retinal scanner.

"Please let this work, please let this work," I mutter to myself. I'm sure Buffy followed the directions she found online to the letter, but this kind of scan is so precise, the science so absolute. One little mistake and we're—

"Unable to confirm," says an automated voice. "Please step closer."

"It doesn't work?" Silver Spoon moves forward.

"I don't know." My hand is shaking now as I look back at the two of them. "Should I try it again?"

"If it doesn't work a second time, it's going to set off every alarm in the place," the Lone Ranger reminds me grimly. Like I could possibly forget.

"Try it again," Silver Spoon says. "It's good."

"Are you sure?"

"Guys, I'm sorry." Buffy sounds gutted.

"Try it again," Silver Spoon urges. "Issa has this."

"I don't know!" she says. "Maybe you should—"

"Do it!" he urges me, mouth tight and dark eyes blazing.

And I do. Because if I'm ever going to trust anyone, now's the time to do it.

I put the photo up to the scanner a second time. This time I can hear the system whirring. And then it says, "Welcome, Dr. Otto," just as the door unlocks.

"Yes, baby!" Mad Max's shouts are echoed by Buffy and Snow White.

But the three of us can't do much more than sag in relief, hands braced on our knees as we take in a few deep gulps of air.

Then Silver Spoon is moving, opening the door and sliding inside. The Lone Ranger and I follow, and our heads nearly explode when we see what's waiting for us on the other side.

18

Owen
(1nf1n173 5h4d3)

It's the most beautiful thing I've ever seen.

I know, I know, I should be appalled, considering what Jacento is doing with all this, and I am. But come on. It's gorgeous, so freaking gorgeous I can barely wait to get my hands on it.

"They've got a Cray XK7," Harper whispers as she walks deeper into the room, and it sounds a little like she's considering genuflecting.

Not that I blame her. Just the thought of being in the room with one of these babies is enough to bring me to my knees. The fact that it's right in front of me...I lock my knees just to be on the safe side.

"Why do they need a supercomputer?" Ezra wonders as he follows her, but there's reverence in his voice too.

"And who the hell has one of these and keeps it offline?" Issa sounds outraged.

"Is it pretty?" Seth whispers. "Tell me it's pretty."

"It's soooo pretty," Harper says, and she's actually petting the thing. Well, part of it, since the XK7 is usually housed in anywhere from four hundred to five hundred cabinets.

"Are you going to kiss it?" Ezra asks her, obviously amused by the way she keeps running her hand back and forth over the cabinet.

"*I* might," I say, moving forward to get my first in-person look.

"Well, this is going to make it faster to download what we're after," Alika says. "But you should still probably get started."

It's the wake-up call we all need, but still. "Always the party pooper, aren't you, girl?" I ask as I pull what I need out of my backpack.

"I prefer *the voice of reason*," she tosses back. "It's not my fault you people tend to leap before you look."

"Sometimes it's better not to know where you're going to land," Ezra tells her as he prowls to the other side of the room. "The servers are over here, guys."

"Awesome. Let me hook into this baby, see what we can do," I tell him as I connect manually. Seconds later, I'm in, running a brute-force attack at the password.

"Want some help?" Harper asks, crouching beside me.

"Why don't you go see what you can do with another one of the servers? Whoever gets in first wins."

These computers aren't uplinked, but they do form their own LAN. Which means once we're in one of them, we're in all of them. And if my hunch is right, they've got the data for all of Jacento—not just North America—on them.

Otherwise, why the hell would they have a Cray XK7 sitting pretty over here? It's got to be the only one. At a cost of tens of millions of dollars, it's not like they've got half a dozen of these babies just lying around.

"How's it going?" Issa asks. "You've been inside more than forty-five minutes now. The entertainment's set to end in half an hour. If you aren't out by then, it's going to get a lot harder to pull this off."

"We're trying," Ezra answers, and he sounds a little testy. Not that I blame him—it's not like we're standing around twiddling our thumbs. I mean, sure, we took a minute to worship at the Cray altar, but we're working now.

Besides, until we brute-force a password out of one of these machines, our hands are tied.

"Hey, who wants to hear a joke?" Seth asks.

No one answers.

"Aww, come on. It's a good one. I swear."

Harper sighs, but then she says, "What's the joke?"

"Okay, are you ready?"

"No," Ezra says, but there's no heat behind it.

"What does one bone say to the other bone?"

More silence.

"We have to stop meeting at this joint!" he finishes triumphantly.

Still more silence.

"Get it?" he asks after a minute. "Because bones meet at joints—"

"We get it," Issa tells him. "I wish we didn't, but we do."

"Hey, that's a quality joke. I got it out of a *Highlights* magazine when I was seven."

"Why doesn't that surprise me?" Alika says.

"Knock, knock." This time it's Harper.

Ezra groans, but I play along. What else do we have to do right now? "Who's there?"

"A cow says."

"A cow says who?" I ask obediently.

"No, silly. A cow says moo!"

It's my turn to groan, and I'm about to call her on the ridiculousness of the whole thing when my laptop dings. "Shit!"

"Hey! It wasn't that bad!" Harper complains.

"I'm in!"

"Are you serious?" Ezra says. "That was fast."

"I guess I'm just that good," I tell him as my fingers fly over the keys.

"Or that lucky," Harper tells me.

"Don't be bitter." But it's a joke, and we all know it. Just like we know that the password shouldn't have been that easy for us to crack. But the fact that the supercomputer is offline and locked in a secure room has obviously made the Jacento IT guys lazy.

Sucks to be them....

"They're running open-source Linux," I say as I dive in.

"UNICOS?" Alika wonders.

"I don't think so. It looks a little like it, but I think it's their own variation."

"Shoot the password over here, will you?" Harper asks.

"I'll do better than that."

A few keystrokes later, and Harper says, "I'm in!"

"Me too. Thanks," Ezra adds.

We work in silence for a few minutes, downloading whatever we can get our digital fingers into. It'd be better if we could upload it to the cloud, but with them deliberately killing any and all internet access in the area, that's not exactly an option. It will be my job, at the end, to go in and hide what we did—so that even if they figure out they've been hacked, they won't be able to tell where the data went.

While the stuff is downloading at a rate so fast it's making my head spin—hell yeah, Cray—I go in and create a back door obscure enough that it'll be almost impossible to find in the middle of all this code. Just two little lines buried so deep that they're almost invisible will give me access to Jacento's servers—and this Cray—whenever I want it as long as my laptop is hooked into the LAN.

While I'm at it, I mess with that too, disguising my port and burying it so deep in the middle of a group of customer service machines that it should take them weeks to find it. If they ever do. And when they do, it'll ghost, tracing back to nothing and no one.

"How you doing over there?" I call to Harper and Ezra.

"Not as well as you, considering you've got the Cray," Harper complains. "But we're holding our own."

"Hey, guys, don't panic, but we might have a problem," Seth says. The fact that he sounds pretty panicked himself makes all three of us sit up and take notice.

"What kind of problem?" Ezra demands.

"The kind where Otto and a bunch of his minions might be on their way to the eighteenth floor."

"Are you freaking kidding me?" I demand.

"You're just telling us this now?" Harper sounds pissed.

"The group of them walked into the building and went straight to the elevators. We're giving you all the warning we can."

"So you don't know for sure that they're coming to the eighteenth floor," Ezra says.

"Oh, no, they're coming to the eighteenth floor," Issa tells us. "They just pushed the buttons for fifteen and eighteen."

"How do you know?" Alika asks. "There's no camera feed—"

"Because I hacked the elevators. Call it intuition, but I had a feeling...." She pauses for a moment, then says, "The elevator just stopped on fifteen. You need to get out of there."

"On it," I tell her as I start covering our tracks as fast as I can.

"Come on!" Harper urges. She and Ezra are already packed up and standing above me.

"I've got to finish this—"

"There's no time, man. Close it up and let's go!" Ezra peers around the corner at the main door. "Where are they, Issa?"

"I don't know. Remember, we're blind out here. The elevator doors just closed, though. They're on the floor."

"Come on!" Harper says again.

I ignore her as I write code faster than I ever have in my life. A few more lines, a few more lines, just a few more—

"Owen, we need to move!" Ezra's in my face now.

"Got it!" I slam my laptop shut and spring to my feet as I shove it into my backpack.

"Hey, Seth. Can you fix the cameras so we can see what they're doing—"

"Already, did, my man. They just logged in at the voice recognition door. And, crap. Now they're inside the secure part of the floor. No more cameras. Sorry, guys. They're in there with you, and I'm completely blind."

19

Issa
[Pr1m4 D0nn4]

"Get to the elevators!" I order.

"How are we going to get out of here without them seeing us—and without tripping the alarms?" Harper hisses.

"You're not," I answer, hoping with everything I have that they're making their way out of the server room *this very second*. "At this point, it doesn't matter if you're seen. The second Otto stands in front of that retinal scan, the whole system is going to lose its mind. A record of him going in two times in a row—without exiting in between—is going to set off every alarm in the place. So make sure your hoodies are up and your sunglasses are on—and whatever you do, keep your heads down!"

"How do we stop it?" Owen yells.

"You can't," Seth tells him.

"So what do we do?"

"I already told you. You run!" I take control of the elevator Otto just vacated and return it to the eighteenth floor. "But you've got to get to the elevators. Now!"

"Shit!" For the first time since I met him, Owen sounds

panicked—even if he is whispering. "They just walked in the server room."

"This way!" Ezra hisses. "Come on."

For long seconds, there's no sound at all as the three of them make their way through the server room—in what I hope is the opposite direction of Otto and his crew. Not that I think they stand a chance in hell of getting out of there without being detected, but whatever kind of head start they can muster is better than no head start at all.

"What's going on?" Seth whispers after about two minutes of total silence.

Alika hushes him—and I get it. The last thing we need to do is distract them right now. But poor Seth looks like he's going to lose his mind at any second, and I totally sympathize, because I'm right there with him. How Alika can stay so cool when it looks like Ezra, Owen, and Harper could get nabbed at any second, I will never know.

"Hey, stop right there! What are you doing in he—"

"Run!" Owen says, and then all I can hear is the sound of feet slapping fast and hard against the floor as indistinguishable but too-close-for-comfort yells make their way through the earbuds.

"Get to the elevators!" I shout, hoping to be heard above everything else.

"The stairs—"

"Will lock down as soon as the alarm sounds. If you manage to get in, you won't be able to get out!"

"So will the elevators!" Harper says, and she sounds winded.

I don't even want to think about how fast the guys have her moving.

There's the sound of a metal door slamming hard against something—a wall, probably—and then more feet pounding and more shouting.

"I've got control of the elevators! They won't be able to lock them down. I've got one open and waiting for you. But you've got to get to it!"

"We're trying!" Owen snarls. "It's like a damn maze up here!"

"I can still see you through your phone! Keep it clipped to your belt!" Seth jumps in to the conversation.

"Not planning on taking the time to remove it right now!" Harper pants.

"I know where you are! Go to the left!" Seth orders them as he stares hard at the building's blueprints. "Now right. Now left again!"

That's when the alarm kicks in, and the whole inside of the building starts sounding like an air-raid siren that's just gone off. Amazingly, outside—from our spot near the cliffs—we can't hear anything. I'm hoping that will buy us a few minutes before anyone outside the building figures out something is wrong, as will the fact that it'll take the guards from other buildings a little time to get here after they get the call. Which—if we're lucky—should be enough time for us to get them out of there.

"You better be right about the elevators," Ezra says, and even he sounds winded now.

"I am," I promise. "Just run!"

"What do you think we're doing?" Harper wheezes out.

"Left again!" Seth yells. "Right! You're almost there!"

"Even if we get them out, they're still going to be sitting ducks," Alika says. "We all are."

"We'll worry about that when it happens," I tell her, as I lock down the other elevators. Yeah, the security guards can use the stairs, but if all goes well, they'll be down and gone before the guards even realize where they are.

"You worry about it later," she tells me. "I'm going to worry about it now."

"Where are you going?" Seth asks. "You're just going to walk away and leave them?"

She gives him a dirty look. "I'm going for the SUV."

"But Ezra has the keys."

"Like that's ever stopped me?" Alika takes off at a jog, and I watch her go—at least until Seth suddenly yells, "Left!" and I realize he's back to staring at his laptop screen.

Something I should be doing too.

"One more turn and you'll be at the elevators," Seth tells them.

"I've got the first one open and ready for you. Just get on it."

"Right!" Seth tells them. And then, "Okay, Issa, they're on!"

"Hurry, hurry, hurry!" Harper chants. "They're—"

I slam the elevator doors shut and get the thing moving.

I can hear Harper panting as Ezra says, "The guards know where we are!"

"It won't matter. I'm going to disguise—"

"Of course it matters. I can see one of the guards waiting for us in the lobby!"

"How can you see that?" I ask, a sinking feeling in my stomach.

"Because it's a glass elevator!" Harper wails. "I can see them looking at us—from the eighteenth floor and from the lobby. We're trapped."

How did I not think about the elevators being glass? I'm an idiot.

Desperate to fix my mistake, I stop the elevator on the closest floor—nine. "Get off, get off, get off!"

"What?" Owen asks, but it sounds like they're running again, so they must have followed my orders.

"Get to the freight elevators on the other side of the building."

"Are you kidding me with this?" Ezra says.

"Do you have a better idea?"

"Don't worry. I still have the cameras on loop," Seth says. "I don't think they've figured it out yet. Just run!"

"We're running!" Harper sounds even more pissed than she did before. "Believe me, we're running!"

"Go right!" Seth tells them. "Then make a left three hallways down."

"This again?" Harper groans.

"I'm sorry. I didn't realize they were glass elevators. I screwed up."

"It's not your fault," Seth says, reaching out a hand to pat my knee.

But it is. I should have paid more attention when I was in the lobby, but I was so busy trying to distract the stupid guards that I didn't even look at the elevators. I mean, usually an elevator's an elevator—especially in an office building.

"Go left up ahead," Seth continues. "The building schematics say the freight elevators should be two hallways over. But you need to move—the elevators are right next to one of the main stairwells."

"Of course they are," Owen mutters. "Because why should anything be easy?"

"I've got the regular elevators locked down so they can't use them, and a freight elevator should be at the ninth floor in three, two, one... It's ready for you!"

"Fine, but what are we supposed to do once we get on it?" Ezra asks. "They know we need to get out—they'll be waiting for us on the first floor when we get there. And we've got to get there eventually."

"Not necessarily," Seth tells him.

"Well, we can't play cat and mouse in this stupid building forever!" Harper exclaims.

"You don't have to. I think—"

"You think they know we're running for the freight elevators?" Ezra asks.

"I'd bet on it," I tell him grimly as my mind races, trying to figure out how to fix my colossally huge screwup.

"That won't matter if we do this right," Seth says.

"By all means," Owen tells him, "let's do it right."

"Send the elevator up," Seth tells me. "All the way to the roof."

"And then what?" Ezra demands. "We can't fly."

"You won't have to," I answer as Seth's idea crystallizes in my own head, becomes a full-fledged plan. "You're going to be in the second elevator."

"Go left here," Seth tells them.

"Don't you think they'll be looking for that?" Harper asks.

"Not if the second elevator is standing still."

"I don't get it."

"Don't worry about it, Ezra. Just trust me."

I wait for him to make a snarky comment, to tell me that trusting me is how they got in this mess in the first place. But he doesn't say anything, and neither do the others. At least not until they make it to the freight elevators.

"Get on," I tell them, and shoot it straight to the roof. "Tell me the eighteenth floor is clear, Seth."

"Give me a second."

"We don't have a second."

The elevator stops at the twentieth floor, but I don't open the doors. "Owen, I need you to get into the panel underneath the numbers."

"I just unlooped the cameras," Seth says. "The coast is clear. It looks like everyone is back down in the lobby or on the ninth floor. But they're running for the stairs now."

"Good, let them tire themselves out."

Just then I hear a shout, and I turn and see three armed guards racing toward the building. Five or six more are behind them.

Okay, think, Issa. Think. I turn to Seth. "Kiss me."

"What?" he asks, turning a little white.

"What?" Ezra squawks.

I ignore them both. "Kiss me, now," I tell Seth. When he still makes no move, I slide my laptop under my backpack, grab his shoulders, and pull him against me before planting one on him.

"Are you kidding me with this right now?" Ezra shouts. "We're trapped in a damn elevator and you're—"

Seth doesn't kiss me back at first, but then he seems to realize what I'm doing and his mouth moves enthusiastically on mine for several long seconds. He's a decent kisser, but to be honest, I'm not paying too much attention to that part of it. I'm more worried about what we look like to the guards running by us. The last thing I want is for them to come over here and start investigating what Seth and I are up to.

"Anytime now!" Ezra says testily, and as I pull away from Seth I can't help feeling a little tingly at the annoyance in his voice. Not that I'm into Ezra or anything, but still…it's interesting to know he doesn't like me kissing Seth.

"They're not paying any attention to us," Seth reports.

"Who?" Ezra asks.

"The guards who just ran by us," Seth answers. "I know it's hard to believe that Issa wasn't overcome with lust for my manly form, but alas, she was just using me to throw the Po-Po off the scent."

"Please don't ever say *Po-Po* again," Owen tells him.

"I can't make that promise," Seth answers.

"Can we focus, people? Owen, I need you to—"

"Already done. I hacked into the control system for this elevator. That's what you wanted me to do, right?"

"That's *exactly* what I wanted you to do!" I tell him.

"So now what?"

"Now we send this elevator back down, and we hold you there. Two minutes later, we get the other elevator moving back up so they think you're going up, while you're actually going down—"

"But without them knowing it," Owen concludes. "Hence the hack job on the control system."

"Exactly. It will look like this elevator is holding steady at seven, when really you'll be getting off on..." I look at Seth inquiringly.

"The second floor."

"What's on the second floor?" Harper asks.

"The cafeteria—including a large outdoor terrace. You can jump from there," Seth explains.

"Did you say jump?" Harper asks. "From the second story of a commercial building? Are you nuts? That's higher than the second story of a regular house, FYI. Just in case you didn't already know that."

"I do know that, actually." I stop the elevator on the seventh floor. "Okay, Owen, do your thing."

I wait impatiently for him to override the system that tells the building's security where the elevator is.

"Got it," he says after exactly one minute and twelve seconds. Not that I'm counting.

"Fantastic." I take them down, while at the same time sending the other freight elevator back up. Then I switch to the other system. I plunge all six of the glass elevators into darkness while simultaneously starting them all up and assigning each one to a different floor. If we're lucky, that should drive security crazy for at least a couple of minutes as they try to figure out who is where.

"Okay, we're out," Ezra says.

"Go to your right," Seth tells him. "Follow the hallway all the way to the end and then turn right again. It should take you to the front of the cafeteria."

"It did," Harper says about thirty seconds later.

"How do we—" Owen starts, but then there's a triple-beeping sound.

"Good idea!" Seth says as we watch Harper finish swiping the badge we stole from Talia. The cafeteria doors slide open.

"Except you just alerted the system that someone's on two," I tell them grimly.

"There was no other way," Owen answers.

"You're going to need to move fast now," Seth says.

"We're moving, we're moving," Owen snarls. "The doors to the terrace are locked. The swipe card's not working."

"They've probably got them locked like all the other outside doors," Seth says.

"So what are we going to do?" Harper asks. "We're not just going to wait here like sitting ducks—"

I glance around, thinking, and that's when I see Alika barreling toward us in the SUV. She's driving the speed limit, doing her best not to draw attention to the big black vehicle, but I'm pretty sure no one's supposed to be driving down here right now. I figure we've only got a minute or two before she attracts attention.

"Come on!" I tell Seth, shoving my laptop in my bag and climbing to my feet. "Our ride is here."

"What ride?" Ezra asks.

"You've got to find a way out, guys. Can you maybe jimmy the doors—" I break off as a loud crash sounds.

Seconds later, Harper says, "Owen slammed a chair through the glass door. We're out."

"Good. Now get to the edge."

"Next time, you guys are so going in the building," Harper mutters.

"I really hope there isn't a next time," I answer.

Alika pulls up beside us, stopping just long enough for Seth and me to dive into the back seat. "Where?" she demands as she hits the gas.

"Around that corner." Seth points. And sure enough, two of the guards racing toward the building have noticed the SUV and are currently flagging us down.

"Ignore them," Seth tells her.

"I intend to." She takes the curve to the back of the building at close to fifty, and I swear I feel the SUV's right tires leave the pavement.

"There they are!" I point to where Harper is climbing over the terrace railing.

"We're coming!" Seth shouts. "Do you see us?"

"I see you!" Harper answers.

I glance out the back window, watch a security car barrel around a corner several hundred yards back. It's coming straight at us.

"Hurry up!" I shout at Alika, who then does something I never in a million years saw coming. She pulls the hand brake on the SUV and sends us careening into a spin—one that ends only when the back of the SUV is right below the terrace and the front is facing the road we just raced down.

"Wow! That's some *Fast and Furious* stuff right there!" Seth crows.

"I took an evasive driving class before I got my license," she says. "Part of the whole daughter-of-the-secretary-of-state—"

Suddenly there's a loud thump as something hits the roof. "That's Harper," Owen says grimly. Seconds later there's another, bigger thump, and the roof above our head buckles a little.

"And that's me," he continues.

There's a pounding up front, and Alika shouts, "Open the sunroof!"

I scooch forward and slam my hand against the button. Seconds later, Harper falls in headfirst. I try to break her fall, but Seth beats me to it.

As soon as she's out of the way, Owen's legs appear in the opening. At the same time, there's another big thump as Ezra hits the roof.

"Hurry up, get in!" I say to Owen, but Alika's not waiting. The second she confirms Ezra made it onto the SUV, she hits the gas—leaving Owen and Ezra clinging to the luggage rack as we speed toward the exit.

20

Owen
(1nf1n173 5h4d3)

"Hey!" Ezra shouts as he tries to pull himself farther up the luggage rack. "You could give a guy some warning."

"No time!" Alika yells through the open sunroof as we careen around a corner going way too fast. As she does, another security car falls in behind us, which only makes her go faster.

"She's going to kill us!" Ezra complains, and I'm not exactly in a position to argue. The only reason I haven't flown off the roof is because Issa and Seth are holding my legs, which are currently dangling inside the car.

"Give me your hand!" I tell him, holding mine out so that I can pull him toward the sunroof and, hopefully, inside the SUV as I slide into a seat.

He takes a few seconds to think about it—not that I blame him, considering the death grip he's currently rocking on that luggage rack, but in the end he nods. Seconds later, he's pulling himself forward with one hand and making a grab for me with the other.

As my fingers lock around his wrist, I'm grateful for

football—and the incessant weight training it's put me through for the last five years.

"I've got him," I shout to the others. "Pull me in!"

They start tugging and so do I, grabbing Ezra's other wrist and yanking him toward me with every ounce of strength I have. Seconds later, we tumble through the sunroof.

I've got about half a second to register landing on something warm and soft—Issa—before Ezra's weight is on top of me. Issa makes a short, strangled sound before I feel her stop breathing altogether.

"Sorry, sorry!" I say, shoving a dazed Ezra off me. He lands in a heap on the floor in front of us.

For long seconds, we're all too stunned to say anything. Except for Alika, who's cursing like a sailor in the front seat as she barrels toward the exit gate.

"Don't stop!" Harper yells as the red-and-white bar stays firmly down.

"I wasn't planning on it!" Alika guns the engine and plows straight through the EXIT sign and continues racing down the road, three Jacento security cars hot on our heels.

"A little warning would be nice the next time you plan on auditioning for freaking NASCAR," Ezra says when he finally gets his breath back.

He starts to push himself up from his spot between the seats, but Alika takes another turn at crazy speed, and he ends up back on the floor in an even more jackknifed position.

"Dude, maybe you should just stay down," I tell him.

"You think?" He doesn't sound impressed.

"Which way do I go?" Alika screams as we finally approach the main road that runs in front of Jacento's headquarters.

Before anyone can answer, an automated voice says, "*Turn left in one thousand feet.*"

"You're seriously Google Mapping this?" I ask Seth.

"You got a better idea?" he shoots back. "I don't know my way around here. And Ezra was hanging off the roof, so it seemed like the best bet at the time."

"Hang on!" Alika calls, and then we're all falling against the right side of the car as she makes the turn without slowing down.

"We're all going to die," Ezra grumbles as he rubs his head where he bumped it when we all went flying.

"Stop being such a drama queen," Alika tells him as Google Maps instructs her to make yet another turn. "We're not going to die."

"No, but we are going to prison," Issa says, pointing out the back window.

I try to see what she's pointing at, but I can't see much from my place on the floor, wedged between the front and back seats. Shoving myself up, hard, I crane my neck to try to get a view of what's happening behind us. And then curse up a storm as I realize she's right.

Because not only is Jacento security in pursuit of us, we've now added a string of cop cars to the chase as well.

"I'm on it," Harper says, and for the first time I notice her bent over her laptop in the front passenger seat. "When I get to three, swerve around that red Prius," she tells Alika.

"It's going too fast—"

"Just do it. One, two, three."

Alika screams as the Prius stops dead in front of us. She swerves at the last second and barely misses slamming into the Prius's back bumper.

"What the hell are you doing?" Ezra yells, but I get it. Oh yeah, baby, do I get it.

"The green Tesla," I shout to her as I shrug out of my backpack and reach for my laptop, hoping it hasn't been damaged in all the rocking and rolling we've been doing.

"It's a different hack," she shouts back. "I haven't got it yet!" Then she tells Alika, "Blue Prius V in three, two, one."

Alika swerves as the Prius screeches to a halt. Seconds later, one of the cop cars plows straight into it.

"Oh God! Sorry, sorry, sorry!" Alika cries. But she's already back at work.

"I'm on the Teslas," I tell her, racing to pull up their diagnostics.

"Jesus." Seth whistles long and low. "You guys are actually hacking the cars on the road with us?"

"Harper is. I'm just trying to."

And that's when it hits me. It's not only the Priuses and Teslas we need to be thinking about here. Any vehicle that's got an onboard diagnostics port can be hacked—meaning any car made in the last few years is vulnerable. Which gives me a crazy idea that just might work.

"Silver Prius," Harper shouts. "Then the black one next to it. Three, two, one."

Alika swerves to the left, then back to the right so fast that the SUV goes up on two wheels, nearly flipping over. She manages to wrestle it back to the ground just as a huge crash echoes behind us.

I take two seconds to glance out the window at the disaster we're leaving in our wake. One of the cop cars got caught in it, but the others are still with us.

"Turn left in one thousand feet." The automated voice lends a surreal quality to this whole mess.

"Another red Prius!" Harper says. "Now!"

Alika swerves, but pulls too hard on the wheel this time, and we end up spinning. Once, twice—she pulls us out before we complete a third circle and then hits the gas again.

"Turn left in fifty feet. Rerouting. Rerouting. Turn left in two hundred feet. Rerouting."

"The gray Prius. Now!"

Another swerve, another crash behind us. But I'm barely paying attention anymore because I'm in. I'm freaking in!

"Turn right in two hundred feet."

"Hold on!" Alika says, and then we're turning. Seconds later, we're slamming the undercarriage of the SUV against the pavement as we race down a bumpy-ass hill.

"Why the hell are there so many hills around here anyway?" Alika complains as she races around a set of hairpin curves way too fast.

I glance behind us to see how we're doing. We lost the last of the Jacento security cars in the latest crash, but now we've got five police Interceptor sedans and three black SUVs on our tail.

"I really hate to be the voice of reason here," Ezra drawls from where he's still on the floor, "but does anyone know where the hell we're going?"

"I'm following the GPS!" Alika says.

"Red Prius," Harper interjects. "Three, two, one, go!"

I brace for the swerve, pressing my legs against the back of the seat, and this time I barely move. Huh. Looks like I'm getting the hang of this high-speed-chase thing, after all.

"And where, exactly, is the GPS leading us?" Ezra asks.

"I programmed in your address," Seth tells him as brakes squeal behind us.

"Seriously? You really think leading them straight to my house is a good idea?"

"You were on the roof of the damn car! I didn't know where else to go!"

"Turn left in eight hundred feet."

"Ignore that!" Ezra barks as he shoves himself up to look out the closest window. It takes him a second to get his bearings, but then he says, "Okay, you're going to want to stay on this road about another half mile, and then you need to turn right, or we're going to end up stuck in really bad traffic."

"I can do that." Alika reaches up and shoves a few pieces of hair out of her face. "But we've got to figure out how to get away from these cop cars. I can't drive forever."

"I'm working on that," Ezra says. "Just keep going for now."

"Turn left in—"

"And turn that damn thing off before I toss your phone out the window!" he barks at Seth.

I write a few more lines of code, then send a quick prayer out into the universe as I hit Send. Seconds later, brakes squeal behind us as the Interceptor slams to a stop, and I peer through the window just in time to see one of the black SUVs plow straight into the side of one of the police Interceptors.

"Hell, yeah!" I say as I pull up the diagnostics for the second police car.

"Turn here," Ezra tells Alika, and she does, just as I hit Send.

More squealing brakes and an even bigger crash ensues, one that sets off a chain reaction of smaller crashes right down the line.

"Holy crap! Are you hacking the *police* cars?" Issa cries as she flops into the seat beside me.

"No," Harper says.

"Yes," I tell her as I send code flying toward a third one.

"How are you doing that?" Seth twists around in his seat to watch the carnage out the back window.

"The same way Harper got the Priuses. I hacked my radar-detector app to get the IP addresses of the cars chasing us, then I exploited a zero day in the Inteceptor's control system and sent in some malicious code. It actually wasn't that hard," I say as I hit Send and take out the last three police cars. We're down to the two big SUVs chasing us.

"Sounds hard," Seth tells me.

"Turn in right up there," Ezra orders all of a sudden, and I look up to see a huge parking garage looming in front of us.

"Dude, you really want to trap us in another high rise?" I ask.

"Do it!" he orders Alika when she hesitates, and she swings us into the entry lane way too fast.

"Go, go, go," he says, and for the second time today she flies right through the red-and-white arm that's meant to block traffic.

"I don't even want to know how much damage we're causing," Harper says when she finally peels her hands away from her eyes.

"So much," I tell her.

"Pull into the first available parking spot," Ezra tells Alika as she barrels up the ramp. "And for God's sake, close the stupid sunroof."

Without a word, Seth reaches over and pushes the button.

"Be ready to move," Ezra continues.

Moments later, Alika pulls into a parking spot.

"Get to the stairwell!" he orders. "Go, go, go."

The others take off running as soon as their feet hit the ground, but he stops at the back of the SUV. After a moment I figure out what he's doing and pull out my Swiss Army knife and use the screwdriver to go to work on the license plate of the car three down from ours.

"Get moving!" he hisses at me as he works on the SUV's license plate.

"I will, as soon as you do," I answer.

"Come on, guys!" Harper shouts. "They're coming!"

Sure enough, I can hear an engine racing and brakes squealing on the level below us. "One screw should be enough," he says. "Just enough to hold it in place."

"On it," I answer, as we switch places. I screw the new license plate onto the SUV as he does the same to the black Jeep I took it from. But by the time we're done, one of the SUVs that was chasing us comes racing around the corner of the parking garage.

With no time to run, I do the only thing I can: drop to the ground and scoot under the car next to ours. A quick glance at Ezra tells me he's doing the same thing with the Jeep.

Within seconds, the two big Navigators squeal to a stop behind the Escalade. But a quick license plate check has them screaming away, aiming for the next up ramp.

By unspoken agreement, Ezra and I wait until they squeal around the corner at the end of the aisle. As soon as they do, we're up and running full out for the stairwell.

"What the hell!" Issa says, grabbing both of us and practically pulling us down the stairs behind her. "Don't ever do that again! You scared me to death."

We're too busy running to answer. When we get down the second flight of stairs, Ezra takes the lead. "We need to get three blocks down," he says as he races across the busy street, dodging cars as he goes.

The others take off after him, and I grab Alika, who has all but stopped dead on the sidewalk outside the garage.

"What's wrong?"

"I can't jaywalk!" she hisses at me.

"Are you freaking kidding?" I look at her like she's crazy. "You just broke every traffic law in existence, and now you're worried about jaywalking?"

"It's not the same thing."

"Maybe not, baby, but we got to go." The endearment slips out, but I don't bother worrying about it as I grab her wrist and gently pull her toward the street. "They could come out of that garage at any minute, and we need to not be out here where they can see us."

Her eyes meet mine, and for the first time since this insane ride began, I see fear there. Like real, honest-to-God fear. Because she has to cross the street against traffic. It doesn't make sense.

She doesn't budge. "Come on, Alika. Trust me. I swear I've got you."

"My sister was killed jaywalking," she says after a few tense seconds. "She took off before the light, and some guy in an SUV..." Her voice breaks and she doesn't say any more.

But then, she doesn't have to. It will cost precious seconds that we don't have, but I'm not going to fight her. Not after she told me something like that. Besides, it's pretty obvious she's not crossing this street here, and it's just as obvious—to me, anyway—that I'm not going to leave her.

"Come on. Let's go to the corner. We'll cross at the light."

"No, go ahead," she tells me. "I'll just—"

"It's fine. Come on. Let's get moving."

Up ahead, Ezra's looking back at us like we're crazy. But I ignore him and angle my body so that Alika can do the same.

"I'm really sorry," she says when we get stuck at the corner, waiting for the light to change.

"No big deal," I tell her. "They're waiting for us." Which they are. Impatiently.

The WALK sign flashes, and we take off at a run, making it down the block fast enough to cross the second street too, before the light changes again.

"What the hell was that about?" Ezra demands when we finally catch up to the others.

"Don't worry about it," I tell him. I glance past them, trying to figure out where we're going.

"BART," Harper quietly answers my unasked question.

Right. The train. Of course. "Smart."

"Occasionally," Ezra answers with a raised brow.

We head inside, but as we stop at the machine to buy tickets, I notice a transit cop nearby. He doesn't seem to be paying any attention to us, but I keep an eye on him anyway.

"Keep your heads down," I tell the others out of the corner of my mouth as we wait for our turn at the machines. It takes a few minutes, but finally we make it to the machine.

Trying to speed things up, I buy all six tickets, then wait impatiently for the stupid things to print. It seems to take forever, especially when I notice that the cop has pulled out his radio and is talking into it.

No big deal, I tell myself. It doesn't mean anything. But then he turns and circles back around, hand on the butt of his gun, and I start to get nervous. Really, really nervous.

And that's before I realize he's headed straight toward us.

21

Harper
(5p3ct3r)

"What are we going to do?" I ask the others almost soundlessly.

I'm trying not to look at the police officer, but I can't help it. It's like I'm hypnotized by the sway of his walk, my head turning a little more with each step he takes in an effort to keep him in my peripheral vision.

Panic is a sick ball in my stomach, short-circuiting my brain and turning me into a sweaty, shaky mess. I can't get arrested. I just can't.

If I do, I'll go back into the system for sure.

Yeah, I have a pretty decent fake ID on me, but fingerprints don't lie. And once they figure out who I am, even if they don't send us straight to jail, they'll send me back into the Las Vegas foster-care system, and I just can't do that. Not ever again.

I learned to hack so I could change my records and get myself out of that system. And after years on my own—free from the never-ending cycle of one horrible house after another—I can't go back to it. I *won't* go back.

Now that we have a little downtime, a few moments to

think, it's sinking in, in a way that it didn't back at Jacento head-quarters or even during the car chase. My panic turns to living, breathing terror as the cop gets closer and closer…and closer.

We need to run, the little voice in the back of my head says. We need to flee and never look back. But where do we go? How do we get away? The SUVs are probably back to patrolling the street by now, and even if they aren't, the cops probably are.

And now that this guy has made us, even if we try to leave, he can tell them exactly where we're starting out.

We're screwed.

Totally and completely screwed.

"Come on," Silver Spoon says quietly as our last ticket falls into the chute. "Let's just start walking toward the train, see what happens."

"What's going to happen is that cop is going to slap handcuffs on one of us," Buffy tells him. But she doesn't have a better idea to volunteer—none of us does—so she follows directions. She starts walking toward the turnstile like she doesn't have a care in the world. Certainly not like she's being stalked by a transit cop.

Soon, we're all doing the same…more from lack of any other ideas than because we think just walking away is going to work.

I don't look back the whole way to the turnstile, but when we get in line to scan our tickets, I squat down and pretend to tie my shoe…and subtly glance at the cop who has been on our tail.

I freeze when I realize that he's been joined by two more officers…and that they're heading our way, this time with a much more purposeful step.

"Come on, come on, come on," the Lone Ranger whispers to himself as he waits his turn. We've divided up two to a turnstile, and I'm with him, waiting impatiently for the tourists in front of us to figure out how to use the stupid scanner and move the hell along.

It only takes a few seconds, but with the police bearing down on us, it feels like forever.

Finally, it's our turn. The Lone Ranger jams his ticket in, the thing beeps, and the gate retracts to let him through. Then it's my turn, and somehow eternity doubles.

"What are they waiting for?" Snow White asks once we've all made it through the turnstiles and are on the escalator down to the train platform. "If they're going to grab us, why don't they do it now?"

"The crowd's often thinner on the platforms," Silver Spoon answers. "They probably want to get us away from the herd, where we can cause the least amount of damage."

"That doesn't really make sense, though, does it?" Buffy tells him. "Maybe we're just being paranoid."

"Yeah, because the fact that there are now three policemen following us is totally normal, right?" The Lone Ranger shakes his head.

"What do we do?" I am trying to fight down the sickness churning deep inside me. I can't believe how bad this has gone—and how fast. *What do we do?*

"I don't know," Silver Spoon says. "But follow me and I'll try to think of—"

"No," Mad Max interrupts, speaking up for the first time. "Follow me."

And at that, he starts moving quickly toward one side of the platform. It's crowded, and I wonder if he thinks we're going to lose ourselves in the people milling around. I don't think it's going to work—the crowd's not that heavy, and I can see the police officers surging ahead, like they're trying to cut us off.

But at that moment, a train comes rumbling into the station. That's when Mad Max yells, "Run, now!" and takes off in the opposite direction—toward a much less crowded part of the platform.

I don't think; I just follow him—the others hot on our heels—as he vaults a bench. Since I'm not as graceful, I do more of a scramble over it, but the result is the same. We hit one of the entrances just as the train comes to a stop right in front of it.

Behind us, the cops are yelling for us to stop, but it's too late. There's a crowd of people between them and us, and the train doors are already opening.

We slide in the back car, then start moving fast between the cars, putting as much distance between the cops and us as we can. They might be bogged down for now, but who knows how long that's going to last? I don't know what we're going to do if they manage to get on the train.

One step at a time, I tell myself as we finally make it to the first car. *One step at a time*.

A warning to stand away from the doors comes through the

train's overhead system, and then the doors are closing and the train is taking off. I stumble at the abrupt change and grab one of the overhead rails as I glance out the window and realize that somehow we managed to leave all three cops behind.

"How'd you know?" Buffy asks as we speed into the sheltering darkness of a tunnel. "How'd you figure out where the train was going to stop?"

"No big mystery," Mad Max answers, holding up his phone. "I pulled up the schedule and just took a gamble."

"Yeah, well, it paid off." The Lone Ranger claps him on the back. "You saved us back there."

Mad Max grins. "Just returning the favor, man."

"What train are we on?" Silver Spoon wonders suddenly. "How long before the next stop?"

"Does it matter?" Snow White asks.

"Yeah, it matters," he tells her. "You think they're just going to let us get away? They know what train we're on and where it's going next. They'll be at the next station waiting for us."

"So we just won't get off," Buffy suggests.

"Yeah," I say as Silver Spoon's point sinks in, "but that won't stop them from getting *on*."

The Lone Ranger is already whipping out his computer. "How long do we have, Seth?"

"We actually got really lucky," he answers. "We're on one of the outside lines, so we've got twenty-seven minutes before we stop. Well, twenty-five now."

"Okay." The Lone Ranger ducks his head and gets to work, his fingers flying over the keys faster than I've ever seen. I'm one of the fastest code writers I know, but he leaves me in the dust. "I got this."

"What are you doing?" Snow White asks, crowding close to look at his screen.

He glances around the half-full car, then lowers his voice. "I'm going to hack into the BART system and stop the train before it gets to the station." He nods to Mad Max. "Do me a favor and Google Earth this route. Find me a good place to stop in the last six or seven minutes of this leg. I'll need at least that long to do the hack."

"What if you can't?" Snow White demands. "What then?"

"Then we're all screwed, so let's think positive for a few minutes, okay?"

"Can I help?" I ask, reaching for my own laptop.

"I'm just trying to brute-force the password—if you want in on it, feel free."

"I've got a bad feeling about this," Silver Spoon says, and he looks more on edge than I've ever seen him.

"Stopping the train?" the Lone Ranger asks. "Because if there's something else you want to try—"

"No, not that. Just…I don't know." He shakes his head, steps back. Then he pulls a gray hoodie out of his backpack— the first time I've seen him open the bag all day—and quickly exchanges it for the shirt he's wearing before adding a skullcap beanie and pulling it low on his forehead. "Just keep doing what you're doing. I'm going to go take a look around."

We all look at him like he's lost his mind. "For what?" Buffy asks.

"I don't know. I just…I don't know."

It's the most indecisive—and inarticulate—I've ever seen him. Which sets off warning bells all over my brain. "You're really freaked out, aren't you?"

"Not freaked out. Just...I don't know, I'll feel better once I get a look around. I just feel like that escape was too easy back there."

"Too easy?" Snow White whisper-yells. "Are you kidding me?"

"Not from Jacento. From the train station. I just—"

"Well, I'm going with you," Buffy says, then holds her hand out to Mad Max. "Give me your hoodie."

"Ummm, okay." He starts to dig through his backpack, but Silver Spoon stops him.

"Don't bother. I'm probably just being paranoid."

"Yeah, well, I like paranoid," Snow White says as she yanks the beanie off his head and pulls it down over her long hair before popping her hood back up. "So let's go look around. Maybe we'll find out what's giving you the heebie-jeebies."

"Do you want me to come too?" asks Mad Max.

"I don't want anyone to come!" Silver Spoon sounds totally exasperated. "But definitely not the three of you—keep doing what you're doing. It's way more important."

"You sure?" the Lone Ranger asks, eyes narrowed as he studies Silver Spoon's face. Silver Spoon stares back at him, and I'm not sure what kind of silent guy communication is going on between them, but after about thirty seconds they both kind of nod and get on with their business.

"Hey, Harper," the Lone Ranger says after the others leave the car, "I think I've found a back door into the signaling system. I'm going to work on blowing it up, but can you do some research on the schematics of the trains? See what it'll take to get the doors open?"

"Won't they open automatically when the train stops?" Mad Max asks.

"Yeah, probably. I just want to be sure we've got it." He sounds so casual that I know something is up. I glance at Mad Max, and the worried look on his face says the same thing— there's something the Lone Ranger isn't telling us.

A part of me wants to call him on it, but we don't have time for that right now. Besides, if this has anything to do with Silver Spoon's hunch, I figure we'll find out soon enough—one way or the other.

So I don't say anything. I just duck my head and get to work pulling up train schematics from the manufacturer. Turns out, though, BART runs trains from five different manufacturers. Since I don't have a clue which kind of train we're on, I'm not going to be able to get much done.

I move to the back of the car and start looking for any kind of logo or insignia, something that might tell me who made this train. Unfortunately, there's nothing except BART information, which is not what I need.

But as I head back to my seat, I see a small amount of raised text along the bottom of the door. Squatting down to get a closer look, I realize it's a gear with the word BOMBARDIER written across it. According to Wikipedia, that's one of the most recent train manufacturers for BART, so I'm going with it.

Three minutes later I've got the schematics to the train pulled up. The only problem? They're in freaking German.

I pull up Google Translate on a split screen and google just enough to know what words to look for on the graphics. But the clock is ticking. We're moving fast, covering a lot of ground, but I'm not sure it's fast enough.

The idea of what's waiting for us at the next station has me searching even faster, scrolling through document after document as Mad Max leans over and starts whispering to the Lone Ranger about where he thinks we should stop the train. I try to tune them out, to stay in the zone, but just then the back door of the car opens, and Silver Spoon rushes in like the whole train has suddenly caught fire.

"We have to move now," he snarls at us.

"We've got ten more minutes," the Lone Ranger tells him, and he doesn't even pause in his coding. "We can't stop the train before that because there's nowhere to get off. We'll get fried on the third rail."

"Yeah, well, we're going to have to figure out how to get around that," Buffy says. "Because Shane is here."

"Shane? CIA Shane?" Mad Max squeaks.

"Jacento Shane, whose real name is Daniel Davies?" the Lone Ranger asks.

"Yeah, and he's got three goons with him. They must have been searching the crowd with the cops, but we didn't see them," Snow White says.

"Yeah, well, they obviously saw us." Silver Spoon looks grim. "They're working their way toward us, looking at every person on every car. I don't think they spotted us, but—"

"It's only a matter of time before they do," the Lone Ranger finishes.

"Pretty much."

"Okay, new plan." He turns to me. "Have you figured out how to open the train doors yet?"

"Yeah, but what good does it—"

"Shoot it over to me." He looks at Mad Max. "There's another train coming this way, right?"

"Yeah. We can't get off until it passes, man. Especially on this rail bridge. Forget the third rail. We'll be pancaked."

"We're not getting off." The Lone Ranger goes back to whatever the hell he's doing on his computer.

"Then what are we doing?" Buffy whispers insistently. "Because I don't really want to get in a fistfight on a train with Shane and his sidekicks."

"If we're going there, I really don't want to get in a fistfight with them at all," Snow White says. "They're very big."

Mad Max nods his agreement. "Not on a train or on a plane. Not in a house—"

"We're not fighting anyone, okay, Dr. Seuss? Get me the exact time that train passes and give me two minutes of peace to finish this freaking thing up, all right?" the Lone Ranger snarls.

"I've already got it. If it's on schedule, the train should start passing us in five minutes."

"Okay, good. Then just let me—" He freezes as the doors at the end of the car swish open.

I don't want to look. I really, really don't want to look, but I can't help myself. None of us can. As one, we turn to find Shane Not Shane standing there, three huge guys behind him and a gun in his hand. One that's aimed straight at Silver Spoon.

22

Issa
(Pr1m4 D0nn4)

There are only about ten other people in the car with us, and they all freak out the second they see the gun. Not that I blame them. I'm freaking out too. We all are. Alika turns so white that I'm afraid she's going to pass out, and Seth is giving new meaning to the word *bug-eyed*. Even Harper looks scared to death, and it's almost impossible to know what she's thinking pretty much ever.

The only two people in the whole car who seem even a little bit normal are Owen—who is still focused on his laptop and working like the end of the world depends on the code he's churning out—and Ezra. Although he's the one with a gun aimed straight at his heart, Ezra seems totally cool. Like this is just any other ride on the train.

I don't know whether to be impressed by his courage or terrified by his insanity.

"Really?" he asks, even as he moves a little closer to Shane. "You really want to wave a gun around on a train?"

"I'm not waving it around. I'm pointing it at a known fugitive, one who is being chased by the police as we speak. There's a big difference. My associates are bringing the other passengers in the car to the other end of the train to let them know they have nothing to fear, that we're government agents apprehending wanted criminals."

My gut unclenches a notch when I hear that—the last thing I want is for some Good Samaritan to get shot trying to stop whatever it is that's happening right now—but that doesn't help the six of us.

Ezra keeps walking, and I want to scream at him to stop, want to beg him to move back here with the rest of us. But even if I did, I'm smart enough to know that's not going to happen. But I can't just leave him on his own up there either. For better or worse, we're a team.

I move forward a little, trying to get close enough to help somehow. I mean, I don't have a clue what I can do, but I know whatever it is won't be possible if I'm cowering in the front of the car.

"Well, you're obviously not planning on arresting the 'known fugitive,'" Ezra replies. "So what is your endgame here?"

"I don't need to arrest you," Shane sneers. "The cops at the next station will take care of that. I just want the files."

"What files?"

"Don't!" Shane says, shaking the gun ever so slightly. "Don't play stupid with me. You were on the eighteenth floor. There's only one thing you could have been doing there."

"Really? You have footage of me on the eighteenth floor? Of what building exactly are we talking about here? Because I've been with my friends all day."

"I don't have to have footage. I know it was you."

Ezra makes a big show of crossing his arms over his chest, of leaning casually against one of the poles running down the center of the car. As he does, he manages to make a bigger target of himself as he covers those of us behind him a little bit more.

The idiot.

Is Shane really crazy enough—or desperate enough—to shoot one of us with the rest of us here as witnesses? Unless they are crazy enough to shoot *all* of us?

As if my thoughts brought it to fruition, the gun shifts a little to the left as Shane looks directly at Owen. "You. Give me that computer. Right now!"

Owen doesn't stop typing for a second. "Do you really think getting this computer is going to do you any good? If we did get into your files, and that's a big *if*, don't you think we'd be smart enough to upload whatever we found to the cloud? And to make about a million copies?"

"You haven't had time—"

"How much time do you think it takes?" Owen demands. But he snaps the laptop closed before standing up and walking slowly toward Shane.

Shane's gun tracks his every move, at least until Ezra starts talking and draws everyone's attention right back to him.

"Tell me what's really going on here, *Daniel*. What is it that has you so freaked out that you're standing in the middle of a train threatening a bunch of kids—in front of cameras and witnesses? Is this whole song and dance because you're worried about your job? Because *that* I get.

"The questions are going to start rolling in about who we are and why we came after Jacento. Aren't they? The big bosses are going to want to know. The police are going to want to know. And what are you going to tell them? That we're just six kids you tried to con? I'm sure the police are going to love that story. As much as your bosses are going to love how poorly you covered your tracks. But come on, you had to know this was coming, right? Because if you didn't, you're even stupider than you look. I mean, what's old Roderick Olsen going to think about this?"

"Shut up!" Shane yells. "Enough of this. I'm not bargaining with you." He waves the gun around, swinging it back and forth between Ezra and Owen. "Now give me the data."

The gun waving is making me really, really nervous. One wrong move, and he's going to end up killing someone. And with the way they're challenging him, I'm pretty sure that some-one is going to be either Ezra or Owen.

"You know what your big mistake was, dude?" Owen asks as he gets even closer to Shane.

"Not killing you all when I had the chance?"

Shane's focused on him now, the gun and his attention trained on Owen with a laserlike precision that makes me sick even as it gives me the opportunity to move in a little closer too.

"Well, there is that," Owen agrees. "But no. Your big mis-take was thinking you could con people smarter than you. It was thinking we were just a bunch of stupid kids you could use and then throw away. And now you're going to pay for that miscalculation—and for trying to use us to do your company's dirty work. All of Jacento, including Roderick Olsen, is going to pay for it."

"You don't know what you're talking about."

"Actually, I know exactly what I'm talking about. And I've got proof."

Owen glances back at Seth, and it must be the cue Seth is waiting for, because suddenly he's standing too—and ushering Alika and Harper down the aisle toward the rest of us.

"I'm going to ask you one more time to hand over the laptop—and the backpacks," Shane says. "And then I'm going to let my friends here take them from you." He glances back and forth among us. "I think I'll have them start with the girls. Wouldn't want anyone to accuse me of not being a gentleman." He nods to one of his guys who is standing at the back of the car guarding the door, and the guy moves forward, straight for Harper.

Ezra moves to block his path. "That's not going to happen, man."

"Screw you," the guy tells him, and goes to push Ezra out of the way. It's the distraction I was waiting for—the distraction we all must have been waiting for—because a bunch of things happen at the same time.

Ezra pivots and kicks the guy, knocking him down.

Owen hurls his laptop straight at Shane with all the power of a Division I–bound quarterback.

Shane's so desperate to get his hands on the computer that he actually drops the gun, which thank God doesn't go off and shoot one of us.

And Seth, using nothing but his phone and whatever code Owen managed to upload, hacks open both sets of doors on our train car.

"Get ready!" Owen says, pushing us toward the open doors. I manage to grab Alika and Harper and pull them with me as the train starts to slow down significantly. Shane makes a one-handed grab for us, but it's Alika's turn to kick someone—and she does, hard enough that he falls to his knees, groaning. I grab the gun off the train floor and aim it straight at the guys coming at us.

"Don't move!" I shout, even as Owen, Seth, and Alika line up across the opening of one door and Harper and Ezra line up at the other.

"Drop the gun!" Ezra yells to me. "Come on! It's almost time!"

I don't want to jump with the gun, but I don't want to leave it for them either. So I do the only thing I can think of—I empty out all the bullets and then hurl them straight at the closest bad guy. A couple hit him in the head. I throw the unloaded gun under a seat.

"Come, now!" Ezra roars, grabbing my hand and dragging me into the doorway with him.

"The train hasn't stopped!" I yell.

"It's not going to stop!" he answers.

"What?!"

"Now," Owen yells.

"Jump!" Ezra tells me, and then he's all but throwing me across the divide and into the open door of the passing train.

I scream as I land, as does Harper, who jumped right

alongside me. About one second later, Ezra's there too, clinging to the right side of the open door as the train starts to speed up again.

"Oh my God!" I scramble for him on my hands and knees and somehow manage to grab him. Harper and I tug him inside, seconds before we pass a BART sign that would have done its best to decapitate him.

He lands on top of me as he falls, and for long seconds we do nothing but lie there on the dirty floor of the BART train. I turn my head to the left, make sure that Owen, Alika, and Seth are okay. They are, though they don't look like they fared any better than we did.

All around us, people are screaming and coming over to investigate, but as I struggle to catch my breath, I can't muster the energy to care. Instead I put my head back down, close my eyes, and wonder how in less than three weeks I went from hacking the College Board and selling SAT answers to this.

23

Owen
(1nf1n173 5h4d3)

Maybe the whole jumping-out-of-a-train-and-onto-another-moving-train thing wasn't such a good idea, after all. Every bone in my body feels like I just got hit by a three-hundred-and-fifty-pound linebacker with serious anger issues.

"You okay?" I ask Seth and Alika, as we start to register that not only are we still alive, but we also still have all our fingers and toes. And our heads, which, for a minute there, is almost more than Ezra had.

"Just dandy," Alika answers as she pushes up to her hands and knees. She doesn't even look freaked out. Instead, she seems energized by the fact that we almost died two different ways in just the last ten minutes. It's nearly impossible to reconcile this girl with the one who was too terrified to cross the street against traffic less than an hour ago.

I sit up, look around, and for the first time realize that everyone is staring at us. Some of them are even holding out their phones and recording. That's the one thing I didn't think of.

I yank my hoodie down farther over my face and pull on

my sunglasses, make sure the others see me and do the same. It's not much of a disguise, but it's the best we can do right now. Telling these people to stop making videos of us won't exactly be effective. If I were them, I'd probably be doing the same thing.

Turning my back to them, I reach into my pocket and pull out my phone—which has somehow remained unscathed through all of this. Thank you, OtterBox.

After swiping in the passcode, I click on the link I sent myself earlier. Then I use it to slow our train down to a crawl as I look out the windows to make sure we're not still on that damn bridge.

We're not—we're in what appears to be an abandoned field. Not the homiest place to stop, but it will do. At this point, anything will.

Seconds later, I stop the train completely, and the six of us jump off, all while doing our best to keep our faces hidden from the many cell phones trained on us. Before any of the other passengers can get the bright idea of jumping out and following us, I restart the thing, and we watch as it makes its way toward the station that started all this.

"We've got about fifteen minutes before that train makes it into the station," Seth says as we start walking.

"That means we've got fifteen minutes to disappear," I answer. But even that's not necessarily the truth. If the people on that train start blowing up their social media with what just happened, we're screwed. I just hope none of them decided to livestream it. And we won't even talk about the calls from the other train about the "fed" with the gun who was apprehending fugitives.

"I think we should split up," Alika says as we start walking.

"If Jacento is looking for a group of six people, we need to not be six people."

"Good point," Ezra agrees. "I say we scatter—stay away from the trains and any other public transportation. And get someplace where there aren't cameras every twenty-five feet so we can ditch these makeshift disguises. Shane and Jacento know what we look like, but until those videos back there get uploaded, the cops don't, and I'd really like to keep it that way."

"What time are we meeting up?" Issa asks.

Ezra glances at his watch. "Let's give it three hours. Traffic's bad, and we might have to walk the whole way, so..."

"Three hours it is," I agree. "If anyone's going to be later than that, they need to text. Okay?"

"Yeah. One more thing, though." Harper looks really worried. "How are we going to make sure Jacento doesn't give our names and descriptions to the police? If they do..."

"If they do, they're as screwed as we are," I assure her. "More, really. Besides, if they go to the authorities, we're totally out of their reach. And that's the last thing they want, especially considering they don't know how much information we got off their servers."

"*We* don't even know how much info we got off their servers," Seth reminds us. "Once we make it back to Ezra's, we need to dig in fast. See what's there."

"We will." Issa holds her hand out for a fist bump, and I connect, not wanting to leave her hanging. "In the meantime, stay safe and stay free."

"Amen to that," Seth replies.

And then we're kind of breaking into pairs—Seth and

Harper, Ezra and Issa, Alika and me. It happens naturally—we just kind of gravitate to each other—maybe because it's how we were paired for the con we were running. I think Seth is probably the lucky one, given the mean right hook we now know Harper isn't afraid to use.

The thought of that makes me grin, but it also jogs my memory. "By the way, should we let anyone else know about the guy we left tied up in the closet? I really hate to just leave him there—who knows how long before someone finds him, with it being the holidays and all."

Issa looks at me like I'm crazy. "Oh yes, we'll just call into the Jacento switchboard and let them know we left one of their employees tied up in his closet."

"I can make it anonymous, you know. I am fairly good at this hacking thing."

"I say we worry about that after we get back to Ezra's place," Issa says. "No use causing more trouble for ourselves when we're being hunted by psychopaths."

I know she's right, but it still makes me a little uncomfortable—and I can tell from the looks on Ezra's and Harper's faces that they feel the same way. Maybe it's harder for us because we're the ones who put that guy in the closest—he's real to us, not just some abstract concept.

Whatever it is, I know Issa is right. Our own safety has to take priority right now. But as soon as we're all back at Ezra's, I'm going to figure out a way to make this right—or at least as right as I can make it.

We split off when we get to the end of the lot, each pair

going in a different direction. It's ridiculous, but walking away is harder than it should be. Especially considering I've only known these guys a few days.

Something's probably there—something anthropological about human bonding during times of extreme emotion. But right now I don't care about anthropology or sociology or anything else. All I care about is that my friends might be walking into a dangerous situation and I won't be there to have their backs.

"So," Alika says as we round the corner and start walking up a really big freaking hill, "we should probably ditch these clothes first. Change into something they aren't looking for."

"Yeah, you're right." I pull out my phone. "Let's see if there's a mall or something around here."

Turns out there isn't, but there is a cluster of vintage shops about three blocks east of us. "Want to try there?" I ask.

"Sure," Alika says, but she looks doubtful.

Not that it exactly surprises me. In the last couple of days I haven't seen the girl in anything that isn't designer—even her pajamas are Gucci or something like that. I'm pretty sure the idea of putting on old clothes that were once worn by somebody else gives her the heebie-jeebies. But it's not like we've got so many other choices right now.

We walk the three blocks in silence, but I think that's because we're both shell-shocked. I know I am. Now that we're out of immediate danger and the adrenaline is wearing off, I feel a little bit like I've been run over *by* a BART train instead of just having jumped off one.

My phone buzzes in my pocket, and I pull it out, expecting

to find a warning text or something from one of the others. Instead, it's my brother checking in—turns out Dad had a really bad morning, so bad that Damon had to take my mom and get the hell out of Dodge. Which meant leaving Dad alone in the house to do God only knows what to himself.

How's Mom?

Shook but OK

When are you coming home?

This is exactly what I was hoping to avoid. Damon's no good with Dad when he gets like this—he just totally shuts off. Which is probably the best thing for him, but it leaves Dad and Mom out in the cold.

I don't know. Couple more days

That OK?

I don't know

You're better with him than I am

He started throwing stuff this morning, almost destroyed the kitchen because he wanted pancakes and Mom had made French toast

You should probably come home

I can't take this, man

It's too hard

I'm probably going to head back to school early

And isn't that just like my jerk brother? He runs halfway across the country to college to escape from our family's problems, and now when he's supposed to be back for just four weeks, he wants to run away as soon as things get difficult.

Fix it, Owen.

I can't take this, Owen.

Maybe we should just let him kill himself, Owen. It'll be better for everybody.

One week. I asked him to take care of them for one week, and he can't even do that without crying to me three times a day about how much he hates it. About how he can't stand to be around Dad when he's like this. About how it's too freaking hard.

Yeah, it's hard. For everybody.

For Mom, who doesn't recognize the man she married but still loves him because she knows he's acting that way because he's sick, not because it's who he is.

For Dad, who in moments of clarity realizes just how far gone he is and hates himself for it.

And for Damon and me, who lost a really good dad somewhere in the madness of this damn disease.

Damn right it's hard. But what are we going to do? Just lock him away somewhere? Just leave him? The whole reason Damon can go to school and have his swanky apartment and his perfect car is because of the sacrifices Dad made. The whole reason none of us will ever have to worry about money is because Dad gave everything—even his mental health—to a game, and a team, that doesn't care about him now.

And I'm just supposed to forget about all that? Forget about who he was when he took me camping and taught me how to play football and sat around the kitchen table helping me learn the multiplication table? All that just goes away because he's sick?

I can't do that, and neither can Mom. What I can't figure out—what I'll never be able to figure out—is how Damon can.

I want to tell him to man up, to stop being such a wimp and deal with it. But if I do that, he really will take off, and that can't happen. I have to be here, have to see this thing through, which means Damon has to stay put. We can't leave Mom alone with Dad for days on end. Maybe he'll be fine, or maybe he'll lose his freaking mind because she put mayonnaise on his sandwich.

Just give me a few more days

Please

You can leave as soon as I get home

But I can't get away now

What kind of scholarship are you going for again?

And why does it matter?

We have the money

Just come home

> I can't
>
> Please don't leave. Please

Fine

I'll stay a couple more days as long as he doesn't lose it again

If he does, you're on your own

Like that's a shock? That's a freaking given. I'm always on my own, and have been since Dad started getting sick. Once the signs of CTE started to show, he went downhill fast. So fast that it feels like Mom and I have just been along for the ride these last three years.

> Fine
>
> Just give me some warning, okay?

Whatever

I want to reach through the phone and shake him, but I can't. It wouldn't work anyway. Damon's never going to change, so screw it. Just screw it.

"Hey, Owen! Look at me!"

I glance up at Alika. She's staring at me with a worried look on her face. "What's wrong?" I ask.

"What's wrong?" She's totally incredulous. "I've been talking to you for the past five minutes, and it's like I wasn't even here. Is everything okay? Who were you texting? Have they found the others? What's going on?"

Suddenly, it registers that she's frightened. That she thinks something's gone wrong. "It's fine. I'm sorry. It was my brother, being a jerk. But it's fine." Very deliberately, I shove my phone back in my pocket. "Nothing to worry about right now."

"You sure?" She moves a little closer then, so close that I can smell the vanilla-and-cinnamon scent of her that seems to drown out everything else, even the stench of sweat and fear that I know must be rolling off me in waves right about now. "Is there anything I can do to help?"

The fact that she means it, that her dark brown eyes are wide with sincerity and worry, gets to me in a way I don't expect. I'm the one who usually does the worrying, the one who helps and tries to figure things out. The fact that she's offering—and really seems to mean it—grabs me in the gut. Makes me feel all unbalanced.

For a second, all I can do is stand here looking at her, breathing her in, wanting to touch her more than I've wanted anything in a long time—except, maybe, to get off that damn BART train alive.

But what I want and what I can have are two different things, especially now when my whole life is so screwed up. It's not like I can tell her about it, not like I can expect her to understand when she's so completely, absolutely freaking perfect.

When I think about it like that, there's nothing to do but lie. So I do, and try not to feel like a total jerk. "Nah, I'm good. Just family stuff. It'll be there when I get back to Boston."

She nods, a little jerkily, but her smile seems real enough when she says, "Of course. I know how family things go."

Most people don't have a clue how family things like mine go, and I start to shrug the sympathy off. But then I remember her face when I tried to get her to cross the street to the BART station, remember what she said about how her sister died. For the first time it registers just how imperfect Little Miss Perfect's life has actually been. No wonder she's such a badass under the prissy designer clothes.

The silence between us is getting awkward now, though, so I glance around. I realize with some surprise that we're standing in front of one of the vintage shops. No wonder she was so insistent on getting my attention—and so freaked out when she couldn't.

"Ready to go in?" I ask, forcing a grin I'm far from feeling.

"Yeah, sure." But she keeps casting dubious looks at the front window—and the nineties grunge look displayed there.

"I promise you don't have to wear flannel," I tell her as I hold the door open.

"Good, because I'm pretty sure I'd rather go naked."

She says the words flippantly, as a joke, but suddenly I can't help thinking about her naked. With another girl, I might say something, might make an innuendo or two, but it feels off to do that with Alika. More, it just feels wrong. Not because I don't like her, but because I do. I really do. And that's probably why I can't flirt with her.

Still, the tension ratchets up between us anyway, like she can see inside my brain to what I'm thinking. Which only makes me think all kinds of other things, like what she'd look like in the tiny little crop top right in front of me.

Damn. I'm so totally screwed here.

In desperation, I grab the first thing I come to that will cover all her good parts and hold it up. "How about this?"

She looks from the shirt to me and back again. "I don't think it will fit you."

"I meant for you."

"For me?" Now she just looks confused. "It's an old football jersey. For the state of Montana?"

"The state of…" Now it's my turn to look from her to the shirt. "This is a Joe Montana jersey."

She looks at me like I'm speaking Greek.

"You know, Joe Montana? Arguably the greatest quarter-back of all time? *Definitely* the greatest quarterback the 49ers ever had. Joe Montana?"

She still looks blank.

Well, that took care of at least half the inappropriate thoughts I was having about her….Shaking my head, I shove the jersey back on the rack. I'd buy it myself, even though it's too small, but I already have three at home. Maybe four.

"What about this?" she asks. She's holding up some kind of seventies hot pants jumper thing in bright red, and not even her lack of knowledge about the greatest quarterback in the history of the game can stop me from picturing her in it.

"Maybe something a little less conspicuous?" I suggest.

"I know," she sighs. "But it's Balmain."

"And I'm supposed to know what that means?"

This time she's the one rolling her eyes. "Just think of him as the Joe Montana of seventies fashion."

"Oh, got it. Well, maybe you can buy it but just not wear it now. Find something else to put on for the next few hours."

"You think?" She holds it up, looks at it front and back, then moves to the closest mirror and holds it against her body. And that's about the time I grab the nearest sundress I can find and shove it at her. "Why don't you go try this on while I look for some clothes for me?"

"Because it's about four sizes too big." She slides it back on the rack, then slips past me to get to one of the other racks. As she does, her body brushes softly against mine, and it takes a lot of self-control for me not to reach for her. Not to pull her against me and kiss her right here in the middle of this crowded little shop.

Especially since she gasps a little at the contact, her body swaying gently against mine for one second, two. And then she's picking up a green KISS ME, I'M IRISH shirt and thrusting it at me. "This might work for you."

"It's December. And I'm not Irish."

"But you could be. Besides, everyone will be so busy looking at the shirt that they won't bother to look at your face. Isn't that what you want?"

"Or they'll see a black guy with dreads walking in an Irish shirt and take an extra long look, just to see what the joke is."

"Maybe you're right." But she's pouting a little as she takes the shirt back and puts it on the shelf where she found it.

I'm tempted to suggest that she can kiss me even though I'm not Irish, but again, I don't want to go there with Alika. She's a badass about so many things, but she's got these good-girl vibes that make me worry about scaring her away by being too bla-tant. Plus the whole I-can't-flirt-with-girls-I-actually-like thing.

Then again, I don't even know what I'm thinking—scare her away? We're in this for one thing only—to stop Jacento from doing whatever the hell it wants to do with our data and the data of every other person on the planet. Trying to pretend this is more than that? Just can't do it. Especially not with my life the way it is.

Alika is the daughter of the secretary of state, for God's sake. Not to mention the way she rocks the "perfect" vibe like it's a religion. No way in hell she's going to be interested in get-ting involved with someone whose life is pretty much the defi-nition of imperfect—especially if you throw in messy and crazy and totally screwed up.

Still, I can't stop myself from watching her as she weaves her way through the cramped store. Everything about her is just so beautiful. Her smooth skin, her full lips, the wicked intelligence that gleams in her eyes when she's thinking about challenging me on some idea or another.

"Hey, what about this?" she asks, holding up a black pin-striped button-down. It's not my usual style—I'm more pat-terns than stripes when it comes to dress shirts—but maybe that's a good thing. Switching up the disguise instead of taking it off completely.

"Sure. Let me try it on." I head back to the dressing rooms, which are little more than one large cloth cubicle turned into two by a piece of fabric draped down the center and tied to a pole on both sides.

Which is fine, until I see a blue-and-white sundress in her hands and realize she's coming back with me. Suddenly, that thin piece of opaque fabric separating the rooms doesn't seem like much. Especially once we're both inside and I can hear the rustle of her clothes as she gets undressed less than a foot from me.

I try to concentrate on something else—like how much it would suck to get captured by a gun-wielding Shane because I'm an idiot—but that doesn't seem to matter when I can smell her and hear her and practically taste her mouth beneath mine.

I am so screwed.

It's my new mantra, and the only thing keeping me from banging my head against the wall right now is the fact that there is no wall. Lucky, lucky me.

"Hey, are you done?" Alika asks, her voice soft and husky.

"Almost," I answer as I fumble with the last couple of buttons before tucking the shirt into my jeans.

"Me too."

Thank God.

I buckle my belt, then practically yank the curtain off the door as I go to step outside—and plow straight into Alika.

She gasps and I reach out to steady her, wrapping my hands around her upper arms. Which only makes her gasp again.

And then we're standing there, eyes locked, breaths mingling, bodies scant inches from each other. I want to kiss her so badly that I can taste it, and for a moment I'm sure that that's what she wants too.

But then my phone vibrates with yet another text, and the

moment is gone. Alika pulls away, turns away, leaves me standing here wishing that once, just once, things could be different. That *I* could be different.

Maybe then I could be like Damon and not care about anything but myself.

But I'm not different, and neither is my life. So I do what Alika knew I was going to do all along. I pull out the phone and text my brother back. Again.

24

Issa
[Pr1m4 D0nn4]

"You doing okay?" Ezra asks me as we make our way down a street lined with brightly painted houses.

"I'm fine." There's something in the way he asks the question that gets my back up and makes me ask, "Why? Are *you* okay?"

He holds his hands up in the universal gesture of surrender. "I'm not being a jerk, I swear. I just wanted to check on you, see how you're feeling. It's not every day a girl points a gun at someone."

"Really? It's not every day that a *girl* does it?" I repeat, brows raised and eyes narrowed.

"Don't get your panties in a wad. When I said 'girl,' I was specifically referring to you, and you happen to be a girl. I wasn't being sexist. If I had to point a gun at someone, I'm not sure I'd be okay either."

"Yeah, well, maybe not. But I'm perfectly fine. And so are my panties, thank you for asking. In my neighborhood, it's not a Monday if you're not carrying a gun, so..." It's a bit of an exaggeration, but he doesn't need to know that.

"Is that right? So you're a tough girl, huh?"

"Tough enough not to get hassled by you," I answer, bumping my shoulder into his in a way that says I'm not going to take any of his crap.

But then I lose the thread of the conversation because we're walking by a purple house. And I don't mean lavender, I mean purple—deep, dark, unapologetic purple that the streetlights show off to great advantage. It's got cheerful white-scalloped trim and boxes blooming with brightly colored flowers beneath every window. It reminds me so much of a poem by my favorite author, Sandra Cisneros, about her house in San Antonio that I can do nothing but stare at it for several long seconds.

"This one?" Ezra asks. "Of all the houses on this street, this is the one you fall for? Really?"

"It's beautiful," I say, and for one second I imagine what it would be like to sit on the swing on that small, sweet front porch with Chloe on my lap. It's so different from the life we have now in our cramped little apartment that I can barely picture it. But I want it, so much more than I should.

Which makes me think. More, it makes me cautious—when from the moment this thing began, I've been nothing but impulsive. Ruled by my gut and my heart instead of my head.

And look where that's gotten me.

On the run from Jacento, from the cops, from my life. I pointed a gun at someone today, something I would never have thought in a million years I'd do. Something I never want to do again.

Still gazing at the house—afraid to take my eyes off it in case it disappears—I say, "I can't go to prison, Ezra."

"We're not going to prison."

"No," I tell him as I stare up at the house—at the life—that I've spent the last two years working to achieve someday, for myself and for my family. "*You're* not going to prison. *Owen's* not going to prison. *Alika's* not going to prison, and probably neither is Seth. But Harper and me? We don't have the same luxury you guys do. We don't have a safety net. So when this goes bad, we're the ones who are going down while the rest of you are bailed out by your parents' spare change."

"Do you really think I'd let that happen to you? That any of us would?"

"I don't think Mommy or Daddy is going to give you a choice, Ezra."

"It's not up to them."

"Yes, it is. The fact that you think it's not shows just how naïve you are. Your parents are not going to let you risk your future just to defend some riffraff from San Antonio."

He gets close and puts his face right next to mine, in an effort to make me look at him. But I keep my eyes on the prize. On the house that is everything I want my brothers and sisters to grow up in. To have a normal life in.

"If you believe that's how I think of you, you don't know me very well." He doesn't sound angry so much as hurt.

"I *don't* know you very well," I answer. "And you don't know me either. So why would I think, even for a second, that you would pay to get me out of trouble? I may not be a fan of old movies, but this?" I gesture between the two of us. "This I've seen a million times, and it never ends well for the regular girl with all the baggage."

"*Pretty Woman*," he tells me.

"Excuse me?"

"That old movie with Julia Roberts and Richard Gere? Where he climbs up the fire escape? It ended pretty well for her."

"She was a hooker. He *bought* her."

"So you did see it."

"I'm old movie challenged, not completely illiterate." I shake my head. "I can't believe you used a movie with a hooker in it to make your point. That says everything about how you see me."

"Oh, no, you're not going to throw that on me. If that's what you got out of that movie, it says more about how you think of yourself than it says about my feelings on the matter."

"Ugh. That's another rich-boy maneuver if I've ever heard one. All I did was put words to how the world sees me."

"That's not what I see," he says as he somehow moves even closer.

"Oh yeah?" I try to sound like I don't care at all, when the truth is, I care way more than I should about what he thinks of me.

He's not falling for the attitude, though. "Yeah," he murmurs as he turns me to face him. Then he slides a finger under my chin and tilts my face up until I have no choice but to punk out or meet his gaze. And since there's no way I'm going to punk out…

I'm not ready, though. Not ready for the compassion I see in his eyes as we look at each other, and definitely not ready for everything else I see there. It makes me feel vulnerable, when I *never* let myself feel that way. Never let myself be put in a position *to* feel that way.

"We should get moving," I tell him, grasping at straws at this point. Anything to protect myself. Anything to make what I'm feeling right now less intense, less real.

Because I know better. God, do I know better. Ezra Hernandez stands for absolutely everything I don't want in a guy, and yet here I am. Letting him cup my cheek. Letting him rest his long, lean body against mine. Letting him whisper in my ear.

"Everything about you is beautiful, Issa."

I start to brush the compliment away—his view of what I look like is the last thing I want to talk about—but Ezra won't be swept aside. Instead, he stays where he is, so close that I can't take a breath without my chest pressing against his. "The way you think, the way you move, the way you code."

"The way I code? That's a new one."

"Maybe, but it's true. Usually, other people's code makes me nuts, but yours is really beautiful. Streamlined and supple and secretly complicated under all the clean lines. Oh, and intriguing. It's very, very intriguing."

I feel myself starting to thaw, my defenses melting away at his words, his touch, the way his body is so warm and strong and perfect next to mine.

Alarm bells are going off, warning me that this is the surest way to mess things up—the surest way to get myself into even more trouble.

And yet, when his thumb comes up and rubs back and forth against my lips, I don't pull away. I don't even protest. I just stand here and watch his dark eyes burn with the same heat I feel deep inside.

He does it again, a little harder this time, like he's actually trying to rub something away. "What—?" I ask, and it's not the most coherent thing in the world, but having him this close—this intense—is giving me all the feels, whether I want them or not.

"I don't like that Seth kissed you," he admits.

I look at him like he's crazy. "That was just a cover, to keep the guards from getting suspicious."

"I know." He rubs his thumb across my lips one more time. "I still don't like it."

"That's ridic—" I break off because he's leaning forward now and slowly, carefully, pressing his lips to mine. And nothing has ever felt so good. Not hacking the College Board, not flying on an airplane, not even getting off that train alive today.

Because, despite everything—despite his arrogance and his brilliance, his ridiculous wealth, and his even more ridiculous propensity for spending it with abandon—kissing Ezra feels like home. If it's the middle of summer and the air-conditioning is broken and every wall in the place is on fire. But still, home.

I bring my hands up to his neck, burrow my fingers in his silky, too-long hair. I should stop him, I know I should. But I can't, not when every nerve ending—every cell in my body—is screaming for him. If this is it, if this is the only chance I have of ever feeling this way in my life, then I'm going to take it. I'm going to stand here and let him kiss me, and I'm going to kiss him back, with all the heat and fear and power I have inside me.

Ezra breaks first, abruptly pulling away to suck shuddering gulps of air into his lungs. "Issa, you—" And then he dives in again, both hands cupping my face as he slams his mouth back down onto mine.

I don't know how long we stand here like this—mouths fused, bodies wrapped around each other. But it's long enough for a few cars to pass by and honk, long enough for my fingers—and my lips—to go numb. More than long enough for me to forget what it feels like to breathe without the musky, slightly spicy scent of him wrapped around me.

And when it's over—when we finally manage to untangle our mouths and bodies and hands so that we can get make our way back to Ezra's condo—it's still not over. Because all that heat, all that emotion, woke up something inside me. Some dormant part that I didn't know existed and don't have a clue what to do with. All I know is that things just got a lot more complicated...and a lot harder to walk away from than I ever anticipated.

25

Harper
(5p3ct3r)

"You made it!" Silver Spoon says as we drag ourselves through the door to his condo. "We were about to send up a flare."

"Yeah, well, it's been an experience," Mad Max responds.

I roll my eyes. "Turns out Mad Max here doesn't know how to ride a bike nearly as well as he claims to."

"I can ride in a normal city, thank you very much, but this place is really hilly. There are almost no hills in Austin, and it's very different riding a bike there."

"Awwwww," Buffy coos as she looks him over. "Did you get a boo-boo?"

"He did. He fell off and banged his knee. Twice."

"You really had to tell them about the second time?" Mad Max complains.

I nod solemnly. "I really did. At least I didn't tell them how you almost fell in the pond and got bitten by a duck....Oops."

"You actually rode bikes to get back here?" Snow White asks. "Where did you—"

"Wait a minute!" Mad Max interrupts, eyes wide. "It just hit me. *That's* my nickname? Mad Max?"

I crack up. I can't help it—he's just sooooo excited to finally know the secret. "Yes," I tell him, shaking my head. "*That's* your nickname."

"It's so much better than Porcupine. So much more badass. I love it, Harper!" He looks so excited that I don't even know how to respond. I take a cautious step back, just in case he decides to hug me.

The Lone Ranger, however, doesn't have any shortage of responses. "She's got a nickname for you, huh?" He wiggles his brows up and down in the most ridiculous way. "Sexy."

Mad Max blushes, and it is totally adorable how this kid can still blush after the day we've had. "It's not like that. She's got one for all of us."

"And they're not sexy," I interject. "I don't do sexy."

"What does that mean?" Silver Spoon asks from where he's sprawled on one of the couches. "You're totally hot."

"I'm really not." Unsure of what to say because I never really expected this to come up, I walk over to the bar and grab a bottle of water from the fridge. Then I decide, *Screw it.* I've never said this out loud to anyone before—never had anyone to say it out loud to—but I nearly died with these people today. If I can't trust them with the truth about who I am, than who can I tell? "But that's not what I meant when I said I don't do sexy." I twist off the bottle's cap, take a long, slow sip as I try to get my thoughts in order. Then I decide simple really is best. "I'm asexual."

"Asexual?" Mad Max asks. "Really?"

I nod. "Really." I look down at the water bottle, start peeling nervously at the label as I wait to hear what they think. Not that it should matter—I barely know these people. And yet, somehow, it does.

"Well, thank God," the Lone Ranger says as he walks over and grabs a bottle of water too. Then he slings an arm around my shoulder and pulls me in close so he can stage whisper, "Ezra and Issa have been drooling over each other since they got back here half an hour ago, and I'm about to puke. At least we know you're still sane."

"Whatever." Buffy makes a face. "Like you and Alika are any better?"

"I don't know what you're talking about!" Snow White exclaims, except suddenly her cheeks are even redder than Mad Max's. "I don't drool, thank you very much, let alone at Owen."

"Sure you do," Silver Spoon teases. "You've been doing it all night."

"I've been in the shower, alone, since you got back. No one to drool over, thank you very much! Don't try to put me on the hot seat just because you can't keep your hormones under control."

"So are you aromantic?" Mad Max asks in the middle of all the chaos. "Or just asexual?"

"I think just asexual," I answer cautiously. "Why, does it matter?"

"Of course not! I'm just trying to get the terms right. This is so cool."

I raise an eyebrow. "It is?"

"Sure. I've never had a friend who was asexual before. Diversity is good. I like it."

"Well, as long as I can be helpful..." I can't seem to stop laughing, and as I look around at this mismatched group that I somehow fit into perfectly, I can't believe I was ever nervous. If I was a lousy hacker, they'd boot me out in a heartbeat, but the fact that I'm asexual is barely a blip on the radar. I kind of love it.

The doorbell rings, and Silver Spoon jumps up. "Dinner's here. Hope you like Chinese."

"I got it, dude," the Lone Ranger says as he climbs to his feet. "It's my turn."

As he moves to grab his wallet off the bar, Buffy sidles up to me. "So, let's get down to the really important stuff...." She gets quiet for a second, and at first I think it's because she's going to ask some personal question about my asexuality, so I brace myself. "You have to tell me. What's my nickname?"

It's so not what I was expecting that I just stare at her for a second. "Really? *That's* what you want to know?"

"Well, *yeah*. You said we all have one. And Seth's is really cool. So what's mine? Wonder Woman?"

"Umm, no."

"Oh." She looks disgruntled for a second, but then she brightens. "Black Widow?"

"That's a good one," I tell her. "But no." And I've obviously got a mean streak because instead of telling her the truth, I say, "Tinker Bell," just to hear her whine.

She doesn't disappoint. "Tinker Bell? Tinker Bell? Seth gets Mad freaking Max, and *I* get *Tinker Bell*? Are you serious? Why on earth do I remind you of Tinker Bell? Is it because I'm short compared to you? Because I'm actually not short, you know!"

"It's totally because of your height," I deadpan. Before I can tell her I'm just joking, the Lone Ranger calls out, "Look at it this way. At least she didn't call you Maleficent. She's a fairy too, isn't she?" he asks, hand on the doorknob. "Or Fairy God-mother. Or—"

And that's when all hell breaks loose.

26

Owen
(1nf1n173 5h4d3)

One second I'm messing with Issa, and the next there's a searing pain in my side. It takes me a beat to register what it is, and that beat almost gets me killed as another gun goes off.

"Look out!" I shout, slamming the door shut as hard as I can. I lock it and slide the chain in place before diving to the side. Considering the kinds of weapons these guys are packing, it will only buy us a minute or so, but that's a minute we wouldn't have otherwise.

"What the hell is happening?" Ezra yells as he comes running.

"Don't!" I scream. "Get down!"

Bullets pound the door, plowing through the wood and heavy beveled glass like it's not even there. I scramble across the floor, trying to get to Alika, while Ezra changes course and heads toward Issa.

"What's going on?" Alika screams.

"Get down!" I yell again, but she's frozen in place, eyes wide and hands over her mouth.

Thank God the others don't have that problem. Ezra throws himself at Issa, taking her down hard while Harper dives behind the bar and Seth rolls over the back of the couch.

I make it to Alika just as another hail of bullets starts up. They go through the holes the first ones made in the door and start tearing up the penthouse. I pull Alika down a second or two before bullets slam into the wall right where she was standing. Others hit tables and picture frames and chandeliers, and glass goes flying everywhere.

Alika keeps screaming, and I shake her, hard, to get her attention. "You've got to calm down," I tell her. "We've got to move. Now!"

The only problem is I don't know where to go. We're forty-two stories in the sky, and the only way out is the door these assholes are currently shooting through.

I'm wracking my brain, trying to figure out what the hell to do, when Ezra shouts, "Upstairs."

"Are you kidding me? You want to go higher?" I yell over the gunfire.

"There's a private elevator in one of the master closets," he answers. "It goes all the way down."

"Up it is, then," Harper says as she peers around the edge of the bar. "As soon as they stop shooting at us, that is."

As if they heard her, the gunfire ceases, leaving an eerie silence in its place. One that lasts only long enough for the front door to swing open.

As three men with very large guns walk through the door, I grab Alika and drag her the last few feet to the nearest chair—a huge overstuffed thing that is, thankfully, just big enough for us to fit behind.

Ezra and Issa are directly across from us, lying facedown behind one of the large sofas. He points to the staircase again, and I nod. But it's all the way across the room. How are we supposed to get there?

"Where you hiding?" one of the men asks in a heavy Scandinavian accent. "You don't actually think you're going to get out of this, do you?"

I slap a hand over Alika's mouth, just in case.

"Come out, come out, wherever you are," the second man taunts, his shoes crunching on broken glass as he makes his way deeper into the apartment. I listen hard, trying to judge where they are, but the whole downstairs is one huge open floor plan, and the acoustics are terrible. Sound rises with the high ceilings, and it's almost impossible to tell where the noise is coming from. I think about sticking my head out to check, but if they see me, Alika and I are both dead.

Especially since the third man hasn't said a word, and I can't even begin to estimate what side of the apartment he's on.

I fight the urge to freak the hell out, but come on. Stuff like this only happens in movies, right? I mean, how are we in the middle of an actual shoot-out right now?

Then again, it's not actually a shoot-out if only one side has guns, is it?

Desperate, I fumble in my pocket for my Swiss Army knife. It's not much, but it's the only weapon I've got. I open the biggest blade, then clutch the handle in my fist as I wait, breath held.

"Haven't you all caused enough trouble?" the first man says. "Why don't you just come out and get it over with? You have to know you can't hack your way out of this one."

His voice is over near the bar, and I freak out, thinking of Harper back there alone, with no weapon at all. I scooch around a little, so that I can get a look at the bar, which is crosswise from where Alika and I are hiding. I get in position just in time to see the guy get to the edge of the bar.

I glance at Ezra, but he's farther away from the bar than I am. I do the only thing I can think of. I grab one of the books lying open on the floor next to my head, and I throw it as hard as I can.

It slams into the back wall of the penthouse, and gunfire explodes yet again.

I wait for the bullets to stop—for them to reload, I assume—then poke my head out just enough to see the guy closing in on the bar again. But this time there's nothing I can do to stop him from finding Harper.

Turns out I don't have to do anything, though, because the moment he gets within range, Harper reaches out and stabs something into his leg as hard as she can. As he howls, she pulls it out and stabs him again. Then again and again.

He falls to the ground, screaming and clutching his leg. He's making enough noise to wake the dead, and it's all the distraction I need. Grabbing a decorative glass orb that landed a few feet from me when it was shot off its shelf, I pop up from behind the chair. Then I use every ounce of strength I have to fire the thing straight into the back of the head of the nearest bad guy.

He drops like a rock, his forehead striking the floor as he falls.

At the same time, Harper grabs a crystal decanter from behind the bar and brings it down on the head of the guy she stabbed. Then she does it again. The girl obviously has some serious anger issues—not that I blame her. I'm feeling pretty pissed myself.

The third guy races toward me, gun raised as he fumbles ammunition into it, and that's when Seth strikes. He leaps up from behind the couch, grabs the only lamp still standing—a huge gray-and-white marble monstrosity—and swings for the fences.

He connects, the lamp slamming into the man's shoulder with a sickening crunch. He drops the gun as he falls to the floor. This time Seth brings the lamp down on his head.

I don't wait around to see any more. Instead, I'm up and running, dragging Alika behind me, and shouting, "Let's go, let's go, let's go!" as I race for the front door.

The others are right with us. But before we can get there, I hear the elevator opening, followed by shouting in some language I don't recognize. That's all it takes to make me change course and race for the stairs, Alika's hand still clutched in mine.

The others follow suit, and we hit the stairs just as two more men burst into the apartment, guns raised. We drop hard, crawling up the stairs as bullets rain down around us. And can I just say, screw Ezra and his damn open apartment with his damn open staircase. Because seriously, this is freaking ridiculous.

Another searing pain strikes my arm, and this time it hurts so bad that both of my arms crumple and my face smacks into the stairs.

"Come on, Owen! Come on!" Alika says as she half drags me to the top of the stairs.

We make it to the top just as the two men hit the bottom of the stairs, and then it's a full-on race to the master bedroom.

Ezra slams the door shut and locks it as I race toward the closet.

"Other closet!" he shouts. "All the way in the back!" He pauses just long enough to slide a huge chest of drawers in front of the door, then follows us into the closet.

I call the elevator, and as we wait for it to come—if it's a private elevator, why the hell isn't it here already?—bullets fly against the bedroom door. They're followed by a loud crashing noise as the chest topples over and hits the floor.

Ezra slams the closet door closed and locks it just as the elevator door finally—*finally*—slides open. We jam into it, and I press the only button I can, P, followed by the CLOSE DOOR button over and over again.

The elevator door starts to slide shut just as the closet door bursts open. The last thing I hear as we start racing down, down, down is the sound of bullets striking the metal doors.

27

Harper
(5p3ct3r)

"Oh God! You're bleeding!"

"I'm fine," the Lone Ranger says, though the blood pouring out of his arm tells a different story.

"You're bleeding," I repeat. "That's not fine."

"I'm aware. But I'm also alive and walking, so the fact that I'm bleeding is the least of our problems right now."

"What *was* that?" Mad Max murmurs, sounding as shell-shocked as I feel.

"*That* was Jacento striking back at us," Silver Spoon says. "And winning." He's currently cradling Buffy's hands in his, and I realize that she's bleeding too. Both her arms and one hand are all cut up, like she rolled in glass. Which isn't totally outside the realm of possibility with what just happened up there.

Before I can comment, though, the elevator opens into the parking garage, and we all pile out.

Silver Spoon dashes over to a locker on the wall and programs in a number, and a key slides out. "Come on, let's get out of here before they make it down to finish off the job."

"Shouldn't we wait for the police?" Mad Max asks.

"Shouldn't they already be here?" the Lone Ranger follows up. "What's the point of having a forty-million-dollar penthouse if they don't even call the cops when somebody shows up to shoot the place to hell and back?"

Despite our questions, we all follow Silver Spoon as he runs to a black Lexus GX and unlocks it.

"They had silencers," I answer as I wait for the Lone Ranger to slide in and then climb in next to him. "On the guns. The gunshots were loud to us because silencers don't actually silence guns, but if the penthouse is anywhere near soundproofed—"

"It is," Silver Spoon interjects.

"Then there's no way anyone but us heard what went on up there. If they came in carrying a pizza after you told the front desk you were calling for takeout, no one would even think something was wrong." I shrug out of my hoodie, then turn to the Lone Ranger. "Did you cut yourself on all the glass, or did you get shot?"

"I'm pretty sure I got shot."

"I was afraid you were going to say that." I wrap the hoodie around his biceps to try to stanch the bleeding.

"Hey, at least I can cross it off my bucket list."

"Good point." I try to grin at him to show him it's okay. "I mean, what kind of boring person doesn't have getting shot on their bucket list?"

Snow White is peering worriedly at him from the front seat. "We've got to get him to a hospital. Now!"

"We can't," Silver Spoon tells her as he backs out of the

parking spot and races toward the garage exit. "They have to report gunshot wounds to the police."

"Fine!" Snow White shoots back. "Let them report it. We need to call the police anyway."

"And tell them what?" the Lone Ranger asks through gritted teeth. "That we're the six people who broke into Jacento today, caused major accidents on two different freeways, and wreaked havoc with the BART trains? I'm pretty sure that doesn't end too well for us."

"We're just going to have to explain," Mad Max says. "Show them the evidence and—"

"Don't you get it? There is no evidence," Silver Spoon barks.

"What do you mean, no evidence?" Buffy cries. "We have—"

"Nothing," he interrupts. "We have nothing."

"Oh no." The Lone Ranger looks like he's going to be sick as the truth sinks in.

"Ezra's right," I tell them. "Unless someone had a chance to upload something to the cloud when they got back to the apartment, everything we managed to get from those damn servers is in the apartment. Or it *was*, considering we left it in the hands of two guys from Jacento. It's probably destroyed by now."

As I explain, I urge the Lone Ranger to hold his arm over his head, then help him hold it in place, as he's weak from loss of blood and being shot. Right away the bleeding turns from steady to sluggish.

"Oh my God," Buffy moans. "Oh my God, ohmyGod, OHMYGOD! You mean we did all this for nothing?"

"Less than nothing," Silver Spoon answers, jaw working

tightly. "Considering you're hurt, Owen's shot, we're on Jacento's radar, and we lost everything anyway."

"And your apartment was just shot to hell," Mad Max reminds him, like any of us could forget. "What are you going to tell your parents?"

Before Silver Spoon can answer—and seriously, what's he going to say?—a fire truck rushes past us. Seconds later, two more come barreling after it. Suddenly I've got a really bad feeling in my stomach.

Turning around to look out the back window, I watch as, sure enough, they stop in front of Silver Spoon's building. "What are the odds someone in the building had a random fire the same time hit men decided to break into your condo and try to kill us?" I ask as he turns the corner and the fire trucks vanish from view.

"Pretty much zero," the Lone Ranger answers grimly.

"Yeah, that's what I thought."

"You think they set the penthouse on fire?" Mad Max asks. "To cover their tracks?"

Silver Spoon groans as he slams his hands down on the steering wheel. "My mom loves that damn penthouse. She's going to be so pissed. And I know that's the least of our worries right now, but *come on*!" He hits the steering wheel again.

He makes another turn, and it suddenly occurs to me that we're not racing randomly through the streets. It's obvious that he has a destination in mind.

I'm not the only one who notices, because Buffy asks, "Where are we going?"

"To a drugstore to get some stuff to clean you and Owen up. And then to the Majestic. My family keeps a suite at every hotel we own."

"There's a CVS!" Mad Max says suddenly.

"It's where I'm heading," Silver Spoon swings over to the curb way too fast.

"But how are we going to pay?" Buffy asks. "All our stuff—"

"I've got my wallet," the Lone Ranger says, his voice fainter than it was a little while ago. "I had it in my hand when the shooting started."

"Thank God!" Snow White climbs out of the front seat, then opens the passenger door and leans in. "Which pocket?"

"The right front one. But why are you the one going in?" He doesn't look pleased.

"Because Ezra's driving, and I'm the only other one in the car not covered in blood. So, looks like I'm nominated."

She's right. Mad Max has been in the back trying to help Buffy, so he's got almost as much blood on him as I have on me. Not to mention he's shirtless, since he obviously had the same idea about stanching the blood flow as I did. And both Buffy and the Lone Ranger look like they've been through a war, and lost, so... she's pretty much our only choice.

"I don't want you going in alone."

She smiles sweetly at him. "Well then, next time don't get yourself shot." Before he can say anything else, she slams the door in his face.

"Dude," Mad Max tells him from his spot in back, "sexism is so last century."

"I wasn't being sexist. I was being concerned! We're being hunted, and she's in there alone."

"She'll be fine," Silver Spoon says as he pulls back into traffic, but he doesn't sound any happier about Snow White going in alone than the Lone Ranger does. Still, it's a no-stopping zone in front of the CVS, so we've got to circle the block as we wait for her to come back out or risk attracting police attention. And since we've spent most of the day trying to avoid just that...circle, it is.

"What are we going to do?" Buffy asks, voice high and panicked, as we drive around the block. "What are we going to do?"

"I already told you—" Silver Spoon starts.

"No, I mean after we get cleaned up. What are we going to do? They've got our IDs, our computers, our clothes. They know where we live—"

"They've always known where we live," the Lone Ranger reminds her.

"Yeah, well, they didn't always want to kill us! So what do we do now?"

"I don't know," he admits.

"Well, we better figure it out! Are they going to go to our houses? Are they going to hurt our families?" She's getting more hysterical with each word she says, her breathing growing more and more ragged. "We can't even get home without our IDs. We have to warn them. We have to—"

I reach over the back of the seat and slap her. Not hard, but enough to get her attention. "Stop it!" I order as she and Mad Max stare at me in shock. "You're panicking so much you're hyperventilating, and that's not going to help anyone, especially yourself, considering the amount of blood you've lost."

"I think I have a right to panic! We're totally screwed here!"

"Yeah, well, freaking out about it isn't going to solve anything, so—"

"What if they go after my family?"

"I think we're all in the same boat when it comes to our families," Mad Max says in a soothing voice. "We need to calm down and try to figure this out—"

"We're not all in the same boat! I have five brothers and sisters I have to take care of! My dad barely comes out of his room since my mom died, and I'm all they have. If something happens to me, they'll be all alone. I can't do that to them. And what if they go after them to get to me? They're defenseless. They—"

"Okay, okay, okay." Just that quickly, Mad Max becomes the voice of reason. "There's no need to panic yet. It's not like they're going to get to San Antonio in the next hour. Once we get to the hotel, we'll get you and Owen cleaned up, and then we'll figure out the rest of this."

"How? How are we going to figure it out? We're completely screwed. How are we going to do anything?"

Before any of us can come up with an answer, Silver Spoon spots Snow White on the curb, and he pulls over to pick her up. She climbs into the car, arms loaded with bags.

"I pretty much bought out the first-aid department," she says as she drops the bags on the car floor. "And I got some juice and candy bars for Owen and Issa," she says, handing me two cold bottles of cranberry juice. I pass one to Mad Max for Buffy, then twist the cap off the other and hold it out for the Lone Ranger. "The sugar will help keep your body from going into shock," Snow White continues. "And I even got a T-shirt for Seth."

She pauses, brows raised, when she realizes how quiet we all are. "What's going on?" she asks. "What'd I miss?"

I keep my mouth shut since I don't have a clue where to start. But neither does anyone else, it seems, so we all just kind of stare blankly at her.

Finally, Silver Spoon says, "We'll fill you in at the hotel. But can you do me a favor and reach into the glove compartment? There's a leather portfolio beneath the car manual. Pull that out and open it to the back. There should be a key card to the Majestic in there."

"I hate to be the one to bring up even more obstacles," the Lone Ranger says, "but how are you going to get Issa and me through the lobby of the Majestic without causing a major crisis? I'm pretty sure they frown on blood on their Italian marble floors."

"We can go from the parking garage straight to our suite, without going through the lobby," he answers. "We try to build all our hotels like that when we can."

I urge the Lone Ranger to take a sip of the cranberry juice, but he's not interested. I've never been shot before, but I'm pretty sure the pain is worse than he's letting on. Still, Snow White's right. He has to drink something—not just for the sugar content, but to make up for all the blood he's lost.

A couple of minutes later, Silver Spoon swings into the Majestic's parking garage. And I have to say, usually parking garages all look alike, but at the Majestic, even the garage is swanky. It's one more glimpse into how the other half lives, and it's strange. I mean, who needs a fancy parking garage as long as your car is safe?

But that's the last thing I need to worry about right now. Silver Spoon stops in front of the elevator and hands me the key card. "Get them upstairs. The suite's on the twenty-second floor, room 2207. I'll be up as soon as I park."

"We're not leaving you alone!" the Lone Ranger argues. "What if we were followed?"

"If we were followed, then we're screwed anyway. So go!" The look he shoots me in the rearview mirror says it's my job to get them moving—and to take care of them. So with a quick glance over my shoulder to tap Mad Max for help, that's what I do.

I climb out of the SUV and all but pull the Lone Ranger out while Mad Max does the same for Buffy. Snow White's not budging from the front seat, but then, I didn't expect her to. The girl's got more backbone than I gave her credit for all those weeks ago.

The Lone Ranger's listing a little by the time I get him to the elevator, and I drape his good arm over my shoulder so he can lean on me. He winces as I press against him, and it's not until I feel wetness seeping through the side of my shirt that I realize. "Oh my God! You were shot twice!"

"I'm fine," he grinds out.

"Shot twice is not fine," Buffy hisses at him.

"Says the girl with the arms and hand cut to hell," he hisses back.

"It's really just one arm," she tells him. "And my hand isn't that bad."

"Oh, because that makes it so much better." He's obviously still got some fight in him, but he's pale, really pale, and it's freaking me out a little. Bandaging his wounds is one thing, but what are we going to do if he needs stitches? Or a blood transfusion?

The elevator comes before I can sink into too much of a panic, thank God. And then we're shooting up to the second floor, which is as high as the elevator goes. It bypasses the lobby, though, so I shouldn't complain—except Silver Spoon totally forgot to mention the whole traversing what feels like a two-mile-long bridge to get to the next elevator.

We pass a bunch of people, all of whom look either horrified or concerned at the sight of us. None stop us, but a couple look like they're planning on calling hotel security. I can't blame them, I guess.

It makes me walk faster even though it means hurrying the Lone Ranger along. He doesn't complain—just bites the bullet and does what has to be done. He must have seen the looks too, even though we're all trying hard to keep our heads down.

But fast is relative, because even though we're hurrying, Silver Spoon and Snow White still manage to catch us before we make it to the tower elevator.

"Sorry," Silver Spoon says as he presses the button, and it's gratifying to see that he's the one out of breath for once. "I forgot about the overpass."

"Obviously."

"How are they doing?" he asks, but he's looking only at Buffy when he asks it. Which, of course. I definitely saw that coming....

"*We're* fine," she answers him as the elevator doors slide open. Two people step out, and they look absolutely horrified as they try their best not to bump into us.

Then we're in the elevator, Silver Spoon inserting the card into a slot in the button panel before pressing 22. I guess it's a good thing he caught up with us, because I never would have known to do that.

Finally, finally, we make it to the suite. Silver Spoon opens it, and we all just kind of fall in the door. I can't remember ever being this exhausted in my life, so I can only imagine how Buffy and the Lone Ranger are feeling....

"What do we do first?" Snow White asks as soon as the door is closed.

"Get Owen to the bathroom," Mad Max says. "We're going to need towels and hot water and a floor he can bleed on."

"The main bathroom is through here," Silver Spoon says, leading us through the lavish suite to an even more lavish bedroom and bathroom. "I'll call down to the front desk and tell them we're here—and also that we'll need a lot more towels."

Then he turns to Snow White. "Why don't you take Issa to the other bathroom and start cleaning up her arms while I do that?"

Suddenly the bathroom's a lot less crowded, but I'm so focused on the Lone Ranger—and on what I'm going to have to do—that I barely notice.

"Before we start, we should get out everything we're going to need," Mad Max says, gesturing to the bags Snow White left behind.

"Yeah, okay. Why don't you do that while I help the Lone Ranger here out of his shirt?"

"Is that my nickname?" he asks as I unwrap my blood-soaked hoodie from around his arm.

"It was that or Desperado. I took a risk," I say as I begin unbuttoning his shirt.

"I like it," he says, but he stiffens as I start pulling his shirt away from his arm. "Though I have to say, this is the first time I haven't enjoyed a girl undressing me. No offense."

"None taken," I answer drily. "Believe me, there are about three thousand, two hundred twenty-seven things I'd rather be doing right now."

"Really? That many?" At my urging, he sits down on the closed toilet seat.

"Probably more. I was rounding down, trying to be nice." I start to poke at his side, then realize I need to wash up first—and, hopefully, put on a pair of gloves, if Snow White thought to buy them.

Turns out she did, because by the time I'm done washing my hands, Mad Max has a pair of gloves on and is holding out another pair to me. I slip them on, then press gently on the Lone Ranger's side as I try to estimate how deep the wound is.

"Owww!" he yells, his whole body tightening up like I just electrocuted him.

"Don't be such a baby," I tell him as I crouch down to get a better look. "It's barely a scratch."

"Made by a bullet," he says sulkily.

"Bullet shmullet. Man up." As I stand back up, I tell him, "Turn to the side a little. I want to see your arm now."

"I'm sure it's just a scratch too," he replies.

"Awww, did I hurt your feelings?" I ask as I poke at the wound.

I take the fact that he doesn't immediately swear at me as a bad sign. Sure enough, a glance at his face shows that he's gone pale and clammy and that he's grinding his teeth together hard enough to permanently damage his molars.

Not that I blame him. His side wound was just a graze, but this is something different. It's still a flesh wound, I think, but the bullet passed clean through, leaving a jagged hole on both sides of the Lone Ranger's biceps. A hole that continues to seep blood.

I exchange a worried look with Mad Max, who starts lining up all kinds of first-aid supplies on the ledge of the bathtub... including a surgical suturing kit.

I do my best not to look at it as I grab the box of Advil Snow White bought and start peeling it open. "So, do you want the good news or the bad news?" I ask.

"Is there any good news when it comes to getting shot?" the Lone Ranger replies.

"The bullet passed straight through your biceps, so it's not like we have to dig for it."

"Well, thank God for that." He glances at the bathtub and—if possible—turns even paler. "I'm assuming the bad news is that we need to stitch this thing up?"

I swallow and try really hard not to puke. "Yeah. I think so."

"Awesome." His tone says it's anything but.

"I think you should probably take some Advil," I tell him, holding out three of the pills. "And maybe some Tylenol too."

"Great. This is going to be freaking awesome." He tosses the pills in his mouth, swallowing them dry before I even get him a glass of water. Mad Max hands him two extra-strength Tylenol, and he swallows them too. "Let's get this over with, huh?"

I nod, even though my stomach is churning. "We need to clean it first," I say, and at this point I'm not sure whom I'm talking to. The Lone Ranger, Mad Max, or myself.

I guess it doesn't really matter, though Mad Max hands me a can of sterile saline wound cleanser. "I think you start with this," he says. "To clean off all the blood and wash out the wound. Then we use peroxide and Betadine to kill bacteria before we stitch him up."

"Right. Sure. Of course." I swallow hard. Then again and again.

"Hey," the Lone Ranger asks suddenly, "you okay, Harper?"

"Great. I'm . . . great. Better than you, anyway."

He laughs. "Yeah, well, you're looking pretty pale there, girl. Don't want you to pass out on us."

"I've never passed out in my life," I tell him. "And I have no intention of starting now."

Still, it takes every ounce of courage I've got to spray his arm with the wound cleaner. He doesn't flinch, but I can tell it hurts from the way he goes silent—and from the drops of sweat that suddenly pop out on his forehead.

After I finish dousing the cut with saline and patting away the blood with sterile gauze, Mad Max hands me a bottle of alcohol, top already removed.

"I'm sorry," I say, but the Lone Ranger just shakes his head.

"Not your fault. I appreciate you doing it—I know you don't want to."

"Yeah, well, we don't always get what we want, do we?"

"Guess not."

"So, here goes nothing," I say, holding his arm out and positioning the bottle above the wound. His jaw is so tight that I'm afraid he's going to break a tooth.

"Hey!" Mad Max interrupts. "Why are ghosts such bad liars?"

"What?" The Lone Ranger looks at him like he's crazy.

"Because you can see right through them. What do you call a pig that does karate?"

"I have no— Son of a bitch!" the Lone Ranger yells as I pour pretty much the entire bottle of alcohol over and around his wound.

"A pork chop!" Mad Max finishes.

For a second, there's absolute silence. Then all three of us start to laugh...a little hysterically, mind you, but it's a million times better than crying.

I reach for the Betadine next, and just as Mad Max asks,

"Why do bees have sticky hair?" I squirt a liberal amount over the wound.

"I have no freaking idea," the Lone Ranger answers hoarsely. He's shaking now, his whole body trembling as I dry off the area around the injury with more gauze.

"Because they have honeycombs."

The Lone Ranger closes his eyes, kind of slumps against the wall. "When we manage to get the hell out of this mess, I'm totally going to buy you a new joke book."

"I'll take you up on that." Mad Max finishes threading the needle, but when I start to take it from him, he shakes his head. "I think you might be shaking worse than Owen," he murmurs softly.

I look down at my hands and realize he's right. There's no way I'll be able to even attempt stitches in this state.

"So, how about this?" Mad Max proposes as he uses one of the clamps from the surgical kit to hold the edges of the wound together. "Owen keeps his eyes closed, I keep my eyes open, and you let him squeeze your hand as hard as he wants while I get this done."

"I'm okay," the Lone Ranger says. Of course he does. And a few weeks ago—hell, a few days ago—I'd have taken him at his word. But if these last couple of days have taught me anything, it's that friendship comes in all forms. It's okay to need someone—and to let someone need you.

So I sit down on the side of the tub closest to the Lone Ranger, and I slide my palm across his. He doesn't say anything, doesn't even look at me, but when his fingers close around mine, I know I've done the right thing.

For both of us.

And if I end up losing a few fingers from lack of circulation… well, at least they've made great strides in vocal recognition software lately.

28

Issa
[Pr1m4 D0nn4]

I can hear Ezra prowling around the sitting room, and it makes me nervous. I don't know why, since he's been nothing but gentle with me since this mess happened. But there's something in his voice, something in the way he can't sit still that sets me on edge. That has me thinking something's really wrong...besides the obvious, I mean.

In the ten minutes we've been in this insane suite, he's called the front desk to let them know we're here and to ask for more towels, room service to order enough food to feed a professional sports team, and his parents—presumably to explain this mess, but Alika and I can't tell for sure because his voice is muffled.

I wince as Alika picks another piece of glass out of my forearm with the huge surgical tweezers she bought at CVS. It's not the glass removal that hurts so much, but that she sterilized the tweezers by soaking them in alcohol for five minutes before she was willing to put them anywhere near my skin.

"I'm sorry," she says for what feels like the hundredth time.

"Your one arm isn't too bad, and I'm almost done with your hand. It's your left arm I'm worried about. There are some really deep gashes. I'm sure I got out all the glass at least, but these cuts must hurt like hell."

"It's okay. It really doesn't hurt that bad. Not like, say, a gunshot wound."

Not for the first time, she glances out the door like she expects Owen to just appear in front of her. "It's totally okay if you want to go check on him," I tell her. "I'd like to know how he's doing too." Plus, I could really use a break. It's taking all my energy to keep up the cheerful front when I'm exhausted—from the pain, the blood loss, and the whole disaster that was today.

"No." She shakes her head firmly. "We're almost finished here. I think there's only a few slivers left, then we'll clean and bandage you up, and you'll be good to go. Well, as good to go as you can be."

She says it with all the sympathy in the world in her voice, and I try not to think about how bad a mess my left arm is…or how long the deep, jagged cuts will take to heal. Just like I try not to think about how I'm supposed to code or change Chloe's diaper or cook dinner or do my schoolwork with only one good hand—especially when that hand is attached to a forearm that's been cut to hell.

It all seems so impossible right now.

But at least I wasn't shot, I remind myself. At least I'm not lying dead on Ezra's floor because some assholes decided they want to rule the world. That has to count for something. Not much, at this point, but something.

"Okay, brace yourself," Alika tells me as she digs for a particularly deep shard of glass. "I think this one is going to hurt."

She's right, it does. And even though I steel myself, I still end up whimpering a little as the sting turns into full-blown pain.

"I'm sorry, I'm sorry!" she says again.

Again, I assure her that it's all right.

But then Ezra's there in the doorway, looking more disheveled than I've ever seen him. "Are you okay?" he demands, gaze hot and voice guttural.

"I'm fine."

He studies me with narrowed eyes, like he's trying to decide if I'm telling the truth, before turning to Alika, like she's more reliable, even though I'm the one in pain. "How's it going?"

"I'm on the last one, I think. I need to wash her wounds off again and check when they're clean, but I really do think this is it," she says as she triumphantly brandishes a thick, half-inch-long piece of glass. One that hurt like hell to have taken out, though I didn't make a sound this time.

"I can help her wash up," Ezra says as Alika drops the last piece of glass in the trash can at her feet. "If you want to go check on Owen or something."

For a moment, Alika looks like she's going to argue. But something changes her mind because suddenly she's stripping off her gloves and sending me a reassuring smile before slipping out the door.

Then Ezra is taking her place, cradling my hand in his palms as he studies the damage for several long, silent seconds.

And I don't know why I feel the need to reassure him when I'm the injured one, but I do.

"It's not as bad as it looks," I whisper as his thumbs stroke the area that isn't cut.

"You don't have to lie to me," he answers, his voice all low and gravelly and too sexy for my own good. "I know what I did to you, and I'm sorry. God, I'm sorry, Issa."

"You saved my life. That's not exactly something you need to apologize for."

"I sent you crashing to the floor in the middle of all that glass. This happened because of me." He looks so tortured that part of me wants to kiss him again and part of me wants to smack him upside the head.

Considering the shape I'm in, I decide to go for something in the middle—namely a firm verbal slapping that might bring him back to reality from whatever guilt-ridden angst he's currently languishing in. "And if you hadn't done it, I might have a bullet between my eyes right now. Given those two options, I'd much rather deal with some cuts. Cuts will heal. So stop beating yourself up and making this all about you, for God's sake. It could have been so much worse—for all of us."

He still looks upset, but at least now he's smiling a little too. "You have a really low tolerance for drama, you know that?"

"I take care of five siblings, including two toddlers and a baby. Believe me when I tell you they give me all the drama I could ever want or need."

"I can imagine. I'm an only child, but in my family, my mom brings just about all the drama I can handle. She can be very…passionate about certain things, and she makes sure my father and I know it."

I wonder if one of those things is the revolving door on his bedroom, as documented by the gossip press, but I'm nowhere near brave enough to ask. Especially not when he gently tugs me over to the sink and starts running warm water over my hand.

The second the water hits my palm, pain explodes along my nerve endings. Involuntarily, I jerk my hand back, but Ezra holds on to my wrist and keeps me in place as water cascades across my palm and between my fingers before slowly making its way down the drain.

"*Lo siento*," he murmurs to me in Spanish, along with a bunch of other words I don't recognize that somehow calm me down anyway.

"What's that mean?" I ask, when he repeats something melodious sounding a few times in a row.

He looks up from the sink, curious. "Are you telling me you don't speak Spanish, Miss Torres?"

"That's exactly what I'm telling you! I didn't grow up speaking Spanish in my house, and I'll have you know that I took French in school."

He chuckles softly. "Okay, then. What didn't you understand? *Dulzura*?"

"Yes."

He ducks his head a little, and if I didn't know better, I'd think he was blushing. "It just means you're sweet."

It's my turn to narrow my eyes at him. "Are you sure that's all it means?"

He doesn't answer me. Instead, he makes a show of checking out my thoroughly rinsed hand and finally, finally, letting me take it out from under the water. I breathe a sigh of relief as the stinging stops, but seconds later he wraps his hand around my left wrist and pulls my forearm under the water to clean it as well. The pain starts all over again, as does the softly murmured Spanish.

When it's finally over, when he's turned off the water and is slowly, gently, *carefully* patting my hand and arms dry with the fluffiest towel I've ever seen, I finally say what's been on my mind for a while.

"You know, you're different than I thought you were going to be."

He stops what he's doing long enough to look up at me with one raised brow. "Different how?"

"When we first met in L.A., you didn't seem to care about anything but yourself, anything but winning. I misjudged you."

"No, you didn't." He grins for the first time since this whole nightmare began. But it's not a warm grin, not the grin I've grown used to these last couple of days. "Don't make the mistake of thinking I'm more than I am. Just because I got involved in this crazy scheme with you doesn't mean you were wrong about me."

He says it so flippantly, so matter-of-factly, that I might actually believe him. If he wasn't simultaneously smoothing antibiotic ointment over my cuts with the softest hands imaginable, taking great care to make sure every inch—every millimeter—of my raw, hurt skin is covered.

I want to call him on it—the difference between perception and reality, including his own—but something warns me against it. Maybe it's because we've had enough tonight. Maybe it's because I'm not ready for that heavy of a discussion. Or maybe it's because I'm scared of digging too deeply. Whatever it is keeps me silent long past when I should have refuted what he said.

Finally, when my hand and arms are bandaged and as fixed as they're going to get, at least for now, he steps back and lowers his hands. I'm not sure if I'm disappointed or grateful, but I do know that I can think more clearly when Ezra isn't touching me. And since I need to think clearly tonight, I guess I'll go with grateful.

I step around him and out of the bathroom, then freeze—terrified—when a knock sounds at the door.

"It's probably just the towels," Ezra tells me, but I notice he's wary too when he walks toward the door. And he makes sure to check the peephole before finally opening the door—with the chain still on.

Turns out he's right, and seconds later he's carrying a stack of towels into the suite's main bedroom and bathroom, where the others are currently working on patching Owen back together.

I can't believe he was shot. Can't believe how close the rest of us came to being shot. To dying. I think about Chloe, and instinct makes me reach for my phone to check on her.

But even before my bandaged hand makes the reach difficult, I remember. I don't have my phone. Don't have my laptop or my backpack or my wallet or my clothes. I don't have anything of mine but the torn, bloodied clothes on my back. Worse, my family has no way of reaching me.

I have to fix that, as soon as possible. The idea of spending money on a new phone and laptop hurts, but not as much as being without them.

An agonized groan sounds from the other room, and I can't help staring at the empty doorway. So far, I haven't gone back there because I figure the last thing they need is another body getting in the way. But I'm worried about Owen, worried about how pale and shaky he was on the way up here. Worried more about the fact that he's been shot and we can't even take him to a hospital.

A minute or so passes and Ezra comes back out, looking a little shaky himself. "Is he okay?" I cry, jumping to my feet.

"He's fine. They're stitching him up—the bullet passed right through his biceps and left a big hole." His smile looks a little sickly. "Guess it's a good thing he's got a big biceps."

He crosses to the wet bar in the corner, pulls out a bottle of water and brings it to me. "Alika bought some Advil. I brought you two, thought it might help dull the pain a little."

"Thanks." I start to take them, struggling to hold the water bottle and the pills with my one good hand.

Ezra realizes my dilemma and sort of whispers, "Open your mouth."

I do, and he puts the two pills on my tongue, then holds the water bottle to my mouth as I swallow them down. My one hand still works just fine, but I let him do it. It's not that uncommon of a gesture—something mothers do with children, nurses do with patients—and yet when Ezra does it for me, it feels more intimate than that kiss we shared earlier.

Like almost everything else that's happened in the last few hours, I don't know what it means. But I'm smart enough to know that I'm not going to touch it either. Not now, when so many other things need to be dealt with.

By the time room service arrives, the others have all staggered into the sitting room to join Ezra and me. Even Owen makes an appearance, in a white terry cloth bathrobe that is almost as pale as his complexion.

"Shouldn't you be sleeping?" I ask as he half sits, half collapses onto the couch next to me.

He just looks at me. "Shouldn't you?"

"Touché."

He tries to smile but it comes out more like a grimace. "Exactly."

Ezra waves at the covered plates resting on the room-service carts against the wall. "I didn't know what anybody was in the mood for at this point, so I got a little bit of everything. If there's something you want that isn't there, let me know, and I'll order it. Otherwise, dig in."

It takes a few minutes—I think we're all kind of shell-shocked now that the immediate danger has passed—but eventually Seth gets up and starts making himself a plate. Harper and Alika follow suit, though Alika brings the plate she made over to Owen.

I'm starving, but my hand and arms have finally stopped hurting. Just the idea of changing that by trying to pick up food or serving utensils or whatever is enough to make me decide I'm not that hungry after all.

It turns out I don't have to do anything, though, because suddenly Ezra is sitting on the ottoman in front of me, a plate of finger foods on his lap. It takes a second for it to sink in that he made the plate for me, and it takes even longer to sink in that he's planning on feeding me himself. Eventually I get it, though, obediently opening my mouth as he forks up a blackberry or a French fry or a piece of cheese and holds it to my lips.

"You don't have to do this," I tell him after a few bites. "My one hand is okay."

He just shakes his head at me and mutters, "Shut up," before shoving more food in my mouth.

When we've all eaten our fill and the dishes and carts have been moved into the hallway, Seth clears his throat and asks, "So are we going to talk about this or what?"

Before he can answer, though, there's another knock on the door. It has me tensing up, has every single one of us freezing as we look toward the door. And when Ezra finally pulls open the door to reveal a waiter carrying a giant pastry basket, "courtesy of the employees," I feel something inside me break. Feel the feelings that I've been carrying around all day coalescing into one loud, resounding "No."

"I can't do this anymore," I tell the suddenly silent room. "I just can't. I'm out, and I'm going home the first chance I get."

29

Owen
(1nf1n173 5h4d3)

It's been hours since Issa's proclamation, and we still haven't talked to her about it, still haven't tried to suss out how serious she is about leaving. Instead we all just kind of wander around the suite staring at one another and deliberately not looking at her.

After all, it's easy to get what she's saying. It's even easier to get what she's thinking—God knows there's a part of me that just spent the last couple of hours thinking the very same thing. Especially when Seth was sewing up the bullet hole in my arm and I thought I was going to pass out from the pain.

But getting where she's coming from is one thing. Actually quitting before we see this through is something else altogether. Which is why I wait all night for somebody else to say that, wait for anybody else to say anything at all. But it's like we're right back in that office building in L.A., when they were all too busy looking at their shoes to actually get something meaningful out of their mouths. When they were too busy staring at what was right in front of them to see the big picture.

And that scares me in a way nothing else that's happened in the last twenty-four hours—including getting shot—ever could. Because it means they haven't learned a damn thing in the last few weeks, the last few days. It means they don't get it, and maybe they never will. I don't expect much from Ezra, because...come on. He's Ezra. But Alika? Harper? Seth, who always seems to know the right thing to do and always wants to do it?

I thought for sure they'd have something to say. Instead it's like crickets in here. And I'm not okay with that. Which is why I do the only thing I can do in this situation. I open my mouth somewhere around seven in the morning and let the chips fall where they may.

"You know, of anyone in this room, I thought you'd be the one to get this the most. After all, you've gone on and on about how you have to protect your brothers and sisters. And yet, you just want to give up? You just want to let them grow up in this screwed-up world that Jacento is trying so hard to be in control of? I mean, seriously, if today's taught you anything, it should be that they can't be trusted to be in control of anything, let alone the world that we're going to have to live in."

Issa stiffens like I slapped her. "Don't you dare use my family against me. You don't know what it's like to be the only one they depend on. To be the one who has to take care of everything."

"And you don't know what I have to deal with! You don't know what my family is like—and you don't even care enough to ask. Instead, you sit there like this perfect little martyr and say you have to quit for them, when the truth is you're quitting for you. You're quitting because you're afraid."

"Hey!" Suddenly Alika's there between us, eyes fierce and narrowed. "Cool it!"

"That seems to be your job!" I tell her. "It seems to be all of your jobs right now. You're so busy enabling her, so busy being caught up in what *might* happen that you don't see what *is* happening. And what is *going* to happen if you don't stand up and do something to stop it.

"Do you think I want to be here?" I gesture to my bandaged arm. "I'm the only one who wanted no part of this from the very beginning. But sometimes what you want doesn't matter. Sometimes life is just about doing the right thing.

"And yes, that means making sacrifices. And doing things that scare you and might not work out in the end. But what's the alternative? Sitting back and letting a corporation like Jacento take over everything?

"You guys created Phantom Wheel, and then you gave it to them on a silver freaking platter. And now they're going to use it to record every keystroke you and everyone else on the planet makes—on your phone, on your laptop, on your tablet, in your gaming systems. Every single thing you buy or search, every person you text, every Tumblr you follow, every Instagram you like. And for what? To sell that info to the highest bidder so they can figure out what you'll buy or who you'll vote for? Or worse, how they can take that information and get you to do what they want you to do? Is that really the kind of world you want to live in?"

I look from one face to another, searching for something. Some evidence that my words are getting through to them, some sign that they're listening to what I'm saying instead of what their fear is telling them. I find it in Harper, who is suddenly the only one willing to meet my eyes.

So I look straight at Harper as I continue. "And believe me, I get it. This isn't what you signed up for when you went to that fake CIA audition. But at some point, we have to take responsibility for fixing what we did, even if that means taking Jacento on. Even if it means getting hurt in the process."

"That's so easy for you to say," Issa says as she wraps her heavily bandaged arms around her knees like she's trying to make herself as small as possible. "If something happens to you, it'll suck for your family. But no one depends on you. No one needs you to stay alive—"

"You know what, screw you."

"I'm sorry," she says with a shrug. "But it's true. I can't afford to think of the world. I have to think of my family—"

"You're such a damn coward I can't even believe it." I look from her to the rest of them. "All of you, sitting here so afraid of what will happen to you that you don't care who suffers. You think this is easy for me? Just uprooting my life to take on Jacento? Because it's not.

"We're pretty damn sure my dad has CTE. Do you know what that is? Do you even freaking have a clue what that is?"

Issa shakes her head, a little wide eyed now that I'm yelling. I tell myself to calm down, to stop yelling, but I can't. Not now that I've finally said those words out loud.

"It stands for chronic traumatic encephalopathy. And what it means is that he's spent so many years getting hit in the head on the football field that his brain is Swiss cheese. It means that my dad—the man I used to look up to, the man who used to do anything for his family—barely remembers us most days. And those are the good days.

"The not-so-good days are when he flies into a rage for no apparent reason. When he throws shit and breaks shit. When he hits me or—when I'm not around to stop him—my mom. When he drives the car into the side of the house. That's what CTE is.

"And it's loving him anyway, even when I'm so angry I can barely breathe. Because the man who does those things isn't my father. He doesn't do them because he has anger issues or because he's violent or because he wants to hurt us. He does them because he's sick, and there's not a damn thing I or my mother or any doctor on the freaking planet can do about it.

"Every minute that I'm at school, I worry about my mother being in the house with him. Every second that I'm here I'm terrified he's going to snap and hurt her, or my brother, who came home from college for Christmas break and said he'd take care of them but can't deal with my father's episodes or the fact that my mother and I still love him.

"But how can we not? He has a disease that's literally breaking his brain to pieces and killing him right in front of us. And if you think I don't want to be home right now, trying to protect my mom, trying to keep my dad from driving his truck into a telephone pole, then you're nuts.

"Because hard as that is, I'd rather be there. At least I'd know what was going on. At least I'd have some kind of control. I wouldn't be worried sick every minute of every day. Because

I'd be there. No matter what happens, I would freaking be there to do whatever I could. Whatever I had to do.

"And instead I'm here, beating my head against a wall because it's the right thing to do. Because Jacento can't be allowed to just get away with destroying any semblance of privacy we have left and doing whatever the hell they want to do to manipulate us. Because what the hell kind of world is that to live in? What kind of world is that for your brothers and sisters to grow up in?"

I push off the sofa because I can't sit still any longer. Any more than I can stand the pitying looks in all their eyes. Including Alika's. Especially Alika's.

I walk over to the glass doorway that leads to the balcony that overlooks San Francisco and stare out the window as I try to get myself back under control. As I try to figure out how to face the others now that they know. As I try to figure out what to say to convince her—to convince all of them—that this is a fight we can't give up.

A fight we have to win.

But the truth is, I've got nothing. Nothing but what I've already said.

"But if we do this, if we go after Jacento again, what's to keep them from going after our families this time?" I hear Issa ask. "What's to keep them from sending someone to my door in San Antonio and killing my dad, my brothers and sisters? We don't have security or any money to pay for protection. There's nothing, Owen, and I can't live with that."

I nod, because that I do get. The fiery throbbing in my arm

is a reminder every second of just how much is at risk here. Just how much we all have to lose.

Leaning forward, I rest my head against the cool glass and close my eyes. Count to ten. Try to figure out how to deal with failing. Again.

"We all have families we're worried about," Seth starts, but Harper cuts him off.

"I don't."

"Okay, but you have a foster family, right?"

"No. I haven't had anybody since I was fourteen years old and hacked into social services to change my records to read that I'd been adopted."

"Wait. You've been alone since you were fourteen?" Alika repeats. "Like totally, completely alone in the world?"

"Yep, totally, completely alone. It beats being in foster care with jerks who thought the money the state gave them to take care of me meant they could do whatever they wanted to me." She stands up, walks over next to me, and stares at the city too. "It's why I started hacking, to get myself out of that situation. I keep hacking now because it's how I support myself while I finish high school, but that's how it started."

She takes a deep breath. "I'm with you, Owen. Whatever you think we should do, I'm in."

I shudder a little at the support, then wrap an arm around her shoulders and pull her in for an awkward, one-armed hug that she only half returns. Because she's come a long way in a few days, but she's still Harper.

"I'm in too," Seth says, springing up from his spot on the

floor. "I mean, I need to call my parents and tell them to be careful, but I'm in." He walks over to where Harper and I are standing.

But when I nod my thanks at him, he gives me the most ridiculous puppy dog eyes I've ever seen. "Hey, don't I get a hug too?"

Harper cracks up and so do I, then we're both pulling him in for a bear hug while the other three just kind of watch.

"You get more than a hug," she says, walking to the pastry basket that's still sitting on the table near the door. "You get the only blueberry scone in the place, since I know how much you like them."

As she holds out the pastry, Seth's face lights up almost as much as it did when she hugged him.

We all watch as he devours the thing in three seconds flat. But once he's done, the silence gets heavy again, until Ezra finally stretches his legs out in front of him and says, "My parents are on their way here to deal with the whole penthouse mess. They'll be here tomorrow night, and I've been told very explicitly not to move from this spot under threat of losing everything I love about my life. But, hey, I haven't done what they've wanted since *I* was fourteen. Why change now?"

He stands up and walks toward us. "I'm in, but if you hug me, Seth—or get crumbs from that damn blueberry scone on me—I swear to God, I'm throwing you off the balcony."

Then he looks at Issa, like he's just waiting for her to make the right choice. And I get it, because I'm standing here waiting for Alika to do the same thing.

"I promise I'll take care of your family, Issa," Ezra says after several long seconds of the two of them just staring at each other, waiting. "Whether you do this with us or not, I'll call up my dad's security team right now, get someone over to your apartment in San Antonio within the hour to watch out for your baby sister and the rest of your family." He glances from one of us to the next. "I can do that for all of you, if you'll let me. It's not much, but it's one less thing for us to worry about if we're going to do this."

"My parents don't need protection," Alika says as she too stands up and makes her way over to us. "My dad's job means they have Secret Service around them at all times."

Relief nearly makes my knees weak—or maybe that's just the whole losing-a-ton-of-blood thing. Whatever it is, I grab her with my good arm as soon as she's close enough and pull her into my chest. I hold her there, refusing to let go. The fact that she makes no move to step away makes it even better.

And then there was one. Issa sits cross-legged on the floor, playing with a tuft of carpet next to her knee and refusing to look at any of us.

We wait for what seems like forever for her to change her mind, and I'm about to say, *Never mind, we get it, go home to them*, when she lifts her head and pins Ezra with the most deadly serious look I've ever seen.

"You swear you'll keep them safe?"

"I swear," he answers. "Call your dad and tell him to expect two security guards at your apartment. And a temporary nanny, if that will make things easier."

"You don't have to do that. They'll manage—"

"I know, but why should they have to?" He holds a hand out to her. "There are a lot of things in life money doesn't fix. But this is one thing it can. Let me do this for you, because God knows we can't do everything we need to do without you."

Her eyes fill with tears, and she nods before slowly climbing to her feet and walking toward us. She doesn't stop until she's right in front of Ezra. "I'm in."

"Thank God." Ezra grabs her and pulls her toward him. Buries his face in her neck and just breathes. It's a tender moment—and a real one—so I turn away, try not to look.

At least until Issa says, "Looks like we're storming the castle, then."

"What did you say?" Seth asks incredulously.

"I said we're storming the castle." When we all just stare at her blankly, she looks offended. "You know, from *The Princess Bride*?"

"Yes, we know from *The Princess Bride*," Harper tells her. "But the quote is 'Have fun storming the castle'!"

"I know that. It's like the one movie quote I actually *do* know. I was just paraphrasing."

"You can't paraphrase movie quotes," I tell her. "Otherwise they're not quotes."

"Seriously?" she replies. "After everything we've been through, and everything we still have to do, this is where you're going to draw the line?"

I shrug. "A boy's got to have his standards."

"Ugh, seriously?" Harper says. "You're quoting *Real Genius* now?"

"Excuse me, but that's like one of the most iconic movies of the eighties," Seth tells her, totally offended. "Maybe of all time."

"Give me a break." She rolls her eyes. "It's got Val Kilmer in it."

"Exactly my point!"

"Are you dissing Val Kilmer now?" I demand. It's ridiculous to have this argument right now, with everything we still have to figure out in the next twenty-four hours, but I do it anyway. Because there's something awesome about putting aside the enormity of what we have in front of us—even for just a few seconds—to enjoy being here with five people I've grown to care way too much about in way too short a time.

"It's Val Kilmer," Harper tells me, like that explains everything.

"Excuse me, but Val Kilmer has been in some of the greatest movies ever."

She looks at me like I've lost my mind. "Really?"

"Yeah, really!"

"Name five."

"What?"

She crosses her arms and leans a shoulder against the balcony door. "List five Val Kilmer movies that qualify for the 'best movies of all time' list."

"Well, *Top Gun*, obviously. *Real Genius. Willow. Heat.* Aaaaaand—"

"*Top Secret!*" Seth jumps to my rescue.

"*Top Secret!*?" she asks incredulously.

"I would have gone with *The Doors* myself," Ezra says.

"Oh, that is a good one." Seth smiles innocently at Harper. "See, there's six."

"It's like you're actually insane," she says.

"Well, obviously," Alika tells her. "Otherwise, what the hell are we doing here?"

That shuts Harper up. Actually, it shuts all of us up. Because she's right. What we're about to do is absolutely insane by every definition I can think of. But if we're lucky, it will be just insane enough to work.

Because the alternative really doesn't bear thinking about.

30

Harper
[5p3ct3r]

"Okay, we need laptops, phones, fake passports, clothes, backpacks, and—oh yeah—six plane tickets to Helsinki for tomorrow," the Lone Ranger says, reading off the list we just made. "Am I missing anything?"

"You mean besides an actual plan?" Silver Spoon deadpans.

"Well, yeah. Besides that."

"Six straitjackets, maybe?" Snow White volunteers. "Because, seriously, where are we going to get all that on such short notice?"

"And how much is it going to cost?" Buffy adds.

"Don't worry about cost right now," Silver Spoon says. "We're saving the world from the threat of evil domination. Whatever it costs is worth it."

"Spoken like the rich boy you are," Buffy taunts.

He gives her a pitying look. "Is this because you're still bitter about *The Princess Bride*?"

"I'm not bitter," she says with a little pout. "But since you brought it up, that quote should totally have counted."

"No, it shouldn't have!" the Lone Ranger argues. "You have to be exact or it's not a quote. Like, 'Of all the gin joints in all the towns in all the world, she walks into mine.'"

"Right?" Silver Spoon agrees. "Or 'Sorry, guys. I gotta see about a girl.'"

"Ooooh, good line," I agree, because it is. And because being a part of something is starting to feel more and more familiar. "But my all-time favorite still comes from *The Cutting Edge*."

"'Toe pick!'" Silver Spoon, the Lone Ranger, Mad Max, and I all shout at once.

Buffy and Snow White look at us like we're crazy. "I stand corrected," Snow White says after a minute. "I'm not sure strait-jackets will hold them."

"I guess you have to see the movie to get it," I tell her.

"You think?" Buffy answers with a snort. "You're on me about storming the castle, and you think 'Toe pick' is a line?"

"You're right. Not bitter at all," the Lone Ranger teases.

"Speaking of bitter," Silver Spoon says, "let's get back to the plan that's not yet a plan."

"Nice segue," Mad Max tells him, with a roll of his eyes.

"Thanks." Silver Spoon flips him off. "As I was saying before I was so rudely interrupted, I'll take care of the plane tickets for tonight."

"Issa and I can take care of the laptops and phones," Mad Max volunteers. "I mean, as long as we get to use Owen's credit card."

"What's mine is yours," he says, tossing Mad Max his wallet.

"I can do you better than that," Silver Spoon says, walking

into the master bedroom. He comes back a couple of minutes later with several bundles of hundred-dollar bills that he tosses onto the coffee table.

For a second we all just kind of stare at it. I've never seen that much money in one place in my life, and he acts like it's nothing. I can't imagine what that feels like. I'm not even sure I'd want to.

But he's right about one thing. Having money does make some things easier.

"If you give me some of that, I can definitely take care of the fake passports," I say. When the five of them turn to stare at me, I just kind of shrug. "I've got a contact in Walnut Creek who can help me."

"In *Walnut Creek*?" Silver Spoon asks incredulously. "You have a contact in the *suburbs* who can get you six fake passports in a day that are good enough to get us into Europe?"

"Yeah. I do."

"Okay, then." He tosses me a bundle of money. "That's ten thousand dollars. Do you think you'll need more?"

"That should cover it. If not, I'll let you know."

He just grins at me. "I don't know why it makes me so freaking happy to know that you have black-market contacts in the burbs, but it just really kind of does."

"Well, as long as it makes you happy, who am I to complain?"

"So what's left?" Mad Max asks after everyone stops laughing.

"Clothes and toiletries," Snow White answers. "Which I can do, if Ezra is willing to drive me to the nearest mall."

"You might want to do that first," Buffy suggests. "Because

I'm not sure how far we're going to get walking around in these blood-splattered clothes."

"I've already taken care of that," Silver Spoon tells her. "Any minute now, the shops should be sending something up for each of us to wear today."

Of course they are. The others all sound surprised, like they can't believe he thought of it. But it's totally Silver Spoon. He may act like he doesn't care—maybe when we first met, he really didn't—but now? Now he's almost always the first one to figure out what needs to be done, and the first one to actually do it. And if that's not caring in some way, then I don't know what is.

"Which leaves me with figuring out the plan," the Lone Ranger says with such an evil gleam in his eyes that, I swear, if he had a mustache he'd be twirling it right now.

"Should we be scared?" I ask, brows raised.

"You should be completely terrified," he responds, deadpan.

"Well, as long as we're on the same page."

A knock on the door makes us all jump, tension filling the room so quickly that it's hard to imagine we were laughing and joking around a few seconds ago.

"It's just the clothes from downstairs," Silver Spoon says. But I notice that he's careful to check the peephole and then opens the door with the chain still attached.

It makes me wonder if any of us will ever feel safe opening a door again or if we'll be haunted for the rest of our lives by what happened yesterday at Silver Spoon's condo. I know I'll never react to a knock or doorbell the same way....

After Silver Spoon distributes the clothes—and we're all dressed in outfits a hundred times preppier than anything we've ever worn before or ever will again—I shove the bundle of cash into the pocket of my denim skirt and slip out of the hotel room.

It's a long train ride out to Walnut Creek, and I want to get this over with as soon as possible.

Case Study:
Issa Torres aka Pr1m4 D0nn4

DOB: 1/12/00
Sex: Female
Height: 5'4"
Weight: 125 lbs.
Eye Color: Brown
Hair Color: Brown with a little bit of purple mixed in
Race: Mixed (Hispanic and white)
School: Denver Heights High School (public), San Antonio
Parents: David Torres and Samantha Lane Torres (deceased)
Personal Net Worth: $3,000
Family Net Worth: Negligible

Most Notorious Hack: Hacking the College Board for SAT answers and the subsequent distribution of them to students in poor communities. Never been done before, and to my knowledge, the College Board still doesn't know it happened.

OBSERVATIONS:

At first glance, Issa Torres is nobody's manic pixie dream girl. In fact, I'm pretty sure that if you looked up the term in Urban Dictionary, a picture of her would be listed under antonyms. Maybe with the warning: APPROACH AT YOUR OWN RISK.

She's got attitude, no doubt about it. But after getting to know her, I've figured out there's more to Torres than meets the eye—even if what meets the eye is a defiant stare, a pair of combat boots, and enough rage to power a small town.

Basically, she's also a lot more vulnerable than she lets on. Not weak, because she's as tough as they come. But definitely vulnerable. Despite all the outer trappings, she's just a good girl trying to do right by her family and make a life for herself.

I don't want to relate to her, but I do.

SURVEILLANCE FOOTAGE:
12/29/18
23:21
PRIVATE HERNANDEZ BALCONY,
MAJESTIC HOTEL
SAN FRANCISCO, CALIFORNIA

Footage begins at 23:21 when Issa Torres is picked up by security camera MH22A as she walks onto the Hernandez balcony, which spans the entire width of the twenty-second floor of the Majestic Hotel (also, incidentally, the length of the Hernandez family suite). One hand is heavily bandaged, as are both arms, as she moves to the railing and stares into the darkness, alone, for twelve minutes and nineteen seconds.

At 23:33, Seth Prentiss joins her on the balcony. Planted audio recording device EH1 provides the following conversation, even when Torres and Prentiss take seats outside the considerable range of camera MH22A (believed to be in the shadows in the back right of the patio).

Prentiss: Hey. You okay?

Torres: Yup. How 'bout you?

Prentiss (*laughing*): I've been better. But at least...

Torres: What?

Prentiss (*after a long pause*): How are your cuts?

Torres: How do you think they are? (*long pause.*)
    Sorry. I'm just...

Prentiss: We all are.

Torres: Not Owen.

Prentiss: Yeah, well, that guy's superhuman, in case
    you haven't noticed....

Torres: Oh, I noticed. Sucks about his dad, though.
    Mine's pretty useless right now, but at least I get
    to hope he'll snap out of it. Owen...

Three minutes and fourteen seconds pass in silence
before the conversation recommences.

Prentiss: Can I ask you a question?

Torres: Yeah. As long as it's not another one of your
    stupid knock knock jokes or–

Prentiss: No jokes this time, I swear. (*long pause.*) Why
    did you come here?

Torres: Uhhhh, because Ezra's penthouse was shot to
    hell and I didn't want to die?

Prentiss: Not to the hotel. I mean, why did you come
    to San Francisco?

Torres: Don't.

Prentiss: Don't what?

Torres: Don't try to make me feel better about going
    to Helsinki. I said I'll go, but I'm scared to death,
    and I'd really rather be on a plane back home.

Prentiss: Believe me, I'm not trying to make you feel better. Especially since Austin is looking really good to me right now.

Torres: Really? You always seem so...

Prentiss What?

Torres: Ready to save the world.

Prentiss: Right. Turns out not so much.

Torres: I don't believe that.

Prentiss: I'm scared, Issa.

Torres: That's because you're not insane. Fear is a pretty healthy reaction to this situation, I think.

Prentiss: Yeah, but...I've been in dangerous situations before, you know? The Habitat for Humanity group I was with in Haiti got attacked by a street gang. I was beaten up, had my wallet and passport stolen. And when we were in Africa volunteering with a Doctors Without Borders group, the local warlord—

Torres: Jesus, you really do think you can save the world.

Prentiss: That's what I'm saying. I've always tried to do my part, always tried to help. But now that it's on us—just us—I want to run in the opposite direction. I feel like a total wimp.

Torres: Seriously? You're horning in on my identity crisis here.

Prentiss: What, we can't both have one?

Torres: No! That's not the way friendship works.

Prentiss: Sorry, I'll try to do better. [long pause.] Is that what we are? Friends?

Torres: Well, we're not enemies.

Prentiss: Wow, damned with faint praise.

Torres: Is that another movie line? Because I swear to God...

Prentiss (*laughing*): I get it. No more movie lines.

Torres: It's going to work out. We're just being paranoid.

Prentiss: You really think so?

Torres: No. But I figure if I tell myself that often enough I won't run away before we get on that plane for Helsinki.

Prentiss: You're not going anywhere...and no, that's not a threat. I just mean, you're not a runner.

Torres: How do you know that?

Prentiss: I may look like a goofball, but I'm actually a pretty good judge of character. And you have a very good character.

Torres: I like the Mohawk. It's sexy.

Prentiss: Oh, really?

Torres: Whoa there, Casanova. Not that sexy.

Prentiss: You're only saying that because you've got a thing for arrogant Colombian boys with a billion dollars in their pocket.

Torres: I don't have a thing for Ezra.

Prentiss: Oh yeah? Because I didn't mention his name. You did.

Torres: Like there are so many billionaire Colombian boys floating around in my life?

Prentiss: Stranger things have happened.

Torres: Yeah, like the fact that we're about to save the world from the worst blended threat ever.

Prentiss: See? You're sounding more optimistic already.

Torres: It's the Mohawk. It spreads cheer wherever it goes.

Prentiss (*laughing*): I'll remember that.

Torres (*after a long pause*): It's going to be okay, Seth.

Prentiss: How do you know?

Torres: Because I've got your back. (*laughter.*) And Alika's got mine. No one in their right mind would cross that girl.

Prentiss: Right? She scares me a little.

Torres: I'm pretty sure she scares everyone. Even Owen. Which she should.

Sound of a door opening, then Alika Izumi appears on security camera MH22A.

Izumi: Are you planning on getting your butts in here anytime soon? Or am I tossing you off the balcony?

Surveillance ceases twenty-three seconds later, when Torres and Prentiss practically trip over each other trying to get in the door.

31

Owen
[1nf1n173 5h4d3]

"I think we should go over the plan again," Alika tells us.

The rest of us groan because we're going on forty-eight hours without sleep here, and tomorrow's going to be a big day.

"We know the plan," Seth says. He's stretched out on his back on the floor, elbows bent so his forearms rest over his eyes.

"Yes, but do we know what we're going to do when the plan goes south?"

"Um, no?" Issa is curled up on the couch, injured hand propped on her knees and eyes barely open. She looks exactly how I feel. Like crap.

"Exactly!" Alika crows. "We should think about what we're going to do—"

"We're going to improvise," Ezra says around a yawn. "Like we always do."

"This is our only shot at this." Alika's pacing now, eyes bright and words coming faster and faster. "We can't afford to screw it up. We can't afford—"

"It's going to be okay," I tell her, pushing myself to my feet.

My injured side and biceps protest the movement, but I ignore them as I cross the room to her. She's working herself into a tizzy, and it's obvious someone has to step in—and since I don't want that someone to be anyone else, looks like I'm elected.

"You don't know that!" she exclaims.

"You're right, I don't." I wrap my uninjured arm around her shoulder and pull her gently into my body. She's so small I barely notice her slight weight against me, but the way she closes her eyes and kind of sinks into me makes the nightmare of the last two days feel almost worth it. "But I know that freaking out about it right now, when we're all so exhausted we can barely stay conscious, isn't going to help anything. In fact—"

I break off as the hotel suite phone rings.

We all turn and stare at it like it's some kind of foreign object. Which, to some extent, it is. It hasn't rung since before the attack. Ezra even orders room service with an app on his brand-new cell.

It rings a second time, and I start toward it. But Harper gets there first, picking up the handset with a hoarse hello.

In the space of a few seconds her face changes from curious to concerned. I feel my own heartbeat start to speed up, even before she says, "I'm sorry, Roderick. Where did you say you want to fly us?"

His name snags the attention of everyone in the room, and suddenly we're all crowded around her, straining to listen to what's being said on the other end of the phone. I'm too far away to hear anything but her sporadic *uh-huh*s and *ooooooookay*s.

"We're going to have to think about that," she finally says. "I have to discuss it with my partners."

My eyes meet Ezra's across the coffee table. *Partners?* he mouths to me.

Think about what? I mouth back.

Harper says a few more things that make almost no sense from our side of the conversation, then hangs up the phone with a very formal sounding good-bye.

Seth pounces first. "Was that Roderick Olsen?"

"What did he want?" Alika adds barely a second later.

"How does he know where we are?" Issa asks, sounding terrified.

"Where else would we go after they destroyed the penthouse?" Ezra replies. "They obviously know who we are. All they had to do was call the hotel and ask for my room."

"Who cares how they found us!" I growl, impatience gnawing at my insides. "What did Olsen want?"

Harper's eyes meet mine, and she's paler than I've ever seen her. Which is saying something, considering the girl normally has the whitest skin I've ever seen on a person. "He thinks we can"—she makes quotation marks with her fingers—"'work things out in a mutually beneficial manner.'"

"Work things out?" Alika exclaims.

"Mutually beneficial?" Issa chimes in. "He tried to kill us!"

"Yes, well, he says he wants to let bygones be bygones. He's flying us to the launch in Helsinki, so we can talk this out in person."

"No, we're flying ourselves out there—" Seth begins, but Harper cuts him off with a look.

"It wasn't a request. It was an order."

• ● • ● • ● •

"Give me a minute," Ezra says several hours later as he leads me out to the balcony. "I want to talk to you, but I need to do something first."

I watch in shock as he walks to a dark corner of the balcony and pulls down a camera. He fiddles with it for a few seconds, messing with the audio feed, before putting it right back where he found it.

"Are you telling me we've been under surveillance since we got here?"

"Looks like," he says, a lot calmer than I'd expect in these circumstances. "Your parents?" I ask when he doesn't say anything else.

"No. They never want cameras in their hotel suites. Too easy to document their affairs."

Alarm skitters down my spine. "Jacento."

He looks thoughtful. "I don't think so."

"Then who?"

He glances inside, where the others are sleeping.

"You think it's one of them? Why would they do that?"

"Lots of reasons." He shrugs. "I don't think it's anything to worry about, though."

"You don't think it's anything to worry about? Someone we're working with is spying on us! What the hell?"

"Whoever it is, I'm sure they have a good reason."

"What good reason could any of them possibly have? It's a total betrayal of—" Who it is suddenly hits me. Of course. "Oh."

He nods. "Yeah."

"You think it makes her feel more secure?"

"I do. And if that's what she needs…"

"Then that's what we'll give her." Still, it grates a little. "You think she's been doing this all along?"

"I think she's been doing it since that first day in L.A. An information-gathering op." He shoots me a look. "It's not like she's the only one."

"That was different. I had to try to figure out who you guys were and what you'd say if I contacted you."

"I'm sure she thinks she has things to figure out too. I mean, she's already figured out a lot, don't you think?"

"I guess." Unwilling to talk about it anymore until I've had a chance to get my thoughts in order, I lean on the balcony railing and look past the city lights to the ocean beyond. "You know this whole Jacento thing is a trap, right?"

"Yep," Ezra responds. "And you still think we should go."

"Yep. And so do you."

He sighs, shoving a hand through his hair in obvious frustration. "It's suicide."

"It's just as much suicide if we don't go. At least if we're in Helsinki, we have a small shot at stopping this thing before Olsen kills us."

"Don't hold back, Heath. Tell me how you really feel."

"Come on, Ezra. You know I'm right. We're just as dead here

as we are in Helsinki. We might have blown smoke up every-one else's asses, but you and I both know that we were dead the moment we showed up on Olsen's radar. Now it's just a matter of when."

"Unless we somehow manage to stop the rollout of those kiosks and expose Olsen and Jacento to international scrutiny."

"Yeah, unless we do that."

He's silent for several long minutes, but I don't mind. There's a lot to think about and nothing to think about all at the same time. It's a strange position to be in, but it's the way things are. Olsen's boxed us into a corner, and we don't have a choice. Not that we ever had a choice. From the minute we found out what Jacento was up to, we've been hurtling toward this moment. Toward this one final shot to somehow make things right.

I accepted it hours ago, but then, I've spent years living with the knowledge that you can't fight fate, no matter how much you want to sometimes. For Ezra, whose world has always been a pretty fantastic place, the lack of choice and the all-but-inevitable bad outcome are a lot harder to wrap his head around.

"If we do this, we're taking them down," Ezra finally says, his voice harsh against the soft darkness of the night. "No screwups, no *can't*s, no *almost good enough*s. If we're going down, we're taking those bastards with us."

"Damn straight we are."

Ezra reaches a hand out and we bump fists, which seems a little anticlimactic considering we just agreed to launch a final strike against a corporation, and a man, determined to grind us into dust.

"And we take our own transportation," he says after a minute. "No way am I giving that bastard a chance to kill us one second earlier than I have to."

"Normally, I'd agree, but—"

"But what?" He leans forward, face incredulous. "You can't seriously be thinking of taking the plane that bastard provides for us, can you?"

"I think it's the only way to keep him from figuring out what's coming."

"That's crazy—"

"Is it? If he knows we're coming on our own, he's going to be paranoid. He'll be looking for the trap every second. But if we let him fly us in, he'll think he's in control. Sure, he'll be wary, but he's a huge egomaniac, and he'll assume he's got us under his thumb."

Ezra starts to argue, but then he shuts up and just thinks about what I said for a few minutes. "It's a big risk," he finally says.

"All of this is a big risk. Didn't we just agree on that?"

"Yeah, but what keeps him from putting a bomb on the plane and detonating it halfway over the North Pole? I mean, if I were him, that's how I'd solve the problem."

"With the daughter of the American secretary of state on board? I guarantee they'll go after the fuselage of the plane, and when they find the bomb—"

"It'll be an international incident, at the very least."

"Exactly." He's finally getting it.

"But it'll be an incident if she dies at Jacento's international headquarters too. You really think the how and why matters that much?"

"Yeah. Because an unprotected girl getting killed on the streets of a foreign country because she was in the wrong place at the wrong time is one thing. An airplane crash is something else entirely."

"I still don't like it."

I laugh. "Who does? But do we really have any other choice?"

He glances back at the glass doors into the suite. "What are we going to do about the others?"

"Whatever we have to do to keep them safe."

"Do you think it's going to work?"

"I don't know."

"Yeah, me neither." He turns to stare at the seemingly infinite ocean. "But I guess there's only one way to find out."

32

Issa
(Pr1m4 D0nn4)

"They chartered a plane to take us to Helsinki."

"It's really not as bad as you make it sound," Ezra replies.

"They chartered a plan to take us to Helsinki. There's only one way for that to sound. This is crazy." I stare at the plane in question and wonder how the hell my life has spun so quickly and so completely out of my control.

I swear to God, at this point if I could kick my own butt, I would totally do it in a heartbeat. Maybe then I could wake up from this nightmare and be back in San Antonio with Chloe and the rest of my family. Except, if I did that, there'd be no Ezra. No Seth or Owen or Harper or Alika. And crazy and disastrous as these last few days have been...I'm not sure I'd trade them. Not when it means having to give up the people who are rapidly becoming my closest friends.

It's a weird feeling to have, considering how hard it's been for me to trust anyone or anything since my mom died. The way she was there one minute and gone the next...the idea of getting close to anyone new after that—except for Chloe—has been nearly impossible for me to imagine.

And yet, here I am, contemplating getting on a jet that seems way too small to make it across the country, let alone to another continent.

"Think about how much faster we'll get there." Ezra's still trying, unsuccessfully I might add, to persuade me that this is no big deal. "It's a direct flight with no layovers, and we've got no waiting here at the airport. We just need to walk onto the tarmac and get on the plane. We didn't even have to go through security."

"This is crazy!"

He sighs, then rubs the bridge of his nose like he's in actual physical pain. "Are you really going to keep saying that over and over again?"

"I think I am, yes."

"Fine." He throws his hands up. "Are you going to keep saying it while we stand here staring at the thing, or are you going to at least let me take you onto the tarmac so we can get going?"

"I don't know." I mean, that plane is small. Not tiny or anything, but compared to the giant planes that fill up the rest of the airport, the Gulfstream isn't exactly awe-inspiring. Or, more important, confidence inducing. "What if we hit turbulence?"

"What do you mean? The pilot will deal with it just like every other pilot of every other plane in the world." Obviously frustrated, he shoves a hand through his hair. "Come on, Issa. Let's just get on the plane. You can argue with me the whole way there if it will make you happy."

"I vote for listening to lover boy," Seth says as he walks by. "I mean, if my vote counts at all."

"It absolutely does," Ezra says at the same time I tell him, "It doesn't."

"What's the big deal?" Owen asks, picking up his backpack and heading for the door out to the tarmac. "We need to get to Helsinki quickly. This plane will do that. I don't see what the issue is."

"See!" Ezra says as he all but drags me onto the tarmac. "You know if Owen and Seth don't have a problem with it, then there's no problem to be had."

"They both want to get to Helsinki pretty badly," I tell him. "I'm pretty sure they're putting everything else on hold."

"You could try doing the same thing," Alika says as she walks by eating a pack of Skittles on her way to the plane. "For simple expediency if nothing else."

"Et tu, Brute?"

"Oh, sure." Ezra has given up on cajoling and has started dragging me toward the door. "That's the quote you know."

"Hey, just because I don't watch bad eighties movies and I go to public school doesn't mean I haven't read Shakespeare."

"Sometimes you just have to go for it, Buffy." Harper slips my backpack off my shoulder and heads toward the plane with it. "So put on your big-girl panties, pick up your big stake, and let's go kill some vampires."

"Kill some… Did she just call me Buffy?" I ask Ezra. When he only grins, I start to follow her. "Hey! Did you just call me Buffy?"

She doesn't bother turning around. Instead, she dangles my

backpack over the railing as she climbs the stairs to the plane. "Get on the damn plane and find out. Or don't, and stay here in San Francisco alone without your new phone or laptop or any money. Your choice."

Well, when she puts it like that...I shake off Ezra's guiding hand and make my way across the tarmac and up the stairs under my own power.

"You just called me Buffy," I tell her once I actually make it onto the plane, because obviously I'm stuck in some kind of bizarre time loop tonight, where I have to repeat everything over and over again.

"Welcome aboard," she answers as she gestures to the seat next to her.

"Is that my real nickname, then? Not Tinker Bell? Or did you change it because you knew I hated the first one?"

She laughs. "I can't believe how serious you guys are taking these stupid nicknames," she says as we buckle ourselves in. "I made them up the very first day I met you. They're no big deal."

"But you still think of us that way, so they are. So just tell me the truth. Was I Tinker Bell first or was I always Buffy?"

She grins. "You were always Buffy. Which is why I knew you'd get on this stupid plane, because Buffy never let fear dictate her actions."

"Wait. That whole thing out there was because you were afraid?" Ezra says.

"Come on, Ezra," Seth says as he settles onto one of the couches and pulls out his laptop. "What did you think it was about?"

"Oh. I'm sorry." He sinks into the chair next to mine. "I couldn't have handled that any worse, right?"

"Sure, you could have. You could have dragged me kicking and screaming onto the plane. That would have been worse."

"Not going to lie. I was thinking about it."

I roll my eyes. "Of course you were."

"Now that that's settled, you two want to join the rest of us in working on the plan?" Owen demands. "We've only got ten hours before we land, and this code needs to be finished."

"Jeez, put a guy in charge of one little plan, and the whole thing goes to his head," I tease even as he helps buckle me in and gets my laptop out for me, since my hand and arms are still a mess.

"I'd tell you to bite me," Owen says with a wink, "but then Ezra might be tempted to beat me up."

"Yeah, right," Alika snorts.

"Hey!" Ezra tells her. "What exactly does that mean?"

"Oh, did I say that out loud?" The look she gives him is all wide-eyed innocence. "I meant to just think it."

"You people are mean, you know that?" He finally fastens his seat belt and pulls out his laptop. "I could totally take Owen if I wanted to."

He mutters the last to himself but it's loud enough for us to all hear. And to everyone's credit, no one cracks up. Though I've got to admit, it's a close thing. Not that Ezra doesn't look like he could handle himself against almost anyone, because he totally does. But Owen outweighs him by a good fifty pounds…and those fifty pounds are *all* muscle.

I want to laugh—which, now that I think about it, is exactly what Ezra wants us to do—and sit here listening to his utter ridiculousness forever. But I have a job to do and it's not going to get done by avoiding my brand-new, state-of-the-art laptop.

Gingerly, I open the beast and take a look at where I am, trying to get my head together so I can think clearly. It's hard because my arm really hurts and I suck at typing one handed. And that's before the captain comes over the loudspeaker, welcoming us to the flight and asking that we not hesitate to make our needs known—which means we're about to take off.

I'm really not sure I'm ready to take off, not sure if I'll ever be ready to hurtle into the air at hundreds of miles an hour with nothing but a seat belt, misplaced faith, and this tiny tin can to keep me alive. A tiny tin can chartered by people who just tried to kill us not that long ago.

Sure enough, we start slowly taxiing toward the runway, and as we do, I can't help looking longingly at the small galley in the front of the plane and wondering if they've got any M&M's. And if it's too soon to ask the flight attendant to get me some if they do.

Probably, I decide, as I try to focus—a task made infinitely more difficult by the fact that Alika's chomping away at her Skittles next to me while Seth crams a whole Kit Kat bar into his mouth before starting on a bag of Doritos. Not that I'm bitter or anything, because I so totally am not. At all. It's not like I tend to eat away my nerves or anything like that....

Screw it, I tell myself as the pilot tells us to prepare for take-off. I'm a big girl with big-girl problems and what I really, really hope will be a big-girl solution. If Ezra, Owen, and Harper can fly—and hack—without sustenance of the pure cane sugar variety, then so can I. Besides, I have enough trouble typing with one hand. Trying to eat M&M's is probably beyond me anyway. And considering what's waiting for us in Helsinki? This flight is going to be a walk in the park.

With that thought, I finally manage to focus on the code in front of me. I installed Linux last night—and ran the Owen-Seth code on all my new devices—so the comp's good to go as soon as I am. My arm is really throbbing, but I take two Tylenol and push through the pain. We have enough going against us right now. The last thing we need is for me to punk out because my arm hurts.

It doesn't take long before I'm immersed in what I'm doing, basically writing code that will exploit Jacento's main servers—*if* the ones in Helsinki are like the ones in San Francisco. If they're not, then we're all screwed. But then, we're screwed even if we can't get to the servers. Because we're running out of places to find the code....

I'm doing the same thing now that I did all those weeks ago—writing code that should let us back door our way into Jacento's particular brand of Red Hat while the others work on ways to exploit my opening. Alika's putting the payload together, Seth is figuring out how to deliver it, and Owen's munching data as he tries to figure out how to get it to spread as fast as possible.

If things go according to plan, we're going to be sending a wicked blended threat straight into the heart of Jacento's network—and straight into the heart of every kiosk Jacento has. One that will ensure those chargers can't so much as charge a phone, let alone complete any of their more nefarious tasks....

I glance at Owen, whose fingers are flying across his keyboard so fast that they're practically a blur. Which pretty much boggles my mind. When I'm on my game, I'm a fast coder, but what he's doing is insane. I can't figure out how he can think that fast, let alone figure out how to bum code at such an insane rate.

It's awe-inspiring and more than a little humbling.

Then again, that can pretty much describe my feelings about everyone sitting around me. I know I'm good—one of the best hackers in the Southwest, in fact. But these people? They've got the most mad skills I've ever seen. Not to mention they're so much more than that. And while I'm not one to get all sloppy and sentimental, I can't help being a little grateful things have gone down the way they have. Because now that these five people are in my life, I can't imagine going back to a time when they weren't.

Ezra glances up then, catches me looking around at the group of them. And, being Ezra, just raises an eyebrow. Which I now know him well enough to understand means *Are you okay? What's the problem?* and *Are you planning on getting any work done anytime soon?* all at the same time.

For a second, I'm struck by how much he's changed, how much more open he is than he was just a few days ago. And I wonder if he's thinking the same thing about me.

Not that I'm about to let him know what I'm thinking. So I

just grin and raise a brow back. It's a definite dare, one I can see by the gleam in his dark eyes that he understands—and is more than willing to take. And for the first time, I let myself think about what happens next. About what happens after this is all over.

I don't know what this thing is between us, don't know where—if anywhere—it's going once we get past today. It's impossible to even imagine a guy like Ezra, with his life, falling for someone like me. Someone with my life. But then he looks at me like that, all deep and intense and cocky at the same time, and I can't help wondering. Can't help falling for him just a little more.

Which is fine. No, it's better than fine, because I've fought this every way I know how and we're still here, still doing what I'm beginning to think we were meant to do all along. So maybe it's time I stop trying to control things that are out of my control. Maybe it's time to forget all the hard lessons I've learned and have a little faith. In myself, in Ezra, and in the universe that brought all of us together.

It's a crazy idea for a girl like me, but as we speed toward Helsinki—Helsinki!—the crazy seems just about perfect. At least until I take out my very professional fake passport that Harper somehow managed to procure, which tells the world my name is Daniella Sanchez and I'm twenty years old.

And then I'm right back to where I started, wondering how I got here and if I'm ever going to reach the bottom of the very deep, very dark rabbit hole we all seem to have fallen down.

33

Owen
[1nf1n173 5h4d3]

We're about to walk blind into the belly of the beast. Not my first choice, as I've always been a fan of control and having backup plans for my backup plan, but right now, it can't be helped. But that doesn't make it easier.

We left San Francisco at 10:00 PM, took a ten-hour flight across the North Pole to Helsinki, and are set to land a little after 6:00 PM local time thanks to the ten-hour time difference. The big black-tie gala at Jacento's headquarters starts at seven, and even in good traffic it's an hour and a half away from the airport according to our research.

Not for the first time since we got on this plane, I wonder how this thing is going to end. All I know is that I'm going to do my damnedest to ensure Olsen doesn't hurt any of the others. I'm the one who got them into this mess, and I'm going to make sure they get out. No matter what it takes.

My arm throbs as I get dressed in one of the three tuxedos that were hanging in the back of the plane when we got on board. It's not the dull pounding of the last day or so, but something sharper, hotter, more painful. I'm no doctor, but I'm pretty sure that I could use some antibiotics—bullets are dirty, and I think I've got an infection going on despite the care Seth and Harper took trying to clean the wound. It's one more thing about this whole night—this whole suicide mission—that just flat-out sucks.

"Are you going to tie that thing, or are you just going to stand there trying to strangle yourself with it?"

I open my eyes to find Alika standing only a few inches away from me in a jade green dress that makes her skin look like porcelain. "Here," she says, brushing my hands away from the bow tie I've been making a mess of for the last five minutes. "Let me do it for you."

"Thanks." I smile at her. "I've never been very good with these things."

"I don't know many guys who are." She evens out the two ends, then crosses one over the other. "I used to do this for my father all the time when I was younger."

"Hey." I catch her hand, hold her in place for one second, two. "I don't think I ever thanked you. For coming with us. For doing this."

"It's the least I could do, considering I'm the one who created the payload."

"No, the least you could do would have been to ignore the message I sent you and pretend none of this ever happened. So thank you, again."

Her lips quirk in the little grin I'm growing to love. "I'm pretty sure we should be thanking *you*. Or cursing you, depending on how tonight goes."

"It's going to go fine," I tell her, though I'm not sure who I'm trying to convince, Alika or myself.

"Yeah, well, let's hope you're right. I look terrible in prison orange."

"Do they even wear orange in Finnish prisons?" Harper wonders.

"If it's all the same to you," I tell her with a grin, "I'd rather not find out."

Before I can say anything else, the pilot comes over the loudspeaker and asks us to take our seats as we're about to land. Alika turns to head over to the seats, but I stop her with an arm around her waist. Then I pull her in close and whisper, "If I forget to tell you later, you look amazing."

Now she's full-on grinning. "So do you. Who knew dreads go so well with a Tom Ford tuxedo?"

"I did."

She laughs as she moves to take her seat. "Careful, or you're going to end up sounding like Ezra."

"Hey, there are a lot worse people he could sound like," Ezra tells her in mock indignation.

"Of course there are," Issa says to soothe him, but she's grinning too.

The usual banter starts flying back and forth, and as I buckle in, I can't help praying that I don't let them down. Can't help praying that my plan works and in four hours we're flying right back across the Atlantic—or at least they are—Phantom Wheel a memory growing more distant with every mile we traverse. I won't be able to handle it if this goes bad and I end up costing all these people more than they can pay.

"Hey." Harper lightly punches my shoulder. "Don't do that."

"Don't do what?"

"Blame yourself for things that haven't even gone wrong yet."

"I'm not—"

"You are," she interrupts. "And I get it. But we're all here because we want to be. So stop thinking of everything that can go wrong and start concentrating on what's going to go right. Because, frankly, 'I'm in the mood to kick a little ass.'"

Ezra whoops. "You and Moira Kelly, baby."

She just smiles. "I told you. *The Cutting Edge*. Best. Movie. Ever. Even if it doesn't have Val Kilmer in it."

There's no time to debate her on it, because suddenly we're on the ground. Olsen's got a limo waiting, and though logic tells me the last thing we should do is accept a ride from him, at this point we don't have any other choice. Not when the four men sent to escort us to Jacento headquarters are all carrying guns— and are more than happy to let them show.

Alika stops when she catches sight of the guns, looking scared for the first time since we got on the plane. It pisses me off, makes me want to slam my fist into one of those bastards' faces. Or all their faces, and then let this unfold however it goes.

But that's a very short-term solution to a problem that will only get bigger the longer we put it off. Besides, bringing Olsen down inside his own headquarters will be so much more satisfying than punching a few of his security guards, no matter how much they deserve it.

So I dial back my anger, settle for wrapping an arm around Alika's waist and pulling her close to my side.

"You okay?" I whisper as I bend down to put my mouth right up against her ear.

"No." She sags against me for one moment, two, and I reconsider trying to take out the security guards. But those few seconds are all she gives herself before she straightens her shoulders. Clenches her fists. Narrows her eyes. "But I'm going to be. So let's get this done."

Is it any wonder I'm crazy about this girl?

I expect traffic to be bad—it is New Year's Eve, after all—but everyone must be taking the train, because the roads are clear. Which is good and bad, I guess. The trip isn't long enough for us to make any last-minute tweaks to the code, but that means it also isn't long enough for us to freak ourselves out any more than we already are.

We end up getting to Jacento's headquarters, where the gala is being held, before the gates even open. That must be Olsen's plan, though, because the security guards wave us straight through. Which makes everything about the beginning of the plan both easier and harder.

"You can let us out here," I try telling the driver.

"You're to be taken through to the main office building," he tells me in his Finnish accent.

Of course we are. Looks like we're dealing with worst-case scenario, then. Big freaking surprise.

I pull out my phone, access the code I uploaded a few minutes before we landed. Then I stay alert, just in case an opportunity presents itself. I memorized the layout of this place on the plane, so when the driver takes a left turn at the small man-made lake, I nearly cheer.

I settle for a sigh of relief and keep my eyes peeled for—

"Stop the car!" I yell with every ounce of authority I can muster.

The driver slams on the brakes. I throw my door open before the limo even careens to a stop and tumble onto my knees in the snow. As I do, I slip a thumb drive to Harper and do my best to make myself puke as a distraction.

Alika throws herself onto the ground next to me. "What do you need?" she asks me in between dry heaves. Seconds later the rest of them pile out of the car too.

"Harper's got it," I whisper back, then groan as I pretend to be wracked by another stomach cramp.

"Get up!" one of the guards orders, and I nod weakly before pretending to try. But I only make it halfway up before I collapse again. Out of the corner of my eye, I see Harper make a run for it, and I groan, loudly, to keep the guards' attention on me.

It only works for a few seconds, but that's all Harper needs. The girl is fast, even in the snow, and by the time they start chasing, she's forty yards away—and right next to one of the VET-Sähkö utility cabinets that provides access to the whole compound.

Uploading my code there is risky—in theory it will eventually work its way into the network, but how long it takes is anyone's guess. And it's not like we've got a ton of time here.

Harper fakes a fall—or at least I hope she's faking. I don't know what happens after that because the guard who stayed with us reaches down and hauls me to my feet. Then he throws me back into the limo with orders to not "throw up on the upholstery."

Alika climbs in after me, as do the others. We watch as the other guards drag Harper back to the car, and while her hair's messed up, she otherwise doesn't look any worse for wear. Thank God.

"What were you thinking?" Issa demands angrily as soon as Harper is back in the car. "There's nowhere to run out here! And were you just going to leave the rest of us?"

Harper looks away, shamefaced, but doesn't say anything. Neither does anyone else. Issa's pretty savvy, so I figure it's just a performance on her part for the surveillance equipment that we're all sure is watching us right now. Especially when she shuts up right after—there's no reason to say any more and maybe tip our hand.

As the limo starts moving again, I glance Harper's way. Her eyes meet mine briefly, and she gives an almost imperceptible nod. Satisfaction winds through me. If my plan worked—to "get sick" right outside the one cabinet on the compound that actually gives us an open, if convoluted, line into the servers— and Harper was actually able to deliver the code in a brute-force attack...then maybe, just maybe, we're in business.

We carefully avoid looking at one another as the limo winds its way through the compound. Partly because of the bug thing, but partly because the quieter and more defeated we look, the bigger surprise it will be to Olsen when we come out fighting.

Or at least that's what I'm hoping.

Long minutes go by, minutes where I feel like I might jump right out of my skin, before we pull up in front of a ten-story building that is ablaze with lights. According to the schematic I memorized, this isn't where the gala is being held; that's in a building halfway across the compound. But this is where Olsen's office is, along with all the other offices.

Ezra reaches for the door, but one of the security guys— the one with no neck and only nine fingers—beats him to it. "Mr. Olsen will see you now."

I just bet he will.

As I wait for my turn to climb out of the limo, I slide my hand into my pocket and check to make sure my Swiss Army knife is still there. It's not much protection against a gun and one of the most powerful men in the world, but it's something. Right now, I'll take whatever I can get.

34

Harper
(5p3ct3r)

We fall into a double line behind two of the four big burly security guards who met us at the airport. The other two bring up the rear behind us, and then we walk—all dressed to the nines in our fancy evening wear—down the hallway. I'm nervous, constantly looking over my shoulder. Olsen might have said this was a civil invitation, meant to make peace between our two sides, but none of us is stupid enough to believe that. This is a trap. We know it, and yet we are still walking right into it. What choice do we have?

"Any luck?" I whisper to Mad Max, who has his phone out and, though it's a long shot, is trying to find out if the code I delivered has made its way from the power grid into one of the servers.

"They're offline, just like in San Fran, so we won't know until we *know*. But we figured it could take a while. There's a lot to check."

"I know. I'm just…"

"Impatient?" he says with a smile.

"Worried. There's too much that can go wrong here, and Owen looks terrible."

"He'll be fine," Mad Max assures me, but I've learned a thing or two about him in the last few days, and I know he's as concerned about the Lone Ranger as I am. He's just trying to be reassuring.

"So, where exactly are you taking us?" Silver Spoon asks as we continue to wind our way down one hallway after another.

"Mr. Olsen wants to speak with you," one of the guards says. "We're taking you to him."

"Yeah, well, we want to speak with him too," Snow White pipes up, even as she reaches for my hand and gives it a little squeeze. *It's all good*, her look says. This is what we expected to happen.

And it is. I know it is. It's just I'm scared in a way I wasn't the last time we did this. Because then I didn't have anything to lose except a stupid college scholarship. Now, suddenly, I have five people that I really, truly care about, and the idea of anything happening to one of them tonight...it honestly terrifies me more than the thought of something happening to me.

It's a weird feeling, but I'm way more scared for them than I am for myself. It's been a long time since I've had anyone to care about, and it feels weird. Not bad, just...weird.

"Yeah," Buffy chimes in, interrupting my thoughts. "We've been wanting to meet Mr. Olsen for a long time."

The guards exchange looks that are about as far from reassuring as they can get. "Well then, tonight is your lucky night."

"Where are we going?" the Lone Ranger echoes Silver Spoon. The words kind of run together, though, and I glance at him, panicked. He's the best coder we've got, especially on the fly. What happens if he's too sick to fix any problems that come up?

"To Mr. Olsen's office."

My heart skips a beat at that. We've been hoping for a chance at the floor his office is on—and the servers housed there. We just never thought Olsen would be stupid enough to give it to us.

"Anything yet?" I mumble to Mad Max, who is once again surreptitiously checking his phone.

"Nope."

"Do you think we could get the code into the servers? It'd be a lot faster—"

"I think right now the only thing we can do is follow along to wherever they're taking us. I'm pretty sure anything else will get us killed."

After an elevator ride and another long walk down a deserted hall, we end up in front of beveled-glass double doors.

"Roderick Olsen's office, I presume?" Buffy asks, all innocent looking.

"*Mr. Olsen's* office," one of the guards stresses. Obviously Rod likes to stand on ceremony around here. Not that that's exactly a surprise or anything...

The doors fly open, and then he's standing there, Roderick Olsen himself. Or Lex Luthor, as I like to call him.

"Welcome," he says, voice warm and eyes absolutely frigid. "I'm so glad you could make the party tonight."

"So glad you invited us," Silver Spoon answers smoothly.

Lex Luthor reaches out to shake his hand, and Silver Spoon

obliges him. A small pissing contest ensues, one that I'm pretty sure Silver Spoon wins, judging by the way Lex is shaking out his hand.

He gestures for us to sit down on the artfully arranged sofas that take up the front half of his office, and we do, warily. There's a part of me that expects him to just shoot us all and be done with it. Sure, he'd have six bodies to deal with, but judging by the look of his security force, I'm pretty sure we wouldn't be the first dead people they've had to deal with.

"So, it seems you've all been having quite a little adventure," Lex says after we're all seated. "At my company's expense."

"To be fair, if you hadn't fought us, it wouldn't have cost you anything," the Lone Ranger pipes up. Because of course he does. The boy doesn't know when to keep his mouth shut, and he never will.

"Yes, well, no one asked you to come barging onto my property and wreak the kind of havoc you did."

"Yes, well," Snow White says, mimicking his very proper voice and speech patterns. "No one asked you to set up an elaborate lie to recruit us and then trick us into creating a virus for you. But that's what you did. What happened after is on you."

Lex Luthor's eyes narrow, and I can't tell if it's because he doesn't like a girl talking back to him or if he doesn't like anyone to do it. Probably a little of both. Either way, the anger in his eyes is both terrifying and strangely satisfying. He deserves every ounce of discomfort we can cause him.

"It occurs to me that you're right. The way we did things was dishonest, and I'm hoping to rectify that tonight."

"By telling us your evil plan?" Mad Max scoffs. "Don't worry, we already know it."

"I never give away my plans, evil or otherwise." Lex Luthor leans back in his chair and crosses his legs, as he gestures at his security guards.

Seconds later, one with a scar steps forward and puts a briefcase on the coffee table between us. "What I do give away, however, is my money. *When* I feel it is earned, and you six definitely earned it."

He glances at the Lone Ranger. "Well, five of you did, but I'm willing to be generous if it means letting bygones be bygones."

He nods, and the guy with the scar opens the briefcase. In it are stacks and stacks of hundred-dollar bills—not unlike the ones Silver Spoon handed out the other day.

And while a few weeks ago I might have been tempted by the fact that my college education would be paid for if I just took the money and shut up, now I can't even conceive of it. I don't have to look at the others' faces to know that neither can they.

"You don't really think we're going to take that, do you?" Buffy asks.

"I do think you're going to take it," he answers her. "Because if you don't, the six of you are going to be very, very sorry."

"Yes, but how do you know we won't just agree that we're all good now and then screw you over anyway?" Mad Max asks.

I didn't think it was possible, but Lex Luthor's eyes turn even more glacial. "I wouldn't recommend that."

"Yeah, well, I wouldn't recommend you upload Phantom Wheel into those kiosks, but something tells me you aren't any more predisposed to listen than I am," Snow White says, and it's obvious that there's something about her talking back to him that pisses him off more than the rest of us.

The guy's a total misogynist.

"I wish you hadn't said that," Lex Luthor tells her.

"Oh, do you now? Too bad I don't give a damn what you wish," she answers. "Let me tell you what's going to happen here—"

"I know exactly what's going to happen here," he says. He reaches across the table and slaps her across the face.

The Lone Ranger, Mad Max, and Silver Spoon explode from their spots on the couch, but Olsen's security forces are right there to take them back down again. I watch in horror as fists plow into their stomachs.

"You should have taken the money," Olsen says as he steps away. "Everything would have been so much neater if you had."

"You never intended to give us the money," I tell him as he walks toward the door.

"You'll never know now, will you?" He casts a warning glance at the guards. "Keep them here until after the gala. Then get rid of them. Quietly."

"You can't do this!" Mad Max shouts as he runs straight for him. He plows his shoulder into Lex Luthor's stomach and sends the guy careening back against the wall.

Lex falls to the floor, and then Mad Max is on him, hitting him in the chest and stomach and anywhere else he can reach.

We're all in shock—even the security guards—that mild-mannered Seth is the one who's snapped. Which is why it takes the five of us a few seconds to react. Once it does register, though, we rush them en masse, trying to help him.

But the guards get to him first, two pulling him off Lex Luthor and then punching him over and over while the others hold us back. I'm furious, terrified, with tears pouring down my face, as I watch them beat Seth.

Beside me, it takes two guards to hold Silver Spoon back and three to hold the Lone Ranger down, despite his wounds. Snow White is swearing like a sailor, scratching and smacking at the guard holding her while Buffy screams the place down.

I'm as desperate to get to Seth as the rest of them, and I bring my high heel down right on the foot of the guy holding me. At the same time I jerk my head back and head butt him in the mouth. He curses, but he doesn't let go. Instead, he tightens his arms around me, squeezing so hard I can barely breathe.

And the guards go on beating Seth.

"Enough," Olsen finally says, after he's straightened his tuxedo jacket and his bow tie. "That's enough for the moment. We don't want to attract any more attention than necessary right now." He moves toward the door, then glances back at Seth, who's crumpled in a ball on the ground. "Tonight, when the gala is done and Phantom Wheel, as you like to call it, has been uploaded, you're going to regret what you just did. More than you can ever imagine."

And then he's gone, sweeping out of his office as breezily as he let us in and ordering his guards: "Lock them in. Three of you stay behind to guard the doors and make sure they don't escape. The rest of you, with me."

The guards let us go, and I rush to Seth, dropping to my knees beside him as the doors slam shut. The six of us are alone again.

"What the hell, Seth?" I cry as I run my hands over his face, checking for injuries. His nose is bleeding—I'm pretty sure it's broken—and one of his eyes will definitely be swollen shut soon. "Why would you do that?"

"What? I jump a guy and now I'm Seth?" he jokes, his voice more than a little strained. "What happened to Mad Max?"

"Right now you're Seth," I answer, because I don't know what to say. Don't know how to say that I can't use a nickname to keep him—to keep any of them—at a distance. Not now, when Seth, my friend, is bleeding right in front of me.

"Let me look at him," Owen says. "I've seen a lot of broken bones in football."

"I don't think anything's broken," Seth says as he sits up gingerly. "Well, maybe my nose," he continues as blood gushes from his nostrils.

"Here, use this," Alika says, grabbing what looks to be a silk shirt out of Olsen's closet and ripping a sleeve off.

"Tilt your head forward a little bit and pinch your nose here," Owen says, placing Seth's fingers on the soft part of his nose. Owen's voice and eyes are clear for the first time in the last hour. Amazing what adrenaline can do for you. "It'll help stop the bleeding."

"In a minute," Seth says, as he pulls his hand away to reach into his pocket.

"Now!" Issa orders him. "You have to let us help you."

"Why would you do that?" Alika asks. "Why would you attack him when all his guards were here? It doesn't make any sense!"

"Because Owen's code came through."

"What?" Ezra, who has been pacing since the guards left, is suddenly still. "What do you mean?"

"I mean," he says as he pulls out a phone I don't recognize and holds it up, "the code hit on the device with Phantom Wheel loaded on it, the device that will deliver the virus to the kiosks. Olsen's phone."

"That's brilliant," Owen says, in awe.

"You attacked him so you could get his phone?" I ask. I'm not a guy, so I'm not nearly as impressed right now as Owen seems to be.

"Can you think of any other way I could have gotten it? I couldn't just casually walk up to him and stick my hand in his jacket."

"Give it to me," Alika says, voice low and urgent. "We need to upload the code now, before he realizes it's missing."

But it only takes a few tries for her to start cursing. "It's not uploading. They must have blocked our devices from the network when they left us in here."

"No wonder he didn't try to take them," Owen mutters. "He's stupid enough to think we can't work around this BS. Give me a minute to find the local—"

"Here, try this." I pull a USB cable from my backpack and hold it out to her. Seconds later, she's done transferring the payload via USB cable from her tablet to Olsen's state-of-the-art Jacento phone. "It's faster than trying to hack something."

"Now, how do we get it back to him?" Issa asks.

"Like this." Ezra grabs it from her and takes it over toward the door, where Seth tackled Olsen. He crouches down, half shoving it under a chair so only a little bit peeks out. "If we're lucky, they'll think we didn't see it."

"It doesn't matter," Alika tells him. "Even if he checks it, he won't see the payload. I wrote it so it would do the same thing Phantom Wheel does, hide in another app until we need it."

"You are..." Owen starts, then stops, shaking his head.

"I am...?" she asks, brows raised.

He doesn't answer. Instead, he wraps a hand around the back of her neck and pulls her against him. And then he plants a kiss on her that has all of us clearing our throats and looking anywhere but at them.

"Okay, okay, okay," Issa says after several long, excruciating seconds. "I hate to break this up, but I'm pretty sure we need to start thinking about how we're going to get out of this—hopefully without ending up in the middle of another shoot-out."

"I like that plan," Seth tells her. "If I never get shot at again in my life, it'll be too soon."

"Right?" Ezra agrees.

"You guys weren't even shot," Owen complains as he finally tears his lips away from Alika's.

"Not our fault we're better at ducking and weaving," she tells him, a wicked gleam in her eyes.

"Keep talking and I won't tell you my idea," he threatens.

"And what idea is that exactly?" I demand.

He starts to answer, but cuts off when two security guards throw the doors open. "Stay right there," they warn as they start scouring the floor. Seconds later, they find Olsen's phone where Ezra planted it. After grabbing it, they storm out as quickly as they came in.

I wait a few moments to make sure they're really gone, then turn back to Owen. "Now, what exactly is your plan and how fast can we put it into action?"

35

Owen
[1nf1n173 5h4d3]

"For the record," Alika says as she stares at the rope I've just tied onto one of the columns in the middle of Olsen's office, "this is not a plan. It's suicide."

"It's a plan," I tell her. "And pretty much the only one we've got at this point. Unless you'd rather take your chances with the armed security guards."

"*I'd* rather take my chances with the security guards," Seth volunteers, eyes wide and Adam's apple bobbing in his throat. "I mean, I know you're a giant football player and everything, but hasn't anyone told you that hackers aren't athletic?"

"I'm not asking you to throw a touchdown pass," I tell him with a roll of my eyes. "I'm just asking you to climb down a rope."

"Yeah, but what you don't get is that I've got as much chance of throwing that pass as I do of not falling off that rope," he answers. "And that's when I haven't just had the crap beat out of me."

I look at the others, hoping for some support. But Issa and Alika are both nodding like Seth is speaking the biggest truth they've ever heard. Harper looks skeptical, but at least she's listening, and Ezra is Ezra, so of course he's not worried about a little rope climbing. Hell, he probably thinks he can just jump down from the third floor and land on his freaking feet.

"Do we even know that this is a sound plan?" Seth continues. "I mean, you are delirious with fever right now."

"I was lucid enough to think to grab this rope off one of the guards! We're using it!"

"And have you forgotten that you just got shot?" Alika asks. "How are you supposed to climb down? There's no way that arm will hold you."

"I can do it one handed. It's not a big deal."

Seth throws up his hands. "Of course you can."

"Look, we've only got a short window of time here. Eventually they're going to come back for us, and I don't want to be here when they do."

The three of them just continue to stare at me with arms crossed.

"Look, I'll even go first if you want me to," I tell them. "That way if you fall halfway down, I can catch you."

"With what, your one good arm?" Issa asks, incredulously. "And your fever?"

She's got a good point, especially since my arm has gone from hurting to being on freaking fire. But that doesn't matter now. Nothing does but getting them down that damn rope.

"I'll go first," Ezra offers. "I'm a good catch, and my arms are both fine. Okay?"

They still don't look impressed.

"Come on, guys," Harper says. "He's right. We're running out of time, and this is our best bet."

"It's *your* best bet. You're almost as athletic as these two are," Alika grumbles under her breath, but eventually she nods. "But fine, let's just get it done." She glares at me. "If I end up hanging myself on this thing, I'm coming back to haunt you. Understand?"

I grin and waggle my brows at her. "I look forward to it."

She just rolls her eyes. "I think you've got *haunt* confused with *provide sexual favors*. That's not what I was going for."

"A guy can dream, can't he?"

"By the time I'm done with you, all you'll have is nightmares," she answers even as she starts to stretch out her arms and shoulders like she's planning on doing the hundred-meter butterfly.

I should call her on it, but I'm glad she's finally decided to see reason. With that thought in mind, I turn to Seth and Issa. "Okay? We good here?"

"No, we're not good here," Seth complains. "But whatever. Gotta die sometime, right?"

Issa glares at Ezra. "If you drop me, I will kill you."

"I won't drop you, *dulzura*. I promise."

She narrows her eyes at him. "Don't you dare try to sweet talk me right before you make me jump out of a third-story window."

"Whoa, whoa, whoa!" I feel honor bound to clarify. "No one's jumping out of anything. There is a *rope*."

She just glares at me. "Potato, po-tah-toe."

"No, no. Not potato, po-tah-toe. There is an actual difference between jumping out a window and going down a rope."

Alika sniffs. "For you maybe."

For the first time I start to get nervous. "Maybe we should rethink this."

Ezra rolls his eyes. Then, very casually, he picks up a lamp and swings it hard through the huge plate-glass window. "Turns out you're not the only one who can break a window," he tells me. "Debate over. Now we've got about three minutes before they get through all the crap we've got barricading the door, so either you're climbing out or we're all screwed."

He grabs Issa and all but throws her onto his back.

"What are you doing?" she shrieks as he grabs the rope.

"You really didn't think I was going to make you climb down that rope with your bad hand and messed-up arms, did you?" He wraps her arms around his neck. "Now hold on!"

It's the last thing he says before he gives the rest of us a quick salute and disappears over the window ledge with Issa attached to him like a limpet. Seconds later, they're on the ground, and he's waving for the next person to follow him down.

"Who's next?" I ask, but Harper's already moving toward the window.

"Screw you, Owen," Harper says. Then she looks down at Ezra and calls, "You better catch me!"

He widens his stance and holds his arms out in an *I'm ready* kind of way. "Damn," she says again as she grabs the rope. And then she's out too, scooting her way slowly and awkwardly down the rope.

She almost makes it all the way down without getting tangled. But she gets stuck in the middle of the second floor, and Ezra calls up, "It's okay. Just let go."

"I don't think I can."

"You've got to!" he tells her.

"Fine! But I want you both to know, you're going to suffer for this!" And then she's falling—straight into Ezra's arms.

"Yippee ki-yay, Mr. Falcon!" she kind of whisper-shouts as he lowers her to the ground.

"What the hell is that?" Ezra asks.

"It's the line from *Die Hard*."

My brows hit my forehead as I stare down at her from three stories up. "That is definitely not the line from *Die Hard*," I call down to her.

She grins. "It is when it's edited for TV."

"Oh my God." I shake my head at her even as I turn back to the others. Behind us the guards start trying to open the doors, but they aren't having much luck. Our barricade is holding. For now. "Who's next?"

"I hate you all," Alika says as she grabs the rope I hold out to her. I try to help her, but she shrugs off my hands—then pretty much glides down the rope. She makes it down even faster than Ezra. The big faker.

Suddenly, the doors crack open, and we've run out of time. There's a bunch of furniture piled in front of them, but it won't take the guards long to get through it. "You've got to go, Seth. They're coming."

"I know. I know." He grabs the rope, then calls, "If I land on you, I'm sorry!"

He doesn't even make it halfway down the rope before falling. "Shiiiiiiiiiiit!" he screams all the way down, and I watch, terrified, as he plummets to the ground. Ezra tries to catch him, but Alika goes for him too, and all three of them end up on a pile on the ground, just as two guards come jogging around the corner of the building.

"Damn it." I launch myself at the rope and start going down. "Move," I yell, and they do, scattering in all directions.

I hit the ground running, literally, taking off in the same direction Alika and Seth are headed while the others scatter in the opposite direction. On the plane, we talked about what to do if we got spotted, and the goal is to split up and try to get to the party, partly because we can blend in with our tuxes and fancy dresses and partly because I figure even Jacento will be reluctant to go after a bunch of teenagers in front of the press. Especially with the story we have to tell.

But Alika and Seth are heading in the wrong direction, and I can't just leave them out here alone. Especially with security closing in. "Turn left!" I yell, as I catch up. And then we're sprinting toward the building where the party's being held, running as fast as we can.

A glance behind me warns that our detour gave the guards a chance to catch up, and they're closing in fast. Grabbing Alika's arm with one hand and Seth's with the other, I all but pull them up the stairs, into the building, and down the hall to the huge rotunda where the party is being held. Thank God for adrenaline.

We're almost there when two men in dark suits come out of nowhere, sliding in front of the double doors that lead into the rotunda. I freeze as I realize it's Daniel Davies and the other guy from L.A., the one I've been trying to identify ever since Issa pointed him out on that footage of Roderick Olsen.

And now they're here, in front of us, aware of exactly who we are and what we're trying to do. Which is probably why they're very deliberately blocking our way. And while I'd normally plow right through them—I didn't play football for a decade for nothing—the two guns they've currently got trained on us put things in a different perspective.

I come to a halt, throwing myself in front of Seth and Alika. After all, I've already been shot twice. Third time's the charm, right?

Except they aren't having it. As one, Alika and Seth step out from behind me so that we're standing shoulder to shoulder to shoulder, making what I'm sure is one really, really large target.

"You need to come with us," the guy from L.A. says in lightly accented English.

"I don't think that's going to happen," Alika tells him. "You need to let us through those doors."

"The only place you're going is to prison," he answers. "Now start walking or I'll make you walk."

"Try it and we'll scream the place down," Seth says. "There are an awful lot of party guests in there who would probably object to you shooting three teenagers. Think of the Jacento brand, if nothing else."

"You should spend more time worrying about your own skin and less time thinking about our brand," Daniel Davies tells us. "Now move."

"Or what?" Alika replies.

Suddenly both guns are trained on her.

Which causes panic to slam through me. I send her a warning glare, but she ignores me.

"Or I'll shoot you right here."

"I'm pretty sure that's called murder. After all, my hands are up, and I'm not making any move to hurt you. Though I should tell you that I'm recording everything you're saying right now."

The first guy laughs. "You think you scare me, little girl? You think I'm some police officer who actually cares about any of that? Where you're going, no one will ever find your recording—or your body."

Panic turns to full-blown terror inside me as he aims his gun straight between her eyes. I start to throw myself in front of her, but Seth beats me to it. He dives straight at the guy, sending him flying against the door even as he knocks the gun out of his hand.

At the same time, Alika kicks Daniel Davies in the balls so hard that he screams—and drops like a stone. And then she's on him, kicking him in the head hard enough to make his eyes roll back in his head.

I turn back to Seth, who is now on the floor with the other guy as they both grapple for the gun. I make a dive for them, but Alika beats me to it as she slams her foot straight into the guy's ribs. I don't think I'm imagining the cracking sound I hear, especially since he lets out a howl loud enough to bring down the roof.

Seth takes advantage of the guy's injury to straddle his chest and starts banging his head against the marble floor over and over again until he passes out. I'd be lying if I said he didn't look a little maniacal, especially with the rolled-up Kleenex hanging out of his bruised and swollen nose.

Suddenly, Davies groans and I turn to take him on, but again, Alika's already there. She kicks him one more time, and then he too is out cold.

For long seconds I can do nothing but stare at them, mouth open. When I finally find my voice, I can't help asking, "What the hell was that?"

Seth shrugs. "I'm just really tired of people pointing guns at me and threatening my friends."

Alika nods as she dusts her hands off on her dress. "Exactly. Now let's move, before the other guards find us. Earbuds in, everyone."

Still in shock, I push open one of the doors and put my earbuds in place as the others do the same. We slide in as silently and unobtrusively as we can. Then we slip into the packed crowd, weaving between people as we try to disappear.

Roderick Olsen is onstage, getting ready to unveil the first kiosk. He's holding the ends of a piece of bright red fabric, just waiting for the signal to tear it off so the world can see the first-ever Jacento charging station. Next to him on the stage are the president, the chairman of the board, and the chief technical and financial officers, all four of them grinning like they've just won the lottery.

A quick glance behind me shows that the guards are causing

a disturbance as they work their way through the crowd looking for us. I duck down a little—thank God Finnish people are so tall—and nod for Seth and Alika to follow me closer to the stage, deeper into the crowd. I look around for the others, but I can't see them—probably because they're hiding the same way we are.

Olsen is speaking in what I assume is Finnish, so I don't understand a word he's saying. But it's obvious from the energy flowing all around us that he's catering to the crowd, getting them excited. And then, just as the music crescendos, he rips the cloth off the charging station.

Applause thunders through the room, even before he hooks his phone up so that everyone can see the welcome Jacento has planned. But the moment his phone touches that charging station, the virus Alika designed takes control. Seconds later, it's not Jacento's triumphant message that scrolls across the huge screen towering above the stage. Instead, it's the very simple one that started us on this whole crazy journey.

YOU'VE BEEN PLAYED

The crowd starts murmuring, and though I don't understand what the CTO is saying, I know he's as confused as the rest of the people in the room. He holds up his hands and mumbles something to the crowd as Olsen fumbles with his phone.

And that's when the first cell phone in the audience pings. And then another. Within seconds all we can hear are the various dings, pings, and buzzes of the phones around us as, one by one, every guest at the party receives a text.

The same text.

I glance at the screen of the woman next to me, who is frowning as she views the message that just came through her phone.

Her screen reads: JACENTO OWNS YOU

She shows it to her very concerned partner, whose own phone beeps seconds later. The woman's phone dings again.

JACENTO WILL SELL YOU TO THE HIGHEST BIDDER

All around us, phones are beeping as the messages Alika and I wrote last night are delivered, one after another:

BIG DATA KNOWS NO BOUNDS

WE CONTROL YOU

YOU'VE BEEN PWNED

All around us people are checking their phones. They're freaking out, trying to figure out what's going on.

Olsen's freaking out now too, as he desperately tries to turn the app off and stop the messages. He pulls his phone off the charger, even tries to turn it off as he babbles incoherently into the mic. But nothing works. Phones continue beeping as the messages keep coming.

People start backing away from the stage, the sound level in the room getting louder and louder as outrage wells up from all directions. And that's when the pièce de résistance starts scrawling across the screen onstage—the letter Alika wrote on the plane just a couple of hours ago.

Ladies and gentlemen,
thank you all for
coming. We're so excited
that you've got front-
row seats to the biggest
fraud ever perpetrated
by a telecommunications
company, in Finland or
anywhere.

Jacento is very proud
of our new charging
stations, a perfect
example of a symbiotic
relationship in today's
global economy. We
charge your phone for
you, and you give us
access to your accounts,
your social media, your
every keystroke.

But don't worry. You can
trust us. After all, big
data is the future.

And the future is NOW.

Olsen takes one look at the letter and gives up trying to explain things away. Instead, he disappears behind the curtains at the back of the stage. Seconds later, the other officers follow him.

"They're running!" Alika starts pushing her way through the suddenly belligerent crowd. "We have to find them!"

"We already have," Harper says, her voice calm and steady in our ears. "They're on the roof."

"The roof? What are they doing up there?" I push our way straight past the security guards, who suddenly have much more pressing problems than trying to find us. People have started yelling, and it looks to me as if they're about to begin tearing the building apart piece by piece if someone doesn't explain to them what's going on.

"I don't know—" Harper starts to answer when the whirring rotors of a helicopter do it for her.

I take off running, straight out the building's main door and into the quad. Seconds later, the others join me. "That's the one thing we didn't think of."

"Who would?" Seth asks, bewildered.

"I would. Or I should say, I did," Ezra says as he pulls his laptop out of his bag and seats himself on the nearest bench.

"You thought they'd try to escape via helicopter?" Issa asks disbelievingly.

"I thought it was a possibility," he answers with a shrug. "My dad's helicopter is never far from him."

"Of course it isn't," Issa replies as the helicopter climbs higher in the sky. More people are pouring out of the building now, coming to stand next to us on the lawn as they watch the helicopter start to fly away.

"So what are you doing?" I ask, crowding close to see what he's up to.

"I'm grabbing their comm signal. And now I'm uploading code I wrote last year when I hacked my dad's helicopter just to see if I could do it."

"Just to see if you could do it," Issa repeats faintly.

We wait for something to happen, all six of us staring at the retreating helicopter, looking for some sign that Ezra's code actually works. And then it happens. The lights on the helicopter start blinking in Morse code.

"SOS?" Harper cries. "That's your big hack?"

"No. That's my way of knowing my code got in. *This* is my big hack." He presses a few keys on the keyboard, and we watch silently as he slowly, carefully, inexorably drags the helicopter right down to the ground.

It's total pandemonium now, people milling so tightly around the helicopter that the men are trapped inside it as the company's security guards try to figure out what to do. The whine of police sirens sounds in the distance, and the crowd starts cheering.

Convinced that they'll make sure no one gets away, the six of us do what we do best—fade quickly, and quietly, into the darkness.

"Well, Ezra, I guess there's only one thing to say now," Issa tells him.

"And what's that?"

"Yippee ki-yay, Mr. Falcon."

36

Harper
[5p3ct3r]

I don't know what to do, don't know how to feel. Don't know what to say to these people who in a matter of weeks have gone from strangers to competition to allies to my closest friends. I have to tell them about how I've betrayed their trust. I don't want to keep my secrets any longer.

A part of me thinks I should wait until we get back to San Francisco. After all, we are thirty thousand feet above the earth in a private jet that Ezra managed to charter for us, and if they get as mad as I think they will, tossing me off the plane might seem like a viable solution to them.

At the same time, though, once we get back to San Francisco, things are going to change. Ezra's parents will be there, and so will Seth's and Alika's. The six of us won't be a team anymore. We'll just be six kids with different lives and expectations who somehow managed to stave off a digital apocalypse. It's hard to imagine, given everything we've just been through together, but once we get home, we'll go back to being who we were before.

That's just the way it is.

Which is fine. Better than fine. I liked my life just fine before, and I'll like it fine once this is all over. But that doesn't mean I don't have to tell the others the truth about what I did. Because we may not be a team for much longer, but we are friends. And that has to count for something, right?

I grab a water from the galley refrigerator—more to give my hands something to do than because I really want it—then slowly make my way back to the main cabin, where the others are sprawled out on the reclining seats.

"Hey, come sit by me," Seth says, patting the chair next to him. "You'll save me from the boredom of watching the four of them moon over each other."

"I object," Owen says. "I am most certainly not mooning over Silver Spoon."

"And I'm not mooning over the Lone Ranger," Ezra chimes in. "He's a little too rugged for my tastes."

Seth rolls his eyes, then moans a little at the pain it causes his battered face. "You know what I meant."

I settle down next to him, twisting the bottle nervously between my fingers.

"Hey, what's wrong?" Alika asks. "You okay?"

"I'm fine. I just…"

"You sure, Buttercup?" Owen asks.

My brows go up. "Buttercup?"

He smiles. "Yeah. We decided you needed a nickname too, and it was that or Casper the Friendly Ghost, so…"

"Casper?" I ask, my throat suddenly so thick I can barely get the word out.

"Yeah, you know, because of your handle? And because of how your code just ghosts," Seth says with a crooked grin. "But we decided Buttercup from *The Princess Bride* suits you better. Everyone loves Buttercup."

Tears well up in my eyes and spill onto my cheeks before I can stop them. Seth's smile falls from his face, and Issa actually gasps. "It's okay. You can be Casper if you want," Seth babbles. "I mean, we aren't as good at nicknames as you are, so if you've got something you'd rather be called—"

"No, no!" I sniffle a little, then wipe my eyes. "Buttercup is great. It's perfect. Amazing. It's just…"

"Just what?" Ezra asks, leaning forward in his seat.

"No one's ever gotten close enough to give me a nickname before." I give a watery laugh. "I'm sorry, that sounds totally pathetic. That's not what I meant."

Alika plops herself down on the seat next to mine and pulls me into a hug. For a second it feels strange, so strange that I can't help but stiffen. But when she goes to pull back, I throw my arms around her and hug her back as tightly as I can. Seconds later, Seth is in on the action too, squishing me in his enthusiasm.

"Well, it's too late for you to back out now," Alika tells me cheerfully, when Seth finally lets go. "You're stuck with us, whether you like it or not."

The guilt that's been weighing me down for days suddenly

becomes suffocating, and I know that I can't put it off any longer. I have to tell them what I've been doing.

"I've got something to tell you," I say, making sure to look them all in the eyes as I do. It's the last thing I want to do—I'd rather duck my head and hide, but they don't deserve that. Any more than they deserve what I did.

"I spied on you guys. After L.A., I memorized your names from the badges. I looked you all up, hacked into your school files and a bunch of other stuff. I spied on you, and kept records, and made stupid assumptions about you. I'm sorry. I shouldn't have done it. I just wanted to know who you were, but then even once I got to know you, I kept doing it. I don't even know why, and I don't have any excuse, except…"

"Except it's not easy for you to trust anyone," Issa says quietly. "We get that."

"What do you mean, you *get* it?" I ask, incredulous. "How can you not be mad?"

"We were when we first figured it out. But by then we knew you, and it didn't seem like such a big deal," Ezra says. "Not after everything you've gone through. Hell, if I had been in foster homes so bad I took myself out of the system at fourteen, you can bet I wouldn't trust anyone either."

"But I do trust you!" I tell him as I battle against the next batch of tears that want to fall. "That's the thing. I didn't at first, but then I got to know you, and…there's no one in the world I've ever trusted as much as I trust you. And I'm sorry that I broke your trust and spied on you. It was a terrible thing to do, and I totally get it if you don't want to be my friends anymore."

"Have you been listening to anything we've said?" Owen asks. "If we didn't want to be your friends anymore, we would have said something when we first figured it out."

Suddenly what he just said, plus what Ezra said moments before, catches up with me. "Wait, what do you mean, you figured it out?" I ask. "You guys knew?"

"I think I figured it out first," Seth replies, and he looks a little embarrassed. "Back at Ezra's, the second day, before everything went crazy. You knew I'd been at Starbucks in the morning, but I never said anything. I didn't put it together right away, but then by the time I did, some of them had also figured it out. We talked about it. We knew, Harper. It's okay. We get it."

"I found the camera you planted at the hotel suite," Ezra added.

I put my head down, tears of shame falling down my cheeks. "So you guys knew this whole time and you were, what, just humoring me?"

Seth's arm is back around me as Alika leans forward and forces me to look up at her. "You're one of us, Harper. We've all got our weird stuff, but we trust you. You're one of us."

"The spying does have to stop, though," Ezra adds. "I mean, if you ever want to watch me shower, all you have to do is ask."

Issa shoots him a look, and without missing a beat, Ezra shrugs and says, "What? She's asexual. Not dead."

And just like that, I am laughing so hard I'm crying. We all are. And this time, I'm not even trying to hide my tears. I just let them roll down my cheeks.

"So do you like your nickname or what?" Seth asks after we all stop laughing long enough to take some deep breaths.

"It's perfect," I tell them.

"It's really not," Seth says. "We know that. But how cool is it that your nickname messes with Issa every time we use it?"

"I still say that paraphrasing counts!" she tells him. "You guys are just mean, right, Harper?"

She looks so hopeful that I want to agree with her, but... "No. Paraphrasing so doesn't count."

"Except in *Die Hard* movies," Owen adds with a grin.

"And how exactly is that fair?" Issa demands.

"Who said anything about fair?" Ezra says, tugging on her hair.

"I did! I said something about fair!" Issa pouts.

"You guys really aren't mad?" I ask one last time, just to make sure.

"Nah," Ezra says. "I've got nothing to hide."

"Yeah, me neither," Owen agrees. "You guys already know my secret."

"My father is secretary of state," Alika chimes in. "The whole world has access to my family's secrets."

"And I don't have any," Seth says. "So, yeah, who cares what you found out. It's all good."

"Besides, you know what they say," Issa tells me.

"No. What do they say?"

"All's fair in friendship and war."

Ezra groans. "That's not what they say."

"Are you sure?" she asks, all wide-eyed innocence. "I was sure that was how it went."

"All's fair in love and war," Owen tells her with a roll of his eyes.

"Oh, sorry." She turns her head a little and winks at me. "How about this one, then. All's well that starts well?"

"That's it." Ezra pulls her onto his lap and wraps his arms around her. "One more and I'm tossing you off the plane."

"You guys wouldn't toss me off the plane," she says, wrapping her arms around his neck.

"Oh yeah? Why's that?" Owen demands.

"Because," I say, quoting one of my favorite movie lines ever, "this is the beginning of a beautiful friendship."

They all groan.

"Jeez," Seth says. "Give a girl a nickname and she gets all sappy."

"I was not being sappy!"

"You were so being sappy," Alika tells me.

"Fine, would *The Cutting Edge* be better?"

"Yes!" Owen says emphatically.

"Absolutely!" Ezra agrees.

"Damn straight," Seth tells me.

"Okay, then."

"Toe pick!" five of us shout together.

Issa just shakes her head. "You guys really are crazy, you know that, right?"

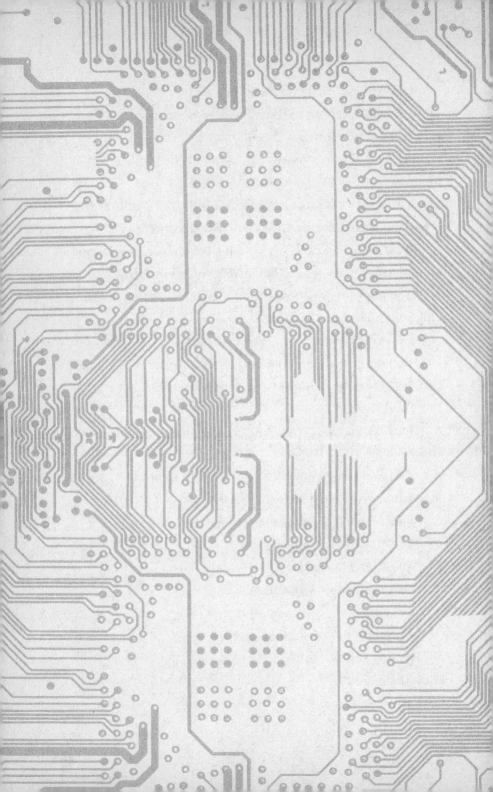

AUTHOR'S NOTE

Every once in a while, if a writer is really lucky, a project comes along that is truly the project of her heart. It challenges her, thrills her, makes her want to tear her hair out, and makes her so incredibly proud all at the same time. For me, *Phantom Wheel* is that project. I am so, so grateful to Kara Sargent, everyone else at Little, Brown Books for Young Readers, and The Gotham Group for giving me the chance to create these characters and write this story. It's the most fun I've had doing my job in a long, long time.

We live in an exciting, fascinating, sometimes terrifying time, one where the power of the internet, and those who wield it, seems practically omnipotent. My goal in writing this story was to explore this idea, to play around with what that kind of power looks like when it's unleashed and how easily people and corporations can be corrupted by greed and the desire for more—more power, more money, more influence. But I also wanted to examine what it means to stand up to that kind of systemic corruption—the strength and sacrifice it takes, but also the rewards that come from knowing you've done all you can to stop something that you know is wrong. I hope I've managed to do a little bit of both in *Phantom Wheel*.

This story wouldn't have been possible without the help and guidance of so many, and I'd like to take this opportunity to thank them all.

Kara Sargent, who truly is the most extraordinary editor. Her ideas and enthusiasm for this project made my job so much easier. I feel so, so blessed for having the chance to work with her.

Daniella Valladares, who has been so helpful and sweet throughout this project, and whose ideas helped me bring the story, and its characters, to life.

Emily Sylvan Kim, who really is the best agent and friend a girl could ever ask for. Thank you for always pushing me beyond my comfort zone and for being there to cheer me on when I am certain that my vision is bigger than my talent and ability to execute. I can't imagine trying to tackle the roller coaster that is publishing without you by my side.

Tom Sanderson, who has given this book the *most* amazing cover *ever*. Words cannot express how much I love it. Thank you, thank you, thank you.

Everyone at Little, Brown Books for Young Readers and The Gotham Group, whose excitement for this project made working on it an absolute joy. You have all been so supportive of me and my vision for this story, and for that I am eternally grateful.

Emily Mckay, Shellee Roberts, and Sherry Thomas, for your unflagging support and friendship. I love you all more than I can say.

My boys, who enthusiastically contributed to *so* many discussions on viruses, worms, operating systems, fight scenes, and a variety of other topics that came up during the writing of this book. You guys really are the best sports, and I'm so grateful that I get to be your mom.

My mom, who is a great sounding board and who does such an amazing job of helping me keep my real life running smoothly even when I'm lost in a fictional world.

The six main characters in *Phantom Wheel*, all of whom taught me something during the writing of this book about the strength and heart that are so integral to the human condition. Ezra's resourcefulness, Seth's deep-down goodness, Owen's bravery, Issa's passion, Alika's dogged search for truth, and Harper's open-mindedness truly are, to me, the most exciting parts of being human—and our best shot at making the world a better place.

And most of all, thank you to my readers. I hope this story excites you as much as it has me.

All my love,
Tracy

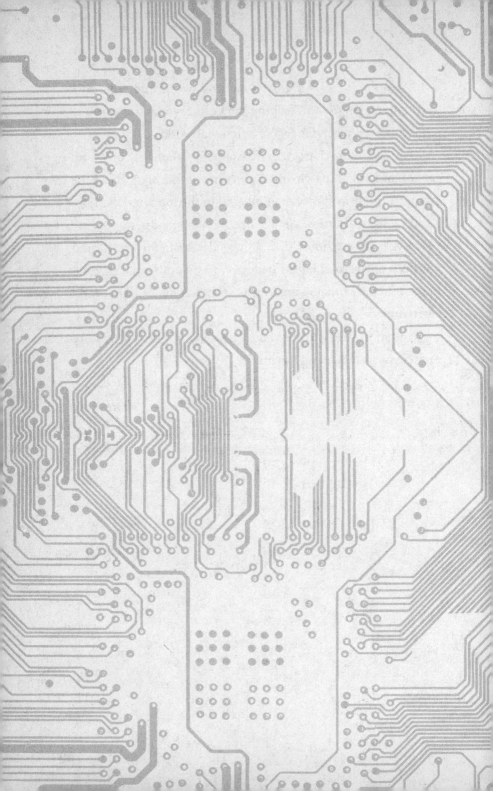

ABOUT THE AUTHOR

Tracy Deebs has written numerous young adult novels, including *Doomed*, which was a YALSA Quick Pick for Reluctant Young Readers finalist and has been on numerous state reading lists. She's the author of the Tempest mermaid series and the coauthor of the award-winning series The Hero Agenda. She is also the author of numerous *New York Times* and *USA Today* bestsellers for adults.

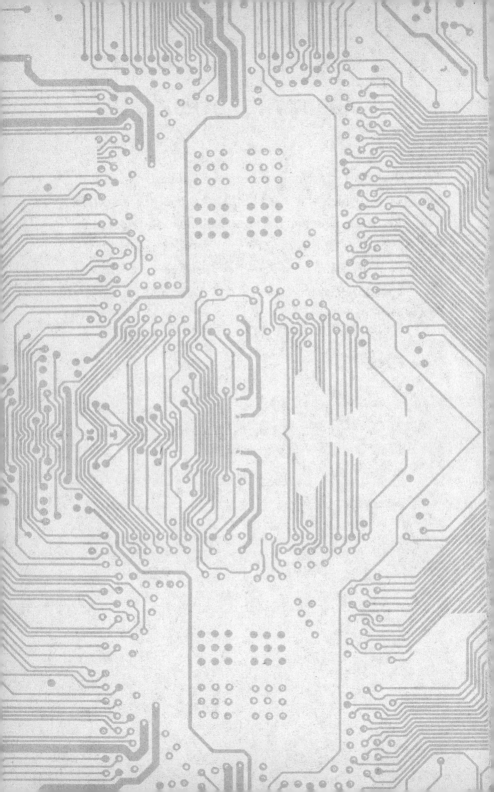